DYING TO GIVE.
GIVING TO LIVE.

AMBER WOLF

LAUREN
PARKER RHODES

DRIARN DUOLOGY

WILDFUL WRITINGS

NSW, Australia

Paperback ISBN: 978-1-7637346-3-0

eBook ISBN: 978-1-7637346-4-7

ALSO BY LAUREN PARKER RHODES

Access Lauren's other books here, or at:
www.laurenparkerrhodes.com/books

DRIARN DUOLOGY
The Wife (short story prequel)
Amber Wolf
Blue Pointed Star

WHEN SECRETS BECKON

TRAITORS DUOLOGY
Traitors' Creed
Traitors' Promise

Author's note: Each of these books, with the exception of Traitors' Promise, were previously published by Lauren Searson-Patrick and have been republished, with permission, by Lauren Parker Rhodes. Traitors' Promise has only been published by Lauren Parker Rhodes.

CONTENT WARNINGS

Amber Wolf is intended for adult audiences and contains mature themes including implied, and attempted, sexual assault. It also contains mention of historical, off-page, pregnancy loss.

For my wildlings, it's never too late – or too early – to chase your dreams.
Even when they change.

PROLOGUE

THEN

My daughter snuggles deeper under the thick patchwork bed covers, the burning candle catching the sparkle of her green eyes – eyes so like her father's they reopen that never-healing wound every time she looks at me. But they're eyes that still hold the innocence of youth and I will do everything in my power to keep it there.

For as long as time will allow.

She looks at me now, expectant of the story to come. This is our ritual – a story and a song to carry her into sleep. I lie down next to her, on top of the covers, pinning her in as I watch the snow fall outside the window. I used to hate the cold. Now, I relish the reminder of how far we've come.

And yet, we have further to go.

'Long ago,' I start, choosing the one she most needs to remember, one that will inspire hope. And faith. 'In a time before stories began, there was a little girl, not much older than you.'

She smiles at me, the way her face lights up drawing my own to my lips.

'A little girl who loved nothing more than to play in the meadows around her. The colours of the flowers and the trees filled her mind with rainbows; the animals that rushed to greet her occupied her days with friends and happiness. But the little girl felt there was something missing from her life. A gap she wasn't quite sure how to fill.

'Until a larger, more powerful animal danced in the shadows of her vision. Every day she would play in the meadow and, every day, the animal watched from the trees. Slowly, carefully, she played a little closer as she continued her games, even as the other animals refused to join her.

'It was as if the animal, whose eyes shone between the trees, called only to her.'

The lids of her green eyes are starting to droop when I look over, pulling my gaze from the snow. I roll on my side to face her, trailing a finger along her nose as I watch the steady rise and fall of the covers over her chest slow as sleep claims her. My heart swells with all I have to tell her and the spaces she fills with love. Spaces I didn't know existed until I knew she was coming.

Another day, I think to myself.

Another day I will finish the story. Another day I will tell her of the animal that stalked the little girl and her dreams, trying to warn her of things to come and guide her way. Of how it so desperately wanted to take her somewhere and all she had to do was follow. How, too late, she found out the destination and it wasn't only somewhere she wanted to go – but needed to.

But that little girl didn't follow, and his song stayed in her heart forever; a melody unheard by any other. One that told her she'd made a mistake that day. That she should have steeled her spine and stepped into that forest.

Another day, I will tell her that some opportunities are missed and some are gained. And it is never, never too late to find your resolve and let the bravery run through your veins. That the bravery won't mean you're not scared, just stronger than your fear. I will tell her it's never too late to follow your dreams and find your destiny. Everything she needs is already inside her.

Tomorrow.

We have tomorrow to talk about the Star.

And we'll follow the wolf together.

I hadn't expected to end up here. So far from the snow and the rolling green hills from my own youth. But looking out of the kitchen window, to the yard my daughter has spent the day playing in, a certain relief starts to creep into my mind. Back home, the differences weren't yet as marked. Here, I can show Adelais the tiny changes so few saw as consequential. Here, I can make sure she knows it's more than our home at stake. And here I can give her freedoms, a childhood she never would have had there.

A tiny chirping finds me from the hallway and I turn, placing my mug on the kitchen table. Despite the heat here, I've never been able to give up my tea. Adelais's unguarded smile shines back at me, the bird she brought back from the brink of death perched on her shoulder. Absently she lifts a finger and strokes its tiny belly; it almost doubles in size as it puffs up under her attention.

I watch as it quickly deflates, attention captured by something out the window, and I wonder if it misses its home too. Giving a final squawk, it takes flight back down the hallway just as a shiver trembles down my spine.

My heart catches, my gaze flying back to the window and scanning the yard.

I don't see anything. But then, I don't really expect to. It's the sense of someone withholding their emotions from me I can feel. The way my gift sparks to attention in the presence of another with similar abilities. Waiting to feel what they do in different touches along my skin.

But it's the muted sensation that makes my heart race. That the presence I feel knows to try and keep their emotions from me.

'Adelais,' I whisper, willing my voice not to shake. 'Let's play a game.'

She giggles as she wriggles under the table and I gently shush her, fighting the urge to snap at her for making any sound. I give myself the briefest of moments to savour the image of her crouched low under the table, her skin flushed with excitement for the game she thinks we're about to begin. A moment to look into those green eyes, even as the pang of loss finds me again.

But even if he was here, he couldn't protect either of us from this.

The smile I draw to my face is forced but I know she's too young to understand that yet and it warms my heart to stare into the face of innocence.

'Stay here until I tell you to come out, okay?'

She nods eagerly.

'That's an important part of the game, Adelais.' My throat is thick. 'Only come out if I tell you.'

I stand up when she nods again, dropping into the hole in the floor. I close the door and drop the tablecloth back down. I knew this moment would come, knew we couldn't hide forever. A surge of fury races through my chest that we've not been allowed the life we should have had.

'Hello, Catriona,' he says quietly as he appears behind me.

I spin on my heel to face him, pressing myself against the kitchen table, its edge digging into my fingers where I grip it to steady me.

'An interesting life you've tried to make here.' He gestures vaguely to the colourful kitchen.

'It's certainly more than the life I was headed for.' The strength in my voice surprises me, fuelled by my anger.

I'd known he'd find us and, yet, the inevitability still makes it hard to breathe. In my fiercest dreams I thought we would have more time. More time to—

Slowly, he shakes his head. 'You had everything, Catriona, but you threw it away for ... for a life punctuated by a gingham tablecloth,' he scoffs, looking at the kitchen table.

'I'm not going back – not yet.' I jam my knees together to keep them from shaking.

He steps forward, the tell-tale pink spots rising on his cheeks, the anger I've been running from for so long surging to the surface before my eyes. His breath on my face is hot and I crinkle my nose, but I don't move away. I will not give him the satisfaction of seeing me cower. Even still, the eyes that were once so familiar no longer hold any affection – only rage – and the shaking in my limbs starts to change from anger to genuine fear.

Fear I desperately try to clamp down so Adelais doesn't feel it.

'You've been incredibly stupid, of course,' he spits. 'But, I suppose, that can only be expected. You have always shown poor judgement. What's been harder to understand is your unbelievable selfishness.'

I stare back at him, cursing how much of this Adelais is hearing and sending her a silent, desperate thank you for staying so quiet. Apologising for loving someone I wasn't supposed to is not something I can do.

Despite what that love cost.

'You're right on one point, at least,' he says, his face still so close to mine our noses almost touch. 'You're not going back.'

CHAPTER ONE

NOW

Raised voices sound from a pocket of homes to our right. I don't need to look at Will to know he's heard it, too, or remind him how quickly a raised voice can turn into a knife in the back. The little shanty town, its dwellings pressing against the original parts of the city wall, looks the same as yesterday. It's been a month since the last super-storm wiped away most of the structures here and the rebuilding of the hovels won't change much until the next one.

'Get out!'

The voice is young and flinty, and Will and I subtly move a fraction faster in that direction, the lines of people begging on the streets not once looking away from us.

I clear my throat as we round the corner. Will and I have an unspoken understanding that these people's lives are hard enough and, where possible, we keep our weapons away. But I would be stupid not to be ready to respond with force if needed.

Just as the group comes into view, they explode into action before us. Two men wrestle in the filth on the ground as a woman's shrill screams pierce the air. A sobbing child watches from a short distance and an older one hovers between the two men and the child – glancing between them, as if torn by where they should be.

'Alright, you're finished now,' Will says as he prowls towards them, broad shoulders stretching out his black guard's uniform.

I stay a step behind to cover his blind spot. Glancing over my shoulder, the small number of onlookers gathering behind me watches silently. Until a man in a torn, sleeveless shirt starts cheering, spittle flying from his mouth.

The others join him, stepping closer.

'You've got less than sixty seconds,' I mutter to Will, glancing between the brawling group and the approaching, growing crowd. Will knows how good I am at reading people, even if he doesn't know why. I just wish he could feel it too sometimes so he wouldn't cut it so fine. But he always assumes the best of people.

The woman stops screaming, shouting profanities at the two men instead.

A glass bottle smashes. Close enough to my feet for the glass to crunch under the soles of my boots as I continue to follow Will.

'Twenty seconds,' I say quietly.

'That was too fast,' Will says, no hint of strain in his voice. 'You always skip count.'

'There's something about having glass thrown at you that calls for it.'

Will ushers the woman away before returning to the two men and hauling the one on top to his feet. Size and training are an advantage out here, but so is access to adequate nutrition. The fighting men are no match for Will, and they know it.

'You done?' Will asks casually.

Despite the violence-hungry crowd at my back, they won't see another fight here today. The steam has gone out of them. Each of their chests heave, blood and muck marking their clothes.

I hope they have others somewhere.

I turn back to the crowd, their cheering turning to disappointed grunts.

'They're done,' I say. 'You can head on out.'

The man who started the cheer is the last to turn away, mock saluting me as he goes.

We tread carefully over the stone road that runs through the makeshift houses on this side of the wall, mindful of the rubbish, rodents, and all manner of bodily fluids I put from my mind. It's better not to know what I walk in. The smell is bad enough, one I can never get used to, and completely overwhelms the scent of the sea. My nose crinkles and a hunched figure snickers at me from the side of the road.

'You'll be sucked dry and die, just the same as us,' she says, but I ignore her and continue to focus on my surroundings.

Our patrol area is mainly made up of the docks and the road leading up to the dockside gate in and out of Rhyton, where we are almost completely exposed to the sun that beats down on us. I'm simultaneously thankful for my guard uniform that's specially made for the conditions, and ashamed that the people who live here don't have access to them.

I look back up to the high, ginger-coloured walls of the city as Will and I weave our way through the slum beyond the gate and make out Phoenix and Hayes atop the wall. Phoenix's head is thrown back in an easy laugh at something Hayes has leaned in to tell him, the sunlight catching the strands of Phoenix's honey-brown hair before he replaces his hat.

The scaffolding, where it is being reinforced against the strength of the encroaching ocean, towers into the sky, dwarfing them. Most of the original coast of Driarn is now under water and the newly coastal cities and towns need to make sure they too don't go under.

The capital, Rhyton, is no exception.

The number of people looking to get out of the city via the dockside gate is invariably less than those seeking to get in. Those on the way out are mostly the more fortunate dock workers and fishermen who have dwellings inside the city. Those looking to get in seek refuge from homes even closer to the ocean than Rhyton, or farmland that is no longer productive.

I see the hope in their eyes, feel the quiet excitement and apprehension that emanates from each of them, and look away.

Shutting myself off to people is something I do regularly; physically feeling their emotions all the time can be exhausting. Often I wonder if it's selfish to not acknowledge how hard it is for people in a less fortunate position than me. But most of them won't find their new lives in this city and knowing their feelings now won't change that.

My feet throb with a familiar ache as our shift draws to a close. My skin is almost crying for a cold shower by the time we head back up the road, on our way back to guard headquarters and our residence block.

The city is framed by a pale pink and purple sky as evening comes; it's harder to see in the in-between time of day and night. Up ahead, the beggar from this morning rocks backwards and forwards, mumbling to herself. It's difficult to understand the words but I strain to hear anyway as we continue over the stones, her demeanour markedly different to earlier today.

A spark of blue flashes in the sunset over Rhyton, briefly enriching the surrounding hues. I stop dead, the soles of my feet pulsing, as a flicker of familiarity races across my mind and the tiny flame I hold in my chest. But it's gone before I can drag it forward for examination.

Will turns back to me, dark brows raised in question, and I start as I realise the beggar is now next to me.

'No more – they can't give any more,' she says, looking at the sky as well, now, too. 'Please, help me, they're dying.'

The crowd gives her a slightly wider berth as her agitation increases until she's screaming at the pastel sky, bringing me back from my lost memories. I take my eyes from her to share a look with Will. Before I can register his face, I'm thrust backwards, my feet slipping on the stone road.

She's too fast and the hands she's fisted in my uniform drive me further away from the city wall. The stench of her breath fills my nose and water lines my eyes. Her teeth are yellowed and her filthy skin disguises her age. For a beat too many, my heart skips until my body remembers its training and I dig my heels into the stone, wrenching her wrists from my front.

But not cleanly enough to avoid an elbow to the ribs.

'They're dying, you must help them!' she screams. 'Just listen to me, please!'

She thrashes and screams in my grasp as desperation pierces through my defenses, running along my skin like nails. Her spit lands on my face and I twist my features in disgust. Will tries briefly to talk her down before slamming the butt of his pistol into the back of her head. It's enough for her to collapse to her knees but not lose consciousness. I release her gnarled hands and she cradles her bruised skull, rocking on her knees. I can feel her anguish, but it's shadowed by my irritation that I didn't see her coming.

The heat rises on my face as my breathing levels out. I refuse to acknowledge the stares of the gathering crowd. When she doesn't move to get up, I kneel before her, even as my heart tries to collect itself once more, forcing myself to look in her face. Her sapphire-coloured eyes pin me in place, their irises ringed with two lines of hazel like I've not seen before.

'Easy, Lish,' Will warns under his breath as he hovers behind me.

'Please,' she begs, quiet now. Her strange eyes bore into mine.

'I'm not going to hurt you,' I say, although there are some Guards she would be right to fear. She shakes her head.

'Please,' she says, her voice thick. I furrow my brow, no longer able to get a good read on her emotions – they're all over the place and empty at the same time. 'You need to help them,' she rasps, scanning my face. Her sapphire and hazel eyes find mine as she gently rests her hand on my arm, pleading with me, the fire gone out of her entirely. She stills and blinks up at me, cocking her head. 'Remember the—you must—' she inhales sharply and places a hand to her chest. 'Oh'—she tries to smile—'you followed the light and you've been found.'

Understanding dawns on me; she thinks I'm someone else. A daughter, probably, maybe a sister, but obviously someone who is now lost to her. Not for the first time, I'm thankful I know exactly where all my loved ones are. The weight of Will's hand finds my shoulder, fingers squeezing gently.

'I'm sorry, I'm not who you think I am.'

Her sorrowful, sapphire-hazel eyes stalk me as I walk away.

'You really need to cover your left side,' Will says, brown eyes flicking to me briefly, as we make our way to Central to debrief after our shift.

I bristle at the criticism but mostly because he's right. I try not to roll my eyes, even as I hope the beggar didn't leave a bruise when she shoved me.

As we walk towards the office, the moments ticking closer to when I can catch up with the rest of our team and go to bed, I'm reminded of last night's dream. The details taunting me as I try to capture them.

Small, bare toes, disappearing in a sea of vibrant green, match me stride for stride down the drab hallway. The laugh of the woman behind me as she swings me into the clear blue sky. My breath catches as yellow wildflowers floating on the breeze dance behind my vision. The wild abandonment of my six-year-old self is an echo in my heart, in stark contrast to the woman I am now.

The dream never lasts long enough for me to see her and I curse myself for letting it slip away, again. Another lost opportunity to remember. It's been more years than I care to count since then and that innocence simply doesn't exist anymore.

She doesn't exist anymore.

Phoenix catches up to us just before we head in, ducking to nudge me hello with a muscled shoulder as he downs the last of his coffee. Heat blooms across my cheeks at both the contact and the way his mouth curls up slightly at the corner.

'How long are you hoping that will keep you awake for tonight?' I ask, looking pointedly at his cup.

'Just enough to keep me interesting.' He winks a green eye at me and I glance away.

Phoenix has a reputation in the Guard and it's not unusual for him to be running on very little sleep. I sometimes wonder if the women he takes to bed are his conquests, or he theirs. A ripple of a feeling I can't place comes from him and I sneak a look at his profile, but it gives nothing away.

'You're insufferable,' Will says with a sly grin.

Phoenix moves to tousle Will's cropped, chestnut-coloured hair, but Will drives a playful punch into his side and Phoenix stands, laughing. Flashing his perfect teeth.

Captain Robard, a robust man, on the shorter side, with a full, dark moustache that's wholly comical, nods dismissively as we walk into Central. Other colleagues of mine – team leaders – and different members of their units join us, their voices filling the room until Robard clears his throat. He launches straight in, and I drag my eyes from his moustache.

'Not much to report from today,' he says. 'Usual drunks, in the usual places, dealt with in the usual way. Security around the remaining gardens has been increased again, following last month's storm. One report of theft from the docks, which is unusual only in that it was reported at all, and a missing girl. It's unlikely she'll be recovered but the night teams will keep an eye out for her, anyway. Between 12 and 15 years old, blonde or brown hair, short to medium height—'

'Sir?'

Robard looks at me expectantly. I can sense his boredom but push it away, drawing on the energy from my little gold flame to ensure my barrier is up. It almost feels like solidifying my skin and I've often wondered if it's the best way to block others out. But it's the only way I could figure out on my own – even if it's not totally impenetrable.

I can't blame Robard for his lack of empathy. It's been a long, uneventful shift, on the whole, and he's looking forward to a retirement with no more night shifts. Understanding flickers in his tired eyes.

'Alice?' He prompts when I don't immediately respond. He sighs, the question must be written on my face. 'The details on the girl are scarce – she's from the orphanage.'

I note the resignation in his tone and a slight flush of shame that he hasn't spared her more thought, but it doesn't mean it sits well with me.

'But someone has questioned the orphanage further, right?' I ask. 'Surely they can do better than that.'

Robard gives me a long look. It would be hard to decipher if I couldn't feel the irritation that ignites in him.

The other team leaders look between us.

Of course other Guards would have questioned them further, it's our job to protect and serve the people of this city. But how well did they execute their duties? A knot winds around my stomach as I hold his stare, but I let the question drop.

Missing people, particularly girls, are not exactly out of character for Rhyton. It's a city like any other with its temptations and seedy underbelly. And no one would blame a girl for leaving the orphanage if she'd run away; the mere mention of it used to tinge my gut with loathing.

'Right...' Phoenix drawls, every face turning towards him. It's easy to see why people fall over themselves for a moment of his time. 'So, we do our standard patrols while looking out for a teenage girl who looks like half the city. Got it.'

Phoenix knows the girl is in the wind and it shows, but he's not wrong. I just hope it was her call.

Having washed the grime of the docks off my skin, I feel at home in a corner booth at our favourite drinking spot. When all six of us on my team are together, I try to shut out their emotions and let them wash around me, not through me, allowing them to express what they will in their own way.

Instinctively, I've always known it would be a mistake to draw attention to my differences. But, somewhere along the way, this group of people wriggled their way under my skin and into my heart. I'm more relaxed about my abilities around them, just not enough for them to actually know I'm not quite like them. They just think I'm great with people. But what would I say anyway? *By the way, did you know I can feel every emotion you have if I want?*

Hayes signals for the next round and Will cackles as Blaire regales us with the adventures of her patrol. She's gorgeous, our Blaire. All long legs, blonde hair the colour of sunshine, and large, brown eyes. She glows in the low light of Pieter's Place and more than one set of eyes in the venue find themselves trailing back to her.

I shift to grab my drink from the barmaid who knows our order by heart and wince at the sensation in my ribs. On the left, of course, which is very unfortunate given Will's commentary on my weakness. He notices my grimace and I wish I remembered the old tales about healing faster.

'Are you going to fill the others in on today, or am I?' he says with a sarcastic grin.

I narrow my gaze at him briefly before sighing and sharing our own stories of the day's patrol.

'That's why you're nursing your left side?' Phoenix asks with a soft laugh, and I try to ignore the quiet concern that brushes against me.

'Leave my left side out of it, we can't all be perfect,' I say, raising a brow at him.

Seated on my right, I can feel the heat of him against my thigh, and I clamp down on the warmth his proximity creates elsewhere.

'I felt bad for her,' I say eventually. 'I reminded her of someone, someone she's lost. And now there's that missing girl Robard mentioned. Did no one seriously notice her missing for that long?' I ask, a tightening in my chest I can't undo.

Riley understands what I'm saying underneath those words, but she responds plainly.

'We know as well as anyone that's entirely possible, Lish,' she says gently, reaching a hand across the tabletop towards me. 'This is Rhyton and girls go missing, most aren't reported for days. Who's to know how many disappear that aren't reported at all?'

I hadn't thought about that angle, and it leaves me with an uneasy feeling. One that's accompanied by the shadow of ringed sapphire eyes I can't shake.

Eyes that ask me to remember.

CHAPTER TWO

Yesterday's patrol is a dark cloud hovering behind my brow. One that only deepens as I struggle to wrangle my unruly brown hair into a bun. So, I called Will. I need to punch it out.

In all the time after I lost my mum – all the time that means anything, anyway – Will has been my counter and my confidant. Actual friends, as opposed to alliances, were hard to make in the orphanage but, once deep bonds were formed, they were incredibly hard to break; and we were no exception. Will delivered my first punch to the face and, while the pain in my nose had been blinding, I'd surprised him by not holding a grudge.

Instead, I insisted he teach me how to hit, too.

We circle each other closely, now, and I lash out at the mitts he holds. He swipes and I throw a kick at his ankles as I duck. Spinning back to full height, I lunge, aiming to drive my glove into the soft part of his belly.

My ribs threaten to crack as I'm driven sideways, legs stumbling, unable to keep upright. The force of Phoenix tackling me to the mat forces the air from my lungs and I land with his weight crushing into me.

'Asshole! That wasn't fair!' I shove at his chest.

'Fair is not what you'll find in this city, Lish, and you know it,' he drawls.

'Well, thank you for that very valuable lesson. Now get off,' I spit.

His face is inches from mine and, even through my narrowed eyes, I notice, unfortunately not for the first time, his full mouth pulled into a lazy grin. His delight ripples against my skin. He's so proud of himself for taking me by surprise. I scowl at him.

Phoenix shifts slightly to prop himself up on an elbow and waits. I clench my fists and take some deep breaths. Something that's not very easy with the best part of his weight still pressing into my ribs.

'Fortunately for your pretty nose I don't feel like getting blood on my clothes today,' I say through gritted teeth.

Phoenix slowly eases himself off me without breaking eye contact, the connection between us going taut. He offers his hand to help me up. I take it and use his anchoring weight against him, driving my knee into his stomach before knocking his legs out from under him. He's already mock surrendering as I roll him onto his back and sit astride him.

'Please, don't tease me,' he laughs, his strong hands on my thighs as his green eyes watch me carefully.

'Go again, this time, we use the knives,' Will orders.

Resigned uncertainty reaches across the space between us, pulling my attention away from Phoenix. Like Will knows something and worries about the road it leads to, but is powerless to stop travelling it. He's given me that look enough for me to know very well what it means by now. I think I'd know what it meant even without the subtle hint of his emotions I let through. I turn that thought away and focus on the smugness that lies underneath. The smugness at having successfully coordinated the surprise attack from Phoenix.

Will's teaching has only improved with age. I can barely raise my arms by the time we're finished and it feels good, a great distraction and a reminder I can actually fight. I shouldn't have let the beggar grab me and get close enough to land a hit at all, I should have been better aware of what was unfolding around us. Next time, it could be Will being jumped, not me. I mull over her words as I get dressed for shift. Who could she be missing?

Robard gives us the usual handover from the night before, his eyes slightly glazed and movements slow with exhaustion. He scratches at his neck and pulls his collar up, hiding a small mark there.

Robard looks at me.

'We've got another missing person – a woman,' he says and the weight in my chest returns. 'Witnesses claim there were sounds of a struggle – so not a runaway, likely a domestic.' Phoenix's broad shoulders stiffen beside me.

'That said, the statements make no sense.' Robard hands me a thin file. 'That's a summary of the discussion with the witnesses by Pike and Lightfoot. You should talk with them again today. There's rumours about gang activity resurfacing and I'd like to make sure this isn't related.'

His eyes don't match his words.

They tell me he remembers my questioning from yesterday, and challenge me to find out more on this case than was gathered on the last.

As we walk out of Central, Phoenix decides he and I are taking the domestic. Will raises an eyebrow at me, the tawny brown skin of his face shining under the lights, before heading out to partner with Hayes.

'You know how lazy Pike and Lightfoot are,' Phoenix says, his words clipped. 'That woman could be right in front of them, bound and gagged, and they'd never notice.'

Phoenix often takes a special interest in domestic violence cases. After one particularly difficult case some years ago, he'd beaten the perpetrator half to death. I'd been tempted to do the same to Phoenix by the time I got him back to Headquarters, but I never managed to get him to admit why it affected him so. We haven't spoken of it since.

His shoulders hold their tension and his lean fingers fidget with the strap buckle at his chest – the one holding the sword in place between his shoulder blades – but I put that down to the nervous energy that can come from being on patrol. I can't deny the sword adds a certain gravitas to his warrior image. Having seen him use it, there's no doubt it serves as more than decoration. But, today, I hope he keeps it away.

As we make our way towards the outer edges of the city to see the woman's family, I am keenly aware of Phoenix's presence in a way I'm not with Will. Will and I have been virtually inseparable since my first day at the orphanage. His young, wide, brown eyes had glowed like bronze in the sun, holding not only kindness but acceptance and a challenge to be my best self. Working with him is like working with myself. I know the moves and decisions he will make before he makes them and vice versa. We've always covered each other, both at the Guard and in the orphanage. Being without him puts me a little off balance.

That could also be because I'm trying not to notice the way Phoenix moves. The way he stalks the pavement seemingly oblivious to the heat, the sun bouncing off his broad shoulders and lighting up the small sliver of skin I can see over his collar. His keen gaze absorbing everything around him.

This part of the city used to be reasonably well off and I sometimes imagine what it would have been like to live here. With green lawns, painted fences, and kids playing in the street, I can only imagine a perfect, peaceful life. The people who built these houses didn't have to think about how exposed the entry and exit points were to the weather, or that they might need a secret escape route, or protected storage rooms for when food supplies ran short.

In today's world, it means these houses are left for those unable to afford any additional protections not only from heat and super-storms, but from those who feel they have no other choice left but to prey on others. They might not be as poor as those outside the city walls, but their lives definitely aren't easy.

Phoenix and I pass a run of deserted houses, the front doors long gone or hanging from their hinges. There's an odd mix of barren, dusty yards contrasted with pockets where the vegetation pervades every surface. Phoenix deflates a little as we approach the address the woman went missing from. I can feel his unease at how these people live and anger simmers below his cool facade. I lean a little closer to him and push a gentle wave of calm forward. The slowing of his breath tells me it's been effective in taking the edge off; if he notices anything strange, he doesn't say. It's not something I do very often – not anymore, anyway.

I'd played around with it a little too much at the orphanage and one of the carers started to take a bit too keen an interest in me. And, in that place, it was better never to stand out. After that, I made myself learn to put up a barrier of sorts to hold other's emotions at bay.

Walking up the stairs, careful to step over the worst of the rotting planks, we flank the door while Phoenix knocks. This house doesn't officially belong to the current occupants, of course, but we do them the courtesy of acting like it does. I suppose, whoever formally owns this property isn't coming back to claim it and it's not worth anything anymore, anyway. Phoenix knocks again.

'It's the Guard,' I call out. 'We would like to talk to you.'

I keep my eye on the front yard and over Phoenix's shoulder as we wait. The door opens a crack and a small nose and one wide, dark brown eye fringed with long, black lashes peaks out.

I crouch down but remain to the side of the door. 'Can we come in?' I ask.

The child assesses us for a long moment before scampering away, leaving the door open. I carefully draw my gun and hold it slightly behind my back as we enter. Phoenix has swung his sword to his hip and his hand flexes at his side. We automatically sweep the two rooms that open out as we enter the house, my pistol raised, and proceed down the hall where we find a small boy in the kitchen. The knife he holds in front of him could be lethal in the right hands, not least because its shaking blade is clearly filthy.

We both know he won't be able to injure us but, exchanging a look, we agree not to make him feel more powerless. I re-holster my pistol, knowing Phoenix's hand won't stray far from his sword – in case there's more than the three of us here. But he does so subtly, tucking it slightly behind his body so it's less obvious to the child.

'We're not going to hurt you,' I say softly. 'We heard there was a distur-bance here last night and we want to make sure you're all okay,' I say.

The boy sags, the hand holding the knife dropping to his side.

'M-m-my sister – she was taken … I don't … I couldn't … I don't know—' he collapses on the floor and sobs. He can't be more than six or seven and I slowly move closer. On my knees in front of him, my words tumble forward softly, without thought.

'I'm here. I'm here. I'm so sorry. We're here.'

I open my arms but don't move closer. Slowly, he raises his tear rimmed eyes to meet mine. Assessing whatever he finds there, he lets the knife clatter to the floor and climbs into my lap. I hold him tight, desperately looking over my shoulder at Phoenix.

'Now what?' I mouth at him.

I don't know how to leave a frightened and traumatised child here. Whoever took his sister could easily return and, even if not, Rhyton is no place for children on their own. The cold, remote faces of the carers at the orphanage come back to me. They are not faces that would look on the little one before me with any kindness. My heart clenches and I squeeze him tighter. I won't be leaving him here.

Phoenix studies me for a long moment, his gaze going between me and the child in my arms. He kneels across from us where he can see the door and I exhale a breath I didn't realise I was holding.

'It's okay buddy, we will keep you safe,' he says. 'But we need to know what happened. I'm going to ask you some questions, alright? You can stay where you are, but I need to ask you a few things,' he says and waits until the boy nods.

'What's your name?' Phoenix asks.

'Nico.'

'It's good to meet you, Nico. I'm Phoenix and my friend here is Alice.'

Nico clings tighter although his sobbing has subsided a little.

'How old are you, Nico?'

'Seven.'

'And who do you live with?'

'Just my sister. She ... she—' he stops.

'That's a little hard to talk about, that's okay. We can come back to that. How long have you been staying here?'

'A few weeks.' Nico sniffles. 'We move places every three weeks, it's the best way to escape the Whispers. We were supposed to move last week but I had a fever and Sofia said we should stay. It's my fault.' Nico's voice is muffled as he talks into my shoulder.

'Can you tell me about the Whispers, Nico?' Phoenix asks.

'They're bad things. I dream of them sometimes,' he says. 'Sofia tried to make sure I never heard the stories but I'm not stupid. I heard them. I know.'

'What do you know, Nico?' Phoenix's voice is low and gentle, and I find myself calmed by it along with Nico.

'I know they take you away,' he sniffs. 'They're monsters you can't see, and they wreck your mind. If they take you, you never come back. They take you to their lair where they torture you and turn you into something you weren't before. They make you a monster as well.'

I can't make much sense of what this means but it's clear Nico believes what he's saying, and I curse those who have been spreading these stories to little ears.

'I know it's really hard to talk about, Nico, but can you tell me what happened the night your sister, Sofia, disappeared?' Phoenix presses gently.

Nico takes several deep breaths. 'I could hear someone talking in my dreams, whispering. And then the banging on the stairs woke me up. Sofia screamed at me to run. I thought she was mad at me, I didn't understand.' Nico's flat voice belies the panic I feel rising in him, and I push back with a calm similar to what I used on Phoenix earlier. But I'm careful not to take it all away. 'I couldn't see anything, it was so dark. I don't know why it was so dark and my hands were sticky on the floor,' he says, pushing harder into my shoulder.

An image of Nico stumbling down the dark hall, beginning to crawl towards his sister, not realising he was crawling in her blood, forms in my mind. But I didn't notice any blood on our way in – or on his clothes.

'And then my head started to hurt so bad I had to shut my eyes and ... she was gone.'

Nico lifts his head and blinks wet lashes at me.

'Where has she gone?' he asks. I have no response and I clear my throat around the lump that forms.

Phoenix gently ruffles Nico's dirty hair.

'You did great, Nico, thank you for helping us. Is there anyone you can stay with for a while?' he asks.

Nico looks at us blankly, the tracks of tears still evident on his face, as he begins to understand what that question means. Phoenix looks at me again and I can feel only warmth coming from him. A small part of me knew he would always take this road and the blockage in my throat starts to dissolve.

'That's okay,' he says after a beat or two, 'you can hang out with us.'

I grip Nico and try to infuse him with a feeling of safety. I don't want to mislead him or take away the significance of the loss of his sister, who I don't believe we will find. But nor do I want to see him in the depth of despair. A hole that would only deepen by a lack of knowing where he will safely sleep for the night ... or nights.

We reach the Guard residence block and Phoenix takes Nico off his back, where he has spent the long walk home. In my apartment, identical to all the others, Phoenix takes charge. He runs Nico a hot bath and disappears briefly to get some clean clothes that, while miles too big, will be a nice change from Nico's filthy rags. Filthy but not bloody, despite his description of Sofia's apparent abduction.

He emerges from the bathroom like a bedraggled scarecrow, with wet hair and far too long pants and shirt. I can't help but smile at him as I roll the sleeves up as best I can, even as my head spins with the implications of the decision we've just made. Robard will be furious, this is not what he would have expected. Not only do I not have any real information on the missing woman, Nico's sister, I've totally broken protocol by allowing Phoenix to bring him home with us. The nerves in my stomach smother the flicker in my heart that tells me Phoenix made the right call. It's the same one I would have made. But that knowledge makes me more concerned, not less.

'Pizza!' Will announces as he bursts through the door.

Nico flinches behind me and I throw Will a look. He pops the pizza on the counter and strides over to Nico and me. He sticks his hand out for Nico to shake, but the boy just eyes him suspiciously. Will chatters away to us all as he returns to the kitchen to prepare dinner, as if this is a normal evening and we bring home stray children every other day.

Officially, there are other avenues we could have taken. Should have taken. But the challenges we face in Rhyton stretch into the country at large. Driarn's welfare system is already immensely strained, and I could never play a part in any child ending up in that orphanage. Even if it earns me more distrust from Robard. I gently guide Nico to the couch and sit next to him while Will and Phoenix get ready for dinner.

'The others will be here in about ten minutes. Blaire is bringing salad,' Will says to no one in particular.

Nico continues to glance nervously around the room but before I can signal Will to call the others off, Hayes, Blaire, and Riley are walking through the front door. Phoenix or Will have obviously given the others a head's up and they each say a gentle hello to Nico as they take up positions on my small couches and floor.

'Make sure there's enough—' Riley starts.

'Salt on your margherita,' Will finishes. 'I got it.' He laughs as he shakes his head.

The apartment provided by the Guard as part of my wages is modest, with one bedroom, an open kitchen, dining and lounge area, and a small bathroom. The seven of us easily dominate the space and it seems quite homely, even with a terrified child in our midst. It's certainly home for me and better than I could get elsewhere. I always feel most whole when we're all together like this.

Phoenix hasn't taken his eyes off Nico all evening, so it's no surprise he is the first to notice his eyes drooping. He nudges me with an elbow and looks subtly at Nico. I take Nico's little hand and settle him into my bed for the night. I will sleep on the pull-out sofa so he can have some space. He looks even smaller nestled into my pillows and white bedlinen and, while his dark eyes are sleepy, they're certainly wary and I can't blame him. He is suddenly without the only person in the world he trusts and is now in an unfamiliar apartment with six strange adults. I sit on the side of the bed furthest from him, closest to the door, and grapple at what to tell a frightened seven-year-old boy whose life will never be the same.

A conversation there wasn't anyone to have with me.

'I know this probably all seems pretty crazy, Nico,' I say, 'but I promise we will keep you safe.'

He watches me through his dark lashes, and I can tell that sleep will take him soon. But it won't be restful. 'You know, when I was little my mum used to tell me about the Blue Pointed Star, have you heard of it?'

He shakes his head.

'She told me the Blue Pointed Star has the power to heal and restore what's been taken. She said it could make our deepest need come true, so I guess we need to be careful about the kinds of wishes we send. But I think wishing to see Sofia again is a very special wish, what do you think?'

Tears leak from the corner of his eyes, and I slowly walk around the bed to sit closer to him, glancing at the timber box that sits on my bedside table. 'Close your eyes and fill your heart with your wish,' I say, stroking his deep brown hair, 'and then let it go. The wolves will find it and take your wish on its journey to the Blue Pointed Star.' I draw a deep breath and look out the window, remembering all the times my mother told me the same story.

'The wolves will take us there, Nico, we just have to look for them.'

Phoenix is waiting at the bedroom door when I leave quietly. 'I love that story, Lish. I've never heard it before,' he whispers.

His forehead furrows with the ramifications of today.

'Why him?' I ask softly.

I'd never take it back. Not now that I've tucked Nico into my bed and told him my mother's story. A story that physically aches to recall because it serves only as a reminder of what I lost. But why Phoenix prompted us on this path is still unclear.

'I just—' His voice cracks. 'I couldn't watch anymore,' he says.

We head back to the lounge room and flop down beside each other on the couch. The six of us look at each other for a moment.

'Holy shit,' he mutters.

'Holy shit, indeed,' I say.

'You two certainly don't do anything by halves, do you?' Hayes says.

'I'm sure she'd take half the paperwork we have to do,' Blaire suggests.

'You are not wrong there.' I gesture towards my bedroom. 'I can't even imagine what this will mean I have to do.'

We quietly talk the others through the events of the evening, mindful of the little ears in the next room. Phoenix exhales heavily and, on impulse, I reach out and squeeze his hand. I linger a moment longer than I expected and, just as I am taking my hand away, Phoenix threads his fingers through mine and grips tighter. Blaire glances at our hands and back to the heat in my cheeks. A beat of envy that's not my own washes over me. It's gone so quickly I wonder if I imagined it. I look harder at her but there is no judgement in her gaze.

CHAPTER THREE

The darkness edges at my vision and my head hurts – but I keep still. I know to keep still. I bite my hand to stop from screaming. I can hear sounds but I don't understand them and my ears start to bleed, the blood trickling down my neck. Beyond the searing sounds in my head I hear a struggle and a wet crack. Time slows and, from where I hide in the hole under the kitchen floor, I see her face tumble into view.

I can just see her in the crack between floorboards. Her eyes find mine but her head is wrong. It's bleeding and she doesn't reach for me. Why isn't she getting me? Her mouth moves slowly as she tries to say something but then she's still too. I'm running again. A hand grasps my arm and I press my knife to his throat.

'Lish. *Lish.*' The voice that wakes me sounds strangled.

Dimly, I'm aware of a dark room pushing into my awareness and it takes me a moment to remember where I am. In my apartment. On the sofa. With Phoenix.

I breathe forcefully in and out through my nose and make myself focus only on the present. The pain of my loss is sharp, a twisting in my chest, as if I'm back there again. As if all these years haven't passed and a thick layer of scar tissue hasn't grown around that wound.

When my vision clears, I take stock of the knee I have pressed into Phoenix's chest. The drop of blood on his throat where my short blade makes a slight but threatening depression. I let the blade fall to the fold out sofa in time with the lurch of my stomach and sit back on his thighs, pushing away the familiar threads between the dream and Nico's story still sticking to me, like an invisible cobweb.

A sense of startled wariness rolls off Phoenix, mingling with my own horror and embarrassment. I don't know how long we sit like that as my breathing returns to normal. He watches me but I only look down at the crumpled pillows. Gently, he takes my hands in his.

'I think you could do with a cup of tea,' he says, moving me off him gently. He puts the kettle on to boil and I gather my senses enough to peek in on Nico who, thankfully, sleeps soundly – he needs it. I take the steaming tea from Phoenix and lean against the benchtop.

'I haven't dreamed of that night in a long time,' I say into my cup. 'I miss her.'

The words are both too much and not enough. My entire world shattered that day and, somehow, I have haphazardly rebuilt pieces of my life and my heart. But it doesn't change the dull ache that permanently resides in my chest. The one that becomes jagged and spreads through my body if I examine it too closely. The pool of 'what ifs' that lie there, the reminder that, while I spend my time protecting the people of Rhyton, I did nothing to help her.

No matter how I've tried to rationalise it over the years, that fact always remains.

Phoenix crosses the kitchen slowly and wipes the tears that have started to fall. As he dries my face, I realise they're not only for her. The enormity of the past few days weighs on me. My mind whirls with the unknowable number of girls and women that have disappeared. I know in my gut this is not a new phenomenon, there is something happening here that's as yet beyond my comprehension. It nags at me. And, as if there is not enough to deal with in Rhyton, I have brought an orphaned child into my home. An orphan raising an orphan is not necessarily a cocktail for success. Not where I am concerned.

I look up at Phoenix, his features filled with a care and understanding that pulls at something deep in my chest.

'What are we doing, Phoenix? With Nico. Despite everything that's happened to him he still *trusted* us.' It's this bit that surprises me the most. It took me much, much longer to work out how to do this. 'But can we really offer him the stability he deserves? I could never send him to that orphan—' I break off, fighting fresh tears.

'Stability? No,' he says. 'Not like he deserves – but certainly more than leaving him on the street with nothing. I know it seems crazy and, really, what the hell do I know about looking after a kid?' he asks, his gaze searching mine. 'But I will look after him until he can look after himself, and even after that. We both know the things life has in store for kids on their own in Rhyton. I don't know exactly how it will work out, but it will. We'll work it out.'

I blink at Phoenix, trying to process the protective conviction that rolls off him. If I'd thought about it, I would have realised he always had this potential. It was just waiting for the right moment.

He steps closer until our toes are almost touching. I take in his face, his kind eyes and where the stubble is just beginning to show on his jaw. He loves women, and there is no denying the feeling is reciprocated. But there is more to him than that and, while I can't quite put my finger on what it is, this situation with Nico more than illustrates my point.

I don't believe it would be uncommon for anyone to wish to save a child from a life otherwise fraught with danger and loneliness. But most in Rhyton would turn a blind eye, their own difficulties too numerous. At best, the child would be delivered to the orphanage – which is its own kind of hell. Very few would actively take a child they do not know under their wing with seemingly every intention of doing the child-rearing themselves.

Phoenix wipes the last of my tears from my cheeks. 'Right now, I'm more interested in talking about what *we* are doing.'

My breath hitches and I stare at him. I hadn't considered a 'we' before, not in any way that seemed plausible outside of the 'we' we make in our team. Of course I've wondered what he'd feel like, particularly that mouth of his, but I never intended to become a notch on his belt.

'What *we* are doing?' I repeat slowly.

He steps closer again and plants his feet on either side of mine. The warmth of his body runs the length of me, and he takes my cheeks in his hands as my heart leaps behind my ribs. He waits and I can't hold onto the thoughts that run through my mind.

'I don't understand.' I frown at him. 'I thought you were quite content sleeping with Rhyton's best.'

He blanches and drops his hands but doesn't step back. Slowly, he shakes his head with a sad smile. The nervousness I could feel from him before, and attributed to his new role as unofficial guardian, now has a disappointed edge that doesn't fit. But, despite my reservations about being someone's conquest, I can't ignore that this feels different to that. I want him to put his hands back, my face feels colder without them there. Boldly, I pop my fingers into the pockets of his tracksuit pants to gently keep him from moving backwards.

'Tell me,' I prompt him.

He sighs.

'I had hoped you'd see through me. There are no 'Rhyton's best', Lish. Or 'Rhyton's worst' come to think of it,' he says, eyebrows quirking. 'Not as often as you're implying, anyway.'

He rubs gently at the crease between my brows, his touch both foreign and familiar. 'You know I grew up on the streets. You don't know what I had to do to get off them. Sex, relationships, none of it is something I do easily. It just became easier to keep the pretence up and not answer difficult questions. Given my background ... I never considered I'd be a suitable partner or husband, anyway. And then – then I realised my feelings for you were shifting.'

My stomach flips as I try to keep up with this change in events. For so long I have reined in my attraction to Phoenix, hyper aware of the lingering gazes that came his way, the late nights I thought he was having. I'd resigned myself to remaining friends, to laughing it off. Now, I try to recall how many women I've *actually* seen him with. I think of the mornings he was far too chipper to have been up all night.

Phoenix has been acting out a charade all this time. In an attempt to protect himself until he discovered he wanted to act on his ... feelings for me. Suddenly I'm giggling helplessly and I cover my mouth to try not to wake Nico. Phoenix's mouth drops a little as he looks at me, his shoulders dropping.

'Well, this isn't quite the reaction I was expecting. Rejection, definitely. But to literally be laughed away?' He makes to pull back from me.

'Wait, wait. I'm sorry.' I laugh.

I gather my self-control and smile at him. I've wounded him and a little sting of his pain takes the rest of my laughter. Gently stroking his cheek with the back of my fingers, the short stubble scratches at my knuckles. I don't know if I am unmoored because of my dream and the hour of the night, or because Phoenix's immediate and unwavering commitment to Nico has awakened a similar something in me. His skin is soft under my fingers despite the slight prickle of his new facial hair and I trace his jaw line.

If I stopped now, I know he wouldn't hold it against me. Our team would never know, and we would never have to navigate the unfamiliar territory of having crossed a line within our own group. As close as we are, I'm not naïve enough to think this won't cause a significant shift in the dynamic that's so important to us all.

I place my palms on his chest and feel it rising and falling. My ability to sense other people's emotions is not something I really understand and I actively try to dampen it with my friends, building a barrier between my feelings and theirs. But, in this moment, I close my eyes, take a breath and let the essence of Phoenix wash through me. It helps that it's already dark and quiet. I focus on the sensation of the gentle movement beneath my hands. I'm not sure what he is making of this, but I feel understanding, warmth, and very genuine care running across my skin as if I'm wrapped in a woollen blanket.

I open my eyes and the sensation subsides, leaving me with just my own feelings. There is only patience left as I look up at him and I wish I could read minds instead of emotions. The affection I felt could be anything. We have been friends for a long time, and he has clearly formed a quick and deep attachment to Nico. My heart flutters and, without quite knowing why, I decide to leap.

'I'm pleased you told me,' I breathe. 'It saves me from continuing to hide my disappointment at being the single person you didn't want,' I say.

He leans forward to touch his nose to mine and closes his eyes.

'Please tell me you're not joking.' His breath tickles my face.

I put my hands back in the top of his pockets and tug him forward so his whole body is pressed against mine. I run my hands up his torso and bury my fingers in his short hair.

'I am anything but joking, Phoenix.'

Remembering what he said about this not being easy for him, I wait. Gradually, he lifts his mouth to mine and brushes my lips. He kisses me deeply – unhurriedly – and I can't help but press my hips against him. Groaning, he pulls back to look at me. Assessing me as he takes a lock of my own wild, cocoa-coloured hair in his hand and tugs slightly.

'What are the chances we'd finally get to this point, only for there to be a small child in your bed?'

CHAPTER FOUR

Having texted Riley with my thoughts last night, she and Hayes are the first to arrive in the morning. My mouth drops at the large boxes Hayes is wheeling on a trolley, his wavy, sand-coloured hair falling into his face as he unloads them.

'Tell me those are not all what I think they are,' I say.

'No,' he replies, and I start to breathe a sigh of relief. 'There's more.'

'Seriously?'

'This is all we could manage to get our hands on so far,' he says, hoisting the first of the boxes onto the kitchen bench and pushing his timber and gold glasses back up his nose.

'Just these were hard enough to get,' Riley says, kicking the door shut behind her. 'I had to swipe Robard's access card to—'

'I did not hear that,' I say.

She laughs. 'Come on, Lish,' she says, 'you were the one insisting we need to look deeper. This is how we do it.'

'I figured this would give us enough to see if there are any patterns or anything else worth looking into,' Hayes says. 'Righto, Nico, you ready to go?'

He's reluctant to leave and Phoenix crouches down in front of him.

'It's just like we talked about,' Phoenix says. 'You'll spend some time with Hayes's grandmother, and then you'll come back here in the afternoon where Lish and I will be,' he says.

Nico looks at him and nods almost imperceptibly. Silently resigned to being shuffled around.

'Ask her for some choc-chip cookies and sneak one out for me,' Phoenix says.

'Only for you?' Riley asks, winking at Nico.

Nico gives me a small smile as he leaves, and I squeeze his little hand. The feel of it in mine warms my heart, even though his is clearly breaking. 'See you this afternoon.'

By the time Hayes returns, Blaire and Will are also in my apartment, and we've sorted the files by date, covering the floor with little piles of paper. We each take a stack to look for anything that stands out. What that might be exactly, none of us are sure. We all started at the Guard at the same time, part of the same graduating class and, while we have mostly been stationed on patrols and raids of various kinds and not investigative work, we have seen enough to know what smacks of business-as-usual-Rhyton versus something unusual.

The volume of files in the boxes Hayes found is immense. Each one containing little more than a single sheet of paper. Almost all seem to have never progressed beyond the initial statement.

Blaire looks through one of the files. 'Didn't you say Nico mentioned whispering in his head?' She peers over the paper at me. I nod. 'So does this one,' she says, frowning.

'This mentions loss of sight and hearing but no visible head trauma.' Will pushes a file across the table as he picks up another.

I glance through the one in my hand. The missing girl was last seen leaving school but there's no mention of anything like Nico's story.

'Nothing in this one,' I say.

'Categorise them,' Hayes suggests without looking up. 'We're looking for leads on Sofia primarily, so let's start by making a pile of the cases that sound most like Nico's account of that night.'

The odd one or two have 'resolved' stamped on them and we put these aside. At some point during the morning, Blaire goes through them and declares they seem to have been solved because of the connections or wealth of the witnesses. They're mostly runaways who are returned, either of their own volition or force – or ransom cases that ended one of two ways.

Of the rest, there are two clear piles. One that contains nothing particularly notable about each file, outside of someone being reported missing. The files in the other pile each contain a reference to something we, and the individual who made the report, can't quite explain.

Given the files are so brief and there are six of us going through them, we pick out some key details relatively quickly from this second pile. It is overwhelmingly made up of girls or women, each of which are described as fair with blonde or brown hair and light eyes. Will is commenting that, while it's not a particularly strong connection, it is a little strange when Hayes interrupts.

'Do the ages of these people seem off to you?' he asks.

My mind snags at his question.

'Yes, actually, now you've said that.' I rub my right temple. 'They don't seem to be restricted in age. There is everything from babies and toddlers to women a little older than us – there's no pattern. Don't these sorts of cases usually have a target group of some sort?'

'But,' Hayes continues, his blue eyes still focused on me. I watch his mind working behind them. 'If we put them back into chronological order, they get older,' he says, and I wait as he puzzles this out. It doesn't take him long.

'I think they're supposed to be someone,' he says. 'Look.' He opens a handful of files, checking himself. 'These early ones are of really young kids, toddlers. Then they shift to school-aged, teenagers, and now we've got women in their mid-ish twenties. Whoever is taking them is looking for someone. And they have been for some time ... minus what could be about a 10-year break. The cases seem to stop here'—he points at a pile on the floor and then the one next to it—'and they pick up again here, including Sofia.'

Will shakes his head, running the palm of his hand over his short, dark hair. 'If we have worked this out in less than a day, what has our supposed Missing Person Unit been doing?' he asks, raising his eyebrows.

'None of this makes any sense,' Riley chips in, putting down the coffee mug that now wears her bright pink lipstick. 'Apart from the clear-cut cases of the shit-hole that is Rhyton, none of these have even been looked into. Are we seriously suggesting that this many women and children have gone missing and the city has done *nothing*?' she asks.

No one has an answer.

'We know Rhyton can be an awful place for a lot of people, particularly women,' Phoenix says, 'but what about the secondary element in these?'

He fumbles at how to capture it. 'They talk of darkness, noises, headaches. Nico talked about whispers in his dreams that were scary enough to wake him. Are they drugging people in some way to cause disorientation and cover their tracks?'

I lean back in my chair and blow out a breath; my head is starting to ache and I rub at it again. Phoenix silently hands me a glass of water and I avert my eyes as our fingers brush against each other. We haven't discussed what we do from here and certainly not if, or how, we tell the team what's begun to unfold between us. Aside from being brand new pseudo guardians.

Blaire heads to the kitchen to make us some afternoon tea, gently knocking a box out of the way with her socked foot as she goes. She grew up dancing and it shows in the way she moves. We'd met in a class she was instructing not long before we joined the Guard. I'd been so hopeless we both dissolved into giggles and she'd had to end the class early, cementing our friendship immediately.

'Do you want to get Nico or shall I?' I ask Phoenix, moving to take the rest of the food back to the kitchen.

'I'm—' Phoenix starts.

'Lish ...' The colour drains from Will's face, a file shaking slightly in his hands.

'What is it?' asks Hayes, brows furrowed.

'It's Lish,' Will says.

'Spit it out, Will. I have to get Nico or—'.

Will hands me the photo. 'I mean it's *you*,' he says.

I look at the photo of a girl who looks to be about Nico's age. She's got messy brown hair, fair skin, and a dusting of freckles just beginning to show. Her eyes are crinkled in a laugh but it's clear they're green. The photo doesn't show what, or who, she's laughing at. There's a lurching in my stomach that makes me feel ill and I quickly shove it back to Will.

'Don't be absurd, that girl could be anyone. And I'm hardly missing, Will, I'm right in front of you,' I say despite the tightening in my throat.

'No, Lish. It's you,' he says. 'My first memories of you are when you looked like that. Without the smile, admittedly, but I would know that face anywhere.'

My legs don't feel like my own and I slowly sink to the floor. Phoenix is quick behind me and puts a chair within easy reach. I look up at them, my eyes searching each of their faces as I swallow away the nausea that comes in waves.

'But that means someone knew me,' I struggle to draw breath. 'They knew *her*. If they knew us, knew me — why did they stop looking?'

Suddenly I am jealous of Nico for having Phoenix and me, two strangers willing to give him the best possible life. For everything I missed and everything I unhappily gained at that orphanage. Part of me doesn't know why it matters. Why now knowing one anonymous person reported me missing has shifted the ground beneath me. But it's more than that. More than my own sense of belonging. This person could have information about who killed my mother. I didn't see their faces and knowing they were never found means my dreams are haunted by shadows.

The rich aroma of coffee fills my nose as Phoenix brings two large mugs over to the sofa and carefully wriggles back under the covers. I roll over to face him, my face pulling into a smile as I run a hand down his chest.

'Morning,' I say, a warm flush rising up my neck and into my cheeks.

He leans down to kiss me in response, his light stubble tickling my face. It's impossible not to smile into his soft lips. The sun is barely rising and Nico hasn't appeared yet, so I snuggle closer, taking my time to feel the contours of his torso. Between Nico, having the team around every night looking into the missing people cases, and one or both of us crashing in exhaustion, we haven't had a lot of time to enjoy being together and explore where that might take us. I continue to let my fingers trail over his dips and ridges. We train hard in the Guard and the effects on Phoenix's form are clear.

'Do you remember when we picked up Nico?' I ask. Phoenix makes a gentle noise of assent in his throat as he sits up to take his first sips of hot coffee. 'He didn't seem like he'd been drugged. He was scared, but he was lucid,' I say.

'Agreed. Where are you going with this?' he asks.

I remove my hand reluctantly and sit up, rearranging the bed covers around my waist before I collect my mug.

'We've been talking about the Whispers as if they are a gang or group who are looking for someone,' I say. 'Perhaps revenge for something, but we don't know. But I can't get this drugging issue out of my mind. Nico didn't have any injuries that would have caused headaches or loss of vision, but he didn't seem to be suffering the effects of drugs either.' I look at him to make sure he's still following. 'Admittedly, any drugging could have worn off by the time we got there but there's also nothing in his version of events that suggest drugs. He talks of being woken from a dream – that the whispers were inside his head. What can have that effect?'

'I understand the question about the drugging, it doesn't seem to add up. But what's the alternative?' He considers his question and I wait. 'I agree there are too many statements for it to be a coincidence or exaggerated,' he says. 'At least, as far as we know, the victims weren't connected in any meaningful way to have corroborated the details. But I can't see what else would cause the physical effects if it's not drugs.'

'No, me neither.' I sigh. 'I just keep coming back to it. It doesn't fit but the alternatives are ... well, crazy.'

The door to my bedroom opens behind us and Nico appears. I twist carefully on the sofa, mindful of my coffee. One side of his dark hair stands on end and the pillow has left its imprint on his face. His brown eyes are still bleary and he looks the picture of innocence.

'Good morning.' I smile at him.

'Did you find Sofia yet?' he asks quietly.

My stomach tightens, of course she would be his first thought. Sometimes my mother is still mine. The sting of the grief has changed, but the older I get the more I realise how much I want to know her. I glance at Phoenix quickly before gesturing for Nico to join us. He perches at the end of the sofa bed.

'We haven't yet, Nico, but we are looking really hard,' I say, conscious it probably sounds very contrary to seeing us in bed with coffee. Still, it's true in that, while we are of course hopeful of discovering what has happened to as many of the other cases as we can, we know the chances of this are virtually zero. So, Sofia has been our focus. She is the most recent that we know of and finding her will now have the most impact on our lives by righting Nico's. But there are no leads for us to go on and, by Nico's statement and what we could get out of the others we found in that street, she falls into the second, trickier category of cases.

Me too, I think and shake the thought away before it can take root.

'Nico,' I venture gently, 'you know there's a chance we won't find Sofia, don't you?'

He visibly slumps.

'But I promise you,' I say, 'that Phoenix and I, and the others, will do everything we possibly can to find out what happened. We will keep you safe while we do that, and I promise we will tell you the truth of what we find.'

He doesn't respond and, not for the first time, I wish I could take it all away for him. He's almost exactly the same age I was when I ended up in the orphanage and I'm struck by just how young that is. I know I can't lie to protect him, but I silently vow to do everything in my power to protect what is left of his innocence.

'Who's up for pancakes?' Phoenix asks, draining the last of his mug and heading for the kitchen, an attempt to distract Nico momentarily.

'Lish?' Nico asks quietly, watching Phoenix walk the few short steps to the kitchen before pinning me with his rich brown eyes. Eyes filled with hurt. 'Do you think Sofia has gone to the Blue Pointed Star?'

'I don't know yet, sweetheart.' My heart breaks for him. I hadn't intended the story to have that effect, but I understand his train of thought. Even now, I wonder where my mum is, and I know for sure she's dead. 'But if she is, I believe it's a wonderful place where she will be safe while she waits for you,' I say, aware of Phoenix's attention from the kitchen. 'And when you're ready to see her again and find the Star, the wolves will lead us there.'

'You don't think the wolves are scary?' he asks, his sleepy eyes lining with tears.

Watching him, I can't help but recall how many times I shed my own tears as I wished for wolves to take me to the Star. So I could make my wish and bring her back. Part of me wonders if I'm just giving him false hope. Whatever the Star of my mother's story is, it's not a place we can get to. But looking at his little face, so trusting and vulnerable, I can't bring myself to do it any other way.

'No, sweetheart, I don't. They're very special wolves, they're the Guardians of the Star.'

CHAPTER FIVE

I pass the city library on my way to pick up some things for Nico, something to wear other than Phoenix's over-sized hand-me-downs, and stop under the fans on the corner of the cross streets. I need some respite from the harsh sun, just for a moment. I breathe in the city as I look around. A vegetable garden that survived the last super-storm fills what was once a car park to my right, the scent of soil mingling with the sweat of the security officers that guard it. Their roles are sadly vital and unforgiving. If they are careless in any way, the whole city pays.

The fans buffet the air down over my hair now I have removed my large, wide-brimmed hat and I shake my head a little to get some air down the back of my neck as well. Peeling my light-coloured shirt from where it's stuck to my chest, I look back towards the library through the crowd of hats similar to mine as others pause under the fans around me. It's old compared to the newer buildings that are quite futuristic in design, all curves and heat resistant materials covered in shining solar panels. But the library is made of hand carved squares and rectangles, sensible shapes that hold stories of their own even though it is the books within that people come for.

The electric train was packed, as always, and even though the station isn't as cool, it does provide some relief of being in close proximity to large numbers of other sweaty bodies.

Like most cities across Driarn, Rhyton grew rapidly as the climate declined and displaced people still flock to the now megacities. The restrictions on travel across the continent of Driarn and the rest of the world has meant each city has been forced to become as self-sufficient as possible. Rhyton has community produce gardens on every block and buildings that were no longer fit for living were torn down and trees planted instead.

The library is no exception. Strips of gardens, mostly housing citrus trees, run between the library and the buildings on either side. Literally setting it apart from the rest of the street.

It's also somewhat of a refuge for those who need somewhere to escape the heat, the librarians having pooled their resources to install additional fans along the long front porch. The widening of the divide between those who can afford to live and those who struggle to get through each day is on every block for those that choose to see.

It's in the hat that sits on the pavement, waiting for loose change, while its owner cowers in the shade, and the luxury apartments that are built over others' land. It's in the little hands that desperately reach through the garden gates at night, and the untouched food from high profile events. It's in the knives that slide through throats for a bag of groceries, and the deeds that can be bought with that bag. I am told there was extraordinary beauty in the time before, but only pockets of it remain.

We are a solar and wind powered city of contradictions.

Thinking about the foreignness of the world as it was before focuses my gaze on the library once more. It's an impressive building in its own right, powered by the city's central electricity supply reserved for government buildings, like the Guard, and those that can afford to pay for it. I gaze at the pale, stone stairs and the pillars rising towards the sky, my mind caught on the abduction of Sofia. Of the possibility Nico was drugged. And the library seems as good a place as any to start looking for answers on what he might have been given. Then I can track where it came from.

Walking through the foyer, I am greeted by the hush that is typical of libraries, as if noise is disrespectful to the pages whose stories and histories beg to be read. My ears thrum slightly from the absence of the sounds of the city; I welcome the embrace of silence and the cool interior as I wipe the sweat from my face. Rows and rows of bookshelves open up beyond the archway at the far end of the foyer, a curved balcony circling the inner rim of the upper level.

Realising I have no idea where to start or what to look for, I search for a librarian. Wandering the rows of shelves, I marvel at the spines that watch me pass by. Many of these books are from before; there are faded patches and titles that are worn by hands past. The breadth of subjects is staggering. Once again, I wonder at people who were clever enough to write everything from gorgeous children's stories and sweeping adventures, to extraordinary medical textbooks – yet still bring the world that sustained them to its knees.

My fingers run along the spines of what appear to be gardening books when the hairs on the back of my neck start to prickle. I turn slowly but there's no one in the same row as me. I continue up and down the aisles but the sensation of being watched remains. I pause at the end of a row and wait. Abruptly, a small man in a moth-eaten tweed jacket appears around the corner and trips over his feet as he spots me waiting for him. I grip his elbow to help steady him and his mouth opens and shuts as if he is looking for what to say.

He clears his throat.

'Can I help you, my dear?' he asks.

I narrow my eyes at him. 'You're a librarian?'

'I am.' His voice is raspy, like he hasn't used it in a long time. 'Can I help you find something?'

'Were you following me?'

He flounders, surprised I've called it out despite us both knowing that's what he was doing.

'Just to see if you'd like some assistance. It's a large library and you've passed by many subjects, I thought perhaps you'd like some guidance,' he says, recovering, but there's still an uncertain openness in his face as he smiles.

I take stock of his slightly hunched figure, watery eyes, and crinkled skin. Oddly, I can't get much of a sense of his emotions but that's possibly due to his age and a greater ability to keep himself centred, especially in a place as calm as the library.

But there is a kindness in his eyes that's unmistakable and, despite myself, he draws a small smile from my lips. He watches me for a moment, his emotions becoming clearer the longer I look back, as if he's giving me a glimpse of himself. What I find matches his eyes, a deep-rooted gentleness even if it's dusted with gentle surprise.

The longer I hold his gaze, I realise there's something different but familiar about it. The colour in his eyes is so pale I didn't notice at first – his blue irises are ringed with silver. Like the beggar's hazel-ringed eyes.

'Yes, please, but I'm not entirely sure what I'm looking for.'

'Well, why don't you start telling me your thoughts and we see what direction they point us in?' he says.

I take a deep breath.

'I'm looking for information on something that causes loss of vision, headaches, and whispers in the mind. I don't believe it's a traditional drug because I haven't found how it's administered and there doesn't seem to be any side effects. Unless it's a gas of some sort ... ' I trail off as I think through how that could work.

'Hmm, interesting.' He studies my face with a hint of wonder that's puzzling. 'Well, no drugs or gasses come to mind with that description but, then, I'm no chemist. I feel there is more to this story, no?' he asks.

'Well, yes,' I say slowly. 'In each circumstance the symptoms are experienced by a witness.'

He waits.

'Of what ... seems to be an abduction of sorts. Each time a girl or a woman has gone missing, the loss of vision and headaches are what the witnesses have in common.'

'That's most alarming,' he says, although surprise doesn't colour his voice, sadness does. He watches me and, noting the absence of judgement from him, I plough on.

'I can't explain it, but something about these stories keeps running over the edges of my mind. My gut tells me there's no drugs involved, and I think the cases are connected – probably looking for someone'—his eyes light up at this suggestion but he doesn't comment—'but it doesn't feel like gang related crime,' I say.

He nods encouragingly, his white hair bouncing gently. 'Let's wander. We may find something in the medicinal section,' he says, beginning to walk away. 'Perhaps you're right and it's not a traditional drug. But there are other resources that might be helpful.'

He chatters away quietly as we traverse the library, the shelves rising up to the high balcony that runs the perimeter of the room. Politely, I answer his questions about how my day is going so far, if I'm surviving the heat. The last one is a question that only older people seem to raise, the rest of us don't know anything other than a heat that just gets hotter.

'Have you always lived in Rhyton?' he asks.

I hesitate.

I'm not skilled at talking about myself to strangers but I've practised my response to this question enough. It's his smile that gives me pause. While I can't read him as thoroughly as I can my friends, a sense of belonging begins to unfurl in my gut. Something I haven't felt with someone new in longer than I care to admit – there's a warmth that comes from him that feels like home.

It's this little spark of warmth that draws different words off my tongue.

'My mother was killed when I was young and I grew up in the orphanage before joining the Guard,' I say, already regretting not using my standard line. There's no reason to burden other people with my history.

'I am very sorry about your mother,' he says softly, that dull ache in my chest getting a little bit sharper.

Walking side by side, I don't have to look at him and it compels me to continue. I focus on the bit that's most relevant for what I'm looking for. The part that really brought me to the library today. That nowhere in my own memories is there a moment I could have been drugged that night. That maybe I missed something crucial in my own research.

'Thank you. I was very young. I was there, but I didn't see it all because—' I close my eyes for a moment. 'Because my vision had gone. It happened quickly.' I say, my voice lacking the depth of emotion it once conveyed when I talked about that day. A day, outside of my own nightmares, I never thought I'd have to revisit. And, yet, now Nico's soulful eyes have witnessed something so similar and I have no choice but to help him.

'Go on, dear,' he says. 'It is a sad, violent story, I know, but you won't shock this old one, I assure you.'

Breathing deeply, I search those faded eyes for a hint of hesitation. Not finding anything but understanding, I continue. 'Someone came in while I was hiding – we were playing – and I could hear them talking but, with the noise in my head, I couldn't make out what they were saying.' My heart starts to race, the images forcing their way back in. 'As she hit the floor, my vision returned and I saw her for the last time through the cracks in the floor.' I huff a soft laugh. 'Now, I wonder if she'd had that trap door put in purposefully.'

He nods and smiles gently, even as his blue and silver eyes seem to water.

'More than once I've wondered if it would have been better if I'd not gone through the door and met the same fate as she. At least we'd be together then, right?'

I blush at the words that stumble out of their own accord. I hadn't intended to go that far.

The librarian quickly grasps my hand.

'Sorry,' I say, forcing a smile, trying to brush off my awkwardness. This is why I don't talk to people about my past.

'No, my dear, it most certainly would not have been better,' he says earnestly. After a beat he drops my hand. 'Ah, here we are.'

We're surrounded by books, most of which look older than the library, with a smattering of shiny new ones. Rows and rows of different coloured spines, many of whose titles I can't make out due to age or the fact they are in other languages altogether.

'These books,' he tells me, 'talk mostly to alternative medicines. Given the symptoms you describe, it could be a good place to start. Traditional medicine is a few rows over.'

He collects a few books from the shelves and leads me to one of the tables set into the quiet sides of the library before heading off to continue his work, leaving me to my thoughts. I thumb through the books and skim over stories of plants and herbs and different things people have turned into treatments for every imaginable ailment. But none of it resonates with my memories or Nico's story and I sigh at the waste of time.

I shut the book I have been reading with a thud and watch as the dust blown from its pages dances in the sunlight beaming through the window.

As I move the last book to my discard pile, a leather notebook looks back at me. Flicking it open, an even thinner book drops out. *Interdependency: an investigation of the relationship between Driarn and the Realm.* I've never heard of a 'Realm' in Driarn but then, like most of the population, I'm not well travelled across our continent.

The existence of the Realm has been debated for centuries. While the accuracy and claims of different accounts varies wildly, underneath the stories a nub of truth seems to survive. The Realm is real. The questions that are harder to answer are why? And what does its existence mean for Driarn? We will begin by examining what we know, and a generally accepted history of the relationship between the two worlds. Before Driarn was known as —

I sit back, slipping the essays back into the notebook and let the cover fall open to the first double page of the notebook itself. It's filled with sloping, handwritten notes in different sections and directions across the thick, aged cream paper. A circled section captures my attention.

Headaches it reads. A line is scratched repeatedly to another bit of text, almost hidden amongst the other notes. *Bleeding ears?*

My heart leaps into my throat.

'Anything?' the librarian asks as he appears over my shoulder.

I gasp as I shut the book quickly, not sure why it feels like a secret. His gaze lingers on the notebook in front of me, a sad look on his face.

I smile and try to hide my shock at his sudden appearance. 'I'm not sure, to be honest, but thank you very much for your help ... can I borrow this one?' I ask, placing a protective hand over the top of the notebook.

The corners of the librarian's mouth tug back gently but it's not a smile. 'Of course. It will serve you well, I think.'

I stand, place the rest of the pile of books on his trolley, and make to walk away.

'I'll walk you out,' he says.

He slows beside me as we make our way to the exit. He quietly tells me about the different sections of the library and my mind wanders to what I am supposed to be doing, buying clothes for Nico. But it's hard to drag my thoughts from the notes I've found. What else they could contain.

The librarian's soft, raspy voice is warm as I keep my pace slow to match him and it's comforting even as I half-listen. I am surprised at how quickly the day has started to disappear. The doors appear before us and I look into his unusual eyes to say goodbye, but he speaks first.

'You found yourself in the cases you're looking into, didn't you?' he asks quietly.

As I watch him, a single tear courses its way over the creases on his face and I inexplicably feel a deep sense of loss.

I nod slowly before I can speak. 'But it doesn't mean very much. There was no information on who made the report, and they obviously didn't look very hard if they didn't find me in the orphanage.'

He holds my gaze, and my own eyes fill with tears at the kindness and sorrow in his face. Somehow, this stranger understands my hurts.

'There is something you must know, my dear,' he says, his breathing seeming a little laboured now.

'The people who love us never stop looking, even if they cannot reach.' He gently taps two fingers against my chest. 'I know you, and your mother, were very loved.' I start to shake my head, I've heard lots of platitudes over the years, and he grips my hands firmly. 'I know it seems impossible, but you are loved, sweet girl, and you are strong. Stay strong,' he says, another tear falling. 'Your strength will be needed.'

My chest contracts at his words and how desperately I want to believe them. My team love me, but it doesn't fill the void my mother has left. Outside of how she made me feel, and the memories that mostly come in the form of dreams now, I know very little about her. The sweet ignorance of being a child when she died robbed me of the opportunity to know her as a person, as my friend.

'I'm sorry there isn't more I can do.' His voice cracks. 'But I will be with you in this life and the next, remember that. It has been an absolute pleasure to meet you, my dear. Everything you need is already within you.'

He presses his hand against his heart and dips his head in a shallow bow. Without another word he shuffles me closer to the doors as I grapple with our interaction.

'Wait!' I can barely hear my own voice as he turns away from the exit. I snag the back of his jacket and he stops abruptly in my grip. 'Did you know her?'

'I —' Redness appears at the edges of his eyes as he tries to speak. 'The book—just—please. Read it.'

I stare at him.

He pulls himself from my grip with surprising strength, even as he wheezes and returns to the depths of the library.

I look down at the hand that held his jacket, ignoring the voice in my mind telling me I let go because I'm afraid of the answers he holds.

CHAPTER SIX

'I'm telling you, Riles, my Pilates instructor would be perfect,' Blaire says as I close the door to her apartment and dump my bag, notebook still in hand. The leather is warm on my palm.

They both look at me and smile in greeting before Riley immediately rolls her eyes at Blaire and she swallows a mouthful of caramel and chocolate slice.

'So, why don't you date him?' she asks, pointing her fork at Blaire who just stares back, clearly having nothing to say to that.

'I met someone today,' I interrupt. They both clasp their attention on me, waiting for me to go on. 'A librarian—'

'Hayes isn't librarian-looking enough for you?' Riley asks.

Blaire laughs until she looks properly at me. Then she tilts her head.

'Wouldn't it be a bit weird for one of us to start dating one of the boys?' she asks tentatively.

A warmth creeps up my chest and I clear my throat, hoping my skin doesn't show too much pink.

'He's a librarian,' I repeat, looking pointedly at them, 'and old enough to be my grandfather.'

'Please tell me he's not married,' Riley says seriously. 'You've been in that sort of train wreck before. I'll kill him if he's married.'

Blaire glances at Riley as I shake my head, desperately trying not to remember the crushing revelation. The horrible cliché of his wife coming home early from work to find me his bedroom. Putting my bra back on in what turned out to be *their* bedroom. I still don't know what hurt worse, the way he looked at her – so full of regret, dismissing me without a second thought – or the way she looked at me.

I bite down on the anger that still comes when I think of him, of the deception of both of us, and that, after close to a year of seeing each other, I was still painted as the one in the wrong.

'Riles,' Blaire says, her voice full of knowing, 'no one makes that mistake twice.' She puts her fork into her piece of slice. 'And I think you missed the bit about him being old? Like *old* old.'

'He was so ... I don't know,' I say, deciding to ignore the married comments altogether and giving them a quick rundown of my visit to the library.

'Look at this.' I place the notebook on the table they sit at, shoving the cakes out of the way. 'He seemed quite happy that I would be reading it. I think.... he may have even written it.'

They both look at the old brown leather and then back to me. Riley narrows her eyes at me and I take a deep breath, forcing myself to voice my suspicions. I know they won't let me walk away from facing my demons.

'I think there's a link between my mum and these cases,' I say quietly. 'The fragments I remember ... I just kept hitting brick wall after brick wall. And if it wasn't a wall, it was literally nothing. Eventually, I stopped looking to save my sanity.' Lead fills my stomach at the truth uttered out loud.

'But Nico's experience, the way he described it ... there has to be a connection, an answer. I need to know what happened to her and I think finding Sofia will take me there.' I jab a finger on the notebook. 'This will help me.'

The frayed bits of hope the librarian summoned float in my mind. Untethered to each other, but gathering.

'This is incredible,' Phoenix says, 'but surely none of it's real.'

'I wouldn't have thought so a few weeks ago,' I say, 'but he clearly wanted me to have it. He effectively gave it to me. And you can't deny the similarities between the stories in this book and Nico's. Not to mention all those files. And my mum,' I say.

The journal is split into two sections. The first contains entry after entry that paint a picture of someone trying to puzzle together or record a number of mysterious happenings. It's not unlike what I would do to keep track of all the anecdotes and snatches of a story picked up along the way. I am mildly surprised that this book refers to the 'Whispers', the same as Nico did, but then most urban myths are based on some elements of truth, and the similarity doesn't end there. These Whispers track and hunt people, although it's unclear to what end, or who controls them.

The book has references to the impact on vision and headaches but it doesn't address why this is. As if this should be understood by the reader, but I am still at a loss. Some entries refer to strange noises heard outside windows before houses are burnt to the ground, their occupants butchered, and animal-like beings that steal people in the dead of night. One of them details an abduction that caused a great stir of excitement amongst the Whispers, only for it to end in a scream of disappointment that shook the world. As if they thought they were about to nab a prize, but the victim was not who they expected.

There are hastily drawn maps I don't inspect just yet, my mind too full to take in the detail, and notes in the margins with all manner of questions that don't appear to have answers. Phoenix pulls out a loose page that looks newer than the others, but it's written in the same hand.

I'm sorry there isn't more.

I shudder at the echo of the librarian's last words to me and close the book.

'You don't want to finish reading it?' Phoenix asks.

'Yes, but not tonight. It's making my head hurt and there are too many reminders ...'

Phoenix squeezes my hand in recognition of the questions that remain around my mother. 'I've been meaning to talk to you about Sofia ... if we don't find her.' He pauses. 'I would like to formally request to be Nico's guardian, if he'll have me,' he says, looking at me.

I smile.

'He'd be lucky to have you,' I say, 'and I will help in any way I can.'

My heart swells as I take him in – this incredible, selfless man – at the same time it aches for Nico's loss.

'I was hoping you'd say that,' Phoenix says, taking my wine glass and placing it on the side table. 'You're a wonderful kind of special, Lish.'

He tucks me closer as my cheeks heat slightly and I kiss him. His lips are warm on mine as we explore each other, and I feel him smile against my mouth. We've been waiting for this for a while and I am more than ready. But I remind myself of his difficulty in relaxing into physical intimacy and I let him set the pace, carefully releasing my hold on my barrier to feel for any unease from him.

I don't find any.

In a smooth action, Phoenix slides me down the sofa bed and kisses me deeply. I wind my arms around his neck and pull him closer, feeling his weight against me. He runs his hands along my side and under my shirt. I inhale softly as he unlatches my bra and caresses me gently. I ungracefully wriggle each of us out of our pants and feel his chest shake slightly against mine. I look up at him, worried I've overstepped a line, only to find him suppressing a laugh. I bite his shoulder in reprimand and to stifle my own giggle, and grip him tightly as our bodies gently come together.

We lie together afterward, and I interlace my fingers with his.

'Did you expect it to be this easy?' I ask.

'Easy?' His eyebrows shoot up. 'Lish, you barely looked at me for years thinking I was sleeping with the whole of Rhyton,' he teases.

'I wouldn't quite say I wasn't looking,' I say. 'I was just trying not to pay so much attention to that great ass of yours.' His laugh is loud, and I shush him playfully to not wake Nico. 'And,' I continue, 'you were trying particularly hard to seem the world's greatest player. Gorgeous as you may be, Phoenix, I do have standards, I'll have you know.'

'Lucky for me,' he says, flicking my nose. 'But, to answer your question, yes? Maybe. I don't know, I guess I hadn't thought this far. I'd fantasised about it, don't get me wrong, but there was less talking in those moments.' He winks at me.

'You really are incorrigible, player or not,' I laugh.

'Really, though, I didn't want to get ahead of myself,' he says seriously. 'I was fairly confident you'd shut it down. Even if you did want me, by some miracle, I wasn't sure you'd take the risk with the team. And I certainly didn't imagine we'd have Nico staying in your bedroom and I'd be relegated to having you on the most uncomfortable sofa known to man.'

Ignoring his comment about the team and Blaire's question earlier, I push him over onto his back and run my hand over the length of him. Slowly I raise myself up to straddle his hips. My brown hair frames his face as I lean down to kiss his soft mouth and I shift my body so I can take all of him once more.

'Easy is good, Lish. This is good,' he says, green eyes fixed on mine.

'Do you mean us 'this' or 'this'?' I ask as I rock my hips for emphasis and stare back at him. He makes a noise deep in his throat and closes his eyes.

'Both. I definitely mean both.'

The low buzz of the shutters closing over the windows sounds throughout my apartment, just as I'm starting to doze off nestled into Phoenix. He shifts beside me, clearly not asleep either, and instead we listen to the sirens in the city.

Within seconds, the shutters are clamouring to break free from their binds. It's too easy for the hand sized hailstones to find them. Yet that's their sole job – protect the glass, and us, from the hail that would shred skin and smash bone.

The crack of the lightning is blinding, even with the shutters down. Nico screams as the thunder that follows shakes the walls and runs out of my bedroom. Phoenix and I scramble apart and Phoenix gathers him up.

'You're safe here, Nico, it's just a storm,' he says.

His eyes catch mine; we know this is not 'just' a storm.

It's a death sentence for anything without proper shelter.

Like many of Rhyton's food sources.

And everyone in the dockside slums.

The clean-up crews will be on today and I shove down the rising bile at the thought of what the casualty numbers will be. With an unexpected day off, the others gather in my apartment after dropping Nico back to Hayes's grandmother. The shadows of last night's storm on their faces, too.

'Blaire and I did some asking around while on shift yesterday,' Hayes says. 'It seems a lot of people know of the Whispers. We obviously all heard the odd ghost story growing up, but I was puzzled none of us seemed to register the term. So, I dug a little further and most of the people who were familiar with them came from outside the city or had family that did,' he says.

I look at him for a moment. 'There's a theory coming isn't there?' I ask, not at all surprised by Hayes's ability to look at a situation differently to the rest of us; it's always been one of his greatest strengths. His blue eyes hold mine as he considers the information we have at hand.

'I think the Whispers didn't always hunt in the city,' he says. 'In fact, I think, for at least a time, they were abducting girls from well outside cities. Now, I think they are very committed to looking for someone and they believe that someone may have come to Rhyton. In the earliest cases we looked at, there seems to be significantly less occasions of missing people with the 'other' factor we've been looking at. The headaches, noises in the mind and all of that,' he continues, 'the possible drugging I mean, increases in frequency about twenty years ago, and then stops, ' he says. 'But something has prompted them to start again. There was another case last night.' He looks around as we all fall silent. 'Who knows what will stop them this time if we don't.'

'I have multiple questions about that statement,' Riley says. 'But, regardless,' she forges on, not giving Hayes a chance to respond, 'we do have to look for them.'

'Isn't that what we're doing?' asks Phoenix, brows knitting together.

'Not just the missing people,' she says. 'The Whispers. Find the Whispers, find the people – or at least what happened to them. I don't hold much hope that any of them are still alive. After all, some of them would now have been held somewhere for the best part of twenty odd years. We know how likely that is,' she says.

We look at each other. None of the scenarios are positive.

Blaire is the first one to speak. 'Riley's right. We could spend weeks and weeks sitting here, trying to unpack the various myths about the Whispers.

We know they must exist, there's far too many missing people with the same circumstances for them not to be real.' She looks at each of us. 'What we have no way of doing is predicting where they will turn up next. The victims haven't been specific enough for us to work that through, nor have we found any connection between them apart from the physical appearance,' she says. 'What we do have, though, is a map.'

'A map?' asks Will, disbelieving. 'You mean the scratching in this?' He holds the leather notebook in his hand.

'I do,' Blaire responds.

I take the journal from Will and flick to the page of the map, laying it out in front of us so we can each see it well enough. Rhyton appears to be marked quite clearly with a capital 'R' in a circle. There are multiple other, smaller circles dotted around the page but no indication of what or where they are. But there is a dotted line from Rhyton, across the deserted farming flats and into Althea Forest. At which point a written description seems to kick in with musings about what to find in the forest.

'Exactly,' Riley continues, 'we go on the offensive. If Hayes is right, and this map certainly suggests he is, the Whispers are coming from outside the city. So there's no way we can stop them from taking anyone else if we stay within the city walls. We will always hear about the abductions after the fact. But there's enough in that book to try and find them. I agree it's a long shot, but it's the only one we've got.'

'Okay,' I say slowly as I consider what they're suggesting. A little spark of hope at finding out something more about my mum flares. 'If we do this, who goes?' I feel Phoenix's eyes on me, his tension beginning to break through my defences.

But not one of my team objects to their going and I don't expect them to. There's nothing we wouldn't do for each other, or the people of Rhyton.

'That probably depends on Robard,' Will says as he spins the journal towards him and leans further over the map, still looking doubtful. 'If he will let us explore this on the books—'

'Assuming he'll look past the fact we're not supposed to have these files you mean?' I interrupt.

Will continues as if I haven't spoken. '—then we can all go. If not, some of us will have to take leave and go anyway. I'm not convinced we'll find anything, but we should probably rule out the possibility.'

CHAPTER SEVEN

I leave the team to decipher the map and the hazy observations – I can't quite call them directions – as best they can and head back to the library to see if the librarian can give me anything else. I can't be certain that he wrote the journal himself, but there is no doubt he knows more than he said on my last visit. There's an urgency growing in the pit of my stomach to see him.

I should have asked him when we first met, pressed him on why he had the notebook. Where it came from. But I'd let my fear keep me silent and now another question rings in my mind as well.

Practically, some help with map would be good, too.

But it was the small, second section of the journal that really struck a chord with me. That I need to ask him about. As I'd turned the pages to find a story about a blue pointed star, my breath caught. Until Nico, I hadn't spoken out loud about the Star or its wolves since my mother died. There hadn't ever been a reason to. I'd always assumed it was a story all kids would be told by their parents but there was little point in discussing it with kids who didn't have any of those. So, to see it in a book that also documented the Whispers was disconcerting.

I need to know what the connection is.

How he knows my mother's story.

The city is quiet as I pick my way through the debris left by last night's storm. Some of it is recognisable, most of it is indistinguishable rubbish. The only remaining question – would it kill someone if the wind picked it up again? More often than not, the answer is yes and the clean-up crews scrape up piles to be discarded.

In the city itself, it's rare to see human casualties. The sirens, shelters, and homes give Rhyton's citizens both time and an escape. The death here is in the gardens. Pulverised fruit and vegetables are now what remain. They, too, will be erased by the crews before they can start to rot in the heat that always follows. It doesn't matter how bad the storm, the heat always returns.

I shudder as I think of the slums outside the city walls and what else the crews have to erase – how many didn't get to the shelters in time. And yet, I can't bring myself to look in that direction, my heart contracting just at the knowledge of what they've had to endure.

My mind drifts back to last night, before the storm, as I walk up the library stairs and into the foyer. Blaire's right, it is weird to be dating one of the boys, if that is what Phoenix and I are doing. But I can't ignore how easy it is, either, and I won't deny it feels good. I've been attracted to Phoenix for so long without really giving any serious thought to what we could be like as a couple. Now we're here and it's happened so quickly, I can't imagine backing out either.

At the same time, the thought of telling the others makes my palms sweat. I know they wouldn't openly reject the idea, but it's a shift in the undercurrent that worries me. I've always thought there was nothing we couldn't survive but that was when we were all individuals and the partners came from outside. Does two of us being together change the power dynamic? Shift the scales in a direction the others won't be comfortable with? The slow fallout of that might not be something I can bear.

It takes me a moment to register that there are Guards stationed at the entrance to the library. I recognise one of them from Will's training sessions.

'Hey, Claire, what's going on?' I ask the woman with an auburn plait draped down her back.

'Oh, there was a murder here last night,' she says. Rhyton can be a rough place but it's still jarring to hear a relatively new recruit talk so flippantly about a murder. 'It was pretty gruesome, actually. An old guy – looks like he was tortured. His hands were smashed and both eyes cut out before his throat was slit.'

'What?' I manage to ask as my blood pounds in my ears. The librarian's face is still fresh in my mind and I—

'Yeah,' Claire says, 'pretty awful way to go, right?'

I stare through the foyer to where I can see the beginning of the book lined shelves and I realise I don't need to go in. The chill creeping up my spine tells me I know who died. And I can't help but think he was killed because of me.

'Awful,' I mumble. Staggering back down the stairs and around the corner, I drop my head between my legs as the city spins around me.

I sit opposite Phoenix and watch the emotions flicker across his face. I appreciate having the time and space to watch his emotions as well as feel them wash through me. He's warring with himself, that would be clear even to someone who couldn't sense everything he felt.

'I don't want you to go,' he says, his voice tight.

'But you also know why I have to,' I say gently. 'It's ... tenuous, I know. But what if'—I steady my breath—'what if I can find out what happened to my mum? The echo of my own experiences that night in all those other reports, and what happened to Nico, is too much. And you can tell me it's not my fault all you like but I know, I *know*, Phoenix, that it was no coincidence the librarian was killed immediately after giving me that journal.'

I'd barely made it out of the library after Claire told me about his death and the manner it was carried out. Somehow, I'd managed to get back to my apartment and found Phoenix waiting for me when I launched into my plan. I didn't know the librarian well enough to be able to claim a sense of loss, but I'd felt a connection to him when we met all the same, and the timing is far too close to be a coincidence. Someone knows he had information that he gave away and they killed him for it. How long until they look for me, anyway? I don't voice that bit to Phoenix, the worry on his face is clear enough. Not to mention the extra energy I find myself pouring into my wall, instinctively knowing it needs more to keep Phoenix's emotions at bay.

'I might even find Sofia, and you know we can't pass up that opportunity,' I say.

Phoenix rubs his face and looks at me. 'I know you're really capable, Lish, but this seriously worries me. I should come but—'

I walk around to his side of the table and take his hands, the devastation on his face making my chest ache.

'I would take you with me in a heartbeat,' I say, 'but you need to stay here with Nico. He doesn't deserve to be left again and he's closest to you.'

'But this is crazy,' he objects. 'The *very* limited information we have on the Whispers is that they are dangerous – really dangerous. The drugging is the least of it, those people were lucky. God knows what they did with the people they've taken. They're not alive, Lish, I assure you.' His forehead furrows.

'I'll be fine. I'll be with Will. You know he won't let anything happen to me.'

'It should be me,' he says in a rough voice.

Sliding myself onto his lap, I snake my arms around his neck. 'Phoenix, you are the sweetest man I have ever known. I would gladly have both of you with me if I could but that would be too unfair to Nico. If you're right and it is as dangerous as you think, we can't risk having you taken away from him for any reason,' I tell him.

He looks at me with a wry smile. 'Don't think I haven't noticed you didn't mention the option of not going at all.'

I press my forehead against his before gently kissing his nose and then his mouth. 'That's because it isn't an option.'

'The answer is no.' Robard's voice is firm.

I open my mouth to protest but he holds up a hand to halt me.

'No, Alice,' he says. 'I'm going to extend you enough professional courtesy to turn a blind eye to you even reading those files.' His eyes narrow at me in disappointment, his moustache flattening over the thin line of his lips. 'But under no circumstances will you investigate this further.'

'Not even if I have a lead?'

He pales and my skin catches on the discomfort that starts to fill the room. I pretend not to notice, but it's enough for me to loosen the grip I hold on the emotional wall between us. Letting a fraction more of him in, I'm now acutely aware of his apprehension.

'What sort of lead?' His voice is gravelly.

I pause, something in my chest squeezing. Robard has long been a supporter of mine in the Guard, helped me win the team leader role, even, but the sands have been shifting. He's been distancing himself, keeping things from me, and I can't pinpoint why. Or even quite when it started. A nagging in the back of my mind tells me I should only share this information, and the notebook, with people I'd trust with my life. I draw a long breath in when I realise I'm no longer sure if I can count Robard in that group.

He fingers the collar of his shirt, absently tugging it higher up his neck. 'What sort of lead, Alice?' he asks again.

'I'll find one.' I make myself hold his gaze.

He leans forward on his desk, rubbing his temples. 'No, you won't. Our resources are far too scarce to have you chasing shadows. Leave it, or I find a team leader better prepared to take direction.'

We stare at each other a moment before I nod curtly and leave his office.

It takes all my restraint not to slam the door on the way out.

My thoughts scramble as I stride the halls to the training room.

Robard just threatened my job. The only thing that gives me purpose and security. I would be a fool to throw it away. But Nico's face dances in my mind, the image of my own face from the photo joining him. My heart beats a little faster. *Find them,* it seems to say.

An urgency flutters in my gut as my heart and mind go to war. I need Hayes. He knows Robard as well as I do but he can be more objective than me. Talking things through with him helps me work through my own thoughts and assessments versus the emotions I pick up from others. I cannot throw my job away on a whim. And yet ...

I scan the training room quickly, forcing a smile to those nearest to me, and spot Hayes sparring with a new graduate. He ducks and weaves but, even from here, I sense him holding back, giving her time to feel out her moves. It won't last long.

My chest burns with impatience as I watch them, stalking close enough to catch his eye but not so close he tries to rope me into joining. He calls a halt to their session after spying me and wipes his face on a towel as he makes his way over. His forehead creases as he takes me in.

'Alright?'

'Robard just threatened to fire me.' I can't believe that's what just happened.

His sky-blue eyes bulge. 'What?'

'I'm ... kind of floored.'

Another Guard team starts a loud session and Hayes guides me to the far wall, his hand resting gently on my elbow.

'What happened?' Concern ripples gently from him but he's never been quick to agitate, his very presence is calming.

'I asked him for clearance to follow the trail of the Whispers. Well, I didn't tell him about them, specifically, but about trying to look for the girls. And—' I break off, thinking. 'Something's up Hayes, I can feel it.'

'What do you want to do about it?'

I smile at him; he's never doubted me. 'That's the hard part. I want to go. I *need* to go. I could find Sofia, find out what happened to my mum. But it seems that I would be throwing away everything I've worked so hard for. How would I survive here without the Guard?'

My mind flares at the thought of everything I would lose. My home, my salary, my food allowance.

'What about leave? You must have loads.'

'I ... yes, actually, I do. But you don't think I'd be stupid to go? Robard might fire me for doing it on my own time, anyway.'

'I don't think you'd forgive yourself if you didn't. Robard ... he'll come around. He always does when it comes to you.'

CHAPTER EIGHT

Until now, I hadn't been focusing on what could go wrong and was more worried about making sure we had our supplies in order. That I'd left things as easy as possible for Nico and Phoenix in my absence. Now, though, the team has come to see us off and I look at each of them, purposefully blocking their emotions.

I didn't want to ask anyone to take leave but Will insisted, even though I put my foot down about anyone else joining us.

Will shakes hands with Hayes and kisses Blaire's cheek. Riley grabs him and pulls him into a bear hug.

'Don't do anything stupid, okay?' she says, before making her way to me and giving me a tight squeeze as well. Her pale, gold hair tickles my nose as I return the gesture. Riley is standing in for me as team leader while I'm gone and I give her a few last-minute instructions. She's so strong-willed, I know she won't take any changes or directions that would negatively impact the team in my absence. She'd prevent harm coming to any of us by sheer determination alone.

'I know, Lish,' she says, mock annoyance in her tone. 'I promise I'll take good care of them, and I'll do my best not to mess up the paperwork.' She winks at me. 'You, however, need to be creating paperwork. The more you find out, the better. I want to know who they are, what their movements are, how many are involved—'

'I know how to build a case, Riles.' I laugh and she points a finger at me, grey eyes narrowed.

'That may be so,' she says in a smug tone, 'but, as of now, I am team leader, and I am telling you I want it watertight. And so compelling Robard won't care you gathered the information while on leave. Because, then, we're going to take it to him and get the resources to bring those bastards down. Properly.'

Hayes steps between us, patting me on the back before pulling me into a quick, hard hug. 'You guys will be fine. But, if you follow that path and find them, do not engage under any circumstances,' he insists. 'We know nothing about the drugs they're using, or how they are administering them. So stay the hell away and gather intel only.' Hayes holds my gaze, glasses back on today, and my stomach flips slightly at the seriousness there. 'Information only, Lish,' he repeats. 'The single most important thing is you both come back in one piece – everything else is secondary.'

I nod at Hayes, letting his message sink in before kissing Blaire on both cheeks, half listening to Will and Phoenix exchange goodbyes. Will looks at Phoenix with narrowed eyes, the latter stumbling over his words but clearly trying to make a point. I drag my attention back to Blaire.

'Please make sure my apartment is standing when I get back,' I say.

'You know better than to ask for things I have no power to deliver,' she laughs.

I'd said goodbye to Nico this morning before we dropped him at Hayes's family home, in case he found the group farewell too over-whelming. His little face was teary as I left and my heart still aches for him, the glimmer of hope in his eyes weighing heavily. It dawns on me I only have Phoenix left to say goodbye to and we haven't discussed what, if anything, we are going to tell the team about us. We're such a tight knit group, I doubt any of them have even thought twice about the fact we've been sharing a sofa bed since Nico arrived. I search his green eyes for a clue for how he'd like to manage this, my heart thumping in my chest. The others are still chatting around us and don't seem to have noticed our awkwardness. Slowly we make our way towards each other and I'm conscious of the noise dying away a little.

'You guys good?' Riley asks, watching us curiously.

My eyes flick to her and back to Phoenix. Shyly he lifts one shoulder at me and I stare back, suddenly at a crossroads. If I show the others the affection I have for Phoenix, there's no taking it back. No way to stop the ripple effect. At the same time, if I reject Phoenix here ... I don't think I'm willing to see the hurt that's sure to be on his face. Or feel on his behalf.

I'd wondered, for a moment, if he would turn away from this but he seems ready to meet it head on. I hesitantly take his lead.

I turn a little so I can see everyone. 'There's maybe something you guys should know.' I say quietly, suddenly realising how much I might lose if things go wrong when Will and I get to that forest. And, if they do, I don't want Phoenix to feel like he was my dirty secret. That is something I will never do to anyone. In any capacity.

Riley lifts a brow, a curious half-grin on her face.

Phoenix reaches out to my hip and pulls me towards him. I lean against him looking up into his gaze.

'I couldn't let you go without another of these anyway,' he says quietly before pressing his soft lips to mine. I savour the feel of his mouth, closing my eyes against the sudden silence of the others. Breathing into the little gold flame in my chest that helps me block everyone else's emotions out. My own feelings are enough to contain at the moment as I say goodbye and chase the answers I've desperately needed my whole life.

'Whoop!' Riley exclaims at the same time Hayes says, 'Bloody hell, you kept that quiet.'

I laugh softly and shake my head against Phoenix's shoulder to hide my blush. I hold him tightly before one last kiss.

'Be safe. Please, Lish,' he says seriously, tucking a strand of my hair from my face. 'I'll be waiting for you.'

I release him and collect my pack.

'God, who packed this damn thing,' I grumble, still trying not to look directly at anyone and give them time to let the kiss they've just seen sink in. Even if it will probably take longer to really process it. Although Riley already seems on board. I can't help the lift in the corners of my mouth at her unwavering support.

'Stay safe, all of you,' I say. 'Don't wreck my apartment, make sure you keep us posted on anything more you hear of the Whispers, and be vigilant on your patrols. Riley,' I continue, 'I know you'll be amazing at the TL role but I do want my job back so don't be too good, okay?' I pause. 'Oh, and look after Nico and Phoenix please. They are my boys, after all.'

I wink as I wave goodbye; a false bravado, I know, but I want to leave them on a lighter note than the worry that's starting to settle in my stomach.

It's not until later, when I've eased off on the barrier I create over my skin and let myself think on the goodbye, that I register the shock in Blaire's fawn-brown eyes.

The Guard Headquarters are roughly halfway between the Dockside Gate and the Northern Gate of the city and, thankfully, the air-conditioned electric trains run that route frequently. The clean-up crews have done their jobs well and none of the tracks are obstructed, meaning we make our way to the Northern Gate in good time. Even if I moan about the weight of my pack often enough for Will to feign sticking his fingers in his ears every time I open my mouth. We've timed our run to maximise the late evening hours, when there's enough light to see by but we don't have to brave the unrelenting daytime sun.

Outside the city walls the landscape is dry and bare, despite the hail last night. There are no more storms forecast for the coming weeks, which will make the heat the biggest threat to the first part of our journey. I focus on that instead of what we might find in the forest, Hayes's warning still ringing in my ears. The librarian's journal has left me with a frayed edge. All the loose ends of my childhood screaming to be tied together.

The land beneath us slopes up gradually towards Althea Forest in the distance, mimicking the subtle change in my heart rate. The rutted road we follow doesn't look like it's ever been sealed, even this close to the city. It's been so long since anyone was able to live on this side, it's all been left as a wasteland.

Dotted along the road, and down laneways that shoot off to the left and right, are old homes, mostly in a state of disrepair. At one time in history, despite Rhyton being a walled city, the world was relatively safe and stable. Properties on the city's edge, with more space for families and a handful of livestock, were highly sought after and seen as a more prestigious holding than some of the higher density urban areas.

Not anymore.

I suppress a shiver at the ghostly old buildings watching us pass.

As we continue along the dirt road, these properties thin out to the entrances of what were once large, productive farms that have now been claimed by drought. The gates caked with dust and left open – if they remain standing at all.

Every last drop has been squeezed from the land here until she literally cracked under the pressure – the fissures running along the hard red and yellow ground as far as the eye can see between the forest and the walls of Rhyton.

The depth of the fissures worsens the further we go and we walk far from their edges. A handful of trees, mostly either dead or dying – their grey trunks a reminder of what eventually claims us all – are scattered across the fields in what remains of the forest that used to grow here, too. Both those and the abandoned houses and sheds are too far spread to offer any cover.

But, despite my constant glancing around and Will's rostered watches on our breaks, we don't see another soul.

The wall on this side wasn't even patrolled.

It takes us a bit over three days to reach the edge of the Althea Forest.

I am sick of the heat and the sweat that clings to every part of me. It sits between me and my pack like slime. We mostly walked overnight and in the early hours of the morning, sheltering under our heat retardant mats during the worst parts of the day, the temperatures out in the open too dangerous to walk in during the hours of full sun. We would normally talk more on our outings together, but even Will doesn't have the energy to engage much as we trudge through the dust.

We walk through the edge of the forest as the sun moves towards its highest point, the trees gradually becoming more densely packed together. Some change to a heavily leaved, darker green, contrasting with those that are in various stages of decay, the dead debris crunching underfoot. I want to sing at the shade they offer.

The deeper we go, the softer the ground beneath us becomes, delicate flowers in blues and purples pop up their heads and moss begins to show on tree trunks. The scratching of the bark on the pads of my fingers as I run them along the trees we pass draws a smile to my face. The air is subtly different here too, as if it hasn't been disturbed by people in a long, long time. My skin tingles in acknowledgment of this sacred place.

'Can you believe this?' I ask as I look up the length of the trees that reach for the sky.

'It's phenomenal,' Will breathes. 'And makes it even harder for me to understand why it was acceptable to destroy so much of it.'

We stop for a drink and Will consults a copy of the map. 'Right, so I think we now shift east a little more and follow the tallest trees. They should make a bit of a path between them that will lead us to the stone bridge the notebook talks about.'

I look skyward where there does seem to be a pattern of taller trees. It's slight, and I wouldn't have noticed it if we weren't looking, but it seems close enough to what the journal describes. What is less clear is exactly what we do once we find the bridge, but I'm hoping that will be more obvious once we get there.

'Please just make sure you know how to get us back out of here, Will. I do not intend to spend the rest of my days wandering around this forest.'

'I shouldn't imagine you would, not with Phoenix waiting for you back home,' he says, an edge in his voice I don't want to identify.

'Ah, I was wondering when you might bring that up. It's only taken you three days.'

'I thought you might first, but apparently I'm going to have to coax it out of you. What's the deal there?'

'Well ... ' I start.

'Hang on, let's be clear. You can spare me the gory details. Save those for Blaire and Riley.'

I laugh. I haven't spoken to anyone about Phoenix at all, as yet, but there are definitely some shareable details about him. And some lovely things I'm very happy to keep to myself.

'Got it,' I tell him. 'Well—oh I don't know. He's gorgeous, Will—'

He scoffs. 'Lish, everyone thinks he's gorgeous. But it's not a good enough reason to jump into bed with him.'

'If you'd let me finish, I mean *he* is gorgeous. His soul is gorgeous. I've had a soft spot for him for a long time, you know that. And I stayed away because I didn't want to be just another number to him, but it turns out that's not all it seems,' I tell him.

Will is quiet for a while as he leans against a tall tree, examining me, and I give him space to think. Changes like this in any group will cause waves, even more so in a group like ours, and it's not something I thought I would ever be part of. Will and I have never been romantically involved, despite many people thinking differently. And Hayes, or Riley, or Blaire for that matter, just aren't my type. As for Phoenix, well, I'd parked the thought of him out of respect for myself. But with that no longer an issue, and I have no doubt he was honest about that, I simply couldn't resist him.

'I'm happy for you, Lish,' Will says, surprising me. I was expecting more of a lecture. 'You're like my sister and Phoenix is my best friend, so this is a little awkward for me ... but I don't want him to get hurt,' he says.

'What?' I ask, not caring about the octave my voice just went up. 'Aren't you supposed to worry about me getting hurt?'

'Oh sure,' he says, waving a hand, my feelings clearly an afterthought. 'That wouldn't be great. But we both know Phoenix is never going to hurt you; he's possibly the nicest person on the planet. And you're tough, even if he did, you've been through worse. It's Phoenix I'm worried about.'

Will twists around to the tree he is leaning on and puts a mark towards the base of its trunk with his knife.

'Thanks for the vote of confidence,' I mumble. 'What are you doing?' I ask.

'You're right about making sure we know how to get out. I can still see to where the trees thin out from here but if it continues to get thicker, it could be easy to get turned around. We can use the notches to figure our way out if needed,' he says.

The moisture in the air licks my skin as we continue deeper into the forest and my heart skips at the reprieve from the oppressive, dry heat. There is no path to speak of, save the taller trees we are following, and we frequently step over tree roots, scramble over large boulders, and carefully pick our way over mossy ground.

I marvel at the difference in the environment here and closer to the city. It astounds me how the environment can change so dramatically in short distances. In the before, I think these changes were slower in nature and this is just another crack in her rhythm we are witnessing. I say a silent thanks to our Premier for marking what remains of Althea Forest as a critical zone, never to be torn down and developed. Part of me wishes it was closer to the city so we could enjoy it more. But the brutal walk across the farm flats puts most people off coming and, really, I don't think it's a bad thing to stop people coming here. The more people admire, the more they want to claim.

Late in the afternoon, we search for a place to stop for the night, having been able to make good progress during the day in the cooler temperatures in the forest. I take out my phone to text Phoenix and the others with our progress only to find there is no reception here – not totally surprising. I grab the satellite phone from my bag, instead, and send a two-line message before flicking it back to power save mode and stashing it away again. We'll need it to have power for as long as possible in case there's an emergency. I don't think about how long it will take them to get here, even if something does go wrong.

We move out of the row of trees slightly, conscious not to lose sight of it, and make a simple camp behind a large boulder. I rub my neck where the hairs have started to prickle and scan the trees. The dark is coming in quickly and it's hard to make out much beyond the immediate area of our camp. Will watches as if he's sensed something as well, and we silently agree it would be best not to light a fire. It's cooler here but not so cold that we will suffer greatly without it. Neither of us have been into the forest before but we know there will be at least some animals here, particularly those that are active at night, and we don't want to draw their attention if we can help it.

But it's the thought of the Whispers frequenting this forest that makes my skin crawl. What they might do to people they find here.

Will has carried the heavier pack these last few days, as we used the supplies out of mine first to help me manage the load, so I volunteer for first watch after our basic meal of bread and pre-packaged snack bars. We sit close together on the forest floor, our backs against the boulder. I expect the stone to be cold but it's strangely warm through my shirt, and I lean my head back to examine the trees and listen carefully to the sounds around us.

Next to me, Will's breathing slows as he rests on the verge of sleep. It's early compared to when we would be heading to bed in Rhyton but these days and nights of walking and scrambling with our packs are tiring and it's now really quite dark.

'Is it nice?' Will asks with his eyes closed.

'What?'

'Having someone who sees beyond the broken bits.'

I turn my head so I can see his profile. 'I see you, Will.'

'I know but ...' he trails off.

'It's different, I know,' I say quietly, and he nods once. 'You'll find your person.'

He smiles a little. 'Do you think it would be too much to wish for the kids and the white picket fence as well?'

I nudge him with my shoulder. 'You'd be an incredible father, Will. You should wish for it all.'

The birds start to quiet down. I enjoyed listening to their various sounds as we made our way into the forest. I don't know what they are, but we don't have such pretty or colourful birds in the city. I smile at the sudden memory of a bright blue bird I had once. It used to come with me everywhere but I don't know what happened to it after that night.

The bird song is gradually replaced with the careful murmurs of night-time and Will's soft snoring. We don't often sleep in the same room anymore, although he does crash on the sofa on a regular basis, but I don't remember him snoring as he does gently now.

I take the jacket from my pack and gently place it behind his head. In hindsight, I should have made him lie down before he could nod off, but he won't sleep deeply anyway. I watch the trees move slightly in the breeze, the leaves rustling a quiet lullaby. Faintly, I think I can hear running water and wonder if it's the river we are searching for. The one with the stone bridge.

My backside is starting to ache from sitting on the ground for so long, my eyes hurting from constantly scanning the forest around us, but I'm loath to move and wake Will. As I lift my head off the boulder to carefully shift a little and relieve the ache, I see them. Or I think I do. Right on the edge of where the trees are too thick and dark to see through, two amber eyes look back at me. I inch my fingers towards the knife I left by my side, too long to stay comfortably on my belt while I sit.

The eyes don't move. I'm not even sure they blink. I brush the handle of my blade with my fingertips and draw it slightly nearer. The amber dims a little and I squint to try and make them out better, but I can't quite bring them into focus. I don't know how I'd explain it to Will if he were awake, I don't even understand it myself. But something about those eyes sparks a deep sense of longing. And while the eyes themselves don't frighten me, the darkness of the forest suddenly seems more sinister and I shiver.

As the sun rises in the sky and I watch Will rouse from sleep, I wait for his irritation I didn't wake him.

'We're supposed to take turns,' he grumbles as he heaves his pack on.

I hand him another of the snack bars.

'You were tired,' I say.

He rolls his eyes before looking around slowly. 'I thought this place was enchanting yesterday,' he says, lowering his voice. 'Now, it's starting to give me the creeps.'

Thinking on the coolness in the air that hasn't shifted and the foreboding mood of the trees during the night, I decide to tell him about the eyes another time.

Lugging my own pack on, I wish once more I'd packed lighter, the muscles in my shoulders groaning with me. I'm pretty sure I've lost skin where the straps of my pack have rubbed, too. We walk long into the morning without talking, the watchfulness of the forest prompting us forward, keen to find the bridge as soon as we can. The running water I heard last night is harder to place during the day, but it seems to be slowly getting louder as we make our way once again along the line of the tallest trees.

We stop for a break and some water under a magnificent tree. I arch my head back to look up at its full height, but I can't see where it ends. I listen to the sounds of the forest as we pack up the few things we had out, the trees are more harried this morning and I turn to check behind us again. Will is saying something I don't catch and I draw my attention back to him.

'What?' I ask.

He looks at me warily. 'I didn't say anything,' he says. 'But you can hear it too?'

We reach for our weapons at the same time – me my pistol, Will palming his throwing knives. The thumping in my chest grows harder and I try to steady my hands.

'We haven't even got to the damn bridge yet,' Will mutters under his breath. 'What's a bet they've found us instead?'

My vision starts to go black at the edges.

'Shit,' I say, and I grip my pistol harder.

Desperately, I look at Will who is shaking his head as if trying to clear his vision and scanning the forest. Sweat stings my eyes as the memories of this sensation come flooding back.

I know what this is.

I know how this ends.

'We have to run,' I murmur, fighting the panic that rises from the pit of my stomach.

Will reaches for my hand, one of his knives now gripped between us and we begin to move, abandoning our packs, the noise in my head increases and drowns out my senses. We stumble through the forest, the branches of trees tearing at my skin as we run. My arm jerks suddenly as Will stumbles but I wrench him to his feet, scrambling forward. I want to call out to him but he won't be able to hear me over the screaming. I am plunged into complete darkness as Will is wrenched out of my grip.

'William!' I scream. 'William!'

The only hint that I am making a sound is the strain in my throat. I can hear nothing over the screaming in my head.

'William!'

I crawl in the dirt to find him. My hands scraping against trees and stones as I seek the feel of him. I don't think it's possible but the noise in my head intensifies. I curl into myself with my hands on my ears. Begging for it to stop. My head wants to explode, anything to relieve the pressure. The pain.

I see her face. The blood that ran down it. The wet crack of my night-mares repeats itself within the noise in my head. I can't see. I can't see Will.

'Please,' I think I whisper. 'Please, don't take him.'

There is a momentary flash of white pain in my skull and then there is nothing.

CHAPTER NINE

There's a ringing in my ears in the quiet. Not quite silence but the screaming of the forest has gone, leaving an echo in its wake. The metallic taste in my mouth slowly makes its presence known and my teeth are gritty with dirt, my cheek pressed against the hard ground. I crack my eyes open a fraction, despite the headache at the base of my skull, keeping my body as still as possible.

My limbs are bent uncomfortably underneath and around me, as if I was thrown – the throb that pulses through my body indicates I was. Darkness still surrounds me but it's different, somehow. Not as dense, as if it's a more natural form of darkness. Perhaps it's night-time. I let my eyes adjust and scan what I can see, without moving my head. I can just make out the edge of what seems to be a metal pole, the edge of bars on a cell – or cage – and dirt.

There's a creak from behind me and I quickly shut my eyes, not ready to give away my consciousness. Two hands grip me under my arms, hard enough to bruise, and haul me to my feet. I let my head flop forward and I don't see the hand that fists in my hair, jerking my head back up.

'Ugh, she's wet herself,' says the one gripping me.

My pants feel dry but, going by the stench I'm just now noticing, he's probably not wrong. I have no idea how long I've been out. The one holding me drags me closer to the wall and shoves me against it, my head bouncing on the hard surface. I wince at the sensation and momentary increase in darkness before my eyes.

'Put that on.'

The second one, clearly not fooled that I'm unconscious, throws a bundle of cloth at me before they both leave, closing the door behind them. I watch them through lowered lids until I lose sight of them in the darkness outside my cell. My gut tells me they don't go far.

Slowly, I shift myself onto all fours and dizziness makes my already limited vision swim. On my knees, I inspect the cloth bundle, expecting some basic pants and a shirt of some kind. Instead, the fabric is surprisingly soft beneath my fingers and unravels to reveal what was once a beautiful, even if now a little old-fashioned, dress. I stare at it, as if this is a puzzle I am expected to solve. But if it's a puzzle, it's a piece that makes my head throb trying to make it fit.

'I said, put it on,' the second voice barks at me through the bars.

I didn't hear him approach and the loudness of his voice makes me flinch. Using the wall for support, I pull myself up, bracing myself against a wave of nausea. I turn away from the cell door and gingerly remove my torn t-shirt. I fumble the dress over my head before removing my pants from underneath. It's a snug fit and my breasts swell over the top. The skirt is full and I'm thankful it's long to help protect me from the cold I can feel seeping in through the dirt floor and what I now realise is also a packed dirt wall.

Another wave of nausea rises from the pit of my stomach after the effort of getting dressed and I sink back down to the floor. I tuck my bare feet under me, seeing no sign of my shoes and socks, and lean against the wall. Groggily, I wonder if being compliant is a good idea – but my thoughts are too slippery to argue.

'Get up.'

The second man is back at the door. Or perhaps he didn't leave. Not waiting for my slow rising, he enters the cell and roughly drags me to my feet. He is agile, despite his bulk, and thrusts me out of the barred room. I stagger along beside him as he drags me up a handful of stairs and along a rough stone walkway, his fingers biting into my arm.

My feet are thick with cold and I stumble along, the hall spinning around me. A large door, rimmed with light, looms on the left and vaguely I hear voices coming from the space beyond. I blink furiously to try and clear the fog in my head. Dimly, I know I need to get out. Get out before I am taken in there. But my body doesn't respond, fear freezing my senses and clouding my mind.

'Time for you to join some friends,' he says, shoving open the door with his other hand. I'm momentarily blinded by the light, my eyes struggling to catch up with the change.

In the light, I can see the man who holds me has short, auburn hair and red-tinged stubble on his chin. A group in front of me talk amongst themselves, only a few turn to me, the others keeping their focus on their drinks. Musicians play in one corner of the pale, stone room, the stools they sit on made of timber, and a small group of women huddle together near where I stand. My head throbs as I look over at them, trying to understand why they'd be so close to the door and not running. Are they part of whatever is happening here? Then, I notice they are also barefoot and dirty. They are not here of their own volition and another realisation tries to claw its way through to my brain.

I scan their faces for hers quickly, even though I know she never left that floor. Desperately, I search for Will instead – someone I know should be here – but I can't see him, either. A sob catches in my throat at what I refuse to imagine might have happened. The fingers gripping my arm bring me back to myself and the red-headed man continues to drag me into the group.

'What do you think?' he says, addressing them. 'Doesn't look like much does she? Got no fire. There'll be more after her.' He laughs but only a handful join him.

Their assessing faces spin around me as bile rises in my throat. We make our way around the fire most of the men are sitting around, my stomach roiling at his touch, and my eyes dart around the room trying to get a handle on my whereabouts. My head is throbbing and I know it would be useless to try and physically defend myself just yet. I'm disgusted at my dependency on this man to keep me upright at all.

Eventually, he takes me to the group of women and shoves me forward, my cold toes tripping me and I slam into one of them. My head spins with the sudden movement and I brace myself to feel the impact of the hard floor. Instead, the woman grips my arms to stop me from falling and I subtly position myself between her and the man as I right myself.

Where are you, Will?

There is a distinct ebb of fear and disgust from the women around me and I desperately try to build my barrier back up. I feel immediately guilty but I'm not strong enough to take on their emotions as well right now. Not when I can't see Will. I close my eyes briefly against the spinning of the room – *a concussion*, I think distantly – and I tentatively seek out my ability to build a stronger wall around me.

I open my eyes and my vision clears a little, my gaze landing on a dark shape towards the back corner of the fiery room.

No.

My hand flies to my throat as ice runs through my veins.

Hung by his wrists, shackles cutting into his skin, is Will. The tops of his feet, shoe-less, like mine, rest limply on the floor and blood has pooled beneath him. I can see only the top of his head as he slumps forward. From this distance, I can't make out if he is conscious. Or breathing. Tears spring in my eyes and the pressure behind my ribs builds to the point of bursting.

My breath comes in short bursts, a sharp pain in my chest. I need to reach Will. I swallow a sob as I look at the men between us and silently beg him not to be dead. Even in my confused state, I know I would be no match for this group on my best day. My muscles shake with tension as I try to clear the fog in my head and work out what to do.

'Breathe,' the woman behind me says in a low voice.

'Breathe,' she says again. 'You will feel worse if you hyperventilate. He's alive ... for now. We just need to get through tonight.'

Time passes like an excruciatingly slow drip. The gathering continues around me and the group of women, statues in a pond of quiet celebration. My heart aches to help them but I know I can't do it on my own and I can't bring myself to focus on them. I need Will. Even with him, we would be greatly outnumbered here. I urge him to give me a sign, any sign, that he is alive.

'Alright.' A male voice reverberates through the room but I don't see where it comes from. He doesn't shout but the noise begins to die away anyway. 'Night's over, he's not coming today.'

The other women, about ten of them, and I are shepherded towards the door into two lines. The woman who spoke to me nudges me towards the door.

'No.' I dig my bare heels into the stone slab floor. 'I need to go to him. Please. I need to see him,' I beg.

'They'll kill you if you do, and likely us as well,' she whispers fiercely.

I still stare at Will, not even looking at the woman, but I make my feet move. For now. Twisting as I walk out with the women, I find Will's shape behind the men that linger by the fire. He remains hanging, showing no signs of consciousness.

Coming to the end of one of the lines, I am herded out the door with the other women. They all wear dresses of good quality like mine. In another life, I imagine we would almost look courtly in our finery. As it is, though, we are dirty beneath the fine materials and vibrant colours and most are nursing hurts of some kind. Not least our feet that are scratched and bleeding from the dirt floor of the cells and the rough stone we walk on now.

We turn right outside the door, flanked by several men. Guards is probably a better term, although they are very different to the members of the Guard that I know. On instinct, I look to my left as we pass through. There is a walkway lined with flaming torches that stretches into the darkness, offering no indication of what, or where, it leads. As we approach the area that houses my cell, I notice mine is close to the stairs that lead back up to the walkway and the fire room beyond. Stretching out to the left and right of me are more cells into which the women are filed off, one-by-one down the row, and locked away.

The guard closest to me gestures to the open door of the cell I was in when I came to, his eyes sliding past me and narrowing slightly. A shiver runs down my spine at the look on his face and I turn to find the auburn-haired one less than two paces away. Reaching us, he puts his hand on my waist and I openly shudder. He is not as rough as he was when he dragged me out of the cell earlier, but I flinch at his touch and inadvertently step closer to the other guard.

'You're alright, I can take her from here,' the red-headed one says, the smell of alcohol on his breath. The guard turns and grips his shoulder, effectively pinning me between them. I press back into him and tremble involuntarily both at the contact and the way the other one pins me with his strange eyes. There's something familiar about them.

'Odhran,' the gentler guard says, 'the favour he did you by bringing you here does not extend to taking liberties. You do not want him to remind you of that again.'

Odhran scoffs. 'But did he do it as a favour, or just so he could keep me where he can see me? We don't report to that bastard, you don't need to tell him anything.' He pauses and I don't need my gift to feel the tension between the two of them. 'I'd let you watch, if you asked me.' He winks at the guard as his hand drifts below my waist and grips my ass.

Gathering the small amount of my returning strength, I drive my free elbow into his stomach and wrench myself from the other guard's grip before landing a second blow to Odhran's gut with my fist. Odhran is too drunk to react quickly. The gentler guard puts a hand on Odhran's chest to keep him from me as Odhran recovers and spits in my face.

'You bitch,' he says.

The guard laughs. 'I thought you said she had no fire?'

He resumes hold of my elbow, gentler again than Odhran, and ushers me back into the cell. Refusing to look at him, I retreat to the furthest corner and sink to the floor. My body feels too heavy to be mine, numbness seeping through me.

I'm so sorry, Will. Hold on. Please hold on.

My vision swims as exhaustion tightens its grip on my bones. I try to focus on the details to keep me awake. The dirt wall at my back, curving slightly where it meets the floor. The metal bars making up the remaining three walls of the cell. The other cells that border mine. The outline of a woman in the one to my right. Her position mirroring mine. It's my job to protect people but the thought of saving them at the cost of Will makes me ill. Somehow, I need to do both.

The gloom here settled in a long time ago – well before I arrived I'd wager – although it's interrupted by the torches that line the opposing wall. I can make out more than before, now that I've had time to sit and breathe. It makes me wonder again at my concussion and if it was the cause of the earlier darkness. Looking into the cells on either side, I can see through the barred walls to the next, and the next, and more after that – but I can't tell where they finish. Like looking into too many reflections.

Muffled voices filter down the walkway outside the row of cells; the silence of the women around me feels like they're all holding their breath. I am. Three men manhandle Will into the cell next to mine. My heart leaps in my throat and I rush at the bars between us.

'Will?' I whimper. 'Will, please talk to me.'

He doesn't respond and the men ignore me. They dump him towards the back of the cell before locking him in and leaving us. Only the guard who brought me down remains. I stare at Will, terrified I'll miss something if I look away. Vaguely, I think I can make out his chest rising and falling in shallow breaths – but my eyes might be playing tricks on me, showing me what I want to see.

Please be okay. Please be okay.

'Will?' I say a little louder. He groans softly and I drop to my knees, my head light.

'Oh god, Will. I'm here, I'm here.'

I feel the attention of the guard and drag my eyes from Will's form.

'Let me help him,' I beg. 'Please.'

He presses a finger to his lips as a hooded figure steps into the walkway.

Glancing both ways, I don't think he's come from the direction of the room where I've just been. Which means there's something else at the other end of this run of cells. And, if he can come in that way, we can go out.

The hooded man waits, looking at me, I think, but I can't see his face in the gloom. The space between us strains and the moment stretches before he snaps it and turns away. Slowly, he moves to each of the occupied cells. Some of the women keep their distance, a couple meet him at the doors to their cells.

But not one of them is scared.

Eventually, he reaches Will's door and my vision narrows to Will and the man, the sound of my heart loud in my ears. The bars between us cut into my hands.

'What are you doing?' I whisper as he looks once at the guard and opens the door to Will's cell. 'Don't you dare touch him.'

Slowly he raises his hands, palms out as he approaches Will.

'I will fucking kill you if you hurt him,' I spit. My voice is higher than normal, a scream building in my throat.

The man in the hood, his face still obscured, kneels before Will and places his hands on his chest. My own chest tightens in response.

I shake the bars but they refuse to give.

'No. Please, don't.' My voice cracks.

I want to look away. But the only way I can be with him is to watch.

For a moment, nothing happens. I wait, praying to all the gods I can think of for the hooded man to leave Will alone. As I watch, Will's breathing begins to steady and deepen into a more regular rhythm. With care and ease, the hooded man manoeuvres Will closer to the bars I am still gripping and places him on his side, not dissimilar to the recovery position. I can't tear my eyes away from the hooded man, my mouth gaping, as he walks out of Will's cell and towards mine.

He stands there at my door, his head still covered by the dark hood of his cloak, and I wonder why he needs to hide. Perhaps he's the only sensible one. I've marked every one of these bastard's faces – and their strange eyes – and I will stop at nothing to take them down when I am out of here. A soft, gentle sensation reaches my awareness and I can't tell if it's in my mind or actually touching me. But it's definitely coming from the outside of the emotional barrier I've layered up from my toes, blocking people out. This feeling is searching for a way in. I blink in confusion, the hooded man still staring at me. It takes me a moment to realise this is how Nico and Phoenix must feel when I push emotions over them.

I try not to gasp as I flatten myself harder against the bars between mine and Will's cell. The emotions pulsing against me feel foreign and I push against them. They're not mine.

This isn't right.

A beat of surprise runs through me as I realise I can feel him despite my barrier. Fuck. Even my abilities are messed up in here. Underneath what he's trying to send to me, he's angry. Really angry, and I don't want to examine why. Will is lying in that cell, barely breathing. Calm is not how

I feel. I imagine the foreign thread of emotions as a rope I can hold, and I carefully place it outside my barrier. As if it was a physical thing I can gently put away.

'Do you need any help?' he asks quietly, nothing in his deep tone giving away that he knows what I've done with his emotions.

I stare at him, wondering how best to answer this question. Of course we need help. But I don't want to walk into a trap, either. Not that I have a lot of options to try right now. So, I go out on a limb.

'Yes,' I say, taking tentative steps towards him. 'I need to get us the fuck out of here.'

My skin tingles where I can still feel the edges of his emotions and I drag harder on the flame in my chest to block them out. But it's not totally successful and it takes far more energy than normal. Still, what I can feel makes me understand the others were genuinely unafraid of him. He didn't force them to feel that. While there is anger there, it's not directed at any of us.

He doesn't want us here, either.

He remains outside my door, looking back once at the other guard, who's paying close attention to the walkway to the fire room, then walks away.

Back the way he came.

He placed Will close enough for me to reach through the bars and hold his hand while I watch and wait for him to rouse. I know Will's face as well as my own, although I still sometimes marvel at the handsome man the young boy I knew has become. Even with the blood on his face, he's handsome.

It's now been several days since we left Rhyton and he is showing definite signs of a beard. Several days. Not even close to when the others would start getting concerned but, still, I hope they do not come looking for us. I think about Nico and Phoenix as I run my thumb over the back of Will's hand and an ache begins to radiate from my chest. Closing my eyes, I imagine myself back in my apartment with Phoenix, his arms around me, and it brings me some small comfort. Until I question when I will see him again.

Most of the men here have shown us their faces, I know one's name. They have no intention of letting us go home.

'I think it's safe to say we found the girls and the Whispers,' Will says in a thin voice, squeezing my hand, and my heart skips a beat.

'Given we were supposed to be doing reconnaissance only, I'd say we got a little more than we bargained for,' I whisper, fighting a sob. 'That was so naïve,' I say.

Will eases himself into a sitting position and retakes my hand.

'Go slow, Will. You look awful,' I tell him.

'So much for the rugged handsome look I was going for,' he smirks.

I frown at him, trying to assess what he's covering up but he seems ... okay. Certainly more okay than I was expecting.

Questions swirl in my mind about the hooded man and what he's been able to do. Why can I feel him despite the barrier? How can he send me a wave of calm when he thought I needed it?

'How do you feel?' I ask.

'Strange,' he says. 'I should barely be alive after the beating they gave me. But I almost feel ... good. Stiff, but I'm alright.' He looks at me, worry clear on his face. 'What did they do to you?'

'Nothing, I'm fine. I don't know if I can say the same for the other girls, but I'm fine.'

'We have to get out of here, Lish,' Will says. 'They might kill me, but I think it's better than what they might do to you.'

Will squeezes my hand.

'Food,' he says nodding towards the stone bowls that have been slipped between the bars. We collect our bowls and we sit as close to each as we can, the bars of our cells separating us. I watch Will carefully, amazed at the ease in his movements.

Breakfast, or maybe lunch, is a luke-warm gruel of some sort. I try not to think about what it's made of as I force it down. The women from the fire room are also in their cells and Will and I each have a neighbour.

The walkway has been clear of guards since the food arrived, and Will and I start to talk to the women beside us, passing messages up and down each run of the cells on either side. Peta, next to my cell, is soft-spoken and tells me in a broken voice that she's been here for a couple of weeks. Her resigned devastation ripples between us.

There is a loose routine here, she says. They are mostly left alone during the day, before being taken to the fire room each evening; they seem to be waiting for someone to arrive but she doesn't know who. They don't get to talk a lot as a group, but whispers are passed up and down the line of cells. Rumour has it we are in a holding pen of some kind while they decide where to send us next. Will's discussion goes much the same way.

'Lish,' Will whispers.

I walk over to him, already sick of sitting in the dirt. He grins at me as we meet at the bars between, his bronze eyes dark in the gloom.

'We found Sofia.'

My hand flies to my mouth. 'Are you sure?'

'Definitely,' he says. 'She's a few cells down, but they've passed names up to me. I got them to ask about her family and guess what?'

'She's got a little brother,' I say in amazement.

Having seen the group of women, I'd wanted to hope but, in my profession, that can be a hurtful thing. Will watches me through the bars and I know he's thinking the same. 'We need to find a way out of here,' I say.

We talk for hours, whispering in the near darkness and asking different questions of the women as needed. Will and I each grill them, as best we can when we can only talk directly to one other person each, on as many details as they can recall. Everything from how long they've been here; how often they're fed; if they ever go anywhere else to wash; have they had any other clothes delivered; who guards them and what they are like. And of course, how often the hooded man comes and if they know why he comes at all.

'Could we trust him to help us?' Will wonders out loud. I told him of the man's actions last night and it's hard for either of us to totally ignore the possibility of his help. More than that, I think of the other women's responses to him and the other guard compared to when they were in the fire room.

'It's a huge risk to show our hand to any of them,' I say. 'But there must be a reason he's been checking on them so often.' I ignore the questions that what he did to Will raises for now.

Will's quiet as he thinks it over.

'You said there was one that keeps watch, right?'

'He was making sure the hooded one wasn't found. He was totally relaxed about all of us. They're definitely working together and keeping it from the rest of the group.'

'What if I ask the hooded man to help us?' Will looks at me from where we now sit at the back of our cells. 'He's helped me already, right?'

A tightness takes hold in my chest.

'And if it's a ruse on his behalf?'

'You're the best judge of character I've ever met, Lish,' he says. 'If you don't think he's dangerous, I trust you. And, if he is, me asking keeps the attention off you and the rest of the women.' He frowns. 'Although, I don't want to leave you to figure it out on your own if it goes south.'

'So … plan b …' I let my voice trail off.

We're silent a few minutes before I talk again.

'The other one – the one who kept watch – he must have the keys. The hooded one can't have left with them. If he was trusted with them, why hide?'

Will makes a sound of agreeance.

'He's not as experienced as you or me,' I say, thinking on how the young guard positioned himself too close to me without being prepared for any attack on my behalf. 'I can get the keys off him when he has us out, and we all go the way the hooded man came from.'

'How do we know what's down there?' he points down the hall.

'We don't. But we have to hope it's better than whatever's going to happen in that room. Better than who they're waiting for. But we'd need to be prepared to run into the hooded one on our way out.'

I look to Will as he nods, the back of his head scraping gently on the dirt wall.

'There are two of us,' he says, turning his gaze to me. 'We do what we need to do to get them out.' The intensity in his eyes is unsettling. But not wrong.

'Tonight?' he asks quietly.

'When they bring us back from the fire room and leave us for the night,' I say, a familiar flicker of nervous excitement starting in my fingertips. Just like when we take on a big job at work. I smile at Will. 'I can't wait to see the look on Nico's face.'

Will smiles softly back.

We don't talk about what happens if we fail – I will do anything to get us out. To get Will and Sofia back where they belong. The memory of my mother's bloodied face forces itself behind my eyes and I squeeze them shut, as if I can force it away. She didn't come this far. I don't know if that's better or worse. But I won't let them take Will from me, too.

CHAPTER TEN

In the fire room, the women and I are lined up near the door, watching the fire from afar; I am again reminded of the stories of royal courts. My dress, I have discovered today, is a deep gold that's fitted through the torso before skimming my hips and falling into a full skirt that swishes heavily around my ankles. It's almost the colour of the little flame I imagine lives in my chest. Beside me, Peta wears a pewter dress that's more shift-like in style with cropped sleeves, the woman on my other side is in knee-length red velvet. Dressed as we are in fine but dirty gowns of varying eras, we jar against the backdrop of dirt and flames.

I try to glance down the line to find Sofia, but I can't see all their faces. I look away again, not wanting to draw attention to us. Searching out the gentle guard, a feeling of quiet anticipation settles in my stomach. I'd prefer not to hurt him, but I will do whatever's necessary to get those keys when he walks me out of here. I think over the timing, again, and again, ultimately deciding I'll wait until he puts the key in my door before I make my move. At the midpoint of when he can take me elsewhere or lock me in.

Odhran brought me to the fire room, something that didn't surprise me at all, digging his fingers into the flesh of my upper arm harder than necessary as he pulled me along. I resist the urge to rub at the spot on my skin that's tender in case he notices. I won't give him the satisfaction.

The flickering light comes from the large fire in the middle and the numerous lit torches around the walls. High up on two sides are long, narrow openings just above ground level, probably for ventilation for the fire. Like the cells, this part of the compound is also underground. Perhaps Will and I were walking around on top of it without even realising.

The musicians have already started and a light, jovial melody drifts towards us. Will is again shackled, with his arms raised to meet the chains that hang from the ceiling, but at least he is still standing this time.

With a clearer head than when I arrived, I take in the details of the men. They are mostly young in appearance and wear a simple uniform of slim legged black pants, a form fitted black t-shirt and heavy black boots. There are no markings, although one or two wear cloaks with hoods hanging at their backs. It's clear to me now that they are soldiers by the way they move, the hierarchy that seems to be in place, and their matching black clothes. What isn't clear is what war they're fighting and what our role in it is.

At an unseen prompt, the soldiers stiffen and draw themselves up to their full height. If I wasn't so disgusted with them, I would be impressed with the image they cut. Heavy footfalls sound to my right but I take my lead from the soldiers I can see and don't turn my head. A figure dressed in a black cloak enters my peripheral vision.

As he walks further into the room, I can see he's quite broad and the hood on his cloak is thrown back. White hair is tied low at the back of his head and flows down between his shoulder blades; it's at odds with the pale, smooth skin I can see on the side of his face. He's much younger than the white hair suggests.

The white-haired man turns slowly on his heel and looks straight at me. I blink, unsettled by his sudden awareness of my presence.

'She's new,' he says, to no one in particular, before making his way to me. His movements are graceful, like a cat stalking its prey. Stealth that overlays the rippling power underneath.

'Yes, General,' Odhran answers. 'We picked up her and her friend in the forest,' he says, his voice cutting through the music.

As they come closer, my stomach begins to skitter nervously, my very body telling me to get as far away from the white-headed man as possible.

They pause in front of me, the General close enough to reach out and touch me. I raise my face to look at him and take an involuntary step back. The cold emanating from his startling, purple-ringed mauve eyes sucks the breath from my lungs.

He cocks his head as those strange eyes shrewdly travel the length of my body, appraising what he sees. His expression is unreadable when he once again reaches my face. I hold his gaze and raise my chin ever so slightly. I won't back away again. His eyes crinkle slightly at the edges but he doesn't smile. Extending a pale hand towards me, he presses a finger in the soft spot at the base of my throat. Swallowing becomes harder but that is nothing to the burning of my skin.

Deliberately he runs his finger across each of my collar bones, the pain searing my flesh. Biting the inside of my cheek to stop from calling out, I taste blood. My breathing comes hard and I blindly reach for the flame I hold dear and beg it to help me stay calm as the General traces an invisible line from my throat to the top of my breast. But instead of helping me, my flame stills and then ever so slightly flickers towards the man. Reluctantly. As if he's calling to it but it doesn't want to answer. Instinctively, I push energy into my barrier. But this time it's not to keep emotions out, but my flame in. Something I've never considered doing before. As quickly as it began, the pain disappears as he lifts his finger from my skin. My knees go weak with relief and I gasp for air. Burns like those should scar but the sudden absence of pain and the lack of stench of charred flesh says otherwise.

He turns to Odhran.

'Interesting,' he says walking away.

The General takes his seat in the ring around the fire pit. It's large and made of stone, clearly setting him apart from the others who have timber stools.

Drinks start flowing and the conversation around me slowly increases in volume. The General's gaze regularly drifts back to me, where I still stand by the door with the other women. The dark eyebrows that contrast with his white hair furrowing slightly as he searches me for something. Something I know I should hide. Something I think he just found anyway.

If only I knew what it was.

Odhran shifts in his seat and assesses the room, as if he's preparing to make a speech. 'General, if you will allow?' Odhran looks to the General who nods subtly and the music dies away.

My throat tightens.

'We have a fit, clearly combat trained individual in our midst. However, he has not been trained in our ways. I suggest we see just how good he might be. For our own training purposes, obviously.'

Hot anger flares in my chest at the smug smile on Odhran's face.

I look at Will, hanging by the ceiling once more. He's glaring at Odhran, goading him to go first. I have every confidence in Will's ability but something in Odhran's face when he looks at me sets me on edge. The General waves his drink in bored agreement and Odhran claps his hands.

'Unshackle him,' Odhran demands.

The two soldiers closest to Will release his binds. He shakes his arms to get the blood flowing again and rubs at the raw spots on his wrists. Odhran makes his way to Will.

'Now, as we are all a couple of drinks in and he is not, I think we should apply a handicap,' he says, turning to look at the unit again.

'You asshole,' I mutter, and I feel Peta stiffen beside me.

Odhran collects a rope from the side of the room and returns to Will, gripping his right hand and roughly tying it behind his back, the rope wrapped around his middle.

'Who wants to go first?' Odhran asks the group.

Silence greets him, the soldiers either looking between each other or tentatively at the General. One deliberately turns his back and engages the man next to him in conversation – the blonde one who was with the hooded man. Odhran points at a heavily built soldier with mousy brown hair and motions him forward.

'You can start,' he says.

The man reluctantly circles Will, forcing him to turn tightly to maintain line of sight. The General scoffs at him for taking too long to make his move and he lunges forward to punch Will in the stomach. Will blocks the attack with his free hand and spins out of reach. Odhran laughs.

The contender lashes out in a flurry of short, sharp blows with alternating fists into Will's torso. Having only one free hand, Will is able to deflect some of the blows but the others land heavily in his ribs and middle section. He has to choose to defend or attack. He is struggling to do both.

The attacker moves like he was a born fighter – I imagine they all do, judging by the look of them – and he lands a perfect kick to the ribs, driving Will backwards with another blow to his gut. Will folds in half. My breathing falters as I watch the impact to his body.

Will refuses to back down, despite everyone in the room knowing he will not win this. Himself included. He staggers back to face his attacker. Taking a moment's pause, the contender smacks Will in the jaw, dropping him to his knees before he walks away. A groan escapes my mouth. But if I intervene, I run the risk of turning Odhran's wrath on the women beside me. Including Peta and Sofia. Nico's little face enters my mind and my heart breaks at what he would think if I let them hurt Sofia.

'Very good. Very good, my friend.' Odhran laughs. 'Who's up next?'

Will slumps back to his knees, blood streaming from his mouth and nose. All visions of Nico flee my mind. I can't sacrifice him. Not for anyone.

'Enough!' I scream.

None of the soldiers make a sound and surreptitiously look to the General. The whole room seems to stop and the music fades away.

'Enough?' the General asks, cocking his head.

With a show of confidence I do not feel, I step towards him and meet his stare. 'It is enough. You've had your fun, let him be.'

The General laughs and a chill runs down my spine.

'That's quite funny, you know. I do like a funny girl,' he sneers.

Someone snickers. Probably Odhran. Fucking asshole.

'But you see, I thought he belonged to me,' he says slowly, 'as do all of you, now. And I will do with you as I wish.'

Now it's my turn to laugh. I level him with my gaze.

'I do not belong to you,' I say. The General's mauve gaze watches me for a long minute.

'Tell me then, who do you belong to?' He gestures around the room and I stiffen. 'Ah, I understand. You belong to our punching bag,' he says. My heartbeat pounds in my ears and I say nothing. 'Well?' he snaps. 'You must belong to someone here, an unattached woman can be in a very perilous position indeed.' The implication of his words hangs over me.

'Yes, I do belong to him,' I point to Will, willing my voice not to shake. 'As he belongs to me. And I will never belong to anyone else as I belong to him.'

The General deliberately stalks over to Will. I move to go to him, but Peta grabs my arm. I whirl at her.

'Let me go.' I try to keep my voice calm before I force her to release me but the fear in her eyes makes me freeze and I'm relieved I've blocked her out. Forcing myself to take a breath, I take a small solace that Odhran hasn't instructed anyone else to beat Will. Staring at Peta, I will myself to be strong enough to keep harm from these women as well. I turn back to Will, my mind grappling for another option.

Any option.

The General watches Will as a hawk watches its prey. He bends to him and pulls him to his feet, supporting him from behind. Will's already torn shirt now barely hangs together and there are deep purple bruises already forming across his torso. His abdomen looks slightly misshapen and the thought of internal bleeding sharpens in my mind. Our eyes meet and his gaze widens, his mouth opening as if he's about to speak. His body jerks. Too slowly I realise what's happening and silence thrums in my ears.

'I guess we'll see who you belong to in a few minutes,' the General says, pulling the knife from Will's ribs.

'No!' I scream at him.

My stomach falls away. I yank my arm from Peta and race to Will. No one tries to stop me. The General has dropped him back to the floor and I slide on my knees across the stone floor that's now slippery with his blood.

No. Oh god, no.

'Will, look at me. Stay with me.' I place him on his side and tear a strip off my dress to try and stem the bleeding. The fabric against the gash in his back is soaked in seconds and deep red blood seeps through the gaps in my fingers. Clumsily, Will reaches for me.

'It's okay, Lish, it's okay,' his voice is already strained.

'This isn't happening, Will, you're not leaving me.'

My eyes and nose stream but I don't dare move my hands to wipe them.

'No,' he whispers, 'but you need to leave me. Go. Like we planned. You can do this.'

'Help me!' I look at the soldiers who keep their distance, most of their expressions are pained. I don't look at Odhran but desperately try to find the guard who takes me back to my cell instead.

He's gone.

'Please,' I say anyway, 'help me. I'm begging you. I will do anything, please help him.'

The General looks at me. 'Anything? Such a tempting offer.' He smiles.

Will stops trying to hold me and lies limply on the ground. This can't be real. I can feel the backbone of my existence starting to crack. It's inconceivable he could slip away so quickly. My hands are slick with blood and the more I push against the hole in his back, the more blood appears. I've never seen so much blood from someone I love before.

Not even hers, not even then.

My heart knows he does not have long, and it begins to cleave. The pain as strong as if I'd taken the blow instead.

I wish I had.

'Oh god, don't do this. Please help us,' I sob.

'God? I am God here,' says the General. I don't take my eyes from Will. 'You said 'anything'?' he asks, his voice agonisingly slow.

I try to stifle my sobs, but my chest is wracked with crying.

'Any-anything,' I say, 'please help him, he needs a hospital, a doc—'

'Would you stay in his place?' he asks casually.

'Save him. Let him take the girls home, all of them. And I—' I pause to gather my breath, the hope of getting myself out with the others crumbling away.

'I imagine you have approximately two minutes before any bargain you might make will be useless—'

'What the fuck is this?' a deep voice asks.

Numbly, I look up to find the hooded man, his hands frozen part way to the covering over his head as if he was about to remove it. Dropping them back to his sides, he turns on the General.

I glance back at the women but they look away, as if they don't want to show any recognition. One shifts on her feet. He gives every indication this is the first time he's seeing any of us here, despite coming to the cells, and I tear my gaze from him. I have an opportunity to get Will out, I'm not going to lose it by showing the General I've seen the hooded man before. But underneath his fake surprise, the anger remains. And I now know who it's directed at – the white-haired man.

'This—' his voice is full of the rage I can feel rippling off him, despite my barrier. 'This is supposed to be finished,' he says to the General, pointing at the women. 'You stopped this madness years ago!'

'Always deciding who others can and can't have,' Odhran mutters under his breath.

The General ignores him and looks at me.

'I asked you a question,' he says.

'Save him,' I say, holding his stare, 'let the girls go home. They all go home safely. And I will stay,' I say.

The undercurrent of the hooded man's feelings warping their way through me are overwhelmed with remorse. My own emotions are nothing. Will grips my hands weakly and tries to remove them from his stab wound.

'Lish,' he whispers, 'you can do this without me. Get them out. You can let me go.'

'William Thomas Fitzpatrick,' I scold him gently, sniffing. 'You know full well I will never let you go.'

I chance another look at the General. His face is impassive, cold purple eyes watching me.

He nods once and the hooded man is at Will's side before I can blink.

'Turn him completely on his front,' the hooded man instructs.

Understanding of what this man did in the cells pushes at the edges of my mind. It should be impossible but now impossible is all I have to hold on to. On his front, the bloody strip of fabric removed, the severity of Will's wound turns my stomach. The side of his face presses against the ground as he struggles to keep his eyes open. I kneel by his side stroking his face and hair, trying not to look at the blood on my hands. The hooded man lays his hands on Will's back, one directly over the wound.

A gentle wave of calm and support pushes its way through. I feel as if I'm being smothered and I fight again to remain breathing. I instinctively want to reject this barrage of foreign emotion. But, whether he knows it or not, they provide an anchor for me to hold. A way to steady myself as I watch the colour leaving Will's face. And I don't know how to fight both my fear of Will dying and the intrusion.

Resolving to use the soothing warmth that washes over and through me for now, so similar to what I can do, I bury myself under the blanketing other presence. I recognise a note of relief at my yielding as my heart rate slows and my breathing evens out, my body forgetting the panic even if my mind has not.

I put my head against Will's and murmur to him. I talk about all the things he will get to do at home, retell funny stories of our team, reminisce about Hayes's cooking and Riley's inappropriate jokes. Words and stories tumble forward as I try to keep him here.

Here with me, even as I feel him slipping away.

Even if I will lose him again soon in a different way.

At least he will be alive. If the impossible is not, in fact, impossible.

'I'm tired, Lish,' his eyelids start to droop.

I look frantically at the hooded man. The top of his hood is all I can see as he maintains his focus on Will.

'Please tell me something is happening. He needs help, please,' I beg. The colour in Will's cheeks continues to fade.

'Did you steal the snacks again?' he asks deliriously. His words run together; I can barely hear him.

He inhales sharply as the hooded man pushes harder into his back. There's a faint thrum in the air around us as the tension rolls off the man in the hood. Abruptly, he reaches for my skirt and jostles me as he rips several more pieces from it. He winds these around Will's middle before asking for help from one of the soldiers to move him closer to the fire.

Numbly I follow them and no one attempts to stop me. They are all focused on Will and the hooded man, almost respectful in their observation. Except Odhran, who watches the hooded man with nothing but contempt. He lays Will down carefully at the edge of the fire and I crawl forward through ash and blood to resume my position near his head. The hooded man kneels next to me and I can feel his warmth seeping into my bones.

'It was close,' he says quietly. 'It will be a little while until we know for sure.'

Silently I lay down and curl around Will, closing my eyes. I ignore the soldiers in the room and the General, who I know is watching intently. I seek out the foreign feelings and give myself to the numbness and relief of having my jagged emotions smothered with someone else's calm. It's a small relief that I don't have to explain that I need this help, so I don't break down completely. That the calm is helping me be strong for Will.

I sense rather than see the hooded man turn his head to me, as I pull tighter on the rope of feeling he sends my way. A small voice in my head hopes he won't leave Will and me with the General, but I don't know what's more dangerous – the General or the hope we will be saved.

CHAPTER ELEVEN

A large hand squeezes my shoulder softly and my eyes fly open. My arms are stiff from clutching Will and panic fires across my senses before I register they're warm.

Warm from the heat of Will's body.

I hold him tighter and let my tears fall. Tears fat with relief.

'It's time.'

The voice above me is deep, but gentle, and one I now recognise as the hooded man. I peer around the room and note that the three of us are alone. For now.

'The others don't yet know he's finished healing,' he says quietly. 'I thought you might like some time to say goodbye before they come.'

I look up at him as he crouches beside Will and me, initially uncomprehending but it comes back fast enough. A sob tears my throat as the reality dawns on me. With Will's life draining away before my eyes, I barely considered what I'd given in exchange. Not that it would have mattered, I would never have chosen a different outcome. My life would mean nothing without him.

There is a hint of stubble on the man's square chin and absently I note I can now make out the end of his nose, but the rest of his face remains in shadow. Alone with him and Will, his emotions are even harder to block out. I've become accustomed to doing it with others in Rhyton but, here, this man's are loud and complicated. But most clear are both the anger and sadness on my behalf.

'Thank you,' I say, my own voice barely breaking a whisper.

Taking a deep breath, I wipe my tears and clear my throat, steeling myself for the impossible task ahead of me. In a normal world I would question if I really had to do this, but there is nothing about this world that feels normal and I am not naïve enough to think the General is anything less than serious in the agreement we made. Will would have died had I not said I'd stay. Only hours ago, I was desperate for the impossible. Now I want to run from it as fast as I can.

In that other world, I might have held on until the last possible moment to say goodbye. Now, though, with the aching wound of thinking I would lose Will still hammering in my chest, I find myself pulled with an urgency to get him and the others out of here before anyone changes their mind. Before the General realises he's made the wrong choice. That he didn't need to make a deal with me because he already had me. Sending Will away is a loss I don't know how to bear but I won't survive if Will doesn't. The faces of the General and Odhran swim behind my gritty eyes.

I sit up, bumping Will a little in the process.

'You need to wake up,' I say quietly.

I poke him in the ribs in a way that reminds us both of a time when all we had was each other. I don't know how sore he might still be but, now I know he's alive and as well as can be, I don't have much room for sympathy. He needs to get out of here. I poke him a second time and he drives an elbow down to protect himself.

'Will, you need to get up,' I repeat.

'You're a hell of a task master, Lish, you know that?' The words grate in his throat. He opens his eyes and pushes himself into a seated position. 'I almost died earlier, you might recall. Pretty sure I saw the pearly gates themselves.'

He rubs at his tired face but the colour has returned to his dark, tawny brown cheeks.

'Well, unlucky for whoever dwells within those gates, you're not ready for them just yet.' I swallow the fear that rises up to meet his words.

Will eyes the hooded man, suddenly letting the seriousness of the situation show. 'I suppose I have you to thank for that,' he says cautiously. The man dips his head fractionally. Will turns to me, his eyes disbelieving before shifting to a scowl.

'You on the other hand, I don't thank at all.'

I ignore him and get to my feet. He's quick to stand so he looks down at me and I shake my head, amazed at the lack of lingering effects of being beaten and stabbed. If I wasn't trembling with the effort of letting him go, I'd think I'd imagined it.

'That was so stupid, Lish,' he whispers fiercely. 'You should never have tried to make a deal with that man. He probably thinks you're going to follow through with it as well.'

Next to me the hooded man rises from the ground and places his hands behind his back. He takes a step away, but his face remains turned towards us.

Will presses his lips into a thin line, reading my face before I speak. I step forward and take his hands, I don't care what the hooded man hears me say. He's already seen the rawness of my desperation to save Will.

'Will,' I start. 'I—'

'No, Lish, I will not accept that.'

He inhales deeply through his nose, trying to quell the panic I can sense building behind his ribs. I want to reach out and ease it, take away his pain. But my own well is trying to burst and it's taking all I have to contain it. Selfishly, I want him to hurt too. I want him to feel us being torn apart because sometimes how much it hurts is equal to how much it means. This man before me chose to be my family when no one else would. And now I have to tell him goodbye.

'It's done, Will.'

'No. We will find another way,' he whispers.

'Will—'

'I said no, Lish.' His eyes start to shine, and I hold his sorrow close.

'I'm sorry,' I tell him quietly. 'I'm sorry I didn't realise how dangerous this search was when we started. I should have thought more about it. It just seemed so ... fanciful.' My voice starts to crack, the well walls beginning to crumble. 'I wasn't confident we'd find Sofia, I thought I might find more answers about myself and why I was in those files. It was so selfish, Will, I can't—'

'But we *did* find her. That doesn't mean I'm prepared to trade you for her. There must be another way.'

He looks carefully at the hooded man who remains silent.

'We don't have time to argue this, Will.' I shut down his foolish hope that the hooded man can help in any other way. 'I said I'd stay, I'm staying. You need to take them home.'

'I can't lose you, Lish. How am I expected to function without you?'

'You can and you will,' I say tearfully. 'I need you to ... tell the others I'm sorry. Tell them they are to look after you. Don't get up Robard's nose and you'll be a shoo in for every promotion. You were always better than me at that job anyway.' I try to smile but the stricken face that looks back at me tells me I failed.

'Lish, stop,' he says, his voice beginning to waver. 'You're starting to give me your laundry list as if—'

I place a hand on his chest to stop him.

'Tell Hayes to give his grandmother a kiss for me and ask her to keep sending Nico and Phoenix those cookies I love, that will give them something nice to remember me by.' I can't stop the tears from overflowing now. I stare into Will's bronze-brown eyes, wanting to commit them to memory. 'Ask Sofia if she's happy for Phoenix to stay part of Nico's life. He could be good for Nico, and it will break his heart to say goodbye to him.'

Will pulls me into a tight embrace, my ribs cracking, and I hold him back just as fiercely.

Drawing back slightly to look at him again. 'Tell Phoenix I—'

The hooded man's curiosity spikes against my skin as he listens and I'm not sure why I pause. Will looks at me expectantly, his brows drawn over eyes that have already seen too much sadness.

'Tell Phoenix I'm sorry.' My tears fall heavily now, thickening my voice. 'Tell him not to wait for me.'

'Oh, Lish,' Will says, his own tears streaking his face and muddying the blood that remains there.

'And you. You just be the fucking best you can be. I'm so thankful to have had you to give my life meaning. And I'm so grateful I got to tell you goodbye. I love you.' I lean into him again so he can't see any more tears and I feel his dropping down the back of my neck. 'Find your person, Will,' I whisper.

The hooded man steps forward. 'I'm sorry,' he says, sorrow in his soft voice. 'But we really must go now.'

Will presses a long kiss to my forehead before we reluctantly face the hooded man, our hands held between us. The hooded man motions us forward before following behind and taking me to my cell first.

Will grips my hand tightly and opens his mouth to speak. But I shake my head silently at him. His mouth clamps shut, and he covers it with his free hand. I watch his chest rise and fall as he composes himself.

I give him one last squeeze before letting go of his warm hand and walking into my cell, the door closing behind me.

I'd thought the cells were quiet before but, with me their only occupant, the silence is deafening now. I don't know how much time passes as I sit against the cold dirt wall, my knees pulled into my chest.

The tears have dried.

I've grown used to the smell of my vomit.

My mind has emptied of all thought.

All I have left to do now is wait.

A soldier crouches outside my cell. I don't have to look at him to know it's the hooded man, the sense of him is now familiar to me. There's a constant ebb of emotions that comes from him that my barrier seems oblivious to. Most of the other soldiers here are almost impossible to read. But this man's presence creates a gentle hum in the air around me.

I continue to stare at the floor.

'Thank you,' I whisper. There's nothing else I can say.

'You shouldn't thank me.'

'What do you mean?' I ask raising my head, worry lancing through me.

'He's safe. I didn't mean that, he got out.'

I exhale and put my chin back on the arms I have crossed over my knees. Minutes pass before I speak again.

'He should have died on that floor. How did you do that?' I saw more than enough to know it was no fluke. There was no way Will was going to survive that wound on his own.

He hesitates. 'It's ... something some of my people have been able to do for a long time,' he says.

Questions swim in my mind but I don't have the strength to form them. Will is alive, that's the only thing I can focus on right now. There are either too many or too few variables for me, so I hold tight to the knowledge that Will is out. He will be back home, and he will see the safe return of all the other women he took with him. I have no doubt of that.

'Thank you,' I say again, 'for saving him.'

'Was it worth it?' he asks.

'It will always be worth it.' My heart beats in sad acknowledgement.

'Even if you condemned yourself in the process?'

'Even then.'

He stays watching me, crouched by the door. I wonder how he sits like that for so long; my knees would have started barking in protest well before now. But he remains.

He came from the other end of the walkway again tonight and the gentle guard, as I have come to think of him, stands watch again. I think on the visit he made here when Will and I first arrived, how he visited each cell. How he asked me if I needed any help.

'Why have you been doing it?' I ask.

'What's that?'

He feigns ignorance but I feel the skip of surprise from him. I remember the first time I felt his emotions wash through me – I'd gently pushed them away, unwilling to bend to them. He laces his fingers in front of him and lowers his hooded head, so it appears he looks at the floor. There's a slightly unguarded feeling to his emotions and I wonder if he knows I can sense him when he's not meaning me to.

'Helping,' I say quietly.

He turns his head in the direction of the fire room before looking back to me. 'That's something I need you to keep to yourself, please.'

I nod slowly, a tightening in my chest at his response. It wasn't an answer but doesn't it also mean he's not intending to stop, either?

'What's the deal with this?' I wave my hand vaguely between us. 'You … sending me things.' It's ineloquent but I've never talked about it out loud before. Not that I really remember anyway.

'I didn't expect you to notice,' he says after a moment. 'Most people aren't perceptive enough.'

They don't when I do it either. At least when I do it right. I want to ask him what he means about 'his people' and how they managed to develop their healing abilities. But, aside from acknowledging the faint relief and immense curiosity I'm no longer the only one I know with abnormal abilities, there are more pressing matters I need to focus on.

Like what to expect from my promise to the General.

And how I go back on it. But that's not something I'm prepared to ask him, yet; I need to figure out what I can on my own.

My hands begin to tremble slightly and the hooded man sends a gentle wave of care through the bars. It's intended to cocoon me and invoke a sense of safety.

I laugh softly at him.

'You know it's not the same when I know it's not real, right?' I ask, the foreign emotions ebbing away.

'How'd you get your bruises?' he asks after a moment, changing the subject. Anger starts to ripple off him and I run my hands over the exposed parts of my arms.

'Friend of yours,' I mumble against my knees.

'Would you like me to fix it?' he asks, death in his voice.

'No, thank you.' The lingering pain feels good, without it I will feel nothing at all.

Slowly, he stands to leave.

'He's not my friend,' he says quietly before he walks away.

CHAPTER TWELVE

I observe the passing of time as if I am watching from afar. There is no daylight down here. I haven't seen or felt the sunlight since the day in Althea Forest when my ears started bleeding. My understanding of the rhythm of time is based on the movements of others as I spend the days in my cell, on my own. No soldiers bother coming down here during the day, I assume they have training, or missions, or some sort of actual work to do during these hours. I try not to think of the women they are likely tracking, hunting, or have already abducted while I waste my life away in my cell.

Instead, I focus on the women who were able to get away. Guided by Will back through the forest and into Rhyton where their families welcomed them with open arms. I use the time I am not watched to train as best I can. Will's voice in my mind spurring me on through multiple rounds of squats, lunges, push ups and crunches. At times, my thoughts dwindle to just this rhythm.

Squats. Lunges. Push ups. Crunches.

Squats. Lunges. Push ups. Crunches.

And then, the sting of the small rocks in the palms of my hands and soles of my feet prompts me to rest, unable to muster the energy to try anything more creative in my workout routine. I don't know if I will ever get to use my body for a purpose again, but I am not prepared to give up on myself entirely yet.

The hooded man comes to my cell most nights, after the noise of the fire room has quietened down. I haven't been back there since the night I met the General. I don't hear any more from the soldiers once they've finished for the night and I guess their barracks must be far from here. But he comes and sits outside my cell door.

A couple of times, Odhran has ventured this way but, on seeing the hooded man, has sneered and walked away. The first time he came down was the night after Will left. The hooded man and he had a tense conversation before the hooded one pointed at Odhran's face. Odhran spun on his heel and walked away.

I know it's because of Odhran that the hooded man comes each night, just to head off any temptation Odhran might have to put me in my place. But it also feels like he's waiting for something.

'Why are you here?' I ask, stretching my legs out along the ground in front of me.

The skirt of the gold dress ends at my knees, the skin below is filthy and covered in tiny scratches from the earthen floor and walls.

He glances at the other guard who often accompanies me to my cell but whose name I haven't yet learnt. They'd possibly tell me their names if I asked but the hooded man is so secretive about being down here – mostly coming from the other direction and always wearing his hood – I don't want to spook either of them. At this point, they are my only source of information.

'Because we believe in something better.' His voice is quiet, as always, but his honesty sparks something in my chest.

'Something different from the General, I take it?'

I sit towards the front of my cell, close enough to the hooded man to hear him but not so close I can touch him. He never opens the door, and I almost prefer it that way until I can round out the edges of my plan. It's more or less the same as the one I made with Will – take out the gentle guard when he is returning me from the fire room and run down the other end of the walkway. But there are a few challenges with it so far. Firstly, I haven't been let out since I watched Will walk away; secondly, as skilled as I am, I'm not sure I could take them both down at the same time without drawing attention.

But waiting to see the General again is wearing on my nerves. I want to be gone before he returns from wherever he's been and realises he doesn't need to keep me alive.

The man considers my question.

'A different perspective on the same thing, I think,' he says.

'And why are you here? With me?'

The other one laughs softly at that, the sound reaching me from his position near the walkway to the fire room. 'Because we don't leave anyone behind,' he says. It's hard to make out his exact colouring in the light down here but I've seen his cheek-length blonde hair in the fire room. 'And you're the last one here. Even if you did make it particularly tricky to change that fact.'

My eyes go wide.

'*I* made it tricky?' I fight to keep my voice low. I shouldn't be engaging them in this way but there's something easy about their presence. 'I didn't exactly have a choice, did I? You know who does seem to have a choice here, though? You two.' I point at each of them. 'So, enlighten me, if you have *different perspectives*'—I make air quotes with my fingers—'to your boss, the questions stand: why are you here'—I gesture around my cell—'and why are you with me?'

The guard looks at the hooded man and shrugs, turning back to the door.

I hate that I can't see his face but I know he's watching me.

'Because,' he says, 'we have a job to do and it's not finished yet.'

'That's putting it mildly,' the standing guard says with his back still turned.

I lean back on my hands.

'And what job might that be?' I ask.

My skin starts to tingle under the attention of the hooded man, I can feel his own surprise that he's even been this open with me, but I can't leave it there.

'The General is looking for someone,' he says.

I nod.

'You're not surprised?'

'Will and my team,' I say, heart aching as I speak of them, 'we discovered that. We just found out the hard way who was doing the searching.'

'Well ... we're looking for someone too,' he says. 'But we won't be leaving a trail of destruction while we do it. If we can help you in the meantime, without drawing extra attention from the General, we will.'

I listen to the sound of food being slid between the bars. It's better food than when the others were in the cells with me; perhaps, with only one prisoner, it's just easier to serve the same food as the soldiers. I never see who leaves it. I tried to stay awake a few times to see if I could catch them but sleep inevitably came and I would get hungry waiting. So I no longer try to see them.

Sweat stings my eyes as I finish my last repetition of exercises and I begin my weapons practice. It's probably quite pointless, given I obviously have no weapons to train with, but I practice different sequences anyway. If nothing else, it helps keep my mind active as I try different patterns of movement. In my mind, I always use either the General or Odhran as my target.

'You move well,' says that deep voice as my skin tickles with the hum of emotions that accompanies him.

'As well as I can in this dirt square that is now my life,' I say. The tension surrounding him starts to prickle my chest. 'What is it?'

He doesn't beat around the bush. 'The General has returned and wishes you to join him for dinner.'

My heart lurches into my throat. 'Will I be a guest at dinner, or just dinner?'

He snorts a thin laugh that belies the hatred coming from him. 'Tasty as you may be, I think he will take his chances with you as a guest for tonight,' he says. 'I can't promise he won't try to eat you later, though.'

The false lightness of the conversation is jarring, and I can tell he feels the same. I don't know what dinner with the General will entail. But, for hurting Will, if I had a weapon, I'd make sure it was his last. I will never forgive him for that, for tearing Will away from me—

'Aren't I lucky,' I say to interrupt my spiralling thoughts.

The hooded man opens the cell door and motions me out. I cock my head at him in query; I haven't left this cell for what feels like a long time.

'Now?' I ask.

'I have orders to ensure you are presentable for tonight,' he says. 'I'm afraid you don't really fit that bill right now and I don't particularly wish to be dinner, either.'

I can't help but glance down at myself, suddenly hyper aware of the conditions I have been staying in.

Stepping towards the hooded man, I properly size him up. I've been paying attention to the breadth of his shoulders every night but, when he's been crouched or seated in front of my cell, it's been trickier to get an accurate assessment of what I might be up against.

He's tall.

And broad.

Bigger than anyone I've fought before.

I look down the hallway where he seems to appear from in the evenings and I note he came from the other way just now – the direction of the hall and what I am starting to think of as the 'official' entrance to my cell block.

I'm two steps away, looking at him again, and running through the ways I could try and take him down, when he clears his throat. The hum around me warms.

'What are you thinking?' he asks.

What would you do if I just ran? The words are almost off my tongue before I find my senses. He said he would help. That drawing attention to the help he's given so far would be bad. And I want to believe him.

'I didn't realise how much I was looking forward to being clean again,' I say instead.

He's left me on my own in the bathroom but I can still sense him on the other side of the door. I pause for a moment to let the feeling of security that brings wash over me. I'd long given up on wishing for any sort of washing and I savour the anticipation of water on my skin.

The bathroom is also made from packed dirt but it has a high opening in one wall, similar to the main hall with the fire. Tears spring to my eyes and my chest hollows out as I make out the sky outside. It's grey and misty and every now and then branches sway into view.

I've lived in Rhyton as long as I can remember, until now at least, but open spaces always called to me. Now, looking at the grey sky as I cry, I can almost feel the clouds beneath my fingers and my heart seems to beat more strongly. I take a mental picture of this beautiful sky and tuck it away for times of need. I know they are coming.

Should I have run? Could I even outrun him when he clearly knows what the other end of that walkway holds and I do not?

But the tears come heavier when I let myself acknowledge the truth: I don't want him or the other guard to be punished for my escape. The blood draining from Will's face as I watched him bleeding out will stay with me a long time. I want to say it's for selfless reasons that I don't want more people around me harmed. But, as I think over my mum, the librarian, Will, I know it's largely because I don't want to add any more visions to my nightmares.

There are two free-standing baths in the middle of the room but no taps to be seen, the water clearly having been carted in from somewhere. Burners sit underneath one of the baths, heating the water. Far below the opening in the wall runs a bench where I find towels and a washer, a firm brush, and bundle of clothes. Ignoring the clean clothes for the moment, I peel the now squalid gold dress from my skin, collect the brush and hop into the cold bath. The water is bracing and I swear as I force myself in. The door cracks but he doesn't poke his head in.

'Alright in here?' he asks.

'Yes,' I breathe, the freezing water making talking hard. 'Out.'

The door closes again.

I scrub myself raw, beginning with the dirt caked between my toes all the way up into my hair, submerging myself in the freezing water. My teeth are chattering by the time I am ready to leave this bath and, dripping water on the floor, I ease myself out. The water I leave behind is black. Having found toiletries on the bench as well, I grab these now and hop into the hot bath. Warmth caresses me and I sink as low as I can so the water laps my chin, my knees tipped to the side so as little as possible of my body is escaping the water. I moan as I rest my head on the edge of the bath.

The man's presence tightens slightly on the other side of the door and I ignore him. I do another number of rounds of washing and spend some time untangling my hair with my fingers and the conditioner. I get a reluctant hurry up from the hall and I grudgingly pull myself from the warm water.

As good as this is, I don't want to anger the General by being late.

Opening the door to the bathroom once I'm dressed, the man stumbles slightly, as if he was leaning against it, before resuming his more formal posture and leading the way to the General. I've braided my hair, to keep it out of my face and do what I can to keep the tangles at bay for however long it is until my next wash. The clean gown tonight feels like it's been tailored just for me. It's fitted through the bodice, similar to the last dress, and feels firm against my breasts and waist. The long skirt drops almost to the floor, but it's just short enough to not drag in the dirt. The deep green velvet is glorious to the touch and I can't resist running my fingers along the bodice as we walk. I even have soft gold slippers. I will be surprised if they last the night, they're so delicate, but the reprieve of not feeling the cold dirt and stone directly beneath my toes is nothing less than joyful.

I glance at the hooded man, who seems to be grappling with something. He's certainly trying to reign in his emotions and my own anxiety about tonight crashes back to me. I'd been able to park those thoughts in the simple joys of seeing the sky and becoming clean, but I can't avoid it now and it's clear my guard is also on edge. He knows the General and so his apprehension along with mine makes me almost blind with fear.

Without thinking, I reach out and grab his arm.

'Stop,' I gasp, 'I can't breathe.'

He stills at my touch and I quickly withdraw my hand before placing my elbows on my knees and dropping my head between them.

Inhale.

Exhale.

I force myself to breathe deep and curse at showing my weakness. I have become complacent with him, but it takes me several moments to gain control over the rioting that fires in my nerves. Slowly I draw myself back up and clench my fists at my side as we walk on, the path inclining as we go. The hooded man doesn't turn his head my way, but I don't miss the concern he tries to suppress. Or that he seems physically closer than before, as if he can shield me from whatever is about to come.

CHAPTER THIRTEEN

The hooded man pauses outside an imposing door, purposefully giving me time to try and compose myself. His hand halts on its way to knock on the door and he looks in my direction, his face still obscured by his hood. My internal struggle must be clear because I nod at him and the stream of foreign, and yet now so familiar, emotion bleeds its way into my core. Taking a deep breath, I take what he offers to help steel my nerves. I clench my stomach muscles in an attempt to hold on tighter to what I have no doubt will be my lifeline as we enter on the General's command.

It takes a moment or two before my eyes adjust to the new light, after the dark hallways lit only by torches. The light in the General's large room is soft and I unwittingly emit a low gasp. Directly opposite the doorway is a wall of glass through which are velvet green hills, not unlike my dress, and the sky. Still grey, as it was from the bathroom, but the contrast of the sky with the gently blowing grass is almost mystical. It reminds me a little of the fields from my dreams, the only place I've seen so much green.

'Sir.'

The hooded soldier's voice startles me from my reverie and I see the General lounging in a heavily cushioned chair to the right of the window, a pile of papers on his lap. In front of him, a fireplace is built into the wall and sends a lovely, welcoming heat into the room that's at odds with the apprehension in my gut.

'You may sit,' the General waves a hand at the large dining table. 'I'll be with you in a moment, I just need to catch up.'

I take in the colourful wall hangings from where I sit. They're quite lovely, really, and I'm sure took great skill to complete; but wish I could see out of the window, instead. Tonight might be the last time I see the sky.

Surreptitiously, my eyes find the hooded man, who stands ramrod straight by the door. I stare at him and my heart rate steadily evens out a fraction, as if I can steal some of his strength. I can't be sure with his hood on, but I feel as if he is staring straight back at me. The thread of emotions between us thrumming. The General appears at my side and hands me a drink. I make myself look away from the hooded man and take the drink, inclining my head in forced thanks to the General.

A deep red liquid fills my cup and I inhale. Wine. It smells good but makes my heart ache as memories of my time with Phoenix make themselves known. That was when I last had wine. Before I said goodbye to it all, without even knowing. The General holds my gaze, his purple eyes set under dark brows, before looking suddenly at the hooded man.

'Leave,' he commands. 'You're dismissed for the night.'

I clench my stomach harder, holding to the connection, silently begging him not to leave. How did I end up with a soldier as my only potential ally? I try not to look at his back as he walks through the door and terror trembles my hands. His blanketing emotions that hide my fragile inner flame remain but I do not let the small relief show on my face. A small voice questions if holding on is a good idea. For all I know, that could be playing right into his hands, or the General's. Perhaps they are the same. But, even if it is a false hope, it is the only one I have.

'Stand,' the General commands.

I rise, not game to break eye contact and reveal even a whisper of the fear that is growing now we are alone. He steps toward me, a hand outstretched and I have a flash of memory of the burning pain that accompanies his touch. Stepping back, I knock into the chair I have just left. It's timber legs scraping against the stone as it moves slightly.

'What is your name?' he asks, dropping his arm back to his side.

'Alice,' I say, righting myself.

'That's your real name?'

I nod.

'You weren't known by anything else?'

I think of what my mum used to call me, but I won't give that over to him. The name the lady at the orphanage couldn't pronounce properly.

'No,' I say.

He nods slowly, a soft smile coming to his mouth. The purple, ringed eyes are a fraction less cold than I have seen them before. I remember, now, why Odhran's seemed familiar. They all have ringed eyes like the beggar. Perhaps the hooded man keeps his hidden because his are not.

The General takes another step towards me and, just like when he came close the first time I met him, I find my resolve to not back away again. He lifts his wine glass up and towards me.

'We should drink to our new arrangement,' he says, smiling.

I stare at him, unsure what I am supposed to do here.

He reaches out to touch the elbow of the arm that holds my drink and I try not to flinch. But there's no pain. Instead, he applies a gentle upwards pressure to direct my glass closer to his.

I take the not-so-subtle hint and clink my glass to his.

'To us,' he says.

My stomach turns.

'Let's sit.' This time he gestures to the large, plush chairs arranged around the fireplace, the window to my left. 'I'll be frank with you, Alice,' he says. 'I did not offer for you to stay simply out of the goodness of my heart.'

I try to school my features into something that doesn't betray my shock. Did he really think I thought he was being kind? I fight the urge to lower my barrier to try and read him. I don't know how many things I can do at once with my gift and letting go of the other man's calmness … I don't think I can.

'You don't know me very well, yet, but I would like to correct that.' He leans forward and reaches towards me, placing two fingers on my knee.

I stiffen.

His fingers move in a tiny circle on the dress, as if he's also captivated by the velvet. Bile rises in my throat.

'I asked you to stay because we are to be bonded.'

My brows lift.

'Bonded?' I hear myself ask and he smiles like this is a good reaction. A strand of his white hair falls around his face. The hint of lines around his eyes are just beginning to show.

'Yes,' he says. 'I know it is slightly more ... unusual now for this to happen so quickly, but I feel like I have known you for a long time. I can't help but think we have been destined for this.'

I shake my head, blinking.

'I – I don't know what that means.'

He frowns. 'You said you'd stay, bonding just makes it official.'

'Oh,' I breathe.

Standing, he places his glass on the small table beside his chair. He takes my hand and pulls me with him. Everything in me wants to stop. To fight. There's nothing about his purple, ringed eyes I trust.

But I remember how easily he drove that knife into Will. I'm too far from my cell to imagine I could run from him easily. My body starts to shake with the effort of staying this close to him. He rubs his neck, scratching something there before cupping my cheek. I swallow the acid in my mouth.

'We'll do wonderful things together,' he whispers as he leans in, his mouth approaching mine.

I shove him back. Hard. He crashes into his chair but straightens before I can blink, striking me with the back of his hand across my cheekbone, whipping my head to the side. I didn't even see him move back to me. My cheek stings and I lift my chin.

A white noise in my mind is getting louder. I had thought it was the result of being struck but it should be disappearing by now. Sweat breaks out on my palms and my knees shake below me. Flashes of that day clamour in my mind. My mother telling me to hide, smiling, the blackness, the blood that started to drip off the end of her nose onto the floor. And the sound, over and over. The sound of something smashing in her skull.

My vision starts to swim and I can't tell if it's the memories or happening now. I don't have any recollection of the General, but then, I didn't see any of their faces. Was he there? Did he do it? Does he know me? The sound in my ears is now at screaming pitch and I jam my hands against them to try and stop it; but it's coming from the inside. He grabs my shoulders and the searing pain shoots down my arms.

'That wasn't polite, Alice. I asked you to bond with me. The correct answer is "yes".'

I shouldn't be able to hear his voice, I know I wouldn't be able to hear mine. Burning hands grip my face and I scream. Blindly, I grapple for the safety of the well of emotions inside me, it's all I have to hang on to. His fist slams into my stomach, doubling me over and I hit my head on something on the way down. I can't see what. He kicks me in the stomach before I'm yanked upright, my hands still desperately trying to stop the screaming in my ears as I'm pushed against what feels like the wall. My breathing comes hard, the wind knocked out of me, and he lands another blow to my torso. The room spins around me, blurring. He places both palms on my chest and my flesh burns. I expect to feel it dripping from me. Pain eddies around me, choking the breath from my lungs. The smell of burning fills my nose.

The time he touched me in the fire room felt like nothing compared to this. This actual searing of my skin.

'If you will not admit who you are and join me willingly, I will simply take you,' he says, pressing his molten hands harder into my skin. I struggle to understand. And then the tiny little flame I've been instinctively protecting slowly makes its way from under the blanket of the hooded man's emotions. Emotions that have thinned as if he's too far away to reach.

Gold flickers towards the General's hands.

I'm lying on the floor when I blink into painful consciousness. The General crouches over me, his long tan boots at my eye level. He's not touching me, but the white-hot burning remains on my skin and I whimper. The heat in my chest pulses through my body and I fight to remain conscious; the darkness at the edge of my vision tinges with purple.

The silver cloak the General wears tonight is pooled out behind him like moonlight. His eyes find mine and I refuse to give him the satisfaction of looking away even as my vision blurs.

'I'm sorry,' he says quietly. 'I just – she was everything. Instead,' he pauses and I close my eyes, my mind giving way to the tidal wave of pain, 'she wanted to run away with that human bastard and reduced me to this.'

He hoists me up.

'I don't want to hurt you, Alice,' he says. 'I never wanted to hurt her, either. But we will be bonded. Even if I have to keep bringing others in here, day after day, to show you what I will do until you agree ... we will be bonded. I would suggest you do so before I have your friend brought back here, too.'

He drags me to the door, gently shoving me out and shutting it behind me.

On shaking legs, I stumble my way along the fire lit hallway, stunned I've left the General's room. That he let me walk away after that. My skin is on fire, nostrils filled with the scent of burning skin, fabric and hair. My laboured breath drags in my chest. I'm not sure where I'm going, I can only focus on moving away from the General. I need running water. If I can find my way back to the bathroom, the dirty bath water might still be there. I round a corner and collide with a solid figure. A soldier.

Please not Odhran, please not Odhran. Although even he might take pity on me, now. His face morphs into horror as he takes in my burns.

'Please, help me,' I whisper. 'I need—'

He reaches towards me and I flinch away. I can't bear the thought of being touched. I make to move past him, but he disappears down the hallway at a run. I try to follow but my body won't cooperate and I slide to the floor.

Out of the darkness, the man reappears, like an apparition. On his heels is the hooded man and I let myself feel a little flare of hope. He saved Will's life; he can stop my burning.

Wordlessly, I look up at him and wish I can't feel his overwhelming emotions when he looks at me. The concern and worry that's almost drowned out by his barely contained rage. I'd give anything to be able to turn them off. He slowly reaches his hands out and I try to scramble back, my head spinning and sweat from the pain dripping into my eyes.

'Lish,' he says in a low tone. I don't think he's used my name before, I didn't know he knew what it was. 'If I'm going to help you, I'm going to have to touch you. If you can walk, I don't have to do that just yet,' he continues, 'but I need to get you someplace else, and I will carry you if I must. Okay?'

I drag myself to my feet and take a hunched step towards him, my face and body screaming. He takes this as agreement enough and begins walking. He sets a fast pace and I push myself to keep up. The other man follows behind.

My mind is shifting, out of reach. All I can feel is burning.

Arriving at a narrow door, the hooded man thanks the other and asks him to remain outside. There is a small bed and I stumble towards it, suddenly desperate to lie down. The hooded man approaches, and I close my eyes, tired of fighting the waves of pain that try to suffocate me. The thick thread of emotions he gave me earlier is stronger again and I imagine wrapping myself in it, giving myself to the embrace and gradually my heart rate slows.

'I'm going to have to place my hands on your chest,' he says. I can't decipher what's in his voice.

He waits a beat for my subtle nod, and I hiss at the contact of skin on my burns. I don't need to look at myself to know I have two handprints there. The heat that radiates from his hands is excruciating at first, adding to the burning already in my skin. Pushing away the vision of those mauve eyes that feel as if they have burned not just my skin, but my soul, I give myself to the pain.

It hurts to open my eyes, so I don't. Breathing is hard and a sharp pain in my side says my ribs might be broken; but the blows to my stomach fill me with particular disquiet. It seems stupid now, but I'd dreamed of children once. I don't know how much my broken body will take and still be able to deliver on that dream. Tears gently make their way across my cheeks to the bed beneath me as I let it sink in that it doesn't matter how broken I am or not, I will now never have the opportunity to try.

The General will never let me go.

The familiar hum and crackle of the hooded man's energy brushes against my senses but I pay as little attention as I can to his emotions. He places his warm hands on my side. I can't help but sigh into the gentle touch, a sensation I didn't realise how much I'd missed. His fingers tense slightly on my skin.

'I'd wanted children once,' I whisper. His hands still before they resume their soft exploration of my different hurts. 'I imagine he will have made that impossible now.' I don't know why I say it, but I can't bring myself to be a stranger to this man. The one whose emotions I am learning like my own and bury myself in every day. The one whose face I don't know.

He draws a long breath.

'I will heal you as best I can ... if you ... want children ...' His voice is quiet before he trails off, unsure how to finish that sentence. The warmth of his hands is spreading through me like a gentle fire now, coaxing my little gold flame back to life as the pain starts to subside.

The laugh that escapes me is hollow.

'And whose shall I have? The General's?' I ask and he flinches at the loss and anger clear in my voice.

I give in to the darkness behind my eyes then and I dream, not of mauve eyes, but amber.

Pieces of conversation filter through to me and I grapple to hold onto the words that try to slip back out of my mind. Gradually, the hum of the hooded man's emotions returns to me, even before I've opened my eyes. The steady buzz along my skin when he's not trying to send me additional strength. Then it's more like a coil of rope. But neither are things I have felt before and I'm still not sure what to make of it. If I wasn't currently at the mercy of the General and the Whispers, I'd be more interested in finding out more about how this works. How there are others like me.

But, in my current circumstances, it doesn't seem particularly important.

'... the fuck did this happen?'

'Best I can tell,' the young one says, 'it was going fine and something made him lose it.'

'Well, that's fucking obvious,' a prickle of anger reaches me. 'But why? He's normally so controlled.'

There's a pause and I concentrate on breathing, this room smells so different to my cell.

'He actually burnt her,' the hooded man says. 'Since when has he gone from painful touch to burning touch?'

I crack my eyes open and find the large man with his back to me, talking to the younger one. The one who has been part of my guard most nights.

I let my eyes run back to the larger one, the breadth of his shoulders. How he takes up much of the space in the room. His dark hair.

He flicks the hood back on.

'I need—' he starts.

'He said he wanted to celebrate my staying,' I say, the hooded man whirling to me, 'and I shoved him.'

I push myself up to sit and all of sudden he's crouched in front of me, steadying me by my shoulders. My head spins slightly and I close my eyes again until it settles, breathing into the warmth his hands spread through my limbs.

Hesitantly, I brush my fingertips across my face and chest and both arms through the holes in the dress. The skin there is soft and raw but not textured as burn wounds would be. I blow out a breath slowly as I release the thread of the hooded man I'd somehow kept coiled in my gut even as consciousness failed me. The gentle hum that exists when he's near crackles in places along my bare arms.

'I'm okay,' I whisper and I feel him step back as I open my eyes again, dropping his hands from my shoulders.

'Well,' the young one says, 'I guess we know why he lost control.'

'We need to bring things forward,' the hooded man says, looking towards him. 'She can't stay here any longer.'

The other one nods slowly, clearly considering what needs to be brought forward and my heart leaps.

'Why would you help me?' I ask. 'What makes you so sure I won't give you both away?'

The hooded one turns slowly to me.

'Would you?' His voice is quiet but there's a lethality in it that sends a shiver down my spine.

I stare at him, where I imagine his eyes would be. But while what I say is important, I can tell by the sensation of him that he knows I never would.

'No.'

I watch his chest fall with his exhale.

'I need to go,' he says. 'Haryk will take you back. There's something I need to take care of.'

Haryk, I think. I smile. It's nice to know his name. I can't feel him like I can the hooded one so I've felt like I don't know him as well. Not having his name amplified this gap and now it's a tiny bit smaller.

CHAPTER FOURTEEN

Back in my cell, I listen to the filtered fragments of sound coming from the fire room.

Do those soldiers have families to go home to? I wonder.

I can't imagine sitting at home while my husband or partner abducted an innocent woman and tore a different family apart. Or burnt her face and beat her. Not that being someone's partner is still an option for me.

But the hesitation to take part in Odhran's abuse of Will, the apparent discomfort I've noticed, makes me wonder how happy they are to be here. If this is the official role they are supposed to play.

I physically shudder at the thought of the 'bonding' the General thinks we are going to have. I've waded through these past weeks totally naïve. Simply waiting away the hours was never going to be enough to prepare me for the full extent of the General and, deep down, I know he is only getting started. The feel of my scorched flesh sliding off my chest will haunt me until I die. The smell will stay with me longer.

But more than that is the cold realisation that I am totally powerless against him and his ... methods. Experiencing what he and the hooded man can do should be enough to convince me, but my mind still wants to reject this reality where people are capable of impossible things. I'd thought I was an anomaly. That there was no particular reason for what I can do. Now, I wonder what I've been missing, what else she wasn't able to teach me.

I long for the deep crevasses in my heart to ice over. Now, it is my only hope of salvation. But, instead of icing over, those ravines are slowly filling with an impotent rage. All my life I have dreamed of finding out what happened to my mother. Now, I am faced with a man who likely dealt the killing blow himself, or knows who did.

And I am completely incapable of destroying him.

The torch closest to my door goes out and the hairs on the back of my neck stand up. Someone stands in the darkness, knocking something against the bars. They laugh and all at once I know who it is ... and what they want. My stomach sinks as he steps forward and into sight, running a baton backwards and forwards along the bars in front of him.

I should be frightened, but exhaustion dampens my senses. The hope that flickered in my chest during my conversation with Haryk and the hooded man remains. But, looking in each direction, I can't see either of them.

A hollow sensation starts in my stomach. Did they change their minds? Worse, did something happen to them because they were going to help me?

'No sentry tonight, then?' he asks.

I remain silent, the metallic thudding loud in my ears.

'It's a shame he won't get to watch,' he says. His speech is slightly slurred. 'But there's enough liquor in him to see him through to morning.'

A stone settles in my stomach.

He unlocks the door and walks towards me. I let my mind empty, my thoughts trickling away. I will face the trials of today later. Right now, I focus on his movements instead, the tiny part of me that's not ready to die yet coming to the fore. And I'm certainly not going to let him take me as he's previously suggested. I force my legs to stand. He's stealthy, if a little wobbly, but that weakness alone will not be enough for me to best him. And he's certainly angry enough at me to push him through any faults in his attack.

My own rage builds.

At Odhran.

At the General.

At the life I have been forced to give up. I will not give any part of myself to this man.

Not today.

'You disgust me,' I say.

He laughs to himself. 'Like that matters. The General is never going to find who he's looking for, she's dead or gone, and that means every woman that steps foot in here is as well.'

I let him get closer, thinking I am frozen in fear, but he doesn't realise I am now trembling at the injustice. He's two paces from me when I attack.

After so long practicing with nothing but my own company, it feels good to hit someone. I savour the impact of my blows reverberating up my limbs. I've caught him off guard but the shock doesn't last long and he lashes out with the baton. I duck, only to catch a fist in my left side. The hooded man healed my physical wounds but I am tiring quickly after my time with the General and so long without proper movement. I am somehow tender on the inside.

I skip out of his reach and try to catch my breath.

Odhran rises onto the tips of his toes, gasping. The hooded man has the baton at his neck and holds firm. The ire from the hooded man skitters on my skin. I back away until the wall presses against my back.

'Of course,' Odhran chokes out. 'Of course, you would be here.'

'And, of course, you're exactly where you shouldn't be.' The hooded man's voice is low, his mouth almost against Odhran's ear.

Odhran grips the hooded man's arms, trying to loosen the pressure against his throat.

'You've given it away now, you know.' Odhran's voice is strangled.

The hooded man presses harder and Odhran chokes.

'What's that?' The hooded man asks quietly.

Odhran attempts a laugh but coughs instead. 'You took the one thing I wanted. Now, I know how to repay you.'

The hooded man presses his face against the side of Odhran's head. 'Your decisions here do nothing but confirm I took the right action when I did.' He squeezes the baton back harder again. 'And you have *no idea* how to repay me. I suggest you do not try.' His voice is more like a growl and it drags down my spine.

He pulls back hard with both hands, definitely not liquored up as Odhran claimed.

It doesn't take long for Odhran to slump into unconsciousness, or perhaps the hooded man has killed him. Given Odhran's clear feelings towards me, I don't particularly care. But I do care about the hooded man's intentions. What he took from Odhran and how. I didn't notice him arrive in the dark and he moves more quietly than a man should be able to. Before I register, he's in front of me – one hand extended and holding a short-bladed knife.

I look between his covered face and his hand.

'It would be helpful ... when they find him ... if there is some of your blood in here. But I understand if—'

I snatch the blade from his hand and drive the tip of the blade into soft skin below the crook of my elbow, dragging it down my arm. My stomach turns as the blood starts to pulse from my wound and I awkwardly wipe the cut along a small section of the bars. Grimacing at the throb in my arm, I flinch as I yank some hair out and carefully stick it to the blood to dry in place.

It's not especially realistic, but it might buy us some time.

I look at the bloodied blade again and slowly hold it between us. Not quite claiming it but my fingers grip it tightly.

'Keep it,' he says, not missing a beat and handing me a sheath as well, 'it's my sister's.' Slipping the blade into its holder, I slide it into the top of my dress, releasing a breath.

He holds his hand out to me once more. 'We need to move.'

'I can't leave,' I say suddenly, the thought crashing into me painfully. My feet are stuck to the floor, torn between the thought of what the General will do if I leave. And if I stay.

His mouth opens and shuts like he's grasping for words.

'He said he'll go after Will again.'

'I've taken care of it,' he whispers and it's my turn to be at a loss for words. 'It's why we couldn't go sooner, but we really need to go now.'

'If I go with you,' I say, pausing to take a deep breath, 'on a fucking hope and prayer this isn't some sick game, I will literally be putting mine and Will's lives in your hands.'

The thought of this going wrong churns in my gut. He still holds his hand to me and takes a slow step forward.

'I have held both of your lives in my hands before and each of those times worked out, didn't they?'

Closing my eyes momentarily, I pray my instincts aren't wrong as I reach out and take the hooded man's hand. He stops for a moment, looking down at where our outstretched hands now join across the space between us. A single squeeze is all the warning I get before he tugs me forward and we run.

We head left out of my cell past where Will was being held. Sweat trickles down my spine as I imagine an alarm being raised and soldiers coming after us. We run past the empty cells the other women were in. In the time since, no more have arrived.

When we reach what looks like a dead end my pulse quickens, desperate to get out. My skin crawls with the need to feel fresh air in my lungs and see the sky. And I long for my family. For Will.

He releases me and runs his hands along the dirt wall. The sound changes as he scrapes along packed dirt to timber. A narrow door is set in the far recess of the end of the cell row. He turns sideways to go through and, following, I find myself in a storeroom of sorts – although I can't imagine what is kept in this clearly long forgotten place.

The dust of centuries coating every surface is illuminated by a thin strip of window at the top of one of the walls. Except a worn path on the floor. He moves some of the timber crates slightly, to disturb the space as little as possible, and reveals a small opening in the far wall. It seems to be a tunnel. For a child.

I hold my arm up before me, blood dripping from my elbow, and he quickly steps back to me.

'May I?' he asks.

Gently, I place my arm in his outstretched hands and let the warm fizzing from his hands encircle me.

'What about Haryk?' I ask as I watch my skin steadily coming together and the throbbing starts to evaporate. He carefully puts my arm down.

'We need him here, his cover is still good. You first,' he says nodding his head at the small, dark hole.

I gape at him, what I can see of his shape in the dim light anyway, and the outline of his apprehension starts to prickle the air around me, mingling with my fear. He grabs my elbow and pulls me forward firmly but gently.

'I know how scary this is, but if we are found here it will be the end for more than just the two of us,' he says. I think of Haryk and get down on my hands and knees to peer into the tunnel. It's like an abyss and impossible to tell how far it goes.

'Do not tell me what things live in here,' I say as I start to wiggle my way in, arms outstretched.

There is just enough room for me to slide in on my stomach and use my body to make my way forward. I try not to think about the fact I can't turn around. If something came towards me, I would have to meet it face on or back out to the storeroom. A series of quiet grunts comes from behind making it clear I won't be getting back out that way.

The tunnel quickly begins to steep upwards, requiring more effort to drag myself along with my elbows, knees, and toes. I lose skin from both elbows and all my toes, my gold slippers not having survived my encounter with the General, and dirt rains down on me, filling my eyes, nose, and mouth. The tunnel widens slightly as it comes to a steeper incline and my fingers connect with what feels like stone. Scrambling closer I run my fingers around the edges confirming the way is sealed shut.

'Is it supposed to be closed? I think there's a rock of some sort over the end.' I spit dirt.

'You'll need to push it off,' he says. Wriggling closer so I can use more of my body weight as leverage I strain against the rock.

'I can't shift it.'

'I'm coming up.'

I try and flatten myself against the wall to give him space but there's still barely enough room for one person in here, let alone two. And certainly not one as large as the hooded man. I'm thankful for the total darkness as he clambers against me in the tunnel, each of us swearing and grunting at different times. He's facing me and I can feel every inch of him pressed against me. He puts his arms out to press against the stone, catching my chin with an elbow on the way.

'Ouch,' I mutter.

We push against the stone, and each other for support, and – bit by bit – it starts to move. Through the hole we've just made I can see the sparkling of starlight and it takes my breath away.

'We're not out yet,' he says. 'They're bugs you're looking at.'

I've never seen anything like it and I scrabble out, trying not to touch too much of him – although I'm suspicious I might have kneed him in the nose on the way out. I spin slowly, rocks crunching beneath my feet. The pain of the sharper ones digging into my soles is temporarily lost as I take in what's around me.

The domed ceiling emits a soft, pulsing light, as if millions of stars have suddenly come to life. Reflecting them is a pool that's so still I can make out individual lights – bugs – in the image on the surface. The hooded man pulls his hood off and I watch the dark outline of him make its way to the edge of the pool, shaking dirt from his cloak. I hobble over the rocks to join him, watching our reflections.

I glance at him but it's too dark to make out any of his features. 'This is incredible,' I breathe, not wishing to disturb the quiet.

He speaks just as softly. 'The next bit's not quite as easy, I'm sorry. I hope you can swim.'

My vision of this as a peaceful place is suddenly shattered as I study the water. The inky black that seconds ago seemed magical now has an edge of malice. I suppose my hesitation to the water is not unlike my concerns about the tunnel. I do not wish to be set upon by things I cannot name or see. And my swimming is fine for splashing around at the beach but, no, I would not consider myself a swimmer.

'Just tell me what we need to do,' I say, forcing a deep breath.

The water laps at my ankles as I draw some steadying breaths and walk into the pool with the man by my side. It's warmer than I expected and not completely unpleasant, if I can put aside the thought of what lurks beneath. The first part is straightforward, although the weight of my velvet dress is hard to pull through the water. Too late, I wonder if I should have taken it off but I have no alternatives. Reaching the other side of the pool, I realise the water doesn't get shallower again but appears to be cut in half by a rock wall. He fumbles along the wall as we tread water looking for some kind of marker in the rock.

'Here,' he says.

Floating on my front, I use my arms to guide me over to him, allowing me to keep my feet as shallowly in the water as possible and away from any lurking predators. He finds my hand and lifts it to the wall, forcing me vertical in the blackness. I repress a shudder. He flattens my hand against the rock and I start to feel the surface as he did. It's cold and rough to the touch but under my ring finger, there is a groove. It's smoother than the rest of the wall and, from what I can tell in the dark, it runs straight down into the water. I follow it beneath the surface as far as I can reach without submerging my head, but I don't feel where the wall might end.

'How do we go through?' I ask. The water eddies around my legs and my arms are beginning to tire from the action of keeping the weight of me in this sodden dress afloat.

'There is no through,' he says, 'we go under.'

'Under?' I splutter. A spike of fear breaks through the wall of ignorance I have been working hard to build. My heart hammers in my chest. 'How far down?'

'It's a way but we'll be fine. You will hold on to me and not let go, understand?'

I nod slowly but remember he probably can't see the action.

'You will feel when we go under the wall. Once we're on the other side, kick like mad to get to the surface. But never let go. Of me. Don't let go of me.'

I wish I had memories of diving off piers and spending days in the water to draw on to get me through this. But my childhood days were mostly spent in the orphanage, there were no pool or beach excursions there. The memories I hold most dear more often feature grass under my toes and the sky above my head. And I can see. I can see everything I could care to see.

The total blackness I'm now literally up to my neck in is anything but that. I can't even see my hands below. I tell myself that's not the water itself but the cavern we're in and I try to imagine the water as it would be in the daylight. Sparkling clear to its rock bottom. He tells me to take a deep breath and hold it. Exhale. Inhale and hold. Then, as instructed, I take a few more sips of breath without releasing the air already in my lungs, mimicking what I can hear him doing in front of me. He grips my hand

and squeezes to tell me it's time to dive. I don't open my eyes. I know I won't see anything anyway and I'm mildly concerned how the water would feel in them.

The temperature of the water drops suddenly and knocks some of the air from my lungs. The man is a strong swimmer and shows no signs of slowing which can only mean we are nowhere near the bottom of the wall.

Blackness crushes me and the sodden dress constricts my chest.

I have to get out.

I jerk out of his grasp and desperately kick for the surface, blindly swimming for what I hope is the top. Something grabs my ankle sending ice through my veins like lightning but it doesn't slow me. I just need to get to the top.

I need air.

My chest burns.

I break the surface and gulp down air, flailing against the wall to try and find a grip. My dress tries to drag me back down. Less than a second later the man breaks through as well.

'I'm sorry,' I gasp, coughing. 'I can't do this.'

My voice breaks and I curse myself for not holding it together but my mind is in overdrive. Thoughts of the General, and burning, and Odhran's intentions are drowning me. Funny, I almost think, to be both drowning in fear and literally drowning.

'You can, Lish, and you will,' he says patiently.

He moves to me and braces one hand against the wall while placing a knee under me, taking my weight and I'm thankful for the help it provides in keeping me afloat. He doesn't use my name a lot, but it sends warmth through me when he does. Like he sees me. After all this time of being no one in those cells.

I find his hand in the water and hold it firmly, absorbing his warmth and strength. I draw the largest breath possible and feel his chest expand against mine. He believes in me. Perhaps he has no other choice, now we're here, but I take that belief and hold it as if it's my own.

This time, I don't panic at the change in temperature and keep hold of the man dragging me down. I kick my legs hard to help propel me to the bottom. He pauses and pulls me closer, knocking me gently into the wall.

Understanding, I run my hand along until I feel a lip. The edge we are supposed to go under. I hold the sensation of my burning flesh in my mind to push me forward.

Because I certainly cannot go back.

The rock scrapes along my back as we pass under. I focus on the feel of the hand around mine, the bones in my fingers crunched against each other as he grips me tightly.

Just a bit further, Lish, I tell myself. *Just a bit further*.

The pressure in my chest and throat begins to take over all other sensations. I hold him tighter and stars appear behind my eyelids. My breath simply won't hold any more and air begins escaping from my nose, the bubbles tickling as they go. Soon, my body will draw its next breath and I will be powerless to stop it. Vaguely, I feel what might be another edge of rock on my back and the man banks us up sharply.

My thoughts slow even as I mentally shout at my legs to kick harder, harder. The distance between us grows until he is no longer beside me but above, pulling me along.

I do not dare to let go.

I will not be alone in the darkness.

But it sings to me all the same and I'm tired.

So tired.

CHAPTER FIFTEEN

'Dammit, Lish, breathe!' he shouts at me.

I don't recall him shouting at me before, I observe from far away. That's a strange thing for a soldier and prisoner relationship. Although, I guess by now I should be well aware this is no normal soldier.

Reality comes crashing back to me as I draw a sudden breath. The air tears down my throat and I can't get it in fast enough. He helps me sit up and I turn myself onto all fours to steady the spinning in my mind. Rocks dig into my palms, similar to those I walked over on the other side of the wall. And it's just as dark, perhaps darker. There are no starlight bugs in here.

The dizziness subsiding gradually, I resume my sitting position. The hooded man breathes heavily beside me. I can barely make out his shape but I can tell he's looking at me and I let myself properly focus on the emotions I can feel from him.

'I'm sorry, I didn't mean to frighten you,' I say softly, and the emotion is immediately dragged away. 'Are you alright?'

'I'm fine.' His tone is brusque. 'Okay,' he breathes after a moment, 'you had me a little worried but we're fine. We're both fine,' he repeats, more to himself than me. The hold he has on his emotions doesn't last long and I feel his shock that I picked up his fear for me.

'Please tell me there's no more,' I whisper.

He chuckles, a rich, deep sound, and I'm pleased he can't see the tug it creates at the corner of my mouth despite our circumstances.

'Definitely no more underwater walls for you,' he agrees.

He guides me over to the edge of this second cavern where a wall feels like it's been made of fallen boulders. It's a difficult climb in the dark with a waterlogged dress, but far less terrifying than the water. As I pull myself up over a large boulder, the hooded man helps me to my feet before lightly resting his hand on my lower back to keep me from slipping backwards.

Ahead of us is a field awash in moonlight and my heart leaps at the same time dread begins to unfurl in my gut. The thought of being in fresh air, of freedom, is exhilarating but it clashes with worry that this is not real. Some elaborate trap set by the General. What better entertainment than to give a girl a sense of freedom only to snatch it away again? And, if it's not a trap, the prospect of being out in the open on that field and the General catching us is equally frightening. The hooded man begins to move towards the opening of the cavern and I reach out to catch his arm, his cloak wet underneath my fingers.

'Wait,' I say. 'How do I know this is real?'

'Real?' he asks, surprise tinting his voice. 'You think I would do all of this just to return you to General Siosal?' he asks and my skin prickles with the offense he's taken.

I remain silent, the name rolling around my head. I want it to make the General seem less frightening but, somehow, giving him a name makes him more real. More likely not to be contained to the prison I have just left.

'I'm sorry, I know he really hurt you,' he says quietly.

'And you are under his command, are you not? What happens when he orders my return? Despite your *different perspectives,* you have participated in keeping me prisoner for the last—' I stop, realising I don't actually know how much time has passed. He begins to fill in the time and I interrupt. 'No, I don't want to know how long. Not yet.'

The muscles of his arm clench against my palm.

'I am supposed to be under his command,' he says carefully. 'He thinks I am under his command. Technically, I was due to leave for another mission tonight, so he is expecting me to be gone for a time and he won't be surprised to find Odhran in your cell.' He runs a hand through his hair, an action that snags my attention. It's far less formal than I've seen him before. 'Siosal knows what drives Odhran, Mother knows he's used it to his advantage often enough.' Anger edges his words. 'But surprise will be the least of his feelings when he can't find you.'

'But ... I'm still not sure I understand,' I stammer. 'Why me?'

'I ... I don't know,' he says. 'Haryk said you challenged him in that room with your friend?'

The concern in his voice is now also in the emotions I'm constantly aware of in his presence. I'm not sure he realises just how easily I can pick up on them.

'I mean why help me? Why go against him at all?' I ask.

'Look,' he says, glancing out the mouth of the cave, 'we should really keep moving. But I made an oath to protect, and leaving you there ...' I can feel him shake a little and anger pricks my skin. 'It wouldn't have been right, Lish. But I needed to try and do it in a way that wouldn't put others in more danger.'

Haryk, I realise. Maybe Will.

'It's just,' he continues. 'It's just not who I am ... to leave someone behind.'

The feel of Nico's arms around my neck as Phoenix and I decided he wouldn't be left alone, either, returns to me; the leap of faith we asked him to have in us. And I let the truth in this man's words wash over me. I want to trust him. I run my fingers down his arm until I can take his hand. I don't want to be alone in the dark.

He slides his fingers through mine and squeezes. 'As for if, and when, he orders you found,' his voice is barely more than a whisper, 'he'll have to go through me first.'

I let the weight of his words find me along with the pressure of his fingers gripping my hand.

'Let's go,' I breathe.

We pause at the mouth of the cavern. Looking back, I can see no sign of the pool below, it looks like a shallow cave. We scan the field for any sign of movement. Not finding any, the man whistles softly. I glance at him but it's still too dark for him to read the question on my face. I am sick of darkness. And hoods. A knicker sounds, as if in response to the whistle, and a horse appears out of the night.

I gape at him. 'You've got to be joking,' I say. 'What are you? Some kind of magical being?'

He chuckles and my heart warms a little. I enjoy the sound of his laugh.

'It's the horse that's made you think that?' he asks. 'Not the fact I brought your friend back from the brink of death with my bare hands?'

I have no response to that. He reaches out to the horse who snuffles its nose in his hand, the moonlight glinting on her coat.

'Meet Niamh,' he says as he moves down her flank, stroking her neck and body as he goes.

Instinctively, I slowly reach my hand towards her nose and still, letting her come to me. Her large nostrils flare as she takes in my scent, her breath warm on my palm. Tentatively, she puts her mossy soft nose against my hand and I stroke the other one up between her eyes, listening to him murmur lovingly to her. The love he has for her envelopes me and the softness in him eases some of the hurt I hold inside.

He places a hand on mine and runs it down her side, drawing me beside her. Leaving me touching her on my own, he bends in front of me with his hands interlaced before him. Recognising the stance from different patrols and training with my team, I hoist my skirt and place my right foot in his hand using my left for upwards momentum before throwing it over her side.

Swiftly, the man lands behind me on the horse and I sit up straight, suddenly self-conscious at his proximity. He shuffles me forward slightly, so I'm higher up towards her withers, and settles himself against my back, his arms reaching around me to grab her mane.

'Try not to tense your legs too much and hold on tight to her mane. You won't hurt her.'

His breath tickles against my neck. I wrap my fingers in her wiry mane as his thighs tense around me. She moves beneath us and he directs her across the field and into the trees. He wraps an arm around my waist helping me keep my seat and, before I can register, Niamh begins to move like lightning.

I clumsily try to match her rhythm before I realise relaxing into the movement works better and I flow with her rocking motion. It helps to have the man holding me to him and the horse, and I grip the arm at my waist with one hand and her mane with the other. My hair whips my face and my eyes stream with our speed but I can't bring myself to close them.

The moonlight has bathed the field in silver, the trees illuminated like beacons of safety. I drink it in. Leaning my head back into the man, I can look up and see the sky. We're moving so fast I expect all the stars to be a blur, but I can make some of them out. A blue one winks at me and, suddenly, it's not just the speed that's making my eyes water. I leave my head bumping gently against his shoulder so I can watch the stars as we fly underneath. The tears are torn from my cheeks and I imagine them taking my pain with them, disappearing into the blanketing darkness behind us.

The loss of Will hurts the most, but I feel violated by General Siosal, by Odhran, and from simply being held in that compound. The questions rising about all I learned there take up too much space in my mind and I push them away for now. Which leaves me thinking about the tether that seems to be tying me to this man and the way I can feel him like I can't feel anyone else. That, despite everything, his presence and his laugh feel like they piece little parts of me back together.

We ride hard, for what feels like hours, and Niamh's sides heave beneath me. She slows under some command of the man's I don't pick up and we steady to a walk now that we've reached a heavily treed wood. He brings her to a stop at the edge of a stream and slides off. He wraps his hands around my waist and I support myself on his shoulders as he gently pulls me off Niamh, placing me on the ground.

My hands leave his shoulders of their own accord and I let them trail to his broad chest to steady me. My legs are aching from our ride, not to mention that god awful swim, and they tremble slightly under my weight. The sky is starting to gently lighten, the sound of Niamh drinking heavily behind us joining the quiet twittering of the night.

His hands haven't yet left my waist and I look at my own where they sit on his chest, rising and falling with his breath. His fingers tighten around me, but he doesn't move. I'm close enough to feel him hold his breath and my cheeks warm at the thought of him feeling my blood thrumming through my veins.

He lowers his head slightly to look at me and I draw my own head back a little to take him in, now he's not wearing his hood.

The small wave of amusement that pushes against me makes it clear he is very aware of my initial reaction. I try to school my raised eyebrows and gaping mouth back into neutrality, holding my features firm. His face looks like it's been carved by a very talented stone mason – from his chiselled chin and cheek bones, and a long, broad nose down the middle. My eyes drop to his mouth next. I've seen it before, the shape of its fullness quite familiar from all the times I tried to see more of him under that hood.

It's his eyes that are particularly striking. His irises are molten pits of black with dual copper rings, one large around the outside of his black iris and a smaller one that circles his pupil. The longer I look at them, the more the colours dance and I'm undecided as to whether they are primarily dark or light. They almost remind me of the amber eyes from the forest. His dark hair has partially dried, pushed back from his face.

'Why do you keep yourself hidden?' I ask, realising it is well past time I said something.

His breathing returns, but it's still shallow.

'Siosal's orders,' he says, watching me. 'He doesn't want the Whispers to forget who they report to.'

I think on him challenging Siosal in the fire room after Will's beating. How the others looked to him as if they were hoping for something, the respect on their faces as he healed Will. Odhran's comments about not reporting to him. It fits with how uncomfortable they seemed to be with the General and his orders that this man would be a threat to him.

'Would it be too much for me to know your name now, too?'

'I wasn't sure you wanted to know,' he says quietly. 'You never asked.'

'I'm asking,' I say, still fixed on his eyes.

He looks at me for a long moment.

'Lochlain.'

I rise on to my toes once more, my breath mingling with his, his fingers tense on my waist.

'Thank you, Lochlain,' I whisper as I place a kiss on his cheek.

He holds me to him momentarily, his chest pressed against mine, before taking an abrupt step back leaving regret in his wake. Mine or his I'm not sure.

We agree to rest for the short time there is left before full dawn but to have no fire. Much of my dress is still damp and the cold is once again seeping into my bones. Just like in the cells, although at least I was dry then. I never experienced cold like this in Rhyton and my teeth clack together. The hooded man, *Lochlain*, takes pity on me and covers the two of us in his cloak. It's only marginally drier than my dress and we lie next to each other without touching. I doze fitfully for a time but visions of General Siosal chase any real sleep away.

I wake gradually, careful to take in my surroundings before I move to make sure it wasn't all just a figment of my imagination. My forehead is warm and, almost overwhelmingly, I feel safe. My chest constricts and I squeeze away tears of relief. Opening my eyes, I find myself staring at Lochlain's chest, his arm thrown across my hip. My breath catches and I slam my eyes shut, forcing my breathing into a normal rhythm so I don't give away I'm awake. I just want to savour this feeling for a little longer.

As the land around us wakes and the light of dawn makes its way through the trees, despite having only slept for what feels like minutes, Lochlain says it's time to go. How long he was awake while we lay like that I don't know, but he is purposefully avoiding my eye this morning. Thoughts of Phoenix pop into my mind and, suddenly, Lochlain's not the only one that feels ashamed.

We spend the day on Niamh again and Lochlain mostly lets her choose the pace. We speed over open areas and she picks her way more slowly through the thicker parts of the wood. I had wondered yesterday if this is the same forest Will and I had entered but, in the light of day, it is clear it's very different. There are more varieties of trees and plants than I can count and flowers of all colours cover the forest floor.

The closest I have been to a place like this is in my dream of the green meadow. There is certainly nothing in Driarn like this. Nothing as *alive* as this. I'd spent some time worried that Niamh's trampling of these flowers would leave a clear trail for General Siosal to follow. But, testing my balance to look around behind Lochlain, the flowers were regathering themselves and wiping any trace of our passing. The little flame that sits in my chest flickers at how far I must be from Rhyton. But the apprehension that should follow doesn't come. Instead, an unfounded hope makes it burn a little brighter.

We stop for rests several times to give Niamh a break from carrying us both. I offer to walk at different times, even though I'm not sure my sleep-deprived limbs could carry me, but Lochlain insists we need to put as much distance between us and where I was being held as possible. While we let her drink and graze Lochlain tells me about the different plants and animals that can be found in this wood. We have no food with us, but he won't hunt anything here, claiming it's a sacred place. My stomach grumbles from time to time but I don't begrudge him the sentiment. There is something about this wood that whispers gently to me.

We're seated on a fallen tree and I'm once again hyper aware of his presence and the crackling thrum that runs over my senses. Sitting in front of him on the horse has become a welcome time. It feels less confronting to be physically close when I don't have to look at him. I have spent so long not looking directly into his eyes, I still find them a bit disconcerting now that I have seen his face. There is something about them that makes me feel stripped bare. But, now I am out of that cell, I am becoming increasingly impatient for answers.

'Lochlain.' I like the way his name forms in my mouth. 'Where are we?'

He looks at me out of the corner of his eye. 'The Court of Airlie.'

'And where is that in relation to Rhyton? Is it far?'

He lifts his brows. 'I think this conversation is best held over wine.'

I laugh softly. 'I would certainly not say no to wine right now. But, seriously, I need to know how far from Rhyton we are.'

'It's hard to explain, Lish. We are both near and far. We're in the Realm.'

'I don't know what the Realm is.' *The existence of the Realm has been debated for centuries...* The memory comes the same time the denial falls from my lips.

'It's – it's not a place most people know about,' he says.

'Right ...' I frown. 'So how did we get here? *Why* am I here?'

'Siosal – he wasn't supposed to go back to the continent—'

'Driarn?'

He nods. 'He left when I wasn't there to intervene, took a small team and they ...'

'Picked up their search again,' I finish bitterly.

'I thought I'd put a final stop to it years ago, but some scratchy information came in about who he's looking for and he couldn't let it go. And, obviously he's from the Realm, which is why you were all brought here, too. As for how you got here – you would have crossed over when they'd knocked you out, so you probably didn't notice the shift.'

My head starts to whirl.

'How do I get back to Rhyton from here?'

A coil of dread starts to form in my stomach. He turns to me on the log, his knee pressing into mine, and takes both of my hands in his. His face is solemn and my heart sinks knowing what he's going to say.

'Lish.' He strokes a callused thumb over the back of my hand as his black and copper eyes find mine. 'You cannot go back to Rhyton. Siosal will turn that city upside down looking for you. He will work out it was me that helped you get out and that will be all he needs to never give you up.'

I search his face for a different answer, but I know in my heart it's true. The dread in my stomach starts to feel much more like nausea as I think about the danger Will and the others are in by my escape alone. I can't fathom what my return would do. The promises in the General's eyes when he looked at me will not be easily forgotten.

'Why, though?' I ask.

He lets out a long breath. 'Because, a long time ago, he lost someone. Someone he thought was unfairly taken from him. And now he goes to great lengths to control those in his life ... and how they leave.'

An icy finger runs down my spine.

'You said you'd taken care of Will and my friends, what did you mean?' I ask.

'I have people looking out for them.' Before I can ask more, he continues. 'We will look out for them until it's no longer needed,' he says.

'And when will that be?'

'I don't know yet.'

'So ... if I can't go home, where are we going? What am I supposed to do?' I ask.

He stares at me and I can feel his regret at what must come to pass.

'I'm going to take you somewhere safe for a night or two so you can gather your strength and supplies. And then you need to leave. Leave the Realm and not return to Rhyton. You will find somewhere far from here to live your life,' he says. 'It's the only way for you and your friends to stay safe.'

I take a hand from his, leaving the other still in his grip, and run a finger over the yellow wildflower that skims my ankle, searching for another solution. It sings to me and I long to give it something in return. Ignoring the thoughts that clammer for attention, I find the memory of the warmth Lochlain sent me as I healed. A warmth like the first kiss of the Rhyton sun. I smile slightly as I stroke this little flower with memories of gentle sunshine and it blooms more brightly under my touch. Or I think it does anyway, it's been a long time since I've tried it myself. Smiling at my success, I drag my eyes away from my momentary distraction and back to Lochlain's wide eyes.

I stare at him as I realise I've just shown him he's not the only one with gifts. He blinks as he looks between the flower and my face, his brows furrowing, but he doesn't say anything.

The afternoon's ride is fairly quiet, each of us sorting through our own thoughts, Lochlain vigilant as always. Niamh seems to be holding up well and we decide to keep riding through as much of the night as she's able.

I try to hold on to the details of the trees we pass through, how the colours of the flowers around us change. But I'm lost. Even if I did have anything to anchor my bearings on from the General's compound, it's well and truly gone now. A sharp pang of the memory of Will marking the trees hits right between my ribs.

I just know our destination, the city Lochlain told me we are making our way towards, lies ahead of us somewhere.

'What's in Elenlea?' I ask.

'I grew up there,' he says, his voice rumbling behind me. 'I've spent a lot of time working away at various times, but it's always home.' There's a small smile in his voice when he talks. 'It's the capital of the Court of Airlie and my sister has a house in the city. We'll be able to stay there briefly.'

'Will you go back to him when I leave?'

'Siosal and I aren't finished yet, no ... but will I go back in the way you're asking?' he considers this for a moment. 'I don't know yet. That will probably depend how badly I compromised my cover.'

'By getting me out?'

'Yes, but I can deal with that part of it. What I won't do is return and put Haryk or any of the others at risk if they will be implicated with me.'

'But Haryk already is.'

'Siosal doesn't know that,' he says. 'I just need to talk with my team before I make any more moves.'

A surge of something runs through me. A combination of missing my own team and a curiosity of what his might be like.

'Are there ... other people like you in your team?'

'How do you mean?'

'You have ... abilities – a gift or something ...' It feels so strange to be talking about it. Something I'd never uttered out loud since my mum died. Until I met him.

'So do you, it seems.'

I shiver at the breath I can feel on my neck.

'I guess,' I say, and his chest moves against my back as he chuckles. 'I just don't know anybody else that does.'

'It's very rare in Driarn,' he says, 'but it's not totally unusual for our people to have come together at different times. It's likely you have some of our heritage in your blood. Here, everyone has ... abilities as you call them. It's just normally a question of how much.'

Everyone. Everyone here is like me.

I let out a breath.

'I've seen two people with eyes like yours before,' I say, 'does that mean they had abilities too?'

He goes still behind me. Automatically, I sweep my gaze around the area, tensing at what he might have seen. Pressure builds in my chest. If Siosal—

'Sorry,' he says, laying a hand on the one I realise I now have clutching his thigh. 'There's no one here. I just – I didn't realise you'd seen – yes, they probably did have some.' He's quiet for a moment. 'Did they use them on you?' There's a faint sense of alarm in his tone.

'I don't think so.' But would I know if they did?

We stop for a final rest, this time for both us and Niamh. Much of the ride was flat with a gentle incline throughout the night. Our breath is illuminated by the bright moon as Niamh steams next to us from her exertion.

'You should try and sleep,' Lochlain says.

I shake my head mutely. My mind is so full there wouldn't be any point trying. Instead, I settle at the base of a tree and he comes to sit next to me. The warmth of his body so close to mine, a beacon in the night.

'How long has it been since Althea Forest?' I ask.

'You mean the night you were taken?' He hesitates but seems to realise there is no way to sugar coat it. 'About seven weeks.'

The weight of my head slowly sinks into my hands. Seven weeks. It feels like a lifetime. Turning my head to look at Lochlain, I marvel at the way his eyes shine even in the low light. They're almost amber in the dark.

'I need to say goodbye to them,' I say. 'My friends deserve to know I am alive.'

He watches me, weighing his next words. I don't need his permission, but I do need his help to get there. I have no idea where I am, and I will never find Rhyton on my own. But, given his betrayal of Siosal, it puts him at risk as well. All of this is putting him at risk and my heart clenches at the thought. Of Haryk who remains with the General.

'You've done so much for me, Lochlain. I will never be able to repay you and I won't ask you to take me. But directions—'

'You don't have to ask me.'

'What?'

'You don't have to ask me to take you to Rhyton,' he says with a sigh. 'I will take you. And then you will leave.' His eyes darken to more of the black from the first time I saw them. 'Give me your word, Lish. One night in Rhyton, say your goodbyes and leave. I don't—he *cannot* find you.'

It's Will's face I think of first. Even though, strictly, I've already said goodbye to him. Getting out fuelled a hope I'd be going home to my family.

But I'll never endanger them again.

'I promise.'

Just like that, I commit to breaking my own heart.

"You've done so much for me. I don't that I will ever be able to repay you
and I won't ask you to take me. But there you—"

"You don't have to ask me."

"What?"

"You don't have to ask me to take you to Rhyton. I'm going with you.
I will take you. And then you will see." His eyes darkened in the center of the
blackness the first time I saw them. Give me your word I let...the night
in Rhyton say your goodbyes and leave before—because I will you
[...] take a think of me. Even though I...yet, I've already said
goodbye to him. Getting out of bed. A hope I'll be going home every family.
But I'll never see any of them again.

I promise.

I'm like that I come...a beating in your own birth.

CHAPTER SIXTEEN

We walk the rest of the way, the incline becoming too steep for Niamh to carry us both safely. The darkness of night is starting to recede when we crest the hill, and the view stops me in my tracks. Below us, hugging the foot of the hill, is Elenlea.

It stretches before my eyes, a large, sprawling collection of houses and stone laneways. It's much smaller than Rhyton but what strikes me most is how ... flat it is. There's not a high rise building in sight. It's a city still mostly asleep, although there are lit windows scattered throughout. From this height, I can make out a silver lake on the other side of the city, and a wide stream snaking away from it into the darkness.

As we make our way down the slope that's much gentler on this side towards the city, the birds start their morning song and the woods behind us slowly come to life. More life than I've heard prior to being here – the Realm, whatever that means, is bursting at the seams with it. Mornings in Rhyton were filled with the sounds of the Guard beginning their training, weapons clashing, coffee machines starting, and the constant whirring of fans. There was no birdsong, no scurrying of creatures in the undergrowth, and certainly no gentle breeze on my face. Rhyton was only ever scorching heat or crushing storms.

Niamh huffs in the cold air, stirring the fog that laces around our ankles. Despite the devastating promise I made last night, what I need to leave behind, the vision of Elenlea shines a little light on my heart.

Lochlain leads me through the outskirts of the city. Niamh, walking beside him, sets a pace that says she knows where she's going and is eager to get there. The houses we pass are mostly two or three storey homes with colourful shutters and doors. Balconies grace the fronts of the houses like eyelashes, pots of overflowing flowers bursting with colour on each one. The stone paved street we walk down is quiet but I imagine a horse would not be out of place here, even at its busiest time. Not like it would be in Rhyton.

As we walk, people start appearing on those balconies with a hot drink in hand or in the street to begin their days.

'Nice to see you back, sir,' a voice calls down from one of the balconies.

An older man is joined by a woman dressed in a vibrant pink and red robe. She smiles down as Lochlain waves back at them, tugging her robe closed a bit tighter. Lochlain keeps walking but I can't drag my eyes away as the man turns to the woman and a mug of something floats towards her open hands. A move it appears they've made a thousand times.

Looking back to the street and the other houses, there's a joy here I don't remember seeing in Rhyton. Time to drink in the breeze and savour a moment – but that could be a product of my captivity. We turn down a narrow lane-way, Niamh's hooves a rhythmic clopping on the cobblestone that's cool beneath my bare and dirty feet.

Halfway down, Lochlain takes us through a wooden gate and leads Niamh into the empty stables on the right. Setting her up with feed and water, he brushes down her pale caramel coat and dark mane while I sit on the haystack outside her stall and wait. The full swing of morning is just around the corner when Lochlain puts the brushes away and sits beside me.

'Ready to meet my sister?' he asks.

His body is close to mine and the usual hum sings between us, asking me to lean into him. Perhaps it's the sensation of the magic that runs in his veins.

'Are you sure this is safe?' I ask, not really answering his question.

'It is for the moment. Ciara knows what I do. We ... work together,' he says, and my eyes fly to his face. Even if I couldn't feel his affection for her, it's written all over him. My heart clenches. 'Siosal won't look for us here,' he says and I like the way his use of 'us' slides warmth along my chest. 'Not yet. He doesn't know I was still there when you left and Haryk will be helping to subtly suggest Ohdran. But he'll work it out'—he glances at me—'and you can't be here when he does.'

I bump his arm gently with my shoulder.

'Would you think it weak of me to want to stay in this moment and not go inside?' The air ripples around us and he breathes deeply.

'Weak is not how I would describe you, no. But why would you want to stay and not ... move on with your life?'

I sigh.

'Because everything is behind me now,' I say. 'My life. My friends. Will.' I breathe through my nose. 'Because the General – Siosal ... what he can do and the things he said ... no one should be able to do that and he ... thinks he knows me.' Lochlain tenses but my need to say it out loud remains. The thought of losing my tie to this man is a stone in my stomach.

'The moment I step into that house,' I say, inclining my head towards where he wants us to go, 'I start the process of leaving everything. The only family I have, but ... also any opportunity I have of finding something about my past.'

'Do you know him?' he asks, the surprise clear in his tone.

'No,' I say. 'Definitely not.'

Lochlain doesn't move, the tension in his shoulders mirrored in the sensation in the small space between us. His thoughtful gaze runs over my face, as if I'm a problem to be solved.

'There's just something—' I laugh sadly. 'You'll think I'm crazy.'

His eyebrows furrow further. 'Why would I think that?'

I don't answer and he nudges me with his knee. 'I won't think that.'

I glance at his dancing eyes and back to the hay beneath us.

'I just know – I *feel* – like I'm closer than ever to answers that have eluded me my whole life. And now I'm having to walk away from that, too. To save my life, sure. But – well, that doesn't feel as important without those I love. Once I get off this prickly haystack'—I examine the ground—'any dreams I had for my future are gone. I will simply cease to exist.'

Lochlain waits a moment before speaking. 'You will always exist, Lish, especially to those that love you – and it's clear there are those that do.'

He considers his words and I close my eyes against the warmth coming from him. If I let it in I might not ever leave, and I can't risk his safety, too.

'They will never stop looking to you, even if they cannot physically reach you, and their hearts alone yearn for you. You will always exist.'

Tears line my eyes as his words start to resemble those of the librarian – another person snatched from me too soon. Another I should have helped in time. Another I didn't know needed my help before it was too late.

'Someone said something similar to me once,' I say. 'But I didn't get a chance to know him well.'

His eyes widen slightly and then he nods slowly, as if he suddenly understands something.

'Well,' he says, hopping off the hay and dusting it off his cloak without looking at me. He clears his throat. 'For what it's worth, you will always exist to me. I don't generally try to drown most girls, so I'll always remember that, at least.'

I smile softly at him and he looks up, his eyes dark and holding his hand out like he did at the compound.

'And you can ask us anything you like,' he says. 'Shall we?'

Lochlain knocks softly four times before the door is swung wide by an incredibly beautiful woman. The resemblance between them is remarkable. She has the same full mouth and liquid eyes, although the rings in hers are more gold than copper, and a glossy, dark brown plait over her shoulder. A narrow, intricate tattoo runs up the side of her neck. Her gaze rakes over me quickly as she motions us through the door.

'You've got a story and a half to tell,' she says to Lochlain as he moves to walk ahead of her.

Following, I find myself in a cosy blue and white kitchen, with an island bench that looks over a casual sitting room. I pause to take it in, the homeliness of the house calling to a long-lost memory.

She walks to me slowly, her face open and friendly. 'I'm Ciara,' she says with a gentle incline of her head.

'This is Lish.' Lochlain pauses and she looks at him sideways.

I offer what I hope is a warm smile. Despite the uncertainty in my heart about where the road after this leads.

'It's lovely to meet you, Ciara.'

She studies us for a moment before deciding that we each need to be cleaned up, eat, and sleep before any stories are exchanged. Lochlain is left to his own devices while I am ushered upstairs and quickly given a large, plush towel. She shows me the main bathroom and the room I will be staying in just down the hall. With an instruction to take my time and sleep before I re-emerge downstairs, I plan to do exactly that. After a delightfully warm, running shower, I pad my way to the bedroom where I pay no heed to the things around me and make straight for the large, inviting bed.

It's about mid-afternoon when I wake, marvelling at the cloud-like softness of the bed. I pull the covers around my neck and turn to face the window. Part of me wishes to stay here forever, cocooned in softness and warmth with a view to the outside. The part of me that wants to deny what I have to do, ignore the questions that are clambering in my mind. But the greater demand in my heart is to keep my friends safe from General Siosal and, to do so, I need to disappear.

The bedroom is soothing, with softly patterned wallpaper and plush carpet. There is enough room for a large bed and a wing-backed armchair in the corner, separated by a well-loved rug. Ciara has left a pile of clothes on the chair and I discover a pair of thick, soft black pants, warm socks, and a cream-coloured, wool jumper. I hug the fluffy jumper to my chest and smile through a smattering of tears. The absence of a vintage dress is what makes this feel real.

A framed, full-length mirror leans against one of the walls and I hesitantly take myself in. I'm surprised to find I don't look all that different. My brown hair has dried in soft, messy waves where I slept on it after my shower and I shake it out to try and make it a bit more presentable. It's grown since I last saw it this way and now hangs just below my shoulders. I'm not quite as curvy, which I had expected, but the cut of Ciara's clothes certainly makes the most of what there is.

But, despite the similarities, I'm looking at a stranger. The last time I saw this face was the morning I left Rhyton. The green in my eyes might be a little bleaker but I can't be sure. Lochlain has healed my body well and no marks remain, which is incredible in itself, but the reflection does not show the heartbreak I nurse – or the panic and rage that simmers just below the surface. I could walk into Rhyton right now and no one would know the difference between the woman that left and the one that stands here now. I don't know if that makes me happy or just incredibly lonely.

CHAPTER SEVENTEEN

I find Ciara in the kitchen, her gold eyes flicking up to me as I make my way downstairs. 'Thank you so much for the clothes,' I say, 'they're far more comfortable than those damn dresses.'

She smiles. 'I thought we'd need wine. And maybe some cheese,' she says, placing paper wrapped parcels on the bench. 'And chocolate.'

'Sounds perfect.'

Maybe it's because she looks so much like Lochlain, or, more likely, that I can find no duplicity in her stare, but I feel compelled to trust her.

'I assume you know where I've been?'

She nods. 'Loch filled me in while you were resting.' Her face lines with sorrow but, while my gut says I can trust her, when I open myself further I can't read any more of her. 'I'm sorry that happened to you,' she says. 'We worked really hard to stop that practice, it's just … devastating to know he's picked it up again.'

I watch her carefully as she prepares different platters of food.

'I'd like to know more about your work,' I say. 'Who he's looking for.'

She stills momentarily before resuming her slicing of a hard cheese.

Ciara places the timber handled knife purposefully on the benchtop and looks at me with her black and gold eyes.

'I will tell you what I can,' she says slowly, eyeing me. 'But it's not solely up to me. I said we worked hard to stop him. We've worked just as hard to keep the details of what we do secret, so we didn't endanger anyone – and we can't stop now.' As her gaze shifts behind me, I feel the familiar brushing of his presence against my senses. 'But Lochlain will fill in what he can, too.'

As I turn to look at him, this time it's his eyes that widen before he can smooth his expression away. He doesn't shy away from my gaze though.

'I'd appreciate that,' I say, conscious to keep the conversation going.

He's in light coloured pants and an emerald-green, long sleeve top. The image he cuts is a world away from the black-hooded man, although the way his presence brushes up against mine feels the same. The round neck jumper he wears is closely fitted around his chest and shoulders, the deep tone setting off his dark-tanned skin and copper eyes. His rich, dark hair is freshly washed and curls frame his face. There's a faint outline of straps crossing his chest under his shirt and contemplating the weapons they hold sends a pleasant shiver down my spine. Dimly, I wonder if they would be better on the outside of his shirt, but something tells me these are ones he keeps there as a last resort and not the only ones he would take out with him.

He takes a step towards me and moves to take the platter from my hands.

'You look good clean,' he says with a soft smile. His fingers brush mine and I try to ignore the sensation it triggers.

'I'd hope so,' I say, 'seven weeks in a dark hole probably doesn't do anyone many favours.'

I'd intended the remark to be light, but it sounds like a barb and he lowers his gaze as he takes the platter over to the coffee table.

'Right, wine,' Ciara says, having watched our exchange and now handing me a glass. She takes hers and Lochlain's to the table.

The couches are positioned around a blazing fireplace and the heat washes pleasantly throughout the room. I swallow hard and force myself to turn away memories of my skin burning. Ciara sits in a large armchair and, without thinking, I sit next to Lochlain on a cosy two-seater lounge, the draw to him as natural as breathing after so long with him as my companion. The rustic scent of his shampoo fills my nose.

Ciara and I make small talk for a while; she's mostly interested in Rhyton and my experience in the Guard but she delights in including some stories of her and Lochlain's childhood.

'I was *not* responsible for all of those things,' Lochlain says, rolling his eyes.

'No,' Ciara smiles, 'just the disappearance of father's ceremonial sword.'

'Something I paid for dearly, if you recall.' He slides his gaze to her. 'And I still never gave you up.'

She pulls a face, even as she tries not to laugh.

The wine flows and I slowly relax into the late afternoon, although I am careful not to drink too much. It's been a while since I've had wine, I don't recall what happened to the glass General Siosal gave me, and I don't want to be muddled or have a headache in the morning.

The conversation reaches a natural pause and I take a deep breath. 'Can you explain the magic?'

Ciara turns her full attention on me, and I silently curse myself for the blunt question. Maybe 'magic' isn't the right word for what I've seen ... what I can do.

'You don't know?' She glances at Lochlain. 'But I thought you said she could—'

'She's only met two of us before,' he says. 'And they didn't make their abilities known.'

She looks back to me. 'You're in the Realm, Lish. The Realm of the Calahi.' She pulls a different face, one less amused than earlier. 'What's left, anyway. Overtime, our magic has been diminishing for one reason or another and we are what remains.'

My eyebrows shoot up as I try to let this sink in.

'So you're not ... human?' I look at Lochlain whose eyes flash copper. 'You didn't think to mention that small fact when you told me where we are?'

'Is that really so hard to believe?' Ciara asks but Lochlain answers before I do.

'You've known it for some time now, Lish,' he says. 'Forget what your head is telling you is possible, listen to what you know in your heart.'

I let that comment go, ignoring the flutter in said heart, the recognition from my gold flame.

'And the Realm is what, exactly? A magic kingdom?' I ask.

'It should be a magic queendom actually,' Ciara says, her gold eyes sparkling.

'I still don't understand why there's magic or how it works,' I say, looking between them. 'Can you two do the same things?'

Ciara shakes her head but it's Lochlain that responds. 'No. The degree of magic varies between bloodlines but the abilities themselves can differ. There are basic things we are all taught ...' he pauses to think through them before continuing, 'creating defensive shields, everyday activities like—'

'Things around the house,' Ciara says. 'But then there are our primary affinities. Like Lochlain can heal.' She looks at him and he nods along, my skin flushing with the memory of him doing just that. 'Physical healing is his speciality, but he can soothe some emotional wounds as well.'

I grapple to think of the possibilities. 'What are other affinities? What's yours?' I ask Ciara.

'There's a number and it's not necessarily rigid – some Calahi might have a blend of other abilities and that becomes their primary.' She lifts one shoulder. 'It really depends on the individual.'

'And you?'

Her eyes flash a little and she shifts in her seat. 'Different things,' she says. 'But I mostly focus on communication with our team.' She sighs at what I can only imagine is a completely blank expression from me. 'It's complex but yes ... it's mental and no, most of us can't do it.'

I stare at her for a moment but her face shutters and it's clear the topic is closed.

'So, why do the Whispers all do the same thing?'

Lochlain looks at me, a ripple of confusion on his features and I wave my hands around my head gently.

'You know,' I say, 'the noise – the pain.'

'Oh,' he says and I wonder if he's ever had to explain this to anyone before. 'It falls under our defensive skills. Most of us who are trained, like in the Whispers or the Royal Watchmen, can do it to varying degrees. But, in the Whispers, there is generally one who is strongest at it in each of the units and they create the incapacitation.'

I sit quietly for a moment, looking between Lochlain and Ciara. Trying to work out where in my mind these pieces of information are supposed to fit.

'So, regular Calahi don't have magic?' I ask.

'No,' Ciara says, 'they do. But how much we all have and how we use it depends on bloodlines and the training we do. What occupations they decide to take.'

Perhaps it's not so different to the people of Driarn – most can throw a punch but physical ability and training will determine how well they do it. And not everyone joins the Guard or the armed forces.

'Where – where does it come from?'

'The Mother,' they say at the same time.

'The Mother?' I ask, trying not to let my disbelief colour my voice. 'And that would be ...'

'Nature,' Ciara says. 'She's our source, hence the decline in our abilities.' Her gaze turns sad again when she looks at me. 'The Calahi are intrinsically linked to our world and it's an honour we would die to defend.'

I try to let that sink in.

'I take it you didn't have someone to help you with yours?' she asks. 'What about your parents?'

I swallow, trying not to be overwhelmed by what this means.

'No. I didn't know my father and my mother died when I was young, I barely remember her. It was ... trial and error,' I say, and they each pin me with their stares.

'So ... who raised you? Do you have a family? Where are they now?' she asks, eyes narrowed, and I can't help but smile at her questioning. She's genuinely interested in my story.

Lochlain watches me carefully as I recount how I met Will in the or-phanage and a tentative friendship became something else. About gor-geous Blaire and her unwavering consideration for all of us, of how smart she is and her terrible taste in movies. About Riley and her brashness and ready laugh, and how I fit in between them somewhere. I talk of Hayes and his amazing ability to see things differently and his delightful grandmother. And I tell them how they each make up the cornerstones of my life.

I raise my eyes in question to Lochlain when I get to the part of Will being stabbed and he subtly nods his head. So I tell Ciara of my agreement with General Siosal and Lochlain saving Will's life. I can't help a tear escaping when I talk of saying goodbye. Lochlain's gaze reluctantly leaves my face and he exchanges a meaningful look with Ciara that I can't unpack.

'And I obviously haven't seen him or the others since,' I say, wiping my cheek.

'I have a lot of questions about this,' Ciara says. 'It's not every day my brother brings home—' she glances at Lochlain, who's gone stiff beside me, and seems to change her mind about whatever she's going to say. 'Someone I haven't met.'

Her body is relaxed but her acute attention doesn't waver.

'So, they are the reason you're running from Siosal?' she asks. The question makes me feel like a coward. But what other choice do I have?

'I'd do anything for them.' I turn the now empty wine glass in my hand, willing my fingers to stop their faint tremble. 'Siosal said he'd go after them if I tried to escape and go back. Lochlain assured me he has people looking out for them. Meaning ... I can have both, I guess. My life and theirs.' The words sound as empty as my glass. 'Just not together.'

'And what do you want from your life, Lish?' Ciara crosses one leg over the other and I'm suddenly reminded of the interrogation role plays we did before we graduated in the Guard. 'Do you have a partner to run with you? To keep you warm at night?'

Lochlain chokes on a cracker. I can't bring myself to look at him as I realise I left out mention of Phoenix earlier. I hold Ciara's gaze instead. They glint with mischief as she pointedly ignores Lochlain. I smile but am serious when I answer her after a moment.

'I don't know.' My voice is soft. 'Possibly not.'

She waits for me to go on.

'I did. When I left I mean.' Lochlain's pulse of emotions pulls away as if he's trying to recoil from me. 'But I asked Will to tell him not to wait for me. So ... I don't know. Will would have told him the truth, he would have known I didn't have a choice, so he may be waiting anyway. He's ... very loyal,' I say, my regret flushing my cheeks.

Lochlain looks at his hands and shame floods over me. I swore I'd never be that person.

'Do you want him to be waiting?' Ciara asks.

I look at the fire then, before looking back to her.

'I don't know.' I close my eyes against the hurt that brings as I realise it's the truth. 'So much has happened since then, I'm not sure I'm the same anymore. I'm not sure ... I would deserve him.'

Lochlain lifts his head to look at me then and there is a sorrow in Ciara's eyes; she moves the conversation on again. She has a knack for this, I realise. I try to follow her lead and put aside the disquiet coming from Lochlain.

'How did you and Will come to be looking for the Whispers?' Ciara asks.

I blow my breath out heavily as the missing person's report flashes into my mind.

'That's a story for another night, I think,' I say, knowing full well we will not have that opportunity. 'How about you tell me what you know about them instead? Like why you're putting up a front of working with them, Lochlain, and why you blew it by getting me out? Or who they're looking for?'

He shifts a little in his seat so he can face me, but he doesn't touch me like he has before and I feel the absence of the pressure on my skin.

'The Whispers,' he continues, 'are a group of specialist warriors who undertake specific missions for the safety of the Court of Airlie. They are currently led by General Siosal.' Anger ripples from him. 'In normal circumstances, he would answer to the Throne.'

He looks again at Ciara and I wonder what the look means. He takes a deep breath and looks me in the eye, the copper rings in his reflecting the fire.

'However, no one currently sits on the Throne of Airlie so he *reports* to the Custodian. I have served the Throne, faithfully, my whole life, including my time in the Whispers.' He seems to search for words. 'But the direction of the Whispers started to shift when the Throne was ... vacated. And, now, I serve in a different way.'

'This is the different perspectives you've talked of before.'

'Yes.'

Ciara's gold eyes watch me closely. 'It is public knowledge in all the Courts of the Realm that the Custodian of the Airlie seeks the one who should be upon it. But how General Siosal conducts his search, and his real motivations, are not known by the Custodian, or most citizens of Airlie.'

'So the Custodian has endorsed Siosal to find the Queen ...' I trail off.

'Or her young one,' Ciara adds.

'Right,' I say. 'So Siosal is looking for the Queen, or her child, on behalf of the Custodian but he doesn't know Siosal was – is again – forcefully taking and killing untold numbers of women?' I ask.

'Yes,' Lochlain says.

'I find that pretty hard to believe,' I say and they share a look. 'Sounds like he's just trying to make sure the rightful holder of the Throne doesn't come back. Where did they go anyway?' I ask.

Ciara leans back in her chair. 'No, I think the Custodian is actually getting quite desperate for the Queen to return. The other Courts in the Realm are increasingly restless without a proper ruler here – having someone appointed by the prominent families isn't the same as having the right Queen. And there are some rumours they might march on us if she's not found,' she says. 'As for the Queen herself, it's a pretty sad story, really. She was fiercely loyal and it was said she'd taken a human lover—'

'Human?' I cut in, the word ringing in my mind in memory of how the General spat it. 'As in like me, different to you? And that would be ... bad for a ... Calahi?'

She looks at Lochlain and I hold my breath.

I had gathered enough about how General Siosal felt about humans but it hadn't occurred to me that could be more than just the rantings of a psychopath and I might be seen as different, too. Slowly, I make myself look at Lochlain. He waits for me to meet his eyes before he responds, the hammering of my heart almost too loud to hear him talk.

'There are some among us who would say that, yes.' His gaze holds mine, copper rings blazing. 'Ciara and I do not feel that way.'

My chest releases and I try to ignore the relief that follows his statement. I blink as I realise perhaps I'm not solely human anyway.

Ciara's eyes slowly leave Lochlain's face and she looks back to me. 'So, everyone thought she had a mystery human lover. But, because she was a relatively new monarch, she was also under immense pressure from the prominent families to bond a Calahi – they had more say in how Airlie was run then. And they selected Siosal, before he was General.'

'Wow, that would be—' I blow out a breath, I can't even imagine it.

'Siosal was very happy with the arrangement,' Ciara continues, 'power has always been his goal. Then he fell for her and insisted, forcefully, that she get rid of the human. But, by that point, she was well and truly in love with him and, rumour has it, with child. So, she ran and General Siosal has hunted her and her young one ever since.' She takes a long sip of her wine. 'I feel sorry for him sometimes, honestly,' she says. 'To him, he lost the love of his life and the life he was destined for in the blink of an eye. But his distaste of humans coloured his ability to see how she really felt. That she never would have been able to love him, anyway. Yet, it hasn't stopped him wanting her and the young one back.'

'What happened to the human man?' I ask.

Ciara's eyes mist over. 'General Siosal found him and ... well, I'm sure you can imagine how that ended. The Queen never announced it, obviously, but I am absolutely certain that was the final push for her to run. She wouldn't have risked her young one here, in case Siosal would kill them, too. Which is precisely why that Calahi can not have any more power. And why he needs to pay for his actions. For the Queen, her child, and all the human women who have suffered at his hands.' Her eyes darken as I look at her. 'He could have left it at just a search. But, instead, he's used it as an outlet for his hatred for humans.'

I watch Ciara pour herself another glass of wine, as if the steady, scarlet stream could help me wrap my mind around it all.

Lochlain levels me with his stare as I turn to look at him.

'So, his goal is good – Airlie needs the Throne properly occupied,' Lochlain says, 'but his motives – and his methods – are not. As to why I got you out,' he continues, the hum turning sharper with his anger, and I think even Ciara shifts forward in her seat. 'We've talked about that; I don't leave people behind.' His gaze wanders my face. 'I never would have left you there. Airlie deserves the best of us and that practice isn't it.'

The food Ciara ordered for dinner materialises in the kitchen then, leaving me gaping at the space it occupies. Listening to Lochlain and Ciara reminisce as we eat draws a pang of hurt in my chest following the memory of my promise to Lochlain. And to myself. I'd do anything to protect my friends.

About midnight, I call it a night and start to head up the stairs.

'She's not a prisoner anymore,' I hear Ciara call out.

'Old habits,' Lochlain calls back as he climbs the stairs behind me.

Having seen me to the entrance of the bedroom, he leans against the door, filling the space, arms crossed over his chest. I can't help but watch him as I've done many nights before. This time, though, there are lights and no hood. I take in his face and the shape of his arms through his shirt, my gaze snagging on his broad chest, the strapping still faintly visible.

'Am I really different?' I ask, my face heating at the implications of my question. I both do and don't want him to think I'm different, but not because I'm human. At the same time, I'm ashamed of how different I now am where Phoenix is concerned. Lochlain's black and copper eyes drift over me.

'Yes and no,' he says softly. 'It's up to you to work how different or otherwise you want to be.'

My fingers drift towards the straps on his chest and I move to trace one. He watches their progress and breathes into my touch slightly as my fingertips find his shoulder. I marvel at the softness of the fabric.

'You would, you know.' His voice is like gravel and he curls his thread of emotions away.

'Would what?'

'Be deserving of him,' he says. I blink, dropping my hand as my chest tightens. 'Do you want to be?'

'Do I want to be deserving of him?' I frown at him, madly trying to clear my thoughts. 'Well, yes. He's a wonderful person, why shouldn't I want to be deserving of a wonderful person?' I ask. 'And his name's Phoenix.'

'I know his name.' A fact he seems to regret. 'And that's not what I meant. I meant him. Do you want to be his?' The air disappears from the room.

'I don't know,' I whisper, angry at the truth of it. 'I don't think I can be.'

He keeps his emotions tightly away from me but the murmur between us is static on my skin.

'Goodnight, Lish. Sleep well,' he says, before turning on his heel and walking away.

CHAPTER EIGHTEEN

I'm sitting at Ciara's kitchen bench, nursing a steaming cup of something I can only liken to tea, when the back door slams. I jump, spilling hot liquid over my fingers. Lochlain's by my side in less than a blink and my heart leaps for the second time.

'Shit,' I curse. 'You scared me.'

Lochlain visibly relaxes as Ciara appears in the kitchen. Her gaze immediately goes to the spilled drink, reminding me of the heat in my fingers. The room starts to contract around me as the sensation spreads up my arms and across my chest. Ciara blurs in front of me as I recall when I last saw General Siosal. The feel of his burning hands on me.

A soft scream builds in my ears—

Lochlain lifts me gently from the stool and walks me around the other side of the bench to the sink. Cold, running water covers my hands and warmth fills me. I dimly recognise it as Lochlain healing me, even as the water cascades into the sink. My mind is full of burning and healing. Burning and healing.

Slowly, the room returns to its normal size and the screaming in my ears quiets. As my mind clears, I realise the burn on my fingers wasn't actually that bad. It was just tea. Water alone would have soothed it.

There's a warm pressure running down the back of my body. Lochlain. Pressing himself gently against my back as he holds my hands under the water so I can feel the cool sensation, arms wrapped around me. Embarrassment edges at me but I feel too safe here, surrounded by this huge man, to pay it much heed.

I shut off the tap and turn into him.

'Sorry,' I whisper.

He takes my hands and inspects them. His calluses gently scraping my palms and fingers. I keep my eyes lowered but I can feel him watching me carefully.

'You don't apologise to me.'

He breathes deeply as if inhaling me before stepping back.

Ciara clears her throat gently. 'You okay, Lish?'

I run a hand over my face and attempt a smile. 'Yes, yeah – I'm fine. Sorry.'

She takes the mug from the benchtop and the spill, which now seems very minor, disappears.

'I'll get you another,' she says. She watches me for a moment. 'There were Whispers at the market this morning.'

Lochlain whirls to her.

'What?' he demands.

I wait for the panic to return but it stays quiet.

'Shit,' Lochlain says. 'We're out of time.'

'Relax,' she says. 'We all knew what we were getting ourselves into and you had no choice.' She gives him a long look. 'We knew they'd be here at some point.'

I look between them.

'It's time for us to leave,' Lochlain says, still looking at Ciara, a pained look on his face. 'I'd hoped we'd have a bit more time.' He turns back to me. 'I – fuck.'

My heart sinks but I know he's right. In the short time I have been here, I've become quite attached to Ciara and I now need to add her to the list of those I won't put in the line of General Siosal. I hug her goodbye and she squeezes me hard. She leans back to look at me and there are tears in her black and gold eyes.

Releasing me, she turns to Lochlain. 'Loch,' she says softly. 'Look at me.'

He reluctantly pulls his eyes from my face and meets her gaze.

'Are you sure about this?' she asks. 'This could be it. There is no turning back from here.' He closes his eyes for a moment, his emotions tightly held. His eyes are black pools when he opens them again, staring at Ciara. He nods once and Ciara's shoulders sag as she exhales. She looks back to me and leans forward to kiss my cheek.

Her gold eyes blaze when I find them again and I have to drag myself away from the regret there. Like she doesn't think I'm doing the right thing. She definitely doesn't seem to think Lochlain is doing the right thing, but I can tell she loves him too much to fight him. Whatever the issue might be.

I turn to Lochlain. 'I don't think you should come. The Whispers are already here. You need to complete whatever mission Siosal thinks you're on and go back. I will go on my own.'

Lochlain's expression is like watching a storm even as he tries to keep his emotions in check. His eyes are dark and anger rolls off him.

I take a step towards him.

'You know I'm right. You and your family have done more than enough for me, someone you don't really even know. I'm just one woman, Lochlain. There are others that need you.'

Ciara's footsteps retreat a little, I don't watch how far.

'I know you better than you think,' he says.

I smile sadly at him. He's right but that's not the point.

'Thank you for everything, Lochlain,' I say. 'But mostly for Will.'

'You need to stop thanking me,' he grumbles but takes my hand and leads me out the back door.

We reach Niamh's stable quickly and she whinnies at us. She snuffles at Lochlain's hand and he produces an apple from nothing that she devours as he whispers to her, her soft ears twitching. I stroke her neck absently while I watch him, savouring the sensation of his emotions that prickle against mine despite the sadness that tinges them.

Ciara joins us again and I look at them both in question.

'She's going to make sure you get out of Elenlea safely,' Lochlain says. 'Let Niamh lead you and ride hard after that. She will take you to the edge of Rhyton, it won't take her long and trust she knows the way. When you're there, tell her to return to me. Say your goodbyes, Lish, and remember your promise – one night.' I close my eyes briefly. 'If you head north of Rhyton,' he continues, 'along the coast, there are a number of smaller towns. You know them?' I nod, the six of us have holidayed in some of those coastal towns at various times. 'Move through them but don't stay there too long, they're too close.' He pauses.

I look at him. 'What?'

'Nothing, just don't linger long. And do some research on where you'd like to go from the coast. You will need to cross the sea. He won't follow you over.' He watches me for a moment, his concern running over my skin and evident on his face. 'You can do anything you like from there.'

Except the things I want, I don't say.

I look up into his face, his dark curls falling into it as he returns my gaze. My chest feels heavy saying goodbye to this man. This Calahi. And I can't hide from the sorrow it brings me.

He squeezes my hand and takes a step closer. So close our chests are almost touching. Heat rushes to my face. I swallow. Taking my other hand in his, we stand like that for a moment that stretches into forever, only the hammering of my heart marking the time that passes.

'You're more than just one woman to me, Lish.' His voice is on the verge of breaking. 'I think you're more than you realise ... but you need to go. You need to survive.' My eyes fill with tears and I blink them away, not trusting myself to speak. 'If he loves you, take him with you.' He closes his eyes briefly again. 'You deserve to be loved.'

He steps away, his warmth lingering along my body.

'Keep her safe,' he says.

As Niamh, Ciara and I walk out of the gate he holds open, I realise I don't know who he's talking to.

We walk at a steady pace out of Elenlea, Niamh's shod hooves clopping on the cobblestones, reminding me of the walk in but, this time, we go in a different direction. A small bag of food and an extra knife is strapped across my back, the slightly larger one of Ciara's Lochlain gave me at my waist, under my cloak.

Ciara skirts around the outer edges of the centre of the city and I push down the disappointment at not seeing the heart of Elenlea. But the houses we pass are whimsical and I smile at the thought of the lives inside. In

Rhyton, I have simply imagined easier lives; here, I imagine lives filled with laughter, and children learning magic together, and the chaos that must cause for everyone around them. The flowers that grace the balconies and gardens of all the houses we pass feel like a homage somehow. To nature, the Mother – the giver of their magic.

A small picket fence inside one of the yards captures my attention. The lushness of the vegetables it contains making my stomach grumble.

'Is that normal?' I ask Ciara.

'What's that?'

'For people to have their own vegetable gardens?'

She's quiet for a moment, as if she's not quite sure how to answer but there's a knowing in her eyes when she glances at me. 'It is here. For now.'

I look back as we leave the edge of the city and my chest tightens. Looking at the city from a slight distance, there seems to be a shadow that hangs over it somehow. Slightly dulling its sparkle. But it has left an impression on me, and I already regret my too-quick goodbye with Lochlain.

Ciara can obviously see my expression and she employs her skill of directing conversations to distract me. As I laugh at her imitation of Lochlain, I realise it's working.

'You know,' Ciara says, thoughtful suddenly. 'My mother used to tell Lochlain and me that, if we were lost or unsure of the best way through a problem, the Mother would help us.'

'Nature?' I ask, trying not to look doubtful as I turn to her, Niamh walking at her shoulder.

'She said we should trust in her – give our hearts to her – and she'd send a sign to help us on the right path.'

She smiles at me suddenly. Gently. 'I trust she'll help you, too. If you let her,' she says, coming to a stop earlier than I would like. But there are no more houses around. When I look back, I can now only see the generously sized backyards that back onto the grass plain we now stand on the edge of. The river meandering along to my right, away from the city.

'This is as far as I'll come, you should be alright from here,' she says, patting Niamh's shoulder as I look over the impossibly green expanse.

'Be safe, please,' she presses her hand to her chest. 'The Realm will always be open to you, Lish, should you choose it. It's been so lovely to meet you.'

I am reminded again of the librarian, his final goodbye to me squeezing my chest.

She helps me onto Niamh and I shift on her back, nervousness racing through my limbs and into my fingers,

'Remember,' she murmurs, her hand on my calf, 'sometimes, we find the answers we seek not by going back but by going forward. You need to decide what your forward looks like.'

Niamh and I ride across the flat plain, the hill it's nestled into rising behind us, the large stream I saw from the hill the day I arrived sparkling in the sunlight. Niamh rides hard, as Lochlain instructed, and the rest of the landscape is a blur of green and blue as we race along, her dark mane streaming and occasionally whipping my face. I hold on tightly, amazed I'm able to keep my seat without Lochlain behind me as an anchor. As I feel the gentle Elenlea sun on my face, the breeze howling in my ears as we move at speed, I think this might be the freest I will ever be.

Too soon, I recognise the shape of Rhyton in the distance but it's blurred as if I am viewing it from behind a thick veil. I glance behind me, gripping Niamh's mane.

You're more than one woman to me. The words rumble in my chest.

Elenlea is now a smudge at the bottom of the green hills, the lake and its river shimmering in front of her. With every rock of Niamh's movements, I am taken further away.

This should feel right. By leaving, I have the best chance of protecting everyone I care for. Including those in the city behind me. Including myself. The crushing weight of putting anyone at risk is enough to suffocate me.

But being on the cusp of understanding why some of my answers lie in this Realm, only to be walking away, is a vice in my chest. My heart aches to go back, my gold flame flickering in desperation. Not to find the answers I've left behind – but to take the opportunity to move forward. The opportunity to know who I have become and who I want to be.

As if in response to my longing, a blue light sparkles over Elenlea; but it's gone before I can be sure it's real.

I turn back around as Niamh drops her shoulders slightly and gallops harder. Warm silk drags across my skin threatening to topple me backwards. A sensation I realise I missed when I was brought into the Realm unconscious. I grip Niamh's mane harder and suddenly my vision clears and Rhyton is just to the south of us. The ground has turned to dust and, glancing behind once more, there is no sign of the green fields we have been racing across. There is only the familiar, cracked, wasted farmland.

If I wasn't still riding Niamh I would think the Realm was a dream.

Ahead of us is a narrow strip of sparse trees, on the other side of which is the coast road. Left leads to Rhyton and my goodbyes, right to the coastal cities and the next part of my journey. That road will soon become busy with the foot traffic looking to gain refuge in Rhyton, their towns or properties no longer viable. From there, the best access point into the city is the Dockside Gate that Will and I used frequently.

Niamh takes care to remain as sheltered as possible in the tree line before stopping closer to the roadside edge and I take that as my cue to dismount. It's not too far to walk into the city from here and such a magnificent horse would draw attention. A horse at all in Rhyton would draw attention. I rub her neck in thanks and whisper against her coat.

'Don't forget me, Niamh. Time for you to head home to Lochlain. Be safe, beautiful girl.' She whinnies softly before heading into the trees. I wait until I hear the thunder of her hooves die away and I begin the walk into Rhyton, trying to ignore the fact it might be for the last time.

Despite being later in the day than Elenlea, it's still much hotter here and I remove my cloak and drape it over my arm, hiding my knife, as I walk up the path to the gates in the late afternoon heat. The knit top and boots I wear are stifling. It's close to evening by the time I get to the gates and the sun has dropped enough in the sky for me to strip off to my singlet, having previously been unable to expose my skin to the sun. People around me start to make camp for the night so they don't lose their spot in the line into Rhyton.

The Guard members who patrol the gates look bored and I take my chances on the Guard entrance I used to use. I try to look casual as I make my way through the entrance. I recognise two of them and wave.

'Night boys,' I say, hoping they haven't been told I'm dead, but they just wave back and let me pass.

It's an easy path to Guard Headquarters from here and I readily blend with the people who hurry home from work or head out for the evening. The tall buildings are soulless in comparison to Elenlea but it still has an echo of home. As Headquarters comes into view, my palms begin to sweat. I haven't really thought about what tonight would be like. The excitement at seeing everyone again is very quickly crushed by the thought of leaving them.

I have no reason to believe that Lochlain's motives for my promise were for anything other than keeping me safe. I know he's right. If there's even a small chance General Siosal will come for me – or is already looking – I don't want him here.

I aim for a nonchalant walk as I go through the lesser used entrance near the barracks. Despite my training, it's impossible to stop the backward glances. Searching for any hint of the Whispers. The security here is pretty light given we're Guard members. They save most of the resources for the main buildings, including where the IT infrastructure is. The six of us have come and gone enough from here that I know where the cameras are, assuming nothing has changed in my absence.

Will's room is further from this end of the base than mine and I don't know who is using mine now, if it has been given to a new recruit. Suddenly, I realise I don't know what day it is, or what the rosters are, and I hope they don't have night shift. That will make finding them more difficult but I'll walk all night if I have to.

I arrive at Will's balcony and look around quickly in the growing darkness before climbing over. There are no lights on inside and I convince myself he's just finishing up his shift as I scramble for the spare key he always leaves under a dead pot plant. Walking into his lounge room, I turn the light on, not wanting to scare him to death to find me in here. I'm relieved to find it smells vaguely of his cologne. He still lives here. I pace his apartment and try to keep my nerves in check.

A key turns in the lock and my eyes water at the anticipation. I remain still, though, knowing his first reaction will be to attack if I suddenly launch myself at him from nowhere. The door moves slowly and I know he's registered the light is on. I should call out and let him know it's me, but my throat has closed. I watch the black pistol snake around the door, followed by Will's firm grip. As he edges into the room, I stand in the middle of his small apartment – almost identical to mine – and hold my breath.

'Holy shit.' He slams the door behind him with his foot and dumps the gun on the table before rushing to me, lifting me off the ground in a tight embrace. 'You almost gave me a heart attack!' he says. 'What – I mean, how – fuck. Tell me everything.'

I'm crying and laughing at him and he keeps cursing to himself as he looks me over, holding my shoulders.

I hug him. 'God, it's good to see you,' I say into his chest.

He draws back to look at my face and obviously notes my mixed emotions.

'You're not here to stay, are you?' he asks. I can't stop the tears then and I brush them away roughly. They're too much of a reminder of the last time we had to say goodbye.

'No,' I say. 'I got out, but General Siosal will be looking for me and I can't bring him here. It's a huge risk to be here at all but I needed you to know I'm not rotting in that place.'

'So you got away but we still have to pay the price?' he asks angrily.

I have nothing to say to that, he's right. We are to pay the price for something I don't even fully understand.

'Listen, Will, I won't have time to explain everything, I don't even understand everything. But I wanted to see you. I needed to see you all one last time, do you think you could get everyone together?'

His eyes darken a little at that and I can tell he's furious. His emotions seem louder than I remember and I make a conscious effort to firm up my barrier and let them ebb around me.

'It can't be here, though. I really shouldn't be here but I had no other way to contact you. Is there a new bar or something we could meet at? Somewhere I haven't been with you before?'

'Yes, of course,' he says distractedly. 'And you need a new phone.'

There's a knock at the door and I stiffen.

'Oh,' Will says, a slight darkening of colour dusts the tops of his cheeks. 'There's a lot to tell you actually.'

He opens the door to a young, pretty brunette and kisses her quickly before ushering her inside. A lot to tell me indeed. I smile. As she comes closer, I realise she's vaguely familiar and she's looking at me as if she's seen a ghost.

Suddenly, she flies at me, a barrage of gratitude coming from her. As she flings her arms around my neck, I notice a pronounced scar around her left bicep. I awkwardly return the embrace, patting her back, and look at Will helplessly. His blush grows but there is genuine delight in his face. The girl releases me, and I look at her face. Understanding sits at the edge of my brain but I can't quite grasp it. Will steps forward and puts his arm around her waist.

'Lish, this is Sofia,' he says.

Sofia. *Sofia?* I look between them and he nods. I sink down to the couch.

'Oh my god,' I breathe.

CHAPTER NINETEEN

Half an hour later, I'm seated with Will and Sofia at a new bar in the centre of the city. We'd left virtually straight away, me being anxious not to be at Headquarters for too long. Will called the others and asked them to meet for drinks, without telling them why on the phone, and we talked on the walk in.

Being in the last group of women with the Whispers, Sofia saw everything, including Will's near death. It took them about three days to get back to Rhyton from where they emerged out of the compound and they clearly bonded during that time. When Sofia excuses herself to go to the bathroom, Will shyly tells me they've been taking it slow, given everything they've both been through, but he's pretty serious about her. It shows on his face and I reach out and take his hand over the table.

'I'm so happy for you, Will,' I say.

His eyes slide to the entrance where there are four other faces walking towards us. I am on my feet in less than a second and flinging myself at Hayes and Riley, who are first to work their way through the crowd. Riley makes to let out a loud curse but I hush her with a finger to her mouth.

'I need to be quick and quiet,' I say.

She understands immediately and squeezes my hand before taking a seat next to Hayes, who hasn't taken his questioning eyes off me since the bear hug I got when he arrived. I'm unlikely to avoid his questions all night. After a beat Blaire and Phoenix come through the throng of people in the popular bar. Phoenix is saying something to Blaire, focused on her as if she is the only person in the room. They smile at each other. Blaire is lit from within, her joy pooling around her.

And it dawns on me what's happening.

I swallow the lump in my throat and draw Blaire in for a hard hug as she approaches, her face frozen in shock. But the relief from her is palpable. There are tears in her eyes when I let her go and I wipe them with my thumb. She opens her mouth to talk but I shake my head.

'Later,' I say smiling.

Blaire glances behind her before claiming a seat at the table and suddenly it's just Phoenix and me staring at each other in the crowded bar. The world disappears around me.

'Hi,' I say and push his emotions away.

'Hi.' He reaches for my hand and looks at me as if trying to decide if I am real or not. Abruptly he holds me tight, and I squeeze him back. He pulls back to look at me and I see the pain in his eyes.

'Oh god, Lish,' he says, 'I can't believe you're back.'

He kisses me hard, stunning me into silence.

We order food platters to share and the waitress brings our drinks on a large tray. If I put aside the fact we are quietly talking about the Whispers and Will being on the brink of death, I would almost say this was a nice evening. Will and Sofia, sitting opposite me, have an easy affection. They are almost constantly touching and Will looks at her like – well, like I've never actually seen him look at anyone.

Reflecting on the life she must have led, raising Nico and enduring the Whispers, I'm happy she's found someone like Will. Just as I am overjoyed for him. I can't recall him ever being particularly serious about anyone, the emotional walls he built are a very clear outcome of the orphanage. But I know what a rare soul he has, and it warms me from the inside to see him so happy, even as it tugs on my heart.

While Will knows, I haven't yet told all of them what I must do after tonight. I'd planned to be up front with it but the temptation of letting their stories and laughter flow through me was too great.

'What's really going on, Lish?'

It's Hayes who is watching me most closely, not contributing much to the conversation. He's spoken just to me, but I see Will catch on.

I turn to look at Hayes. His skin glowing in the lighting of the pub, blue eyes not missing a thing. Desperately, I wish I had a choice, that I could make this the first night of my return but I force the words out.

'General Siosal – the one who stabbed Will – he's likely to be looking for me. To make sure I uphold my end of the bargain.'

'Why does he want you?' Blaire asks, her glass of champagne untouched.

'I don't really know,' I say. 'Possibly because he thought I was undermining him in front of the Whispers but it's more likely to be a power thing, I think. Apparently, he doesn't respond well when he can't control how people leave his life.' Somehow, it feels so much worse when I say it out loud.

Hayes nods his head slowly, sadness and determination in the eyes I love. 'So you won't stay here.'

It's not a question.

My heart is heaving. 'I cannot lead him here. Tonight is a big enough risk.'

'Why? Where will you go?' His gaze dances over my face.

'Because he made it clear he'll come for anyone I care about if I didn't stay with him.' I close my eyes briefly at the nausea this calls forth. The selfishness of that statement coupled with being here. 'As for where I'll go, I don't honestly know. My plan is to head up the coast and see where I end up.'

On my other side, Riley has now started listening in, her grey eyes narrowed. 'That's a bad plan, Lish.'

I sit back in my chair with a sigh. Sofia, Blaire, and Phoenix are now also focused on me. I can feel the tears building behind my eyes. Riley's right, it's a shit plan. And it's a shit plan because I haven't wanted to make one.

'I don't think you can run,' Hayes says. 'You had no choice but to leave there so take that worried look off your face. But running? That's not you. We set out to find the Whispers, you did that, so it's on to phase two.'

'Which is?' I ask.

'Take them down,' Riley says.

'When have you ever run, Lish?' Hayes asks.

I look at Will, whose face shadows. 'I know,' I say, 'but you haven't met this guy.' Images of that night with the General coming back to me. But Will wasn't there then, he doesn't know. My chest heats as it remembers the burning. I try not to shudder. I don't want to give them details of that night, they're worried enough as it is.

'We will help you, Lish, you should know that.' It's Blaire talking now, her eyes lined with silver tears.

'I think we need another round,' I say, inelegantly changing the subject.

But their words won't leave me and nor does Phoenix's agonised gaze. I should have spoken to him first.

Blaire is out of her seat almost before I am and follows me to the bar. She leans against the sticky surface next to me. I'm torn between wanting to cry with relief at seeing her and not knowing how to look at her. I opt momentarily for looking at the bar and her confusion crashes into me, she doesn't know what's written all over her face. I make myself meet her gaze and, seeing the hurt in her eyes, I'm ashamed of myself.

'How long have you been in love with Phoenix?' I ask quietly.

She pales but I know she won't lie to me, and she knows I know. She drops her gaze to the bar.

'Longer than is sensible,' she whispers and guilt churns in my gut.

'Why didn't you tell me?' I ask. 'You know I never would have gone there if I'd known.'

The memory of her shocked face when I'd kissed Phoenix goodbye returns, dampening my eyes. Perhaps I would've known had I been paying more attention. More attention to letting their emotions in than blocking them out.

'Maybe I should have,' she says with a small shrug. 'But the thought of the two of you hadn't occurred to me and I never thought he and I ...'

'Have you?'

'God no, Lish,' she glares at me, her voice sharp. 'I would never. He would never. You know that.'

A little of the tension in my chest loosens.

'I do know,' I sigh. 'But I'd told Will to tell him not to wait for me so ...' I lift a shoulder unable to convey the conflict in my heart. 'Do you want to?'

'You're back now, Lish, things can be as they were. It doesn't matter what I want,' she says. I sit on the bar stool that's just become free beside me and swivel to face her, conscious of the gazes that keep landing on us from our table.

'Lish, I – I don't know what to say. I'm sorry. So, so sorry.' She's fighting tears which is unusual. I hate seeing her cry. 'But I won't interfere, I promise. No one needs to know.'

I watch her and it occurs to me I have a choice here and whatever I feel, or felt, for Phoenix is not enough for me to lose my best friend.

'Blaire, you and Phoenix, you ... make sense to me.'

I didn't realise how true that was until the words are out of my mouth but my eyes continue to mist at the thought all the same. Sweet, kind Blaire and Phoenix's unwavering goodness. Tears start to spill over her cheeks now.

'Oh, my Blaire, I didn't mean to make you cry.' I hold her hands in mine. 'Do you think he feels the same?'

She wipes gently at her tears before holding my hand again.

'We've grown closer since you've been gone,' she says. 'I feel sick even saying that. But he's been so torn up over you, Lish, I don't think he has room—'

'I won't lie to you.' I search for the right words. 'It stings a little but, Phoenix and me ... I don't think it's the same as what you two could have together. I don't think we're right for each other, not anymore.'

'Does he know that's how you feel?' she asks and I shake my head sadly at her. 'I'm not going there, Lish, it isn't right.'

'Blaire,' I say, waiting for her to look at me. 'Do you truly love him?' She nods reluctantly and opens her mouth to apologise again but I keep talking. 'Then you need to fight for it. We have so few chances in our lives to seize happiness. If this is one of yours, you will not waste it,' I say, ignoring the conflict it creates in my chest.

We head back to the table hand in hand and Phoenix meets my eyes, his shining. I squeeze his shoulder on my way back to my chair and slide back into the conversation. The night goes too quickly and the bar staff call last drinks.

'Are you sure you won't stay?' Riley asks, a frown creasing her forehead.

'I can't risk it, Riles. I would give just about anything to be able to, but I won't do it.'

'I get it, but it sucks, you realise? You better be fucking safe, Lish,' she says, gripping her electric blue clutch tightly. It was my favourite to borrow.

I kiss both her cheeks in goodbye. I can't bring myself to make it serious and I treat our goodbyes like any other night, particularly with Will and the goodbye we've already had to do. Otherwise my throat might close over altogether.

Phoenix hangs back as the others filter out. This is not a conversation I want to have, talking to Blaire was bad enough – and I meant what I said to her. But I have to tell him something, not about – I can't talk about him. Not when I've left any opportunity of that, too.

'Lish,' Phoenix starts, his green eyes solemn.

My face heats and I grip my hands to halt my squirming as I lead him to a smaller table in the corner, near a large window. I study his handsome face and the thought of what we could have been makes my stomach flicker. But I really can see he and Blaire together, I don't know why it hadn't occurred to me before. At the same time, I can imagine what our life would have been had I not left. Happy, of that I'm certain. But perhaps there is such a thing as too easy. Not that it matters now, too much has happened and I can't stay with him and put him in danger. My own feelings are—

'What are you thinking?' he asks, looking worriedly at me.

I look at the table. 'About what might have happened if I hadn't left.'

His eyes shutter.

'Will told me you didn't want me to wait, but I had no choice, Lish,' he says. 'Why didn't you want me to wait for you?'

There's pain in his eyes and I wish I could wipe it away. We're sitting close to each other and I can feel the familiar shape of him. The hairs on the back of my neck prickle and I check the room quickly to make sure we're not being watched. My heart rate picks up as I feel time running out.

'I'm so sorry, Phoenix, I thought I would die in there. I couldn't have you waiting out here not knowing if I lived or died.'

He blows out a breath.

'And now what do you want?' There's a hope in him that squeezes at my heart. 'We can go back to what we were, Lish. I will come with you.'

'I want you to be happy,' I say tears starting to fall, 'and I don't—'

'I thought we were happy.' He smiles sadly. 'But you're not coming back to me, are you?'

I look at him, careful not to touch him too closely and my heart aches. Part of me yearns to go back to him, back to before I left to find the Whispers. Before my heart started to tug in a different direction. He would make me happy, I know. But somehow, it's not enough. And knowing what I do about Blaire's feelings, I could never stand between them, even to save Phoenix and me this pain. And it is pain I feel, Phoenix is my friend above all else and I'm hurting him just like Will predicted I would.

'No, Phoenix, I'm not coming back to you.'

A tear slides down his face and I can't look away from the anguish it holds. The sense of being watched hasn't left me and apprehension winds its way through my veins. I need to leave.

'Are you okay? About not being Nico's guardian I mean?' I ask.

He wipes his cheek. 'More than okay. You should see him Lish. Having Sofia back has set his little world on its axis again. And ... he sees quite a bit of Will, you know?' He smiles softly. 'I do hope I get to stay part of his life, but it's truly turned out for the best for him. And that's because of you. Don't underestimate the good you did for that little boy. And Will. You've seen him – that doesn't come around every day, now, does it?' he says thickly.

I laugh sadly at that. 'No, it certainly doesn't, he looks like a love-struck puppy.'

He studies my face for a while and I wait, despite my increasing urgency to leave. The intensity in Phoenix's gaze presses on my skin and I look away.

'It's the one that got you out isn't it?' he asks suddenly.

My stomach plummets. 'No, Phoenix – I—'

'Fuck, seriously?'

His hurt is spiking now. He leans away from me and runs his hands through his hair.

'No, Phoenix, not that.' I grip his face to make him look at me. 'I swear to you, nothing has happened. I would never have done that to you.'

'But you wanted to?' he asks, pulling himself out of my grip.

'No.'

It's not entirely a lie, but it's true my thoughts haven't been totally platonic and I hope the guilt doesn't show on my face. I take his hands instead.

'Please, Phoenix, look at me,' I beg him, my palms starting to sweat. 'Nothing happened. But I – I've changed. My time in that ... place. I'm not the same person that went in. And I can't stay here, anyway, I don't know how long for. I – I don't want you to wait for me.'

He stands abruptly like he can't bear to have this conversation anymore. I look up at him, his warring emotions running over me. He wants to believe me, but I feel as ashamed as if I have hurt him in this way. My heart has betrayed him even if my body hasn't.

'I dove headfirst with you, Lish,' he says quietly. 'I will respect your decision, but I can't say I didn't want this to have a different ending,' he says, his voice tight.

'Phoenix—' I start but he looks away from me before drawing a long breath and walking out.

Hayes is waiting for me as I exit the bar and he holds his hand out to me. Looping his fingers in mine he pulls me in and holds me against his chest. I squeeze him with the force I need to keep the tears at bay. I relish this contact with my dear friend; I hadn't realised how badly I needed to be held until he took me in his arms. I never want him to let go.

'He thinks I cheated.' My voice is muffled against his shoulder.

He squeezes harder, cupping the back of my head and resting his chin on top.

'He doesn't really, he knows you better than that, Lish. No one thinks you'd do that.'

'I still hurt him.' Fresh tears burn.

'You did. And it's unfortunate.' He lifts his head from mine and presses me away, holding me by the shoulders. His eyes are a dark blue in the low light of the street. 'But it won't ruin us, or him. Our bonds run deeper than that. Things between the two of you will shift and change but you'll both be okay.'

I nod slowly, not entirely convinced but his words are a balm anyway.

'There's something special about this other man isn't there?' he asks.

My heart catches.

'Maybe,' I whisper. What does it matter if I can't go back to him either.

'I meant what I said before,' his eyes intent on mine. 'I don't think you can run. I don't think you *should* run. Not from General Psycho and not from this other man.'

I open my mouth but Hayes gives my shoulders a squeeze.

'Think on it,' he says. He drops his hands and picks up a bag I hadn't noticed at his feet. 'If you decide to run, I got you a few things to take with you. It will be useful wherever you go. Backwards ... or forwards.'

The city quietens down around me as I pass through, keeping to the shadows. I don't want to draw attention to myself but I still stick to the main streets, there's no need to play too easily into the Whispers hands if they really are looking for me. It will be bad enough being on the coast road on my own.

I drink in the tall buildings, their lights glittering against the night sky, the rows and rows of fans that are so unnecessary in Elenlea and the delightful smells of the Guarded community vegetable gardens. It's not a place that oozes warmth in the same way as the Realm but it houses so many wonderful memories for me, even as the more difficult realities pulse underneath.

Most of the people I pass on my way through the gate and through the slum on the outskirts of the city are climate refugees. I recall the old beggar with the ringed eyes from so long ago and hope she's safe and well. Not one of the rotting corpses from the shanty town that either end up in shallow graves dug by their family members or the city's mass, unmarked graves.

The sea breeze makes the air a touch cooler than inside the city walls. I pull Ciara's cloak back on so I don't have to carry it anymore, despite it still being too warm to wear here. I was alone so long in that cell that I'm not concerned by my own company but the weight of leaving my friends is heavy on my heart. Phoenix's face as he walked away haunting my every step. He wants to believe I haven't betrayed him, but I've still left him and the hurt I've caused is worse than if it was my own.

I also feel the absence of Lochlain, the sting of what I've done to Phoenix more pronounced with this reality. His steady presence was a desperate reprieve in the darkness and I brush my hand across my middle. As if I can replicate the feeling of the thread that helped anchor me. As I walk further from Rhyton, the city lights fading into the distance, the darkness presses against me. Mauve eyes stalk me, flashing in the tree line I follow only to disappear when I jerk my head to find them.

My hand flutters at my throat as I whip around to see what's behind me. The hairs stand on the back of my neck.

I can hear General Siosal's mocking tone as the sea murmurs my name.

Not real. *They're not real, Lish*, I coach myself. But then how do I really know?

The sea pounds against the rocks and calls to me. With nowhere else to go, I find myself standing at the very end of the point staring across the black sea. I lose myself in the sound of the waves rushing to shore and crashing on the rocks below me; it's a wild lullaby that cracks me open and I sob into the darkness. The breeze picks up and splatters my cheeks with sea spray. Right on this very tip, I feel almost free. But the shadows behind me are hard to keep away, how many of them contain Whispers? Are they really looking for me? Can I outrun them? Or have they moved on to other prey, and I am leaving Rhyton for no reason at all?

Sitting on the rocks beneath me as my chest heaves I decide I have nowhere better to be and if they're coming, I'd like to feel the breeze on my face when they do.

CHAPTER TWENTY

My tears ultimately submit to the sea and my eyes begin to clear. Rummaging in my bag, I take out the small box Will gave me before we left his apartment. The timber is familiar and warm under my fingers. It belonged to my mother, one I used to keep on my bedside table, and contains a handful of trinkets and mementos I've collected over time. He's added the librarian's journal and I take it out, using my new phone to see by.

Skimming through the entries on the Whispers, I am struck by a sense of immense gratitude that Will, Sofia, and I all got out. I don't know how many others can say the same and, even if my isolation is the cost, I would pay it several times over to give Will the happiness I can see between Sofia and him. Not to mention the impact on Nico's life.

A fierce wind whips up from the ocean. I hold my hood on with one hand as the gale lashes at the pages in the journal. It's gone as quickly as it came and I squint into the darkness for signs of a super-storm.

Moving to pack the journal away again, my gaze lands where its pages have been thrown open.

A page about the blue star from my mother's stories.

Follow your heart to the Blue Pointed Star, the wolves will guide your path.

Her bedtime stories of wolves as the Guardians of the Star always made me smile. The thought tugs at my mouth now, too, a warming sensation in my soul. I imagine her sitting with me, much like I did with Nico when I told him of the Star that first night. Her long, dark hair falling across her face as she propped herself on my bed with an elbow. Whether it's a real image or not, I can't say. She talked of the Star as a great power that would unlock the most important knowledge of our time. A magic so incredible that even the worst damage could be undone, the hardest hearts turned and the dying set free. But only if it could be found and freed.

As I grew, I often thought of this and wondered if it was her way of instilling a sense of self in me. That I should listen to my intuition and it would lead me. I figured the wolves were creative license.

Being directionless, literally, doesn't sit well with me and I feel paralysed in what decision to make next, despite my promises to Lochlain. He is right. I can't return to Rhyton. But maybe that doesn't have to be forever. And moving to a foreign land across the sea, away from everything I know and everyone I love, turns my stomach.

The journal entry also echoes an idea Ciara planted in our short time together and I have nothing to lose by giving it a try.

I breathe the salt air deep into my lungs and close my eyes, recalling her words.

I open my heart to the sky and let go of the life I thought I would have, Phoenix included, and make a different choice. A choice that frightens me. But one that makes my gold flame burn a little brighter.

I open my eyes and wait for the Mother to give me a sign.

Nothing happens.

There's nothing but me and my now silent tears.

The sky makes its transition from black to a deep blue as dawn begins to break through. My body complains from sitting on the hard rocks for so long and I slowly rise, joints and muscles griping, and dust the sand from my pants. I do the only thing that's an option now and follow Lochlain's advice about heading north through the coastal towns.

The first one will be a good day and a half walk away, particularly as there will be so many daytime hours I will need to shelter from the heat. It's also my best chance of finding a boat or a ship I can take across the sea. The towns get smaller after the first and are likely to have less options for passage. Although they might be easier to access. The restrictions on travel will mean I need to get creative with how to get myself onboard.

Moving across the sea isn't something I've ever seriously considered. There are other continents that sounded intriguing at one point in my life, but that sort of upheaval is not as easy as I believe it once was. When jobs and resources were easier to come by. I will have to start again, literally from scratch, in a land I know nothing about. While knowing it will be just as hard – harder – to return here. Or to the Realm. But I know I need to accept that the Realm is not open to me either. Even if I could find it without Lochlain or Siosal, I will never be able to return.

I've been walking the coast road towards the first town for almost an hour, my feet already starting to ache and the familiar sensation of sweat forming under the band of the large hat Hayes had stashed in my bag, when the hairs on the back of my neck start to prickle. My palms tingle and I realise I am being watched.

It's not a figment of my imagination.

Subtly trying to glance around, I see nothing and move closer to the line of trees on the other side of the road. They are sparsely dotted along the edge, more scrub than anything, but it's greater cover than being on the road. Although, against the Whispers, it will do nothing.

A twig snaps close to me and I draw Ciara's knife from my belt before pressing myself against a narrow tree.

My heart roars in my ears but there is no whispering. Yet.

I peer around the tree trunk and into the wood. Morning has broken but full light hasn't yet reached much beyond the edge of the tree line.

A pair of unblinking, amber eyes stare straight at me.

I whip my face back and press the back of my head against the trunk. My throat constricts at the echo of the Whispers and the screaming in my head.

How long before Will and I were taken in Althea Forest did I see those same eyes?

Are they a precursor to the Whispers?

Closing my own eyes, I listen to the layers of sound around me. Its core is peaceful. Bugs creak and chatter around me. There are no bird sounds but, then, I am no longer in the Realm. I can make out no whispers in my mind, no malicious movement, and no emotions brush mine.

I wait a minute.

Two.

Giving the beast time to move on.

My stomach worries against the thought I could be an attractive meal and I try and recall my training. Is it stay still or run from wild animals? A frantic flutter skips in my heart as I struggle to remember.

I steal another look around the tree to check it's gone only to find those unwavering eyes.

They're pinned on mine as if it never lost sight of me.

I watch it for a long moment and, despite my imagination attempting to work against me, I don't detect any threat.

Silently cursing my likely naivety, I step out from behind the tree.

The amber eyes watch as I take slow step, after slow step, and edge myself closer. I stop halfway between the tree and the animal. The eyes, a long, grey snout, and furred chest comes into view. It's sitting like I imagine a dog waits for its owner to come home but there is nothing domesticated in the way it's watching me. It is wholly something else. Something spiritual. It blinks once at me and silently walks away.

Inexplicably, I feel a tug in my gut to follow.

The wolf doesn't turn around to look at me again, the slight twitching of its ears the only indication it knows I follow. I've not seen a wolf before, I've never even heard of them living around Rhyton. I believe they're pack animals but I can't hear nor see any sign of others. Perhaps I wouldn't know if others followed, though. I shiver.

The wolf pads deeper into the trees. Most of them are dead or dying, a pang of sadness I've become accustomed to taking root, and, briefly, I long for the large, shady trees of Althea Forest. But that forest hid its own horrors I do not wish to repeat.

The slightly thickening trees increase my nerves. I should turn back, there are too many places for the Whispers to hide here. Suddenly, the wolf, larger than any wild animal I've ever seen, stops and raises its black nose to the air as something approaches from the right, just ahead of me. There's something familiar about the sound of what's gently crunching through the wood, but I can't place it. My head shouts to run but my feet don't cooperate.

'Oh ...' I mutter out loud. 'You are an amazing, beautiful girl.'

Niamh whinnies quietly but is still as I approach, her gentle brown eyes taking me in. I glance to the wolf to find it's left Niamh and me alone. She's warm to the touch as I stroke her thick neck. Finding an apple Hayes packed for me, I hold my hand out flat for her to take it, marvelling at her presence.

'I'd love another ride, Niamh, what do you think? Can you take me along the coast?' I place my hand close to her wither, taking a couple of small jumps to gain some momentum before launching myself onto her back as gently as I can. It's certainly not as graceful or easy as when Lochlain was here to give me a leg up, but I make it far enough on to wriggle myself over the rest of the way.

She doesn't waste any time and makes her way deeper into the trees. I tug her mane gently.

'Niamh, that's the wrong way.'

I tug a little harder to my left, but she only shakes her head, mane flying, and ploughs on.

'Niamh, no. I can't – I need to—'

The wolves will guard your path.

My flames flickers and I suck in a breath. Surely not.

I watch Niamh's strong shoulders, striding forward. So purposeful in her direction. I trusted her to get me to Rhyton when I needed to. With an excited flip in my stomach, I decide to trust her now, too. I can't help but smile to myself as I watch the sky pass above us, listening to the sporadic sounds of small animals scurrying underfoot. I don't see any sign of the wolf and its amber eyes but, somehow, I feel it watching our progress. And I smile wider at the knowledge, realising how much comfort it brings.

Niamh begins to move faster beneath me until we're flying through the trees and across the dusty cracked earth she brought me back to only yesterday. I give myself to her and close my eyes, my pack bouncing on my back. The sun bears down on me now we're out in the open and sweat streams down my body, despite having changed into the more heat appropriate clothes Hayes gave me. My nerves should be on edge, but I've made my decision. I want to return to the Realm. The coastal towns and a ship across the sea are just not my path. Niamh will take me to the Realm. She *is* taking me to the Realm.

I think of Hayes's questioning face last night, what I would encourage them to do in my place. My mother didn't have the life she deserved. I don't know what she wanted, but I know it was horribly cut short. I won't have my life severed prematurely as well. I didn't create a life after loss only to walk away from it.

I lift my chin into the scorching heat and exhale.

Niamh knows I will not run.

And now, so do I.

I kick her along, faster, and – abruptly – the sensation of warm silk pulls again at my skin as the temperature drops. She races across the green plain for what seems like days, my thighs and backside barking in protest, when she finally slows. My lower back hurts and I feel much too old to be racing bareback across the countryside.

Gradually, she comes to a complete stop and I take in my surroundings. Rolling green hills rise up in front of me and, not far to the left, is the gently running stream. In the foothills, a city begins on the other side of the lake and hugs its way up the gentle slope.

Elenlea.

I dismount awkwardly, my inner thighs threatening to let me sink to the ground, and turn to look at Niamh.

'We're both going to be in trouble for this, you realise?' I mutter, even as my heart sings to be back. My flame burning.

She snorts and trots off. I shake my head. *Guess I'm on my own, then.*

I walk gingerly the rest of the way to Elenlea, stopping for lunch and a break by the side of the river, not far from where it skirts the edge of the city. The water bubbles along softly and my eyelids droop. Laying back in the grass, I watch the clouds overhead and wonder if anything has ever seemed so peaceful. I don't let myself drop off to sleep, though, tired as I am from being up all night and travelling all day. Would General Siosal expect me to still be here? I try to muster the fear that should accompany that thought but the gladness that fills me takes precedence, instead.

Walking into the city, the sounds of children playing float around me. I pull out the phone Hayes bought me. He's put a photo of the two of us on the home page and I grin at him. He knew what I needed to do before I did. How totally unsurprising.

I log in to our group chat 'Orphan Team Pin Board' and flick a message to the group letting them know I lasted the night. Without seeing if it's been delivered or not, I write another into the ether.

You were right, I can't hide in the shadows and live half a life. I'm going to end this and then I'm coming home. Love you all x

I message each Blaire and Phoenix separately with the same words.

I'm going to try and come home but it doesn't change what I said. Be happy x

I turn it off and stash it back in my bag before I can see if they go through and walk into Elenlea.

It's evening when I wind my way through the cobbled streets, still quietly cursing Niamh for leaving me to do this bit on my own. I don't know Ciara's address and the city is large. But I've come this far, hopefully another stroke of luck will find me. I tug my hood on against the cool breeze, the novelty of which makes me smile, and lean into the music that drifts on the breeze. Instinct has me following the sounds that vibrate in my chest.

Calahi are out on the streets and spilling out of what appear to be underground transport stations. It's a night in the city not unlike I would find in Rhyton but it still seems somehow not at its full beauty in a way I can't quite put my finger on. Like its colours are ever so slightly muted. But even with that, it's more alive than Rhyton. Magic, my heart reminds me, it's magical here. The tiny golden fire that lives in me quivers in response.

The city buildings are lit up in soft, warm light, making them appear otherworldly in the gentle dark of the evening. Lanterns are hung from the sky along the sides of the streets, lanes and buildings built from pale stones line each side, differing in shape and size. Dark-green vines embrace those with pillars. Balconies overflow with coloured flowers and merriment seeps from every corner. Musicians and singers are in the various establishments and stir the part of me that always ignites in the presence of live music.

I don't need to recognise the songs to know they're beautiful.

I flinch as a spike of fear crashes against me.

A firm, male hand grips my upper arm from behind. I twist, slamming my elbow into his throat, knife pressed dangerously along his side, just below the ribs, as I push him back against a wall. A familiar crackle runs over my senses as he rasps softly against the pressure at his throat and raises his hands.

'It's me, Lish, it's—' He frowns, as if thinking I don't know who 'me' is.

'Are you trying to give me a fucking heart attack?' I lower my knife and release him. My heart does indeed feel like it's going to beat straight out of my chest but I send up a little thank you for this particular piece of luck.

He glances sideways at a group approaching, laughing at each other. A tall, attractive Calahi has his arm around the waist of an equally beautiful woman. Something tightens in my chest as I note the ease with which they touch each other. Lochlain brings his eyes back to mine and gently moves us so we trade places, my back now against the stone that's cold even through the fabric of my cloak. He plants his hands either side of my head. I raise an eyebrow at him.

He leans in slightly and whispers. 'You have quite the spring in your step for someone who is very, *very* far from where she should be.'

The sensation of having him so close makes my toes curl, despite the flickering worry in his voice. He leans his head down so it rests against mine and closes his eyes, his panicked undercurrent ebbing away. Heat rises on my face, his warm breath sending skitters down my spine, and I silently curse him for it. The edge of his hood falls across my face as the group passes us by.

He lifts his head, his conflicted face illuminated in the low light of the sky lanterns. A face I missed even in the short time I have been away. I peek up at the copper rings flashing in his eyes. He's a jumble of emotions, although restrained like he's trying to keep them away from me. But it's fairly safe to say he'd like to throttle me simply for being here. And maybe something else as well.

'*Had* a spring in my step until you scared the wits out of me,' I whisper back.

'Trust me, that's the least of what I feel like doing to you right now,' he says through gritted teeth. The heat in my face travels lower, much lower, at what his voice doesn't say. The group has moved out of earshot now but he doesn't move, his eyes traveling to my mouth as if waiting for what I will say next.

I hold my breath.

He drags his eyes back to mine. They seem darker but perhaps it's a trick of the evening light. 'We should get you off the street.'

My knees and backside are complaining by the time we get to the top of the fourth, and thankfully last, flight of stairs. Bloody horse riding. The loft is close to the heart of the city, although Lochlain insisted we keep our hoods up and took us a circular way, in case we were being followed. Apparently, Elenlea can be a little less than enchanting for humans and strangers. And that's without the threat of Whispers looking for me.

I remember the man that called out to Lochlain when I first came to Elenlea and I wonder how many more Calahi would recognise Lochlain without his hood. But still, I enjoyed the longer walk through the city, the music seeping into my soul, and I couldn't help but think he was being a bit paranoid. It's so peaceful here.

'It's meant to make you feel that way, you realise?' he asks as I remove my cloak and hang it over the back of the worn leather couch.

'What is?'

'The music, it's ... designed to make you feel at ease.'

'Well, it certainly did its job then.'

I smile, remembering the notes that found their way to me. Lochlain rolls his eyes, a gesture that seems totally at odds with the person I know him to be. But then, I guess that's the thing, perhaps I don't really know him. My heart and body disagree.

Damn them.

He pours us some drinks as I survey his space. It's simply furnished, with a couch, a cosy looking bed, and a small dining table. The fireplace and exposed beams give it a rustic vibe that suits him. My gaze lands on the bed and my insides warm. The memory of his proximity in the street hasn't left me. I'm thankful the only real light emanates from a lantern hanging over the couch as he catches me looking and my cheeks blaze.

I force myself to look away and watch the flames starting to take in the hearth. It's a relief to be able to see them. Heat that burns without flame haunts my dreams but this is not that.

'Right,' he says, taking a seat on the brown couch, 'out with it.'

'With what?' I ask, joining him and taking the drink he offers.

He looks at me, nothing but seriousness in his face. 'Why, and how, for that matter, are you here?'

'Can I be honest with you?' I ask. It's a stupid question, of course, he has no choice but to say yes if he wants me to answer. But I still feel compelled to ask, I want to hear him say it.

'Of course,' he says in a rough voice and there's truth there. I can feel it. The crackle that exists between us is warm on my skin. I take a long sip of my drink, the deep, burgundy liquid scorching my throat on the way down and starting a luxurious fire in the pit of my belly.

I like counting the fires that don't scare me. Making sure they outweigh the one that does.

'I'm here to stop General Siosal,' I say and his fingers tighten slightly on his glass. 'For two reasons. Firstly, he cannot keep taking women against their will, it's abhorrent and I simply won't allow it. Certainly not because of me. Secondly, because I fought damn hard to let a select group of good – incredible even – people into my life and I will not let them go because a purple eyed psycho may or may not be looking for me.' I take a deep breath. 'I need to be able to go home, Lochlain.'

His eyes close briefly at my last statement but he doesn't comment on it. 'And how, exactly, did you get back here?'

'Well ...' I hesitate, unsure how much I should implicate Niamh in this. But then, his love for that horse probably means she could get away with anything.

'It was Niamh, wasn't it?'

'Maybe.'

'Bloody hell,' he says, 'traitorous damn horse. I should replace her with one from your world.' He throws his drink back, the glass immediately refilling itself.

'Will you help me? Let me join you?' I ask, dragging my eyes from his glass and back to his face.

'You're going to try and do it regardless of my answer, aren't you?'

I don't bother responding.

He leans back against the arm of the couch and I don't falter under the weight of his stare. Welcome it, even.

'Yes, Lish.' The effect my name on his lips has on me hasn't diminished, it seems. 'I will help you. And I will pray I am not sending both of us to our graves.'

I scoot over to him. 'Thank you, Lochlain,' I say, taking his hands in mine. He looks at our hands and brushes a thumb over my knuckles. 'I mean it, thank you.'

Slowly, he looks away from our hands only for his eyes to catch on my knee that's now gently pressing into the side of his thigh. He traces a single finger along the soft part on the inside of my knee. A sensation my skin won't let go of.

'There's so much you don't know.'

He's still not looking at me.

'Then tell me, Lochlain, I'm not going anywhere.'

'That's exactly what worries me,' he says, finally meeting my gaze. He sighs heavily. 'But, for now, you're just about dead on your feet. Take the bed, I'll sleep here.'

I start to protest that the couch is better suited to my size but he holds firm. He gives me some old, soft pants and shirt that I shimmy into in his small bathroom, hyper aware of how close and yet how far he is. They are vastly oversized but ridiculously comfortable and I hop into the bed, which turns out to be just as cosy as it looks. He sits on the edge, not touching me.

'Lish,' he says, searching my eyes.

'Hmm,' I respond, struggling to keep my own eyes open against the pull of sleep. Even my earlier thoughts aren't enough to wind back the need to close my eyes.

'It's unfair of me to say this but ... you know I can't be a second choice, right?'

I look at him in the flickering firelight.

'You were there, weren't you? You followed me into Rhyton.'

If his emotions didn't give him away, his face would do it for him. I realise he's thinking about the kiss Phoenix gave me and perhaps the tears we each had when we said goodbye. When I'd left him.

'I just ...' he starts. 'I needed to know you were safe when you left there.'

I prop myself up onto one elbow, certainly more awake now than a moment ago.

'I didn't just leave there, you know. I left Phoenix too.' I take a deep breath. 'He was waiting for me, and I asked him not to. To just be my friend. Is that what you wanted to know?'

He holds tight to his feelings but they continue to leak through to me. I still don't tell him I can pick them up, anyway, even though I can't with any other Calahi. Maybe he doesn't know that I can read others' emotions at all, only that I can tell when someone is trying to manipulate mine.

'It's not any of my business,' he says. 'But maybe.'

I smile softly and lie back down. He sits there for a moment, letting me drift back into drowsiness, before I talk again.

'Just for the record,' I say looking at him through half closed eyes. 'You, Lochlain, could never be anyone's second choice.'

Sleep drags me under then and I dream of amber eyes and a feather light touch on my cheek.

CHAPTER TWENTY-ONE

Ciara gasps and throws her arms around my neck as Lochlain and I arrive in her kitchen the following morning. A delightful smell fills the room and it takes me a moment to place its rich aroma. It's been an age since I had coffee and my mouth waters at the thought of a hot mug – and the pastries that so often used to accompany it. She looks at Lochlain triumphantly.

'You came back much faster than I expected,' she says, grinning.

'You knew I was going to?'

She shrugs slightly but her gold ringed eyes are serious when she looks at me.

'I was hoping you would choose us, yes,' she says. I blush, thinking of my conversation last night with Lochlain about choices, but she said 'us' not 'him'.

'You listened to my story, didn't you?' She continues, pouring me a large mug of coffee.

Lochlain bristles. 'What story?'

'I might have,' I say ignoring him. 'Does that make me crazy?'

'You ended up here, didn't you?' Ciara says. 'So ... maybe, yes.' She laughs.

'What story?' Lochlain asks again, eyes on Ciara.

'Oh, you know,' she says, a little coyness creeping into her tone, 'the old story about the lost girl who listens to her soul instead of her head and lets the Mother guide her where she needs to go.'

Lochlain narrows his eyes at her and glances at me as if expecting to see an answer in my face.

'Don't worry, Lochlain, as nice a fairy tale as it might be,' I say and he looks at me suspiciously, 'I think I just fluked finding Niamh again. She didn't seem worried about the wolf, though, I thought that would have spooked her.'

They both turn their eyes to me at that, Ciara's mouth open in contrast to the thin line Lochlain has pressed his into.

'Mother forgive us,' he mutters.

'I'd suggest it was the Mother that sent the wolf, Loch,' Ciara says, still staring at me.

I glance between them, missing the point of this sibling exchange. She recovers herself, handing me a plate of thick cut bread with cheese and the mug of coffee.

'Lochlain,' she says gently, 'this is what you wanted. It's what you've been fighting for. It's what we have *all* been fighting for. You can't turn your back on that now just because you'—she waves a hand in the air as she slides her gaze between us—'you know.'

He glares at her. 'It's my duty to—'

She raises an eyebrow at him and he looks away, not meeting my eye. *Duty*. I frown, pushing away the thoughts and questions that try to crowd in.

'And, if she wants in,' Ciara continues, 'she's in. You know full well we can't argue with that now. She chose this.'

'Definitely no point arguing that,' I say slowly, 'but, if we're doing this, you're going to fill me in on what you already know about General Siosal and how you intend to stop him.'

I look pointedly at Lochlain and understanding flickers from him.

'Don't bother denying you've been planning this rebellion for a long time,' I say. 'Having you in the Whispers was clearly part of your strategy. And you're going to stop talking in riddles I don't understand. At least not in my presence. Got it?'

Ciara claps her hands, 'I love her!' she exclaims to Lochlain.

After spending the next few hours talking with Lochlain and Ciara about the Whispers and the General, it's clear finding the rightful occupant for the Throne is something both Lochlain and Ciara are very passionate about. But there's a wariness that coats their discussion about it I can't read – and that I don't recall being present in our first discussion. Perhaps it's tiredness.

Equally clear is their love for the Court of Airlie, and that General Siosal's methods, and how they impact on their Court, flies in the face of what they believe Airlie to be.

'What happened to the ones who turned out not to be the Queen or heir?' I ask, shifting position slightly on Ciara's soft couch.

Lochlain lowers his gaze and tension ripples across his shoulders. 'For many of them, they spent a few nights as entertainment at the compound before they were no longer useful.' His jaw clenches before he goes on. 'A handful of others were sold for other ... uses before they, too, found their end.'

'Fuck,' I breathe.

'When we realised what was happening, I was able to get him to stop. To convince him that's not how you honour someone's memory,' Lochlain says. 'Then, something triggered this side of his search again and here we are.' He smiles grimly at me. 'I can't take any credit for getting out the women you were with. That was all you.'

I'd known, though, and it's that knowledge that makes me feel sickest. That I looked into the eyes of the likes of Odhran and the General and knew what evil lay there. And yet I got away, only to put more women at risk. I think of Sofia and the others. I only know her name and Peta's, no one else's. The shame of that heating my cheeks. I recall the happiness on Will's face as he looked at Sofia, how many others have been robbed of that opportunity? How many more will be before I stop him?

'And you still think the Custodian of the Throne doesn't know about Siosal's methods?' I ask.

'It goes against everything Airlie believes in,' he says. 'The General's methods are the essence of what the Throne is supposed to protect us from. What the Custodian tries to protect us from. He wants the Queen or the heir found as much as anyone, but not like this.'

'So why not build a case against Siosal and take it to the Custodian?' I realise now this Custodian, who I didn't know existed before, is a better audience for a case than Robard.

Ciara blows out a breath. 'Because we've already tried that. The Custodian has a habit of seeing the best in others,' she says. 'Which is wonderful when things are going well. But ... trickier when there are Calahi like Siosal around and other Courts to manage. Other Courts that don't necessarily want to see Airlie stand on her own anymore.'

I rub at the tension running across my forehead. The language Ciara is using reminds me of the reading I did in school about wars. The careful, politically sanitised versions of events used as justification for invading, violently, other countries.

'Stand on her own,' I say slowly. 'Meaning?'

'The possibility of war in the Realm,' Lochlain says and my heart quickens with the stress I can feel from him about this. 'Ideally,' he continues, 'we stop Siosal ourselves and find the heir. Then we can gently move the Custodian on as he is expecting, support the Queen to stabilise Airlie, and deter the Courts of Rothani and Mercasia. Show strength without violence.'

'And have you worked out if you should go back in?' I ask. 'If you don't return from your ... supposed mission, you won't know if he finds them or not?' My gut twists nervously at the thought of him in General Siosal's hands if he is found out for helping me. I will certainly not let him go on his own, if that's his plan.

He glances at Ciara sitting across from him in the armchair. 'No, if I don't go back, I won't know who else is brought in. If anyone is. But we have Haryk ... and others.'

'He said he would,' I say. 'He said he wouldn't hurt me anymore, but he'd keep taking women until I went back.' That twist in my gut turns painful.

'Siosal isn't someone who forgives. Ever. But events may have progressed enough now for me to not have to go back.'

Ciara notes the relief on my face at this and smiles softly. Lochlain pretending to loyally work under General Siosal is something she has endured far longer than me.

'Haryk confirmed Siosal isn't yet looking for Lochlain,' Ciara says. 'He thinks you got out on your own after Odhran came for you. But we'll need to be incredibly careful.'

'Have you given any thought to what you will do if you find the Queen or her child and they don't want the Throne?' I ask.

'We talk about that a lot,' Ciara says, turning her gold and black eyes to me. 'But, really, we have no option but to try. At this point, it seems clear the Queen has gone. But what of her young one? Do they know what's here for them? Wouldn't you want to know, if it was you?' Ciara asks, her loose posture belying the tension in her voice.

Lochlain's eyes flick to her before returning to me.

'Yes, I would want to know. I'd want to choose,' I say slowly. 'But those women didn't have a choice and I can't sit back and let that happen again. Not now that I'm out. Not *because* I am out.'

I lean back, resting my head on the plush couch cushions and blow out a breath. With it I send away the visions of that dark cold cell. My mother's words about bravery come back to me and I close my eyes. She was running, I know that much. I didn't realise it as a child but the different places we lived, the fact there was never anyone else in our lives, that I was only ever allowed to use my gift at home. As an adult, all of those things made more sense. What I never knew was why. Now, I wonder if I'm strong enough to.

'So what's your plan?' I ask, lifting my head again.

Ciara smiles.

Lochlain runs a hand through his hair, his loose curls bouncing back when he takes it away. He watches me like I imagine a predator observes its prey.

'The three of us alone won't be able to stop Siosal, and Haryk has confirmed he will go after more women,' he says. 'It's time you met the others.'

'Maybe Airlie will win you over in the process.' Ciara winks at me and Lochlain sighs. The fear and hope ebbing from him glitters in his eyes.

Ciara leaves to contact the others, whoever they may be, leaving Lochlain and me in the sitting room. I take our mugs to the kitchen and he joins me, leaning against the counter with his arms crossed over his chest.

He's anxious and I force it away to keep myself steady, focusing instead on the faint outline of weapon straps I can see over his shoulders, hidden by his shirt. Slowly I look up and find his eyes already on my face.

Waiting.

'You seem hesitant,' I say quietly, 'about having me join you. Do you not trust me to be part of this?'

He steps towards me, and my pulse kicks up a notch. 'Sort of ... mostly,' he says.

My brows feel like they shoot to the sky. 'Sort of?'

'I trust you're skilled, that your heart is in the right place,' he says. 'But you forget that I *know* you will put yourself in danger to protect those you care about.'

I'm not sure how to respond to that. Is he telling me he knows I care about him or that the fact I do that – and he's not wrong – worries him? A smile lifts the corners of my mouth.

'Lochlain,' I say, 'are you worrying about me?'

'Every moment I'm with you makes me worry more.'

He moves to take another step towards me, halting when Ciara comes back into the kitchen.

'They'll be here in ten,' she says. The force of Lochlain's nerves make me look at him quickly but he won't meet my eyes.

Ciara's gaze flicks between us and she gives Lochlain's bicep a quick squeeze. I look to him for understanding but he only looks back to the doorway.

'Hey hey!' a loud voice calls from the back door, the same one Lochlain and I used the first day I came here.

I'm momentarily thrown by the Calahi who appear in the kitchen a few moments later. Partly because the man is quite possibly the most beautiful person I've ever seen, and the fierceness of the woman sucks at my chest. And then there's the wave of mixed emotions coming from Lochlain.

I stifle the urge to tell him what I can feel, and he reins them in on his own with some effort. No one else seems to notice. Feeling like I can breathe a little better, I turn back to the new arrivals – although it's me that's new, in reality. The shared history in the room sends a flutter behind my ribs, reminding me why I am here. For my own family. So I can go home.

The male Calahi is slightly taller than Lochlain and not quite as broad. The white, long sleeve top he wears shows a body that is either used to maximum ability every day or is slavishly honed to look like it is. With skin the deep brown of wet earth and black hair cropped close to his skull, it's all I can do not to stare. Mahogany eyes survey me.

'Hi,' he says in a rich, curiosity-lined voice.

The woman's steel-coloured eyes flick to me as she comes around the man. Her eyes widen before she looks to Lochlain, who clears his throat, as if remembering himself. He steps forward to introduce me, a hand hovering at the small of my back.

'Rory, Aeyva, this is Lish.'

Rory steps forward and takes my hand, gently kissing the back of it. A prickle of objection runs over my back where Lochlain's hand remains, not touching me, but it's drowned out by his anxiety. Rory lifts his stunning eyes to mine as he squeezes my fingers. Mahogany lined with obsidian.

'Pleased to meet you ... Lish,' he says in a voice I am entirely sure has women and men alike losing their minds.

'Don't mind him,' the woman, Aeyva, says. 'He thinks he's sex on legs. He is, truth be told, but we don't tell him that.'

She quirks an eyebrow at me, and brushes stray strands of her silver hair out of her face. The top section is bound in a tight, complicated braid that hangs past her shoulders. Above each ear a shaved strip about two inches wide shows the tattoos on her skull. Her black bodysuit is not unlike my old Guard uniform. I can't see any weapons on her but there is no mistaking how deadly she is.

'*You*,' she says pressing a finger into Lochlain's chest, 'are one lucky bastard. Sending ...' She shakes her head. 'That was the single dumbest thing you've ever done.' She kisses him forcefully on both cheeks and makes her way to the couch, throwing Ciara a soft smile that lingers. I follow her mutely to the sitting room, my cheeks warm.

Aeyva's steel-grey eyes turn to me and I notice the pale blue rings in them. 'How did you find your way back?' she asks. 'We're normally very well hidden.'

We've all taken seats, leaving Lochlain to sit between Aeyva and me on the couch, facing the fire. He sits a little stiffly between us, as though he's trying not to touch me.

'I probably wouldn't have found it on my own, to be honest. I had a little help.' I tell them about Niamh and the wolf, and they watch me carefully. Almost as carefully as Lochlain and Ciara watch them to gauge their reactions.

'That's a very intriguing story,' Aeyva says. 'It reminds me of an old one I've heard before.'

Lochlain clears his throat.

'A very intriguing story,' Rory chips in. 'I assume that's just the beginning of what we're here for, Kiki?'

Ciara looks at Rory and Aeyva. 'She came back, and she wants to join us.'

Aeyva pins me with a look.

'This is starting to feel like an audition,' I say, meeting her gaze. She looks to Lochlain and he holds her stare for so long I almost think they're communicating in some way I can't hear.

'Join us to do what, exactly?' Aeyva asks, resuming her focus on me. Steely eyes portraying just how lethal she is.

'Lish's goal is to stop General Siosal and return home,' Lochlain says evenly.

'Home?' Rory asks slowly. 'And where is that?'

'Somewhere other than here,' I say gently.

Aeyva narrows her eyes at me but there's amusement there. I tentatively allow her emotions to find me, but they remained obscured. Rory and Aeyva look at me without talking and my skin tightens a little in self-consciousness. I don't know what I was expecting from this meeting but I did think there'd be more talking and less ... visual assessment. I feel like they're looking through me and it sets me on edge.

Wine appeared on the low table as we sat down and I take a sip now to help steady my nerves. I accidentally bump Lochlain with my knee as I set my glass back on the table and he subtly shifts his leg away. Ignoring him, I sit forward and address the others.

'Look,' I start, 'I get the tight group of friends thing and it's hard to let others in. I'm not asking you to let me be bestie number five. I'm saying I'd like to help you stop Siosal. I know enough from Lochlain and Ciara to know you're against him. So am I. But if you're not up for working together that's fine. I will do what I can on my own.'

'Bestie number five?' Rory asks, smirking.

'Listen, Lish,' Lochlain says, 'it's not that we don't want you with us but it's dangerous. There are other ways—'

'Why do you want this at all?' Aeyva cuts him off. 'Loch gave you the opportunity to walk away and never look back.'

I think on that. I know the answer, but I question how much to give them. It's Ciara in the end who makes my decision. I realise I want her to trust me, I want to earn it from her. But I still keep a piece to myself. About how much the possibility of answers drives me, even if I'm not ready to face them all.

So it's her I am looking at when I say, 'Revenge and protection.'

Next to me, Lochlain cocks his head slightly, offended. 'Protection? I—'

'Let her finish,' Ciara says, not taking her eyes off me.

I breathe in and out through my nose and pick my wine glass back up, watching its contents as I swirl it around.

'Whether he knows it or not, General Siosal has taken, or has tried to take, the most important people in my life from me. And I want to protect anyone else from feeling that pain. That's without even going into the moral responsibility I have to help the women he intends to take – nobody should be treated like that.

'I watched the man who may as well be my brother almost bleed out, courtesy of the General's blade. I saw firsthand a little boy's devastation as his only remaining family member was torn away from him. I saw the anger in his eyes as he threatened to burn me into oblivion. And then, I was asked to leave and not return.' I take a shuddering breath. 'The option you put forward, Aeyva, of walking away and never looking back simply isn't in me to do. My friends, my family, are all I have. And if I don't stop him, he's going after them again. I won't risk it,' I say.

A pulse of warmth flows over me from Lochlain.

'Nobody would've blamed you for choosing that path, Lish,' he says.

I look at him and note the sadness in his eyes. 'But I would have.'

My history plays in my mind, and I weigh up telling them they're not the only ones who've had dealings with the Whispers in the past. Perhaps not as often as them but ... certainly life altering.

I take a deep breath. The last person I told of the darkest moment in my life – the librarian – wound up dead. But there's an air to this group that tells me they can more than take care of themselves. Every fibre in my being screams to stop General Siosal. If sharing a painful fact helps me do that, so be it.

'There's something else you might as well know,' I say looking into the fire now. 'This wasn't my first experience with the Whispers.'

Anger and something like worry tinge the emotions Lochlain is grappling with. Absently, I wonder why I can't sense the others like I can with my friends, and everyone else in Rhyton.

'They killed my mother.'

Rory and Ciara sit forward in their seats and Lochlain shifts to face me, turning his back to Aeyva. Devastation ripples from him, but not surprise – he knows I grew up in the orphanage. Feeling his emotions as well as mine bring tears to my eyes as I remember that day and I blink them away.

'I think I'd repressed it, or couldn't make enough sense of it as a kid, but when we began looking into the different cases, it started to come back,' I say. 'When the Whispers took Will and me, there really couldn't be any doubt. And if there was any lingering uncertainty, being ... with General Siosal certainly wiped any last trace of it away. I don't know if it was him personally or not, of course, but I know they were there, and I want to make them pay. I want him to pay.'

Lochlain gently holds my knee. 'Do you know for sure she's dead? She wasn't taken somewhere else?' There's a hint of hope in his voice that hurts.

I look at him slowly and swallow against the sound of her skull cracking. 'She's dead.' I blink the image away.

The others in the room seem to collectively inhale before placing their palms to their hearts in what I assume is an Elenlea way of expressing sympathy. Although it does remind me of the Librarian again, how long ago that seems.

Lochlain's eyes flash. 'I'm so sorry, Lish. I ...' he doesn't seem to know what else to say and I don't blame him.

Several moments pass and I notice how still the Calahi can be.

'Can you fight?' Aeyva asks abruptly.

I look her over. 'Not like I imagine you can,' I say, 'but yes.'

Rory smiles. 'Not many can.'

'No.' Lochlain shakes his head. 'I don't think she should come. The risks ...' A weight drags down the centre of my chest. 'We're talking about fighting full-blooded Calahi.'

And I'm human, I think. Mostly. Who knows how far back my heritage is linked with theirs. How diluted it is now.

Aeyva gently runs a hand over his back, and I try not to track the movement. Lochlain tenses as she looks around him. She stares at me, distracting me from the disappointment that not only did Lochlain want me to leave Elenlea, he also doesn't want me to help now I'm back.

Heat surges to my face and I have to look away.

'We'll help her,' she says. 'We wait until Siosal makes his next move and then we take down those supporting his methods. We know the Custodian won't believe us yet, so we hit Siosal where it will hurt him the most – his numbers.'

CHAPTER TWENTY-TWO

'They're moving,' Ciara announces.

It's been two days since I met Rory and Aeyva and we've been waiting for Siosal's next step. We need to stop him but, now he's started again, Lochlain also wants evidence to take to the Custodian. Even if the chances of him accepting it are slim. But that was the compromise – Aeyva's plan of taking out his supporters and cleaning out the Whispers as well as collecting evidence. So ... a more violent version of what Will and I were attempting to do.

A stream gurgles in the distance, from where I now stand in Althea Forest, possibly the same one Will and I were searching for. So much of the compound we were held in was underground and I shudder at the thought we might have been haplessly wandering right on top of it, delivering ourselves directly to the Whispers. But then I wouldn't be here now, either. I wouldn't have an opportunity to stop them, or an opportunity for answers.

The birds have quietened down or left all together, they know this isn't a good place to be. I look around the grey tree trunks for a sign of amber eyes. They've appeared to me twice now, in different places, but I don't find those either.

We've split up to surround the area the Whispers are supposed to appear. Rory and Ciara make the apex of the triangle. Lochlain and I, along with Aeyva directly opposite us across the clearing, make the bottom two points. I'd suggested I go with her instead, but Lochlain stood firm and none of the others felt the need to argue.

I'm intrigued by Aeyva and I thought she'd be less distracting than Lochlain. But here I am, with my back against a tree and Lochlain's hard body pressed firmly along my side, his shoulders taut with tension. Luckily, the trees are large here, far grander than those the wolf found me in near Rhyton.

I'm wearing more blades than I'm used to, and Rory selected me a light – but deadly – sword as my primary weapon. I'd requested a pistol as well but there are no guns in the Realm. According to Rory, the Calahi are lethal enough without them and there is no honour in delivering that kind of death.

The fear that comes off Lochlain is not for himself, and I elbow him in the ribs.

'Quit worrying. I'm fine,' I say quietly, despite the strain in my tightly wound muscles. He opens his mouth but I cut him off. 'I know, I know, I shouldn't be here,' I say, mimicking his tone from earlier. 'Thanks for being so inclusive, Lochlain.'

He glowers at me, eyes black.

The forest goes still.

Stiller, if that's possible. But there is no screaming in my head. Soft footsteps approach from my left and Lochlain slowly rolls on his shoulder over the trunk, pressing into me so I am momentarily pinned between him and the tree. Physically shielding me. The footsteps move away, and we trail silently behind, Lochlain keeping close enough our arms brush. I can't hear the others but Lochlain's occasional sideways glances through the forest tell me they're not far away. Voices filter through the trees up ahead, not at all concerned they might be found.

We approach the edge of the clearing. There are six women lying unconscious between eleven Whispers, but I can't make out their condition from here.

Lochlain gently nudges me behind a tree. 'Stay hidden.'

His hands shake slightly which takes me by surprise. It's been obvious how dangerous he thinks it is having me here, but I hadn't realised he was *that* concerned for me. He draws his blade and steps into the clearing. One of the Whispers swears as he spots Lochlain and stumbles back towards the group. The others are quick to respond and have weapons out in an instant. They're highly trained as well, have perhaps even done the same training as Lochlain. A jolt goes through me as I realise he can never go back after this. A jolt of relief.

'Would you leave those girls if I ask you nicely?' he says, his deep voice a quiet rumble.

One of the Whispers, a man with short, blonde hair, stops dead.

'Sir—' he starts, but another steps forward, lunging at Lochlain. Before I can blink Lochlain has dropped him and one other.

The blonde one who spoke, steps back, hands raised.

Rory appears behind the group, twin swords out and bloody. Drawing my own sword with the intent to maim feels foreign. But I know how to finish people and, whatever it says about me, I will kill these Calahi if I need to. Perhaps I should stay hidden, I've never fought a Calahi before, but this is my fight, too, and I won't be sidelined.

My eyes on the girls, I step into the clearing. The electric current between Lochlain and I snaps against my skin as I enter his peripheral vision. He whirls to me but is too far into the clearing to push me back to the trees. I ignore him. Instead, I watch the two Whispers between us who have followed his gaze and are now grinning at me.

They approach faster than men should be able to move and I give myself to the calculating calm that descends. I catch sight of Aeyva in the forest, hands held out creating a shield against the power of the Whispers. Making sure none of us are brought to our knees by the screaming in our heads.

Looking back to the two stalking Whispers, I let them come to me for a beat as they cross the clearing. I toss the sword gently in my hand.

Two beats.

I strike.

The first Whisper goes down hard as my blade slashes across his stomach and I block out his dying sounds as he lays on the ground. The second has started to move behind me. I can sense Lochlain's wrath as he makes his way to me, but another Whisper blocks him.

I face the Calahi coming at me and meet him blow for blow, the metal screaming in the quiet forest. My arms ache with the impact as he strikes his sword against mine and drives me back. He's trying to separate me further from the others and while sweat starts to run down my spine, he looks like he's playing. There is nothing but death in his dual ringed eyes and I will never outlast him this way. I wasn't prepared for how much stronger the Calahi are.

Sweat stings my eyes.

I move to punch my blade through his ribs, but he spins and the metal glances to the side. It costs me my balance and I sink to a knee.

The Whisper laughs.

Dropping to a complete roll, I surge up on the other side of him. My boots gripping the soft ground. He spins to face me, a delighted smile gracing his face. Gathering what's left of my diminishing strength, I slam Rory's sword through his front. Blood splattering my face.

I lock eyes with Lochlain and he steps toward me, eyes wide as he watches me wrench the sword out. The Whisper slumps back to the ground with a dull thud.

Lochlain scans the clearing, looking for other Whispers. Only one remains standing, Aeyva's sword loosely pointed into his side.

Lochlain twists back to me. A storm crashes over his face and buffets my chest but he forces himself to soften. His eyes, still wholly black, survey me for injury from head to toe. Coming back to my face, he wipes blood off my cheek with his thumb before crushing me to him.

'Please don't do that to me again,' he says quietly. The desperation in his voice reverberates in my ribs. He holds me for a moment, his breath steadying.

I'm speechless when he regretfully releases me.

I glance back to the others. Rory and Ciara are sharing a look but if it's about Lochlain and me, they don't say. Aeyva's eyes take a long time to leave my face.

'He knew you'd do this,' the remaining Whisper says to all of us. A coolness settles in my chest.

'What do you mean?' I ask.

The blonde Calahi's eyes find mine. They're green with emerald rings and they close slightly when Aeyva's sword digs a little harder.

'He said ... this would be your weakness,' he says, still looking at me. 'He's going to make us do this'—he points to the women behind him—'until you return.'

Breathe, Lish, breathe. You knew this, it's not a surprise.

'We'll pretend you were among the dead today,' Aeyva says. 'I suggest you don't return to Siosal and you move your family from Elenlea.'

'Thank you,' he says. 'I hope you win this.' His eyes are on Lochlain as he talks and then he walks away.

Vomit burns in my throat and I can't help but look at the pile of women and think of the trauma they have already suffered because of me. I swallow and look back to Lochlain's pained face. General Siosal will know I was part of his downfall. I will make sure of it.

Ciara moves away and crouches by one of the women drawing the sharp gaze of both Lochlain and Aeyva. Her eyes flare and, even in unconsciousness, the woman before her relaxes.

I jump as Rory bumps my shoulder, his black hair absorbing the sunlight.

'She's making them forget,' he says, 'but cataloguing what she can of their experiences for the Custodian as well.' I stare at her, fascinated by what she can do. 'Come, we'll leave them to it. Ciara will finish up and bring Niamh home.'

I look for the horse I rode here but she's nowhere in sight.

Aeyva nods in agreement, her gaze flicking between Lochlain and me before she moves to join Ciara.

My head spins, trying to place this into a rational way of thinking, until Rory places his arm around my waist and grips Lochlain by the shoulder. Before I can see what Aeyva does, I'm in Ciara's back garden throwing my guts up.

'What. The fuck. Was. That?' I gasp between heaves.

Rory laughs heartily and Lochlain smirks.

'You didn't tell her?' Rory looks at Lochlain who's helping me up.

'I wasn't sure how long she'd be here, didn't seem any need to complicate things,' he says.

Rory slaps him on the back. 'Oh, my friend, you are doing well enough at that on your own,' he laughs.

Lochlain ignores him as he walks me up the back steps, my head spinning and stomach threatening to deposit more of its contents at the back door.

Cleaning myself up when I'm finally back upstairs, I stare at my face in the reflection, willing myself not to be sick again. The smear of blood on my cheek where Lochlain wiped his thumb is like a stain. Even if I can no longer see it. I've imagined killing the Whispers, or some of them, since I met them in the compound. I've imagined killing those involved with my mother's death longer. But I hadn't considered they'd bleed just like me. I joined the Guard in part to help me from a path of darkness. To give me a purpose – a good one – of protecting others instead. And now I've worn someone else's blood on my face. Listened to the sound of the sword I drove it through them.

But those Calahi were the worst of them, those that enjoyed the hunt. And I'd do it again to save those women. But, if I don't go back to Siosal, how many more will I have to kill to keep other women safe?

We share a takeaway dinner in Ciara's kitchen, which is a base much like my apartment was in Rhyton – except steaming hot food didn't appear out of nowhere in mine. Rory is still chuckling to himself about making me sick.

Afterward, we move to the living room and I find myself between Lochlain and Rory on the couch, Ciara and Aeyva are draped over the two armchairs.

'You had a particularly spectacular stack after that, if I recall,' Ciara says, laughing.

Rory cocks his head at her, a cheeky challenge in his eyes. 'There is no way I *stack* anything, thank you. My gifts,' he raises his hands, 'require immense skill and manipulation and I had a *learning period*. That is all.'

The two Calahi on either side of me take up much of the couch and the warmth from each of them leaks into my sides. But on my right the warmth is just that, warmth. Body heat. On my left, it feels like a living thing, the warmth seeking me out and toying with my senses. Lochlain shifts a little, as if he notices it too.

Exhaustion starts to settle along my limbs, and I say my goodnights. The joy they get from being with each other is clear and it tightens my stomach a little to watch them and recall the nights I did exactly this with my own friends. Lochlain and I are both staying at Ciara's once more, there was no second bed in his loft for me and he seemed unwilling to let me stay somewhere without him close by. As I head up the stairs, I realise I am slowing, waiting for Lochlain to see me to my room, as has become our routine.

He doesn't follow.

CHAPTER TWENTY-THREE

The smell of coffee drifts up the stairs as I make my way down. Lochlain's pants were too big to stay on my hips for more than a night, but I have adopted the shirt he gave me when I arrived in Elenlea for the second time. I'm wearing it and the thick, tight black pants Ciara gave me when I appear in the kitchen, my feet cosy in their woollen socks. Ciara stocked up on some basic wardrobe items for me but I couldn't quite bring myself to let go of the shirt just yet.

Lochlain has his back to me, though I know he hears me coming. Ciara calls out a greeting before passing me on the stairs on her way to get dressed. I need coffee. How quickly it comes back as part of a basic need despite so long going without. Lochlain shoots out a hand as I pass by him to get the milk and snags the hem of my – his – shirt.

'What's this?' he asks, pulling me to him slightly, his eyes on my face.

Copper flashes and melts away into darkness as he glances at my mouth. My cheeks warm and I hope he can't see it, but I hold his stare.

'Oh, just some old thing I picked up somewhere,' I say with a nonchalant shrug of my shoulder, my blood thrumming in my veins.

'Lish,' he says, his eyes darkening further and creating a pool of heat in my core. 'I need to tell—'

I hear Ciara coming back down the stairs and I pull away, finishing the making of my coffee.

'Loch, it's bloody Giving Day, did you remember?' she asks.

His eyes shutter at that and I look to her. She's got her pants on with her pyjama top, the thought clearly catching her mid dressing.

'What's Giving Day?' I ask, the heat I'd experienced just a moment before draining away at the look on Lochlain's face.

'Something the Custodian brought in ... almost 10 years ago now,' he says. 'You know it's nature that gifts us our abilities. Well, she's dying so—'

'What do you mean she's dying?' I ask. My mouth goes dry even as I know the answer. The toll it's taken on Rhyton.

'Nature, our world, it's dying – you call it climate change,' he says. 'Every month we have to give more of our gifts back to keep the Realm running.'

'But, how big is the Realm?' I frown. 'Surely you can't negate the effects of an entire planet being misused?' I ask.

'No,' Ciara says, 'we can't. But the intention was to try and sustain us for as long as we can. We were all in for that idea when it started. But we'—she looks to Lochlain—'don't believe it's working. Not yet, anyway.'

'How would you know?' I ask.

'Our people have never had to do this before, what we gave back naturally used to be enough. In theory, it's a cycle,' he says. 'If we can give back to nature, over time she can give back to us. But each Giving seems to take a little more of us and we're not seeing nature replenish herself. And, without our gifts, we cannot survive either,' he says.

'Are you telling me that once a month you give a bit of yourself, a bit you cannot replenish, and it is slowly killing you?' I ask.

Neither of them speaks.

I go to the Giving with them, wanting to see this for myself. Every individual that Gives is recorded so Lochlain and Ciara have no choice but to participate. Even if they did, I know neither of them would leave the others of the Court of Airlie to carry this burden alone.

Lochlain's tension is palpable at having me out in broad daylight. That Siosal might have Whispers looking for me here. But he was equally tense leaving me at Ciara's on my own and I refused to be left behind.

Ciara talks most of the way over the cobbled streets as I focus on the colour and the Calahi, not to mention the gorgeous buildings, attempting to soak in the beauty and not the roaring in my ears. Elenlea oozes character, its soul far more apparent than that of Rhyton. A storybook town full of small acts of magic. Like the woman ahead of me whose basket floats at her side, or the flowers that water themselves in the garden across the stone laneway, but there is a mix of those who openly show magic and those that don't. Of those who don't show their magic, only their beauty and eyes mark them as different to humans.

A small girl to my right slips on the stones, crashing to her knees. My heart tugs at her soft cry. A woman kneels before her, concern lining her eyes and lifts the child's skirts, placing her hands gently on the grazes. I can't drag my eyes away as a memory tries to make itself known. One of gentle warmth and kind hands and knowledge of pain wiped away. There was a lesson I was supposed to know but it's lost now to time.

We pass the pair and I shake my head, even as the nagging in my mind continues. What have I forgotten from that moment? I wrangle my attention back to Ciara who's still chattering, Lochlain quiet and watchful beside me.

'So, do you have a boyfriend?' I ask when she pauses for a moment, unafraid, given her own frankness with me.

'A dear one? Goodness no,' she says cheerfully and Lochlain bristles. 'I was due to be bonded, once, but it didn't work out. A good thing it didn't, too.'

I glance at her and catch the look she gives Lochlain.

'Bonded?' I ask, remembering Siosal's request of me.

'You know'—she waves a hand—'when you commit your life to another's. He wasn't my Soul Accord but, turns out, he wasn't going to be very good for me at all and Loch ... helped move him on. Loch tried to help him, to give him another direction but he ... is too attracted to the very thing we are fighting.'

'That's what Siosal asked of me.'

Lochlain stops dead. 'You didn't tell me that.' He stares at me, his eyes going black.

I frown, stopping along with him. 'Yes, I did—'

'You said he wanted to make it official.'

'Is it not the same thing?' I ask, frowning.

Lochlain's eyes slide to Ciara's.

'Yes,' she says eventually. 'It is, really. But it's still ... overwhelming to hear it. It's not what we initially assumed.' She touches Lochlain's arm and guides him on again.

I want to ask what difference it makes but I'm not sure I want to know the answer.

The long, hooded cloak I wear helps cover my face and keep me warm – something that's new for me to need. My new riding boots, courtesy of Ciara, wrap my legs from the knees down in chocolate brown leather. In the cold Elenlea weather I don't feel at all out of place, a handful of people around me are in similar clothing. But here they mostly wear an amazing array of colours and textures, many of which I've never seen before, with everything seemingly designed to showcase their beauty. So incredibly different to clothes solely designed for air flow and heat protection.

We line up outside an official looking building, one that's reminiscent of the Rhyton library with its stone pillars. Lochlain and Ciara flank me and Ciara's talking peters out. Lochlain is close enough to touch me but doesn't; I know it's so he can have easier access to the weapons under his cloak, should he need them. The ones he has in addition to what's under his clothes.

We've come early, as I'm told it can take a little while to recover and Lochlain prefers not to be out of action overnight. Many others have obviously had the same idea and there are several groups in front of us and joining quickly behind. It seems an event the Calahi mostly come to with others but there are a handful of single Calahi in the lines as well. They all talk softly, it's not a joyous occasion but one they are used to. I assume it's the same at the other venues they are taking the Giving throughout the city.

'About time someone put an end to this,' the female Calahi in front of us says to the male next to her. Her soft brown hair is pulled up into a braid that runs up from the base of her neck. 'Have you seen this?' she asks as a large piece of cream paper appears in her hands.

I can't quite tell what it is, but it's covered in writing.

'We have neither our Queen,' she continues, 'nor the right General in place. And the Givings just go on and on. They've got so much of our magic. When will they work out what to do with it?'

The male next to her murmurs something, I think in agreement.

'It's no wonder Queen Nakiasha and King Kailoh are taking an interest in us,' the first one says. 'Apparently, the Queen is hoping to visit soon. Scoping us out, is more like it.'

I stiffen as a voice calls out behind me, forcing myself not to turn around as my throat tightens. The conversation in front rapidly losing my attention.

'It's not him, Lish,' Lochlain whispers. 'He's not here.'

My heart thunders as my mind races through the what ifs. The back of Lochlain's fingers brush mine and I know he can feel the trembling there but I can't still them. My breath catches. I hadn't thought this would be so hard, that I would be so terrified to be out in the open with so many people – Calahi – any one of whom could be Siosal.

Lochlain squeezes my hand and turns to me, leaving Ciara to survey the crowd around us. His black and copper eyes burn into mine.

'Lish.'

I breathe into the sensation of his calming emotions. The urge to fight against him is markedly less than when we first met. Now, I welcome them.

'If he tries to hurt you again, I will kill him. Do you understand?'

I nod mutely, my pulse evening out with the gentle assistance of Lochlain. Absorbing the promise of death in his low voice.

'Okay.' I exhale.

Lochlain studies me a moment before accepting what he sees in my face and stepping to my side once more. I turn my attention back to the crowd, still looking for any flicker of purple eyes.

A gruff looking male marks names off a list before sending the Giver into a large chamber teeming with Calahi. He directs us to a long row of tables lined with Calahi in simple, forest-green uniforms. The chairs before them are quickly filled by the citizens of Airlie, to Give before they are dismissed to the waiting area. In the busyness, I slip past the tables and join those who have already Given to watch. As my name is not on the list anyway, they can't worry me for not Giving. But they can wonder who I am, and I fear being discovered here either by General Siosal or as a non-resident of Airlie. And what the consequences may be for either of those things.

From the waiting area, I can see Lochlain and Ciara facing the small tables, Lochlain trying not to look at me directly but marking my every move. The set of his jaw says he is well aware of the distance between us. His desire to protect is palpable.

They each push up the sleeves on their right arms and lay them flat on the small black tables. The uniformed collectors produce what look like medieval, hydraulic syringes. Bronze, with two large, circular finger holes to draw out the magic. Given the flippancy with which that term can be used in Driarn, it doesn't seem to hold the required weight of what I've seen here. But it's still magic.

Everything I have seen so far has been incredible; Will's healing, Niamh's ability to get me in and out of the Realm – which is so close, and yet so far, from Rhyton. Even Rory's ability to make me throw my guts up by zapping me around the place is amazing. But the term 'magic' is somehow not enough for what I feel when I'm here and the sense that it's ... right. That it calls to me somehow, the little gold flame in my chest burning brighter here.

Lochlain's collector is ready first and he braces himself as the needle is plunged deep into the inside of his elbow. She pulls hard and a copper-coloured, fog-like substance fills the syringe. Lochlain pales as she withdraws the needle and places the vial in a case at her feet having crossed his name from her list as well. She fills another two vials, each looking the same. I'm watching Lochlain so intently I don't notice Ciara approach. Holding a patch on the inside of her right arm, she slowly makes her way over to me.

'He is allowed to give less given his official place in the Whispers, but the stronger the magic in a person, the harder it is to have it taken. He'll be out of it for most of the afternoon.'

Over her shoulder my attention snags on a small group of people being forcibly pushed through the row of nurses towards a narrow doorway. They're silent but I can sense their fear from here. Some of them thrash against those that hold them. Others are already defeated.

'What – Ciara, what's happening?' My skin starts to crawl, a chill running along my spine.

She looks over her shoulder quickly before looking gravely at me.

'They're the humans that some Calahi sacrifice instead of Giving.'

My mind goes white. 'What?'

She looks at me, a combination of pain and sympathy.

'There are some who don't wish to, or cannot, Give and can afford to purchase a human to sacrifice instead.' She looks at me, her grief plain to see. 'They used to come from the groups General Siosal took – before we stopped him the first time. It's partly why Lochlain is so on edge having you here in the Realm. Having any trace of human in your blood can be enough for you to be seen as an opportunity. And ... well, no one wants to lose you.'

'But how –' I gape at her, uncomprehending. My vision blurs and the floor shifts. Ciara grips my elbow. *Sofia* I think. This is what I saved her from. Peta as well. But the countless others I did nothing for feels like a fist twisting behind my ribs.

'The life of a human is something ... somewhat magical in its own right, I suppose. And so it can be given in place of our actual magic.' She cringes as the words come out. 'Stopping General Siosal,' Ciara says quietly, 'instating the true heir, they are our best options for saving Airlie from itself as well as everyone else.'

Ciara and I deposit a very pale and wobbly Lochlain into bed, and I insist she rest up as well. Her eyes glaze over slightly as she agrees and heads towards her room. I wander aimlessly around the house for a while, looking at the small collection of photos Ciara has dotted around. Trying to distract myself from the horror of knowing those people at the Giving have been walked to their deaths for a world most don't even know exists. Of the knowledge that the Calahi face a death too, even if it's slower. One that comes on two fronts: the crippling of the Mother that provides them with their gifts, and the giving of it to the Court of Airlie.

There'd be protests in the streets of Rhyton if the people were asked to give something so important for no sign of what it was doing to help. I can't help but think this is part of the dullness that surrounds Elenlea. Not only the loss of their magic but their faith in the system.

I peek in on Ciara, who's sleeping peacefully and looks almost her normal colour, before heading to Lochlain's room to do the same. Cracking the door, I watch him breathing heavily. My feet move before my brain catches up and I find myself sitting on the well-loved, navy pinstripe chair next to his bed. The late afternoon sun stretches across the plush carpet bathing the chair and I soak in the glorious warmth.

Dark curls fall over Lochlain's pallid face, the faint smattering of freckles on the bridge of his nose drawing my smile. They're quite endearing, really, and I can't help but marvel at him. When awake, he's watchful and guarded; but like this he seems so peaceful. Slowly, I reach out and brush a curl back from his face, the silky strands soft against my fingers.

'You'll have to touch me elsewhere if you want me to purr,' he says.

I snatch my hand back and slap his shoulder. Suddenly incredibly grateful he is wearing a shirt.

'You scared me! You're supposed to be asleep,' I say, my heart racing.

He chuckles and opens one copper eye.

'I was, until a certain someone padded their way across my room.' He smirks.

I narrow my eyes at him, but the side of my mouth gives me away and I laugh.

'Sorry,' I say. 'Clearly you're fine and I will leave you in peace.'

He gently catches the tips of my fingers in his as I stand to leave and looks up at me. 'Thank you for checking on me,' he says.

I squeeze his fingers, my stomach skittering.

'Dinner will be ready downstairs when you're up for it,' I say, willing the warm blush to leave my cheeks.

CHAPTER TWENTY-FOUR

Something smashes on the timber floor downstairs, dragging me from sleep. I've slept later than normal. I'd tortured myself for half the night, wondering if Lochlain actually did want me to touch him somewhere else ... and where exactly that might be. Groaning, I resolve I should help clean up whatever has broken downstairs and see how Lochlain and Ciara are faring after the Giving. I haul myself out of bed.

Dread and anger start to uncoil along my limbs and I have to check myself in my sleepy state. But the emotions aren't mine. Lochlain.

I'm halfway down the hall when I freeze. A voice drifts up the stairs. A voice I'd recognise anywhere. Nails scrape down my spine, my stomach churning.

Odhran.

I curse myself for not keeping any weapons in my room and creep to the top of the stairs. Odhran's voice is still murmuring but I can't hear any responses.

'—really think he wouldn't work it out, did you?' Odhran is saying. 'A unit of Whispers totally wiped out. How many people would be dumb enough to give that a shot? And bloody lucky enough to pull it off?' he asks.

There's still no response. Holding my breath, I crawl on my stomach to the edge of the stairs and peer down through the railing as far as I can into the kitchen. I make out the back of Lochlain's head that seems to be bent backwards at an odd angle. His rage envelopes me, and I know he's alive and not injured – at least, I don't think. Yet.

I can't see Ciara.

'Fuck, you're an idiot, Lochlain. I know she's here and I'm taking her. He's had enough of your stupid games. Hand her over and he'll let you live. For now.' Odhran laughs. 'Looks like I will get you, after all,' he says softly.

I can't see who the last part is directed to but the boiling fury that fills the house and burns my skin tells me he's talking to Ciara.

'Tell me, though, why give it all up for a piece of ass? You could have had her in there, you know. I wouldn't have said anything, if you'd learn to share. You could have joined us. Now, you're just on borrowed time.'

My hands start trembling, both with Lochlain's anger and my own. There's also a touch of fear from him seeping in and I focus on the rage instead. It will be more useful. Briefly, I wonder if I should get a message to Rory and Aeyva but I don't know how and I don't have time to wait for them. My only course is forward.

I take the steps lightly.

'Morning! Oh—' I start, my shock not entirely fake.

Lochlain is being held by something I can't see but it grips him by the throat. He gasps softly, his head pushed back. Odhran has a partially clenched fist held towards him. His other arm holds Ciara against his side, a knife pressing into her throat. Odhran laughs in genuine delight.

'I knew you were here, honey,' he says. 'Are you finally ready to come and play with me?'

Lochlain strains against his invisible hold but I can tell just by looking at him he's not back to full strength after the Giving. Which is probably exactly the reason Odhran has chosen today to come.

'I guess that depends what sort of play you have in mind, Odhran?' I ask.

I look at Ciara, her gold eyes are wide as they look back but the terror there is not for herself. Some of the buttons on her shirt are ripped open and dark hair falls around her face. Her nails dig into Odhran's arm where she's gripping it and I can just make out a pink mark on his face where she's hit him. But he has both of them unable to move for fear for the other. And now for me.

'General Siosal has lots of plans for you, don't you worry about that,' he says. I walk towards him and Lochlain struggles as I put myself between him and Odhran. 'Tell me though,' he continues, 'how much have you sullied yourself with him? A woman of your standing shouldn't be fucking the likes of him. Perhaps you've debased yourself too much for us to play before I give you to the General,' he says. 'Maybe I'll take Ciara as well. It's been a while since I've experienced all she has to offer.'

I look between him and Ciara, understanding settling in. The thought of her bonded in any way to Odhran makes me physically ill. But it explains his obsession with getting under Lochlain's skin, there's more history between them than I realised. Odhran is sweating slightly and his dark auburn hair falls in his face. The knife he holds is dangerously close to the soft part of Ciara's throat. I say nothing and harness the anger that rises at his words.

'Did he tell you?' he asks. 'Did you know you were fucking a bonded man?'

My thoughts threaten to empty away but I focus on the nails cutting into my palm. Focus on those and not of the memories of the heart-break and humiliation a different man inflicted in the same way.

Somehow, it's worse now. Worse that it's Lochlain. Even though we haven't – I thought he was different. Special.

Asshole.

Slowly I turn to Lochlain who's looking at me with difficulty. The shame and guilt coming from him gives me my answer. And not the one I wanted. I step close to him, my back completely turned to Odhran, and fumble with the shirt he wears, gripping it with my fists.

'Why didn't you tell me?' I whisper forcefully. His eyes pleading with me. I turn back to Odhran and gently tug my sleeves down.

'No, I didn't know.' I let Odhran see the tears come to my eyes even as I force away the thoughts that accompany them.

'I wouldn't think so,' he says. 'I'd wager there's much he hasn't told you, despite you following him like a little lost lamb. What about the fact his father was the one who ordered your mother killed?'

I don't take my eyes off Odhran. My chest rises and falls heavily. His father. My –

The words rip through me, but I refuse to show it on my face. My stomach falls through the floor. I can't look at Lochlain this time, not even for Odhran's benefit. Lochlain's devastated, I can feel it. And so, so sorry, but I don't care. I won't care. I wanted answers and here they are. I knew they wouldn't be pretty.

But I didn't expect them to hurt quite so much, either.

'No response to that one. Interesting.' He laughs. 'Did he tell you who—' His mouth stops mid-sentence and a trickle of blood slowly starts to leak from the corner.

He drops to the floor, taking Ciara with him in slow motion. Behind me, I hear Lochlain's knees hit the floor as he gasps for air. He tries to call my name. Ciara swears and elbows Odhran in the ribs as she disentangles herself, despite the fact he was dead before he hit the floor.

I threw true.

It was a gamble, to be sure, that it was knives Lochlain wore on the straps under his shirt, but I'd never seen enough bulk there for it to be a large blade. And practicing throwing them with Will clearly paid off. I hit Odhran straight in the heart, slicing the sleeve of Ciara's shirt on the way.

I look at Ciara still unwinding herself from Odhran, blood soaking her shirt.

'Are you alright?' I ask her, my voice devoid of emotion.

She nods silently, her eyes flicking to Lochlain. I face him. Still on his knees, his dark curls falling in his changeable eyes. Right now, they're bright copper, almost as vivid as the red mark around his throat.

'Were you ever going to tell me?' I ask quietly. His mouth opens but I don't want to hear the timbre of his voice.

His eyes plead with me, but he has nothing to say and that's all I need to know.

I spend the day just inside the edge of the wood above Elenlea, where I can see who leaves the city this way – so I will know if they come looking for me. I do not wish to be found. I replay every interaction I've had with Lochlain for a clue; any clue that I misread the situation. That we weren't

... close. Becoming a team. That there would be some reason, other than pure selfishness, not to tell me about his father.

About his wife.

I've felt so stupid, naïve in their presence – these powerful, incredible Calahi whose heritage I partly share. But he's the reason I don't know what that means. That I don't know my family. My history. That I don't know *me*.

I press the heels of my palms into my eyes. I don't want to cry.

But it's spite that's driving that, I know. And the crushing weight of losing her drives the tears from my eyes anyway. Why did it have to be her?

I rub my arms. Even my skin feels dirty as I watch the evening begin to dance across the sky. Despite the suffocating emptiness in my heart, I can still appreciate its beauty. A tiny, furred animal with a white tail appears in the flowers at my feet, tentatively sniffing the ground before it. Warmth blooms in my chest as part of the memory I've been trying to recall these last few days is shaken free.

'See, if you borrow from me, your body will remember.'

I long for the rest to come but it's stubborn. All I can see is the blue bird I used to own, and I don't know why they come together. Perhaps it won't ever be clear, and this will just be yet another fragment of a life that no longer exists. One their father – a stranger to me – violently took from me.

I watch the little creature nibble on the coloured flowers that are closing for the night, loathe to disturb him. Equally unwilling to see Lochlain and Ciara again. But what choice do I have? Lochlain's loft, if I could even find it again, feels far too intimate. And, angry as I may be, I do not intend to spend the night in the wood on my own. Nor do I intend to spend it trapped in a house with Lochlain and Ciara.

To hell with this.

They are both in the kitchen when I arrive and look up expectantly at my approach. There isn't a single trace of Odhran's blood and the questions I once had about the lack of blood when we found Nico seem so prosaic now. The relief on Lochlain's face makes my stomach twist and I look away, heading for my room. I want to sink to the floor but my legs are restless and I pace instead, stopping before the wardrobe and flinging it open. In her shopping trip, Ciara had selected a sparkling dress as part of my so-called 'basic' wardrobe. It winks at me now, beckoning.

'You never know when the mood will strike,' she'd said.

Well, the mood has struck and oblivion calls. The one thing I thought I could hold on to in the wake of my captivity has been false and I can no longer trust my own judgement. So to hell with it. I want to forget where, and who, I am.

I take care to do my makeup, focusing on the details to occupy my mind, before tugging on my dress. It's totally outside what I would normally wear; which makes it perfect for tonight, when I want to forget who I am. I assess the short, bronze dress and the way it fits over my hips and waist. My curves are returning since my time in the compound and it works in this dress. The sleeves end at my wrists and twisting in the mirror I can see my back that's on full display as I pile my hair messily on top of my head.

Satisfied I don't look anything like myself, I grab my cloak and head out. Lochlain's eyes go wide as he takes me in, but he keeps his mouth shut.

Ciara just watches the two of us.

I walk towards the heart of the city and simply follow the music.

It's dark in the establishment I find and it pulses with want. A mood that's all encompassing as I walk through the door. I down several of the fluorescent drinks that hover at my elbow, blinking at their appearance but appreciating it all the same. There are a large number of young, unfairly attractive Calahi filling the different spaces. It's clearly a place designed to meet the needs of its customers and provides alcoves and booths where patrons can do as they please out of sight or, if they prefer, with an audience.

There are plush couches for intimate groups, surrounding a large dance floor in the centre. Chandeliers bob above our heads between trailing plants, hung from beams in the ceiling, and soft rugs cover different parts of the floor. I wonder how often they are ruined and replaced. Or perhaps magically cleaned.

Somehow, my drink is never empty and I chat with several strangers, who offer different coloured glasses during the evening. An unattended human is clearly a novelty and there's not a single Calahi here who doesn't know I'm among them. The effort to ignore them diminishes with every mouthful of drink that dances and pops on my tongue.

A very cute, younger-looking Calahi man with hair the colour of sunshine, like Blair's, waits with me for two drinks before inviting me to dance. The room spins as I get off the bar stool and he slides an arm around my waist and onto my hip to keep me steady. I lean into his warmth and we fight our way through the crowd to the dance floor.

Mahogany black eyes spark from one of the couches and I twist to face them but there's no one there.

The music is a fast, steady beat in my bones and we dance, our bodies finding their own rhythm. He's strong and his muscular arms feel good around me, I wrap my own around his neck. My awareness narrows to the man's hands travelling over my hips, down to grip my ass and back again, a bead of sweat running down the length of my back.

A dull voice in my mind wonders if this is a good idea, if this is really me. I squash it down with a squeeze of the golden man's fingers on my waist.

I took off my shoes at some point and, vaguely, I think I might have stepped on glass, but I don't care. He leans down and whispers something against my neck. I can't make out what he's said but it sounds like a question and I nod yes. He manoeuvres me towards the door and I somehow have enough faculties to grab my cloak – but not my shoes.

His hand runs continuously, slowly, up and down my exposed back. Strong fingers dip under the start of my dress, close to the curve where my ass begins, and caress my skin. I realise we're not out of the club yet and I pull him towards the door. He takes a step back as a large, dark figure walks in. I groan loudly.

'Fuck off,' I say and move to pull my dancing partner around him, but he doesn't budge. Not willing to challenge the bigger, clearly very pissed off, Calahi warrior in front. Not that he has any damn reason to be angry.

I look back at the golden haired one and try to focus on his face. It's possible his eyes are too close together to be really good looking but maybe that's because I lost count of how many drinks I had a long time ago.

'Sorry, Sir,' I think he says. 'I didn't realise ...'

I scoff.

'Forget him, he's just pissy because I know his secrets. Let's go,' I tug his hand again but he shakes his head at me. If I was sober, I might say there was genuine regret there but right now he seems like a coward and I roll my eyes. Fine. I'll leave on my own then.

I push past Lochlain and out into the freezing cold. What the hell happened to my cloak? I'm sure I just had it. The frigid air marginally sobers me, and I realise I'm limping. The glass wasn't my imagination.

Oh well, still drunk enough not to give a shit about that until tomorrow. I keep walking. Two strong arms lift me into the air like I'm a child and, even in this state, I don't have to look to know who it is. I push hard against his chest.

'Let me go, you asshole. Let me fucking go!' I scream at him, thrashing my arms and legs in an attempt to get away. But he's too strong for me and pins me harder against his chest.

The Calahi we pass don't even look uncomfortable. Nothing alarming about a large Calahi man taking a human woman against her will. It makes me sick. He says something in his gruff voice that I don't care to hear and slowly I give up fighting. I need to sleep and I'm suddenly very thirsty. I wish I don't do it, but I lean my head against the soft space between his chest and shoulder and place a palm against his heart. I shouldn't touch him, but I can't make myself stop.

'Why wouldn't you tell me?' I ask quietly, the blazing anger gone out of me. 'I was *six*,' I say, my voice breaking. 'She was everything and she – she was killed. In front of me. I—' Salty tears are escaping now. 'Do you know how long I've spent looking for answers? Fuck. The things I wanted to do to myself when I couldn't find them? Because it was my fault. Because I didn't save her. I realised too late we weren't playing a game and I just *sat there* as she was killed.' I suck in a shuddering breath. 'But it wasn't my fault, and you didn't want to tell me whose fault it was. Even though I *told* you the Whispers were involved. And what about ...' I push a bit harder on his chest and close my eyes. 'I don't – I don't understand.'

I don't know what I'm saying so I stop, tears burning my cheeks. We reach the house where Ciara is waiting. The worry on her face is how I imagine a mother might look waiting for her teenage daughter to come home. A look I never saw. Thanks to their father.

The tears keep coming and Lochlain takes me upstairs. He sits me on the edge of the bath and takes my foot in his hands. They're warm compared to the bathroom floor and I glare at him for it. I wince and swear as he removes a piece of glass, but the pain is gently washed away as my skin heals.

'You need to leave,' I say, 'I'm going to be sick.' He looks like he might stay and I grit my teeth. 'Leave me the *fuck* alone.'

I wish I could leave myself alone, too.

Ciara sits with me, instead, and holds my hair while I vomit and cry. I'm dimly aware that I'm curled into a ball on the bathroom floor while she stays with me.

'Why didn't he tell me?' I ask wiping my nose on the back of my hand. 'Why didn't *you* tell me? I feel like such a goddamn fool, Ciara. So fucking stupid. What am I even doing here? I left everything. *Everything.* Because I *trusted* him. I trusted *you.* And what I did to Phoenix – oh god—'

She shooshes me and strokes my hair.

'It's okay Lish, it will be okay,' she says to me quietly, over and over. I curl into myself more.

'No, Ciara. Her death will never be okay. Lying is never okay.'

CHAPTER TWENTY-FIVE

I don't know what's worse, my head that threatens to split in two or my stomach with its queasy tide. It must be almost evening and I sneak to the bathroom to drown myself in the shower. The thought of going downstairs makes me sick with apprehension but I need to eat. And water, I need water. Painkillers would be good, too, as every step pounds in my temples.

'How's your head?' Ciara asks as she hands me a black coffee. I grimace at it. 'Milk will be no good for you right now, so I wouldn't even try.'

'Do you have any painkillers?' I mutter. I look at her, remembering the look on her face last night. 'You didn't need to stay with me – I would have preferred you not to see me like that. I would have managed on my own.' I try to keep the bristle from my voice but she kept these secrets from me too. Secrets that directly impact me.

She waves me off before tying her dark hair back with her hands; at least she has the gumption to look apologetic.

'Forget it. Not your finest moment, I'm sure, but we've all been there. You sit, I'll make you something to eat.' She starts to busy herself with the task, pausing as she's turning away. 'I'm sorry, Lish,' she says quietly. 'We should have told you our suspicions about your mother and our father. It was a complicated time in our family and some of it has only more recently come to light.'

I can't help but stare at her, weighing my response. 'Why, though?' I ask. 'I don't understand why your father had anything to do with this at all.'

'The role of General in the Court of Airlie has traditionally been held by the same family line – my family, the Wolvertons – who protect the Throne. We are some of the best Calahi warriors you will find.' She smiles grimly at me. 'But Siosal challenged our father for the role before it could be handed to Lochlain. He didn't survive the challenge and now we have General Siosal. Joy that he is.'

'What were the grounds for Siosal's challenge?'

She turns back to me, her gold and black eyes full of sorrow. 'One I – neither of us – really believed at the time. But now'—her gaze drops to the bench—'now I'm less sure.'

I wait until she looks at me again.

'Siosal thought our father ordered the death of the Queen,' she says, 'by giving the Whispers the ability to take out whoever they deemed necessary. Siosal thought the Queen would be ... collateral damage. That she'd never be found.'

I swallow. 'And is that true?'

'At the time, we didn't think so. I don't really know how it all unfolded but, essentially, as General, our father was in charge of the search before Siosal. So the responsibility of anything that happened in the name of the search should have fallen at his feet. But Siosal thought it was more specific than that.' She takes a deep breath. 'And he's never stopped looking. If you were six when your mother died ... that was when our father was at the helm.'

I let that sit for a moment, trying to fold all the pieces into my mind. Work out where they fit.

'So Siosal has been trying to avenge the Queen?'

She shakes her head slightly, dark hair stirring softly around her face.

'I don't know. Maybe. But she was such a gentle person, I can't imagine him really believing she'd be comfortable with his choices. I think it's more likely he was looking to take back the life he thought he'd have and avenging the loss of it, instead.'

'But that doesn't change that your father was involved with the death of multiple women, including my mother. And that you both kept that from me.'

'No.'

I watch the sadness ripple over her features and let the weight of my words sit with her for a moment before I talk again.

'So, Lochlain is supposed to be General?'

'He still wants to be, yes. It's his duty and he is committed to the Throne of Airlie above all else.'

Clearly, I think bitterly, rubbing my temples. A fuzzy image of the Calahi male I almost left with last night comes back. How he called Lochlain 'sir'. How others have greeted him in the street. How Siosal demanded he wear his hood.

I breathe out heavily.

'And Lochlain should have told you about Aeyva—'

'*Aeyva?*' I interrupt. She nods and another wave of nausea hits me. Holy shit.

'Just when I thought I couldn't look any more stupid,' I mutter.

Ciara watches me, gold and black eyes waiting. I think back on seeing them together. They were close, but I hadn't thought they were *close*. I didn't think it was possible but this thought makes it feel worse. That I'd missed something right in front of me. At least last time, I genuinely had no way of knowing.

'I guess it makes sense,' I say after a moment, still looking at Ciara. If she can hear the hollowness in my voice she doesn't say. 'She's pretty incredible. He's lucky.' I don't know if I'm trying to convince her or myself that this makes sense.

Ciara waits, as if she's unsure of what she should say. I probably would be in her position as well.

'Does she—'

I stop as I hear the back door open and Lochlain strides in, halting abruptly before us in the kitchen. I feel his eyes search my face, but I don't look at him. I'm too busy trying not to notice how his presence makes itself known to mine, the soft hum caressing my skin. I am definitely fucked if I can't work out how to stop noticing that. Rory and Aeyva enter not long after and push past Lochlain.

'Oopphh, you look rough, Lish,' Rory says, raising his black eyebrows. 'Heard you had an interesting night, so we brought food.'

'A very interesting night,' Aeyva says quietly, her steel eyes flashing.

Lochlain shoots her a look and she smiles sweetly at him. A look so different to the one the other wife gave me. How did I end up back here? Despite all the promises to myself, how did I not see?

I force myself to look away, the anger probably clear on my face.

Rory waves the paper bags at me. 'These are my favourite,' he says, plopping them on the counter.

The hot, buttered rolls, stuffed with a filling I can't identify, smell delicious and I devour one. Somehow, it simultaneously clears my head and calms my stomach. I groan at the wonderful food in the Realm. I remain downstairs for as long as I can bear before I make a feeble excuse and escape back to the bedroom, the feel of Aeyva's eyes following me is like a brand on my back.

I think I hear footsteps on the stairs and I quickly shut my door.

My head is clearer the next day, thankfully, and I get ready efficiently, finishing braiding my hair as I head towards the stairs. I start making coffee for me and the tea for Lochlain and Ciara, trying to decide if I can face eating breakfast. Inhaling deeply, the scent is vaguely familiar and I remember my mother sitting at a red gingham table, drinking a cup of tea. Laughing.

It was the same table she died at.

Lochlain and Ciara move around upstairs and it's Lochlain who is the first to join me in the kitchen.

'Morning,' I say flatly into my coffee.

I'd considered ignoring him altogether but I opt for distant civility, instead. My goal of bringing down General Siosal hasn't changed and I need his help. I also need Aeyva to think I can be part of their team, not someone who's trying to steal her husband. Their relationship still doesn't add up to me but the scars of being an unwitting third person in someone else's marriage remain. And I don't intend to get any more. I hand him his hot mug, careful not to touch his fingers, and move to the table, leaving him in the kitchen, still unable to meet his gaze. Those damn changeable eyes, they'll haunt me forever.

'Lish,' he starts but I cut him off.

'It's fine, Lochlain, forget it,' I say. 'I've spoken to Ciara – I know your father is responsible for more than just my mother. That doesn't make it hurt any less.'

'Please, let me—' he says.

'Honestly, I'd just like to forget it all.' I remain focused on my cup as his sorrow washes through me and I desperately hope he can't tell what I feel in return.

'All of it?' he asks quietly.

'All of it.' As if there is any other choice.

Ciara appears at the bottom of the stairs, pausing to take us in. She comes to the kitchen a moment later and picks up the mug I left on the bench for her. Her eyes glaze over for a moment and Lochlain stands up straighter, suddenly more aware of her.

'What is it?' he asks.

'Message from Haryk,' she says, her eyes clearing.

I look between the two of them.

'They're bringing back more women,' she says.

Rory gets us to Althea Forest and I take a few moments to let my stomach settle, taking in the death that already surrounds us. The twisted and falling trunks are the most obvious, the muted sound the next. There are fewer green leaves in this part of the forest than where Will and I were taken.

I've paired myself with Ciara this time, Lochlain and Rory go together, and Aeyva is once again on her own. Lochlain tried to insist I stay near him and out of sight, but I wouldn't entertain the discussion and left with Ciara before he could voice more weak protests. While part of my heart warms at his concern, I am not his to be worried for. And I made my decision before returning to Elenlea – I won't stand idly by.

I'm not sure I totally believed Ciara when she told me about her mental communication abilities but, when I hear voices filtering through the forest, it's hard to deny. The forest falls totally silent as the group approaches, the same as the last time, as if it doesn't want to bear witness to the evil they do. The clearing we surround is smaller and I peek around the tree I stand behind.

The sound of metal-on-metal sings around the forest and bounces off the trees, distorting where the fights are happening. But clearly Lochlain and Rory have made their move. Ciara and I step out and I face the Whisper in front me, the connection between Lochlain and I tightening. I glance at him and Rory, who move like two halves of a storm. They're mesmerising. I take a blow to the cheek for my distraction.

'He's going to kill everyone you care about,' he says.

I spit blood.

I fight back with a vengeance, fuelled by humiliation and rejection, and drop him with a knee to the stomach and the pommel of my sword in the back of his head. The wet crack chilling my blood with the song of a memory I have to force back down.

Ciara is liquid through the small clearing, Whispers falling in her wake. I highly doubt she will need any assistance from me, but I stay close all the same. Aeyva remains on the fringe of the clearing. A Whisper edges towards her. I can't tell if she's seen him approach or not. I assume she has but, now I have seen the potential threat, I'd never be able to live with myself if I got it wrong. Especially knowing what I do now – my character is not that questionable.

I look back to Ciara once before breaking away and running across the clearing towards Aeyva. Halfway there, another Whisper blocks my path. I barrel into him, throwing my weight behind my borrowed sword and plunging it into his torso. I keep moving for Aeyva but the Whisper stalking her is too close, I won't make it.

She still appears oblivious.

I drop to one knee, skidding slightly across the dead grass in the centre of the clearing. There's a Whisper approaching behind me but I block him out for now, taking these precious moments to focus on Aeyva at the edge of the treeline. Grabbing one of the throwing knives I'd requested from Rory, I throw.

It catches him in the thigh hard enough to stop his approach. I twist and drive my sword into the Whisper just about on me from behind, using my back leg for leverage. A surge of relief floods through me as I see Rory spot the one near Aeyva. He moves like lightning towards her as two more come to me, grim expressions on their faces. I shove off the dead Whisper and withdraw my sword, grimacing at the sound. Ciara's finished with the one I left her with and races towards the unprotected girls.

Lochlain is behind me somewhere, I can still feel the slight hum of our connection, slightly sharper in this setting, and I can hear him. Looking between the two approaching Calahi, I make a quick assessment. They are almost within reach and I strike out for the one on the left. As he steps back to dodge my blade, the one on the right leaps forward and I take a blow to my right shoulder that knocks me backwards. I stumble as they now effectively pin me between them and circle, like dogs hunting their prey. I spin slowly on the spot, tracking them, my sword arm bleeding heavily and losing strength. I'm out of my depth. They are better trained and faster than I am. One on one is hard enough for me to keep up with and put down. I don't stand a chance with two.

Alarm that's not my own slices through me – it's Lochlain that's seen me first. Angry as I am, I hope he doesn't get distracted by it.

'Lish!' he calls. *Shit. Focus, Lochlain.*

I'm still spinning slowly and he comes into my vision in time for me to see him look away from the Whisper he's fighting. Without taking his blazing eyes from me he plunges his sword into the Whisper's middle. But he doesn't see the short knife the dying Calahi male draws on his way down and slashes across his side. My vision blurs, the surge of terror all my own. I palm my last throwing knife and land it in the neck of one of Whispers circling me.

Rory is with me in an instant and slits the throat of the remaining Whisper. I look back to Lochlain to find Aeyva cradling his head where he's landed in the soil. It crashes back to me that this is how it's supposed to be. She's trying to stem the bleeding as I and the others start approaching, but it's not slowing. Black and copper eyes are trained on me as I kneel on his other side and I wish he'd look to her instead. She's efficient but tender in how she presses down on his chest gently with one hand and lifts his shirt to examine the wound with the other. A large, red slash of flesh is ripped into his tanned side.

'Can you not heal yourself?' I ask quietly, willing the tremor in my voice to still. My arm throbs and I angle it away, out of sight.

'Not since our magic has been fading and being siphoned off at the Givings,' he says. 'We heal faster than humans but no, I can't heal myself like you're thinking.'

His voice is a little strained, but he doesn't sound too bad. I look to Aeyva.

'It's not terrible,' she says, 'but we don't have time to walk back with him like this and the pressure of travelling with Rory could be too much, forcing too much internal bleeding. We need to stop the bleeding here and try and patch him up before he can be moved.'

'None of you can heal him?' I ask, looking around.

Ciara and Rory have reached us now, Ciara looking for all the world like she'll strike him herself for getting injured, and Rory looking around us in case we missed any Whispers.

'Mine is – no. We'll just have to pack the wound and get Rory to shift him,' Ciara says.

The memory of the day with Will in the fire room at Siosal's compound comes back to me and the difference between having a little time to think about what to do with the person before me and none is glaring. I close my eyes.

'See, if you borrow from me, your body will remember.'

I don't think I've thought of those words before seeing the mother heal her little girl in Elenlea. The little blue bird dances in my memory again, my fingers stroking its belly. Its chirp when it shook off its injuries.

'Can I try?' I say quietly.

Aeyva's steel-coloured eyes shift to me, assessing. She glances at Ciara, something passing between them. She nods once. Taking a deep breath, I place my hands on the wound like I'd seen Lochlain do to Will, his skin hot under my fingers. Blood oozes slowly between my fingers and I have to remind myself it is not that day. Not that man. I will not lose anything today. I have nothing left here but my cause, anyway.

Closing my eyes, I picture the bird. It's little round body no bigger than the palm of my tiny hand. Its feathers were the most remarkable blue – sapphire, like the eyes of the beggar woman. I feel the shadow of something then and focus on my breathing so as not to scare it away. I remember the sensation of Lochlain healing me in the compound and the warmth of his hands around my foot in Ciara's bathroom. I can feel Lochlain's eyes on me and the forcefield that exists between us seems to give way.

Gold flickers in my chest and I draw a thin thread from the flame. *Remember,* it sings. *I remember,* a quiet voice sings back. I guide it into my hands and to Lochlain, trusting it to heal him. He's not dying, yet, and so I gently and steadily pour what is now a sapphire stream across and into his wound. Aeyva inhales across from me and Rory swears, a smile in his voice.

Carefully, I open my eyes but I don't dare move my hands. My palms tingle and I think I can feel his breath. I can't bring myself to check. To find the gaze I can feel watching me.

Ciara's eyes are on my face when I find hers instead of his. A knowing there I turn away from. One I can't face just yet.

I find Rory's mahogany eyes instead. 'Did it work?' I ask.

He frowns.

'Only one way to find out,' he says softly as he kneels next to me and removes my hands. He rocks back on his heels and lets out a breath. 'Definitely not just a pretty face, are you?'

Aeyva leans across Lochlain's chest, whispering to him and I dare to take him in. He's starting to sit up and, while still quite bloody, there is now a raised, angry red line across his side. It looks rough but his skin is no longer gaping or bleeding. I hope like hell it's healed underneath as well and he's not still bleeding internally.

His emotions crackle around me but I can't see his face behind Aeyva.

'You're both idiots,' she says without looking at me, but it's clear I am one half of the intended audience. 'And you'—I think she grips Lochlain's chin—'should know better.'

Slowly, I back away and enter the forest, leaving them be. I sink down against a large tree and look at my hands. Hands covered in Lochlain's blood that are now trembling so badly I press them under my armpits as I rock against the trunk. What I've just done is impossible, and overwhelming, and raises so many questions that I can't think straight. I feel whole and empty at the same time.

My mother knew and she isn't here to help me understand. Help me harness it, whatever it is. Without that guidance, I want to run as far as I can. With her gone, my team left in Rhyton, and the others hovering around Lochlain and Aeyva, I cannot hide from how incredibly alone I am.

My sobs now audible, Rory comes to me slowly, like he might approach a wounded animal. The cracking in my chest is painful and for a moment I am that six-year-old girl once more. The one who so desperately wanted her mum to wake up and save her.

'Lish?' he asks, gaze flicking over me.

I look up at him, unable to stop my tears. His eyes flare as he registers what he's seeing and he disappears us back to Ciara's.

CHAPTER TWENTY-SIX

The trembling hasn't left my hands and I rush my eating in the hope the others don't notice. The food sitting like lead in my gut. A headache forms between my eyes as I try to focus on their words. But the images of Lochlain's blood circling down the basin as I washed my hands – and a tiny blue bird – are what dance before me.

I'd tried to wash away the thoughts that crowd my mind, as well, but they remain. A black mark I can't remove.

'I don't think anyone's properly focusing on what the hell went down today,' Aeyva is saying as I gaze vacantly around the table, their faces blurring. 'Lochlain'—she fixes him with a glare—'was so distracted he got himself seriously injured—'

Lochlain opens his mouth to speak but she holds her hand up to him.

'Sure, you weren't dying but it was going to make it pretty damn hard to get you out of there safely. It was a stupid injury to get and for a stupid reason.' She visibly calms herself. 'This is exactly what I was talking about, Loch. You can't be both. Even if it wasn't impossible, one of you will end up dead.' Shame constricts my throat, but I make myself meet her gaze. To listen.

My face heats.

'You're right,' I say, taking a deep inhale. 'It was sloppy and Lochlain shouldn't have gotten hurt.'

My voice wobbles but no one says anything, waiting for me to continue. But looking at these extraordinary warriors before me, I feel so small. So … human and my stomach ties itself in knots. I clear my throat, willing myself to keep moving forward. To take the next step. Warmth caresses my skin as Lochlain's brow furrows with concern. I clear my throat a second time.

'I think the time for these small, reactive attacks has ended. Siosal was clear – I go with him, or he keeps taking them, killing them. Including everyone I love.'

My voice catches on the last word and I flinch at Lochlain's reaction, his unyielding anger flying against me. I rub my forehead where the pressure builds.

'Honestly,' I say quietly. 'What's the worst that will happen if I just go with him?'

'Over my dead fucking body,' Lochlain grinds out, his eyes black.

I place my cutlery down, my hands shaking with the effort not to slam it. Aeyva's steel-grey eyes flick between us. Ciara places a hand on Lochlain's forearm and whispers something I can't make out.

'What would you have us do, then?' I ask and then jam my teeth together.

Silence is my only answer.

Lochlain looks at the table and my injured shoulder throbs in warning as my pulse quickens.

'We need to talk about the challenge,' he says.

Aeyva looks sharply at him and it's like a hand grips my throat. Lochlain wants to discuss the challenge ... the same way Siosal killed his father? Sweat breaks out along my hairline. I have to get out.

My chair scrapes loudly on the floor as I push back from the table.

'Lish, wait,' Lochlain says.

I keep walking up the stairs and down the hall. He catches up to me at the bedroom door and lightly grips my elbow.

'Please, stop,' he says.

I wrench my arm out of his grasp harder than is necessary, wincing at the pain in my shoulder, and turn to look at him.

'Why, Lochlain?'

The copper rings in his eyes catch in the hovering hallway lights as his gaze flicks between my shoulder and my face. He's debating what to say and the jumble of feelings I wish weren't so familiar are now also reflected in his conflicted expression. I throw my hands up in exasperation.

'Seriously, what's the point to all of this?' I gesture between us. 'I shouldn't be here. Whatever is happening is driving a wedge between you and your friends. Your *wife*. And it's dangerous. You could have been really fucking hurt today because you were too busy worrying … about me.' I've cracked the floodgates a fraction and the emotions I've been trying to keep from him start to bubble to the top. 'If Siosal really is going to try and kill me, then fucking let him.' I glare at him. 'I can't be part of this, Lochlain. Of you being hurt. Hurting others. Coming between you and Aeyva; it's not me. But do you know why Siosal won't kill me? He doesn't *want* to. He wants to *own* me.'

My words are hurting him, the sensation sitting uncomfortably against my skin, but I don't try and understand it.

'I'm sorry, Lish,' his eyes are sorrowful, 'I've managed this really badly.'

'That's just the thing, Lochlain. I don't want to be *managed*. I thought you were – I thought we were … perhaps friends.' His face darkens a little and I look away.

'We are friends, Lish,' he says.

'No, Lochlain,' I shake my head, 'we are not. This is a very one-sided relationship, and you know it is. You hold all the keys to the kingdom, and I have nothing but give everything anyway.'

He frowns at me. 'The keys?'

'Forget it, it's just an expression. You get my point,' I say. 'And you should have told me about your father. I – I expected you to be honest with me.'

His dark hair is starting to curl up, framing his face. Absently, I wonder how many people pay for hair like that.

'You have every right to expect that.' He takes a deep breath. 'Because … you matter to me,' he whispers. My chest constricts as if it might fracture in front of him.

'But I can't matter to you, can I?'

'There's … something you don't know,' he says quietly.

'Yes. And you had the audacity to lecture *me* on second choices. You arrogant, self-entitled prick.' I shove at his chest with both hands.

Slowly, as if trying not to spook me, he takes my shaking hands in his and holds them in front of our chests.

'I don't want to do this,' I say. But damned if I can withdraw my hands from his. 'I've been here before, Lochlain,' I take a deep breath, trying to pull myself together. 'I've been this person, the *other* person, and I didn't know. It was – I don't want to be that person.'

And I will not break that vow, even for you.

'You're not that person,' he says softly. 'Not with me, it's—' He looks back down the hall before taking another step towards me, my hands still in his. 'But you're right,' he whispers, eyes searching mine. 'You're right, I've handled all of this so badly. You – you took me by surprise and things have been moving so fast since we got out and I didn't think you were coming back.' He pauses but doesn't look away. 'I'm sorry, Lish.'

My eyes prick with tears.

'I'm so sorry,' he says again, his voice pained. 'I never wanted to hurt you.'

He lowers his forehead to mine and I close my eyes, the sting of tears sharp.

'I made a promise to Aeyva a long time ago that I can't break.'

My breath catches against the pain in my chest.

'But you asked me once what was real,' he says. I keep my eyes closed. 'For me, this is real.'

Several moments pass before I open my eyes and stare up into his face, the hurt still flickering in his eyes and I wonder what's reflected on my own.

'Please come back downstairs with me, I'll talk you all through what I'm thinking about Siosal,' he says. 'Hear me out. And, if you still want to leave, I will take you home. I can ... put provisions in place for your safety.'

I raise an eyebrow at him. 'You mean *you*, don't you? You'd come and watch over me?'

He dips his head in a shallow nod. 'I would never let anything happen to you, Lish,' he says gently, squeezing my hands.

'That's a ridiculous suggestion and how would it even work? You have a wife to go home to remember?' I ask softly.

'It's a long story,' he says.

'I wouldn't know,' I retort.

'You will,' he promises. His hands are warm around mine and he presses them against his chest, pulling me closer. 'Please, don't leave. Not yet,' he whispers. 'I want you to know.'

The field between us threatens to envelope us both and I pull back a little. I don't know what will happen, or what I will do if it happens, and I make myself think of his wife sitting downstairs, probably wondering what the hell we're doing.

'You better pour me a fucking big wine,' I say, and his smile is all the reason I need to stay. I pray to any god that will listen to save me from myself.

'It's time,' Lochlain launches straight in before we've settled on the couches in front of the fire.

Aeyva assesses me with her grey and blue eyes. It could be my imagination, but I think she's both slightly surprised and pleased I returned. Another piece I don't understand and file away for later – wishful thinking, most likely.

Lochlain looks sideways at me. 'Someone said something to me about keys to a kingdom—'

'I don't like where this is going, Loch,' Ciara says, fiddling with the dark braid that hangs over her shoulder.

'I know, Ciara,' his expression is serious, 'but it's time.'

'I don't think we're ready,' she protests.

Aeyva sits forward in her seat and looks at her, gentle concern lining the corners of her eyes. 'If we're not ready now, Kiki, we never will be. So either we work out the details and make our play, or we leave it behind. I, for one, vote for the betterment of the Realm.'

'Me too,' says Lochlain even if his gaze is a little uncertain as he looks at me.

'Well, you know I'm in,' adds Rory, leaning across me to chink Lochlain's glass with his own. They look to Ciara who leans her head back against the couch and closes her eyes.

'Clearly, I am still outnumbered in this debate,' she sighs, 'but you know I will support you.' I stare hard at Lochlain waiting for an explanation. Ciara nods in my direction. 'But you can tell Lish what you're planning, I'm not doing that for you.'

Being the last ones to arrive, Lochlain and I are seated next to each other on the couch. I nestle myself as close to Rory on my other side as seems appropriate in an attempt to touch as little of Lochlain as possible. He said it was real for him. But how do I process that when I'm sitting across from his wife? If Aeyva worries about our proximity she doesn't show it.

Lochlain shifts so his back is against the arm of the couch and his folded leg presses the length of my thigh. I focus on his face and put my blush down to the wine he poured me – very big, as requested.

'The first Ruler of the Realm, Queen Roisin,' Lochlain says to me, 'had a large sapphire that is rumoured to have held incredible power. Legend tells that the power of the sapphire corrupted her soul and, when she died, it was smashed into four pieces. The largest piece remains with the occupant of the Throne of the Court of Airlie – in the crown – and the remaining three are scattered throughout the Realm.

'Our father held one of these pieces while he was General and it was supposed to be passed to me when I took on the role. But the current General challenged him for it and killed him in the process, meaning he took the sapphire and the role. The only way for me to get it back, and take the role, is for the General to die or vacate the role without an heir in place. Or for me to beat him in a challenge,' he says.

My heart goes out to him and Ciara; I understand the pain of losing a parent to violence. But when he was involved in my own violent loss ... I don't know how to reconcile those things.

'A challenge?' I ask. 'And, if you win, you will be General?'

'Yes. I will take my rightful place as General and I can formally, and without losing human lives, find the heir to the Throne,' his eyes burn into mine.

'I'm guessing the challenge is going to be a little harder than a chess game, for example?' I ask. I know what the answer is, but I need him to tell me. It's Ciara, though, who answers.

'Correct, Lish. It's a challenge to death or submission. If the challenger loses, they forfeit the right to challenge again,' she sounds resigned. This is clearly a conversation they've had several times before.

'Why now?' I ask Lochlain and he hesitates. 'The truth, Lochlain,' I say.

I notice a flicker of amusement in Aeyva's eyes and look away from her. He's trying to hold his emotions back and let his words convey the messages but it's hard to ignore the heaviness that settles around me.

'Three reasons,' he says. 'I think you're right about Siosal. He will keep going until he draws you out. It's become too big an issue for him now to walk away from. And I'm done playing in the shadows. It's my duty to protect the Throne and the Court and I can't let it go to hell under his watch.'

He leans back and looks at the others. I wait for a beat, but his third reason doesn't come.

'That was two,' I say.

'What?' he asks.

'That was two reasons, what's the third?' I ask and I can feel the others watching me.

A seriousness settles on his features. 'Because I think we are closer to having the heir to the Throne than ever before ... and I need to be in the role of General to ensure their ability to take the Throne safely. Under no circumstances will I let General Siosal bond his way to King.'

A challenge to death or submission. I'm trying to wrap my mind around this and take comfort in the submission ...

I look away, the other thoughts I haven't been willing to face racing forward in my mind. Trying to demand my attention. But I'm not sure I'm ready for them. If I just had some time to better process, to—

'We need to work out the details, then,' Aeyva says across my thoughts. 'We need to confirm our numbers. Who have we got firmly in our corner?'

'Numbers?' I ask, letting my attention be drawn back to the conversation.

'To make a challenge, I need to have the support of a minimum of eight. Which is a problem,' Lochlain says. 'In addition to the four of you,' he glances at me, and I raise my eyebrows, surprised I would be included in this. That Airlie would recognise me as valid support. But I guess that's not quite true, Airlie should definitely recognise me as support. Even if they don't know why yet.

'We have Nuala,' he continues, 'who'll come back for it, but I don't think we can expose any of the Royalists, not after the loss of Benny. We have support from some of the more influential families, but they are unlikely to stand publicly with us. Not yet.'

'The Elmwoods might,' Rory offers.

'Who are these people? Are there criteria they have to meet?' I ask.

'They need to be willing to show their hand to the current Custodian,' Ciara says. 'Nuala is a Manorynx, and a highly respected one.' She frowns a little at me. 'I'm sorry, I'm not sure there is an equivalent to a Manorynx in your world. I'm not sure how to explain her ... she's like a knowledge keeper. A magically powerful one.'

'The Royalists and Benny,' Lochlain says, 'you already sort of know. The Royalists, including Haryk from the compound, are those that support us in righting the Court. And Benny'—he turns to look at me—'was a librarian in your world.'

My stomach drops away and I know I can't hide from this anymore.

'But the supporters need to be from different bloodlines or Courts,' Aeyva says. 'The prominent families won't stand publicly yet,' she continues, oblivious to my turmoil, 'because, if the challenger, Lochlain, loses, they could be facing the retaliation of General Siosal.'

I try not to shudder at the memory of his touch.

'So,' Rory says thoughtfully, 'if we can't present a complete cohort of prominent Realm families, we'll need a show of warriors. Highlight we have strength on our side as well as Wolverton blood.'

'What if—' I start, thinking of my team.

'No, Lish, I don't think—' Lochlain says quietly, eyeballing me.

'You don't even know what I was going to say and it's a no?' I ask.

I'm in two minds about suggesting it, though, and maybe this gives me an easy out. But there's a growing murmur in my heart that tells me I need to stand up and fight for my home. And that I am working out where that is.

'I know exactly what you're going to say,' he says, 'and that's why it's a bad idea. Siosal can be unpredictable and dangerous.'

'I can ask my team,' I say to the others. 'There is no guarantee they will agree, of course, and I have no authority over them – they're my friends. My family. Even if I did, I would never force them.' Lochlain is shaking his head, but the others look at each other and not him. 'But they will at least hear me out.'

'Could it work?' Aeyva asks Rory, who's resting his chin on his fist. Ciara looks like she knows the answer but isn't prepared to give it away yet.

'I – possibly, yes,' he says. 'I don't recall there being a need for all the supporters to be from the three courts in the Realm. We'd have to be clear they were guests of the Court of Airlie but ... the appearance of an alliance from outside the Realm may actually work in our favour.'

'Right,' Aeyva is decisive. 'I'll contact Nuala, she might have others who will come with her, just in case the humans are out. Ciara,' she looks at her, 'can you work with Lish to get a message to her team?'

Ciara nods slowly.

'But training starts straight away,' Aeyva says. 'We need to be at our absolute best and prepared for anything. Now is not the time for complacency. You get one day to recover from today, Loch,' she says.

He winces. 'Who put you in charge of training?' he asks.

'You did, smart ass, and for good reason. I'm done for tonight, see you soon.'

She leans to kiss Ciara on the cheek and plants one on Lochlain's head. Try as I might, I can't see any heat in their touches. Rory stands from the couch, leaving me to fall slightly into the space he leaves. He laughs.

'Do you want to join me?' he winks.

'Goodnight, Rory,' Lochlain says in mock admonishment.

The sound of Rory's laughter disappears out the door.

The burning sensation in my skin fades as a gentle knock on my door breaks into my dreaming and I gulp down the crisp air and morning sunshine. I'm still out. I'm no longer in there.

But the look on Siosal's face when he touched me for the first time in the fire room stays with me, even in my waking moments. A look he didn't give the other women. Because of what he learned about me.

I can't help my thoughts drifting to Lochlain. Seeing him. His presence, and the sensation of his emotions running along my skin, warms parts of me I didn't realise needed it. Despite his commitment to Aeyva, I find myself wanting to get lost in him. In those black and copper eyes and what I can tell he feels for me. In the realness he said it has for him. Because I know it's real for me. Despite the hurt I still nurse that he didn't tell me about her. About his father.

'You're too polite, Loch,' says Rory's muffled voice on the other side of the door before he bursts in and strides across the room, breaking through the gloom that had started to settle on my chest. God he's gorgeous, and his swagger is contagious. I look up at him through my eyelashes and smile.

'This is a pleasant surprise, Rory. I didn't realise I'd need so little effort to get you into my bedroom,' I say.

'You, my dear, can have me in your bedroom any time you please.' He laughs, enjoying our little game. 'But it's time for you to rise.'

The jealous prickle from the doorway tells me Lochlain doesn't enjoy it as much. I shouldn't torture him but ... part of me wants to see how he'd react. I ease myself out of bed. My singlet and knickers aren't exactly what I would have chosen for this, but they leave little enough to the imagination to be effective and I haven't been able to bring myself to wear his t-shirt again. Rory drags his eyes across my body, almost entirely for Lochlain's benefit I'm sure, and I swear I can almost hear a growl from the doorway.

I stand on my toes and pop a good morning kiss on Rory's cheek. I pad across the room for my robe that's hanging on the back of the door where Lochlain is still standing. Very well aware of his eyes roving over me.

'Good morning to you, too, Lochlain,' I say, unable to hide my coy smile. He tears his eyes away, although they don't miss my hastily bandaged shoulder, and I delight in the blush that dusts his cheekbones.

'Excuse me,' I say as I brush past him on my way to the bathroom.

Rory's laugh booms down the hallway and I hear the slap he makes on Lochlain's back as I walk away.

'Oh, you are in for a world of pain, my friend,' he says.

I don't hear Lochlain's response as I shut the door, grinning to myself.

Aeyva waits downstairs and I immediately regret my little show. I know they're bonded, and I swore never to interfere in this way again. Regardless of what conversations Lochlain and I have about it.

'You're with me,' she says.

'What?' I ask. 'Since when am I involved in training?' Her steel-coloured eyes fix mine.

'Since you decided to join our little band of rebels.' She cocks her head slightly and smiles at me. 'And since you displayed some of your magic traits. You may now consider yourself one of my troops,' she says looking me up and down. 'An out of shape, new recruit.'

My eyes slide to Lochlain who shrugs apologetically.

'He won't save you from me, I'm afraid,' she says. 'I demand the best from my team and, if you are going to stand with us at the challenge, you need to be at your best, too. Airlie will require it.'

Aeyva's regime over the ensuing days is brutal. The worst part is how right she was about just how out of shape I am. We fall into a steady rhythm of training in the early hours of the morning and late evening, using the soft darkness to aid our cover. Lochlain, Ciara and Rory have their own training and teaching, and I spend most of my time with the fifty or so Royalists Aeyva mentioned before. Those who want to be part of whatever might come after Lochlain challenges Siosal for the role of General – to help find the rightful heir. But they can't do that if the whole of Airlie knows who they are. Not yet.

After a particularly rough day, I gingerly lower myself onto the couch. Everything hurts; I copped a number of kicks in the side and a savage blow to my face. The Calahi are fast and brutal when they need to be. I'm pretty sure I've cracked some ribs and I'm a little worried about my cheekbone. The others arrive after Rory brought me back, their session having gone longer, and Lochlain stops dead in his tracks when he sees me.

'Fuck, Aeyva, what did you do to her?' he asks.

'Nothing she can't handle, Lochlain. She's not made of glass.' She rolls her eyes.

He holds his hand out to me. 'Come, Lish, I'll take a look,' he says.

The pain in my face is too great not to accept the invitation.

Lochlain drags over a small stool in the bathroom and instructs me to sit. Kneeling before me as he does, we're about equal height. He lifts a hand to my cheek and I flinch. I'd grumble at him but my jaw and cheekbone are too sore, so I don't protest. A subtle look of concentration crosses his face as his black and copper eyes fix mine. Slowly, the pain starts to subside and I can feel my cheek returning to its normal size. My heart hammers in my chest, somehow I need to stop my fall down this steep, slippery slope.

But a small voice protests that Aeyva doesn't seem to be staking a claim to him. Nor does he seem to have any romantic feeling towards her. Not that I can feel. But being wrong about this would be crushing.

'Your freckles are the colour of dark chocolate, did you know?' I ask.

His eyebrows lift in mild surprise. 'I didn't, no. My freckles are not normally the thing about me people notice. Or point out, for that matter.'

'Oh? You mean there's something better about you to look at than your freckles?'

Not quite the direction I'd intended to take. He looks at me and I desperately try to ignore the thrumming of air around us as he tugs the neck of my shirt away to place his hand on my shoulder.

His eyes narrow. 'You should have told me about this,' he says quietly. I ignore him, the reasons for not telling him too heavy. The dull throb that's hounded me since the last attack on the Whispers slowly slips away.

'Lift your shirt,' he says.

I blink at him. 'What?'

He can't seem to help that stupid half smile that makes my skin tingle. 'Your ribs, Lish, I need to look at them please,' he says.

'Right, of course,' I stumble.

I lift as little of my shirt as possible, and he slides his large, tanned hand up my side. Perhaps this is payback for the other morning. My breath catches at the pain, but it, too, starts to ease and my breathing returns to normal. At least, as normal as it can be.

'You know it's a bad idea, right?' he says. He hasn't moved his hand and I realise I can't actually breathe.

'Yes,' I whisper, searching his eyes.

'I mean your friends,' he says kindly.

Fuck, of course. I need to clear my head.

'Maybe. But I can ask them. For you, I will ask them,' I say.

'You're not going to try and stop me?' he asks.

'Would you?'

'No.'

'Not much point then, is there?' I ask.

'So, you'll help me, instead?'

'It's what friends do isn't it? I think that's what we agreed to be?'

Slowly, so slowly, he runs his hand back down my side and removes it, helping me stand. I sway a little on my feet and he walks me to my bedroom door.

'Thank you,' I say.

He puts a hand on my hip and leans down to whisper in my ear.

'Just for the record,' he says, his breath tickling against my neck, 'I will make you pay for that little stunt the other morning. And, I promise, soon you'll find out if there is anything about me worth looking at more than my freckles. And if we're ... *friends*.'

He walks away without looking back and I slide down the inside of my now closed door. Rory is wrong. It's me that's in a world of trouble.

CHAPTER TWENTY-SEVEN

Ciara greets me with a smile and a steaming mug of coffee. I accept it gratefully and nestle myself into a couch, she has quickly learned I can't function without one in the morning. Aeyva has given me one day off to let my ribs and face shake some of the remaining tenderness. But only one, and I intend to enjoy it, even if I'm plagued by tiredness.

I look out the large windows that face onto her street and catch my reflection. When I first came here, I wasn't sure anyone would notice how much I'd changed in my time at the compound. Now I know they wouldn't. My hair is the same, albeit it a little longer; my shape is much the same, even as Aeyva's training helps it remember its strength. I can't see the details of my eyes from here, but I'd wager they look the same as well – they also don't reflect what I have found about myself here. And yet, my Calahi heritage is undeniable, despite the lack of rings in my eyes.

I listen to Ciara in the kitchen as she prepares food for us and the thoughts I have been avoiding make themselves known. Taking a bracing sip of my hot coffee, I let them come.

Siosal recognised something in me when he touched my chest that first night. Something he hadn't found in all the previous women.

My gaze moves past my reflection and to the potted plants on the balcony beyond, the colours blurring in my distracted vision. Distantly I note how vibrant they are in the morning light.

I swallow, the hot liquid running down my throat reminding me of the burns Siosal made on my skin. The constriction that seems to sit permanently in my chest tightening. There's only one reason Siosal would have made me stay, asked me to bond with him.

He thought I could replace my mother.

The woman Lochlain and Ciara's father took from him. From both of us. If she ever loved him at all. Perhaps my own father was the one who really did the taking from Siosal. But I think of him, my father, in a detached sort of way. I have literally nothing to give me any indication of who he was.

My mother, though, I know she had gifts too. I don't know how similar to mine, but she was trying to teach me how to borrow hers. And I know she was running.

Now, I'm running as well. Just in a different way.

'They were our mother's favourites,' Ciara says as she sits on the armchair across from me. I blink at her.

'Pardon?'

'The pink flowers,' she says, looking out the window as she cradles her own mug.

'They're beautiful,' I mumble, still grappling with my thoughts. Their ramifications.

My back tingles, announcing Lochlain's arrival. Ciara's gaze flicks to him as he comes to sit with us as well. I watch his broad shoulders as he lowers himself next to me instead of his face, my thoughts now well and truly focused on what he said to me last night and trying to contain the heat I can feel racing across my cheeks.

He looks between us, and I take another sip of my coffee.

'What's going on?' he asks slowly.

'I was just telling Lish about Mother's flowers,' she looks at me suddenly and I meet her gaze. It suddenly turns quizzical. 'I hope I didn't upset—'

'No,' I say, 'not at all.'

I smile, trying to calm my hammering heart. I need to say something, but I don't know what the right words are. How do I tell them I think I'm supposed to be Queen of a place I've only just come across? That perhaps the wolf was guiding me here?

Lochlain turns to Ciara and asks her a question I don't hear but she remains looking at me.

'I think,' I start, talking over Lochlain. 'I think I need to talk to you about something.'

The full force of Lochlain's gaze finds me then, understanding the seriousness in my tone. I build my barrier up as hard as I can, but I still feel his expectant apprehension. Sighing a little, I relax my hold against his emotions. It's obviously pointless where he's concerned.

Would have been good if she'd been around to teach me about that better. And how to take on her role as ruler of the Court of Airlie.

I blow a forceful breath out my mouth, very aware of my shaking hands and gripping my mug a little tighter.

Alright Lish, you can do this.

'You know Siosal wanted me to bond with him, right?' I ask.

Ciara nods, Lochlain narrows his gaze.

'I think ... he knew ...' I clear my throat. 'I think I'm the heir.'

Lochlain blows out a loud breath.

'How would he have known?' Lochlain asks.

'He ... touched me,' I say and Lochlain immediately goes still, 'the first time I met him. And ... something in me'—I don't know how to explain how my flame reached for him, just slightly—'responded to him. Like it knew we were similar. He wasn't at all interested in anyone else there, but he seemed to go to great lengths to get me to stay. Is still trying to get me to volunteer to go back ...' I trail off. Ciara and Lochlain stare at me. 'He said he felt like he knew me, that—'

I'm gripped by doubt suddenly and I hold my shaking hands in my lap to steady them.

'I think the wolf was trying to bring me back ... where I belong.' I lift my gaze to them again and look between them.

'He touched you without burning you?' Lochlain asks, anger dancing across his features at the memory of the time I was actually burnt.

'Yes,' I say quietly.

'It's one of his abilities,' he says, turning towards me, eyes going dark. 'To confirm bloodlines – it's why the Custodian leaves him to it.'

I exhale. Part of me thought they'd deny it if I said it out loud.

They exchange a look before Ciara smiles at me, her hand at her chest. Lochlain's face is slightly more subdued, but the pride in it is reflected in his feelings that run along my limbs.

'Wow,' Ciara says, her eyes wide. 'This is – quite huge.'

Lochlain's hand finds my knee, and he gives it a small squeeze.

'Are you okay?' he asks, his eyes sparking with copper.

I press the heel of my own hand into my chest, my heart still beating wildly and a manic sounding laugh escapes me.

'I don't really know yet,' I say, looking between them again. Wondering if I could take Lochlain's hand. 'You haven't challenged me on it though.'

They look at each other, Ciara still smiling. 'We have something for you,' she says. She disappears back up the stairs and I can't stop my hand from falling to Lochlain's where his still rests on my leg.

'Do you think I'm crazy?' I ask softly as I trace his knuckles with my finger.

How is it possible for this to feel so natural when I know who he actually belongs to? But the feeling he creates in my chest could be so much more than the hurt. And so I let go a little.

He laughs softly. 'No. But what we're about to get into might be,' he says, twisting his hand around to lace my fingers in his. I stare at where our palms connect, butterflies dancing behind my ribs. From both my admission and the sensation of Lochlain's skin on mine.

Ciara's footsteps thump gently down the stairs and I take my hand back, swallowing. Lochlain takes my lead and slowly removes his as well. She hands me an envelope and I drain my remaining coffee before taking it and turning it over in my hands.

'What is it?' I ask slowly.

'Open it,' Lochlain prompts gently. He's close to me and, yet, I yearn for him to be closer. To help me through this. Instead, I drag my eyes away and tear the envelope open. The sound too loud in this quiet, waiting space.

My dearest Adelais,

I have arranged for this to reach you in the event two things have occurred. Firstly, my time has come. Secondly, you have worked out, on your own, who you are and who your mother was. It is not something you can be told, and I am deeply sorry for your loss.

I desperately wish we had more time to discuss what all this means but that is not to be. Please know you and your mother were so very loved by your father. His life was ended too soon and we were all robbed of what should have been. There is nought we can do about that now.

Your mother will have told you about the Blue Pointed Star. You need to find it.

If all has gone to plan, you will have part of this already – the Wolverton Pendant.

Your task is a difficult one and I will be as clear as I can: claim your Throne, find the pieces of the Blue Pointed Star. This is a huge weight to lay at your feet and I am immensely sorry for the responsibility you must bear. But there are things that only Roisin's line can do, and you are what remains.

Please know, your identity was never intended to be a secret from you, your mother would not have done that. Her desire was to tell you when she thought you old enough to understand, teach you everything she could and then, when you were ready, return to the Realm with you and take back her Throne. She will have shown you what she could, even if those memories are hazy and I regret there is now so much you need to work through on your own.

I know this will seem overwhelming, but I have every faith in you and I will be with you each step of the way. Even in death, we search for the ones we love as I searched for you, and watched over you, for so many years.

Stay strong, all my love

Benny X

Benny – the librarian. The room seems to tilt on its side and I lean back on the couch, looking out at the sky and focussing on the small white clouds I can see.

I turn my head to Lochlain.

'Did you know?' I ask. My voice shakes a little.

'Not at first,' he says quietly. 'But I started to wonder about your abilities when you made that flower bloom on our way here. On our way out of the compound.' He scans my face. 'But he didn't take you – you were already in the forest, so I hadn't actually thought about it before then. I was still – I was still looking for you and I didn't realise you were already there. When you left, I sort of thought it was possible but ... I wanted you to be safe and it was better not to look too hard at it. But then you came back. And when you told me Siosal asked you to bond with him, it started to make sense to me then – why he gave you the choice to stay.' His chest expands with his inhale. 'But I wasn't completely sure until just now, when you said he touched you.'

'And you?' I ask, looking at Ciara.

'Loch filled me in on the General and the flower just before you arrived.' Her gaze flicks to him. 'I was doubtful, definitely. But, talking with you, there were just too many parallels.' She breaks into a grin. 'And then you were able to find your way back into the Realm with the help of a wolf. It's as if the very land was welcoming you back.'

I look down at the librarian's letter in my hand. Even the smaller parts threaten to overwhelm me. Someone searched for me, looked out for me. What a different life I might have had if Benny had taken me. But one without Will.

There's pain in my chest as it sinks in. I met him, had a connection with this man, and I had no idea. He died that night. The timing of his death propelled me down this path, but I couldn't face the possibility that he knew things about me.

Now, it's abundantly clear he was killed because he helped me. Without his journal, I would have never ended up here. It was significant on the path that has led me to this moment. But the weight of these expectations physically drags at me.

Adelais, he called me in his letter. The same as my mother did. The name the orphanage carer couldn't pronounce and changed to Alice. That a young Will took and created his own version of. Lish. Me.

'How do you even know him?' I ask them, blinking my eyes to clear them of the moisture that's beginning to gather.

'His name was Nathaniel Bennett – Benny,' Lochlain says. 'He was a Manorynx and Adviser to our father in his role as General for many years. After your father was murdered and your mother ran, he left the Court and positioned himself in the human world to look for you.'

The thoughts rampaging through my mind try to drag me out of the conversation. I vaguely recall Ciara telling me there is no equivalent to a Manorynx in Driarn.

'He was part of your Royalist group?' I will myself to focus. To not get lost in all this means.

'Passionately,' Ciara says. 'He was very fond of your mother and supportive of her relationship with your human father. He reported you missing.'

The photo Will found in that missing person's file tugs at my memory.

'Why did neither of you tell me your suspicions?' I ask.

'Because you needed to work it out for yourself,' Ciara says. 'You knew your mother best – what if we'd been wrong?' She looks at Lochlian, who's gaze hasn't left my face. 'And we need your heart because if it's not in this, we will all fail.'

'And you think my heart is in it now?'

My heart is very, very far from being in this. My heart has only just poked out from underneath its blankets. The letter I hold might as well be trying to force it back under.

'It's a lot to take in,' Lochlain says carefully. 'For all of us. But we don't have a lot of time and—'

'Siosal knows who you are,' Ciara finishes for him. 'If he manages to get his hands on you again, you will be bonded to him before you can blink – there will be no more waiting for you to choose. Crowning him as King.' She looks genuinely apologetic. 'I'm afraid that's not something we can allow.'

The violence humming from Lochlain is sharp against me and I suck in a quick breath. Ciara looks between us.

'By that, I mean it's not something you, we, or Airlie would survive,' she says.

Lochlain's eyes flash and his fists clench and unclench on his knees, as if willing himself to calm down. I watch him as I push a comforting sensation through him, a reassurance that I will never bond myself to Siosal. It's an intimacy we shouldn't share, but his gaze is grateful as I look back to Ciara.

'So, if I let my heart be in it as you say, how exactly am I supposed to do these things?' I ask, waving the letter. 'He says I should already have a pendant?' I ask.

'We'll figure it out,' Lochlain says. 'Together, we will figure it out. The first step though, is for me to take my role as General, that's how we get the Wolverton pendant back. And I – we – need you to have someone you ... trust to protect you. Having me in the role is the first major step to being able to crown you Queen. I know I – you can trust me, Lish, I promise.'

I think of the role his father had in my mother's death. Of his bonding to Aeyva. Is he the person I trust to protect me as I do this? As I close my eyes to focus on sorting through his emotions, I realise I don't need to.

I already know.

Sleep is hard to come by that night. I spend hours thinking through what the challenge could entail and weighing up if I should really bring my team into it. It's not their problem but, despite that the Realm didn't mean anything to me not so long ago, it's been drawing me in.

I can no longer hide from my responsibility to it. Even as I avoid thinking about the letter and what it means has to come after. There's an answering melody here that calls to me. To the little flame that shimmers.

The house is quiet as I head to the backyard to clear my head, seeking Niamh's presence to soothe the sharp edges. And I'm not alone. Ciara sits on a bench, looking at the stars, and I silently take a seat beside her. She doesn't bother to wipe away the tears that reflect the moonlight.

'The stars are beautiful here, don't you think?' she asks softly.

I lean back and watch them with her. They're incredibly vibrant in a way they never were in Rhyton, as if someone splashed luminescence across the night sky. They remind me of the nights I spent with Will in Althea Forest, before we were taken. When I could appreciate the beauty.

'I take it there's no talking him out of it?' I ask in return.

'No,' she says, the sadness in her voice is crushing. 'This day has been coming since Siosal challenged our father. We knew he would never win, but he was too old and proud to submit. He wasn't prepared to hand over his last remaining dignity as well. But I wish it didn't matter so much to Lochlain.'

'He really thinks it's important enough to risk his life for?'

'To Lochlain, honour and loyalty are everything,' she says. 'He was bound to the Throne before he was born, and he will serve it until he dies.'

She sighs. 'Two of the greatest risks to Lochlain are General Siosal and this stupid challenge and his duty and ... love for Airlie.'

'Which worries you the most?' I ask.

She laughs gently.

'You're astute, Lish, I'll give you that. The challenge is terrifying of course, and I will never recover if we lose him that way. But, at least in his view, he will have died with honour and attempting to serve what he loves. But, how he manages his sense of love and duty, if he can't bring those things together ... I fear that would break him in a way nothing else could.'

'So, why take the risk at all? Why not leave the Custodian where he is?'

'Because we're running out of time. We can't have a Custodian indefinitely. One of the other Courts in the Realm – Rothani most likely, but possibly Mercasia – will come to take us over, or the Givings will mean there is nothing left of us, anyway,' she says.

'Is that where the visiting Queen is from?' I ask, remembering the conversation I overheard at the Giving.

'There's a rumour about that, yes,' she says. 'But I don't know anything officially. The three Courts have, at least in recent history, a fairly stable relationship. But their interest in Airlie has been increasing. I fear it won't be long until one of them decides to move against the weaker Court – us – and add to their borders.'

She turns to me, her dark hair unbound and falling delicately around the blanket she has wrapped around her shoulders. There's a silver patch on her hair where the moonbeams reach and I can't look away.

'You really care about him, don't you?' she asks.

I scoff. 'You mean my drunk tears didn't give me away already?'

She remains quiet, watching me in the silky darkness and the knowledge I can tell her anything without judgement descends.

'I feel like such an idiot knowing how obvious it is to everyone and I'm sick to my stomach at what Aeyva must think of me. But yes'—I sigh—'I care about him. I haven't worked out how to turn it off yet.'

'Would you want to? Turn it off I mean?'

'It would make it easier, wouldn't it?' I look up at the stars again. 'But I honestly don't think I could let him go if I tried.'

She takes my hand.

'He needs you to hang on, Lish. That sense of duty makes him his own worst enemy. But don't let go. Not yet.'

'Why, though?' I ask. 'He has Aeyva.'

I don't know if I really want to know, but their relationship is a question with no answer for me. A question I'm unsure I can bring myself to ask.

'It's not a story I can share,' she sighs. 'I know it probably seems like a strange thing to say, but if you can wait...' She doesn't finish but gives my hand a squeeze before leaving me in the dark.

The loneliness and fear from earlier in Althea Forest come back like waves on the shore, each one hitting harder and harder, choking the air from my lungs. It takes me several minutes to collect myself enough to go back inside.

I let the steam fill the bathroom as I sit on the cold floor of the shower, trying to leave the day behind. Hopefully, it will help me sleep. My head spins. The parallels between the librarian's – the Manorynx's – letter and my mother's own stories are undeniable. Not to mention the things I have been able to do. The healing Lochlain did in the cells should have been impossible. And then I repeated it. I *borrowed* his power and my body mimicked it.

The countless occasions I have bent other's emotions flash before me. Something I never remember learning, just an innate ability to help. I drop my head to my arms and let the scalding water pound over my shoulders and neck. What a different life I would have had if my mother had lived. So many secrets I wouldn't have had to face on my own.

Self-pity sits uncomfortably with me. Just one more thing the orphanage frowned on, and I found out on my own that it doesn't do me any favours as an adult, either. So I force myself to stand and turn off the shower. The sudden cold prickling my skin.

I dry myself roughly, ticking through the reasons I shouldn't be a Queen.

CHAPTER TWENTY-EIGHT

I hand my dead phone to Ciara. It hasn't had any reception in the Realm and I eventually stashed it in one of the drawers in Ciara's spare room. Her brow creases as she holds it momentarily and it pings into life. Shuddering in her palm as the messages flow in.

'It won't last indefinitely,' she says, handing it back to me. 'The magic will close back over and shut out the … signal.'

A slice of pain furrows its way into my chest when I open our group chat, the morning sun gently warming my window. Unable to read the multitude of messages I've missed, I keep scrolling and ask if they would meet me in a secluded spot outside the Realm.

Ciara explained no one can enter the Realm without being a guest of a Realm resident, so they can't enter on their own. Something that never occurred to me when I arrived on Niamh with no Calahi escort. In theory, we should also be harder for General Siosal to stumble across outside the borders. But his primary hunting ground is outside the Realm, so I don't find that argument particularly compelling.

The conflict I feel about even talking to Will and the others about this, what it opens them up to, churns in my gut. But they serve Rhyton just as I did, and I know they won't stand the injustices of General Siosal either. And of course, Will and Phoenix have personal reasons to want to stop him as well. I would be disrespecting their ability to decide for themselves if I didn't ask the question. I would be livid if they didn't ask me.

Riley is the quickest to respond. *Lish! Where the hell have you been?! Of course we will come and chat. Consider me intrigued …*

I drag myself to my bedroom knowing full well sleep will elude me, despite another day of Aeyva's training.

My heart leaps into my chest and I yelp. I'm not alone.

Lochlain sits in the navy armchair beside my bed.

'Sorry,' he says. His gaze travels the length of my body. 'How are you feeling? About everything?'

I laugh, the sound a bit hollow.

'Like I'm falling down a spiral staircase.'

He smiles softly.

I should stay where I am in the doorway, my whole body trembles having him in here. In this space I have come to call my own. The only patch of space I have. Letting him in here flings open the door to me being, feeling, like the worse version of myself. I didn't choose to be the intruder in a relationship last time, and I certainly didn't this time. Even if I can't see the romantic connection between he and Aeyva, there is still the lie. That he let me end up here without a warning. Without an indication this was a dead end.

But then, perhaps that's not quite true anymore either. He said I'd know. That it's real for him. And bit by bit my anger at him is fading away. He's not his father, just as I am not my mother.

He watches me, caution on his face, and I know he's assessing my indecision. He runs a hand through his hair, disrupting his loose curls and my feet move without instruction. I've taken a single step when he's out of the chair and reaching around me to shut the door.

The air leaves my lungs as he stands before me.

'Are you okay?' he asks quietly.

'I don't know,' I whisper.

He cups my head and strokes a thumb over my cheekbone. I close my eyes and lean into his touch, just slightly. Tears well behind my lashes.

'I can't be a dirty secret, Lochlain, I – I don't want to be a stain on your life.' I keep my eyes closed, I can't bear what I might find in his.

'Oh, Lish.' He exhales and takes a step closer. Close enough I can feel his warmth radiating along my skin. 'I would never ask that of you. You know there's no love there, from either of us ... but it's a story I promised never to tell.' He takes a deep breath. 'When I made that vow, I never thought I'd ... know someone like you. Care about someone ... like I care about you.'

The weight of his emotions and my own threaten to buckle my knees.

'What would you ask of me?' I'm not sure I've spoken aloud.

He groans. Tipping my head back, he leans down and places his forehead on mine. Breath tickles my face with his exhale, the heat of his body running the full length of mine. The tears escape then, and I squeeze my already closed eyes.

'I ...' he says slowly, 'would ask things of you that aren't fair. Things I don't get to ask. Not of a queen.'

My eyes fly open at that and immediately find his black ones, the copper burning around them.

'What if I want you to ask? What if I want to decide for myself what's fair?'

His fingers shift into my hair and tingles run down my spine.

'What happened to my shirt?' he asks.

I blink.

'What?'

'The shirt you claimed, you're not wearing it.' His eyes drop to my mouth to watch me respond.

'I – it felt too intimate. After.'

'Do you still have it?'

'Maybe.'

His full mouth pulls into a gentle smirk. My stomach flips. He drops his head to where my neck meets my shoulder and my head falls back. He runs his nose up the side of my neck and places his mouth against my ear. Goosebumps explode on my skin and heat pools in my core.

'Don't let go of it,' he whispers, his soft lips caressing my ear.

He pulls back, grinning, and walks away. Leaving me a trembling mess.

I bounce slightly on my toes as we wait, my heart hammering with impatience to see them. I place my palm against the dying tree next to me, looking at the forest floor that's now mostly dirt. My chest aches at the destruction here. There's been no violence, but the decline weighs on me heavily.

On impulse I push a small wave of my gift, whatever it is, into the trunk. Green leaves burst forward, outlining my hand, tiny white flowers dancing at their intersections. I snatch my hand away and blink. They remain. A question explodes in my mind—

Riley is the first one to spot me and she crashes through the thick wood, crushing me in a hug.

'Oh god, it's good to see you, Lish,' she says against my hair.

'You too, Riles.' I squeeze her back just as hard. She draws back from me, her gaze cutting away immediately. She sucks in a gentle breath as she takes in the group of Calahi and moves away to introduce herself.

Will, Sofia, and Phoenix are the next to appear, with Hayes and Blaire just a step behind. Will rushes to me and lifts me off my feet momentarily in a bear hug. Phoenix hangs back to let Hayes go first and I feel Lochlain's eyes on me as Phoenix takes a step forward, my heart fluttering in my chest.

'Phoenix, I—'

'I know,' he says tightly as he presses me firmly to his chest.

Pushing his emotions away, I grip him. That he even came after how much I hurt him is an incredible relief, one that gives me a small hope we might be able to find our way back to being friends. I didn't expect to see Sofia but it's a very happy surprise and I hug her too. Blaire has tears on her face as she approaches.

'I missed you, Lish. So much,' she says.

I'm still holding her hand as I introduce the two groups. The immediate, gravitational pull between Rory and Riley on the periphery of my senses. Will takes a step towards Lochlain.

'I take it you are ...' Lochlain dips his chin and Will grasps his hand. 'You're different without the hood. Thank you,' he says.

Sofia appears at Will's side, effortlessly linking her fingers in his. She leans into him slightly but emotion overwhelms her and whatever she was going to say to Lochlain. Tears well in her eyes as she covers her mouth with her free hand. Lochlain presses the heel of his palm to his chest and lowers his head, making my chest contract at the enormity of bringing them back together. Of what we escaped, and Will found.

Watching them all together, I notice subtle differences I hadn't before. The Calahi move differently to those from Rhyton. There's a fluidity, a grace, to the way their bodies cut through the air, almost predatory. Hayes watches them with narrowed eyes. His hand, I know, is not far from his knife. He probably has a pistol tucked away somewhere as well.

The space is tight, but I roll out the picnic rug we brought and start popping out lunch. If I could look past the thinly veiled apprehension of both groups, and the weapons everyone carries, we almost look like a group of friends out for some fresh air. Almost.

Lochlain sits beside me, across from Aeyva. Will and Phoenix both pretend not to notice, Phoenix's body practically singing with tension.

'Much of this is going to sound crazy,' I say, looking at my friends. They look back intently.

'Don't censor on our account, Lish. Just tell it like it is.' I look gratefully at Riley.

I hadn't thought I would be nervous about telling them but, now, the words to describe the Calahi – and magic – are stuck in my throat. How to tell them I am supposed to be royalty in this strange, magical world totally defies me. And I am definitely nervous of their response.

I want to help Lochlain, but the thought of possibly sending him to his death is more than I can comprehend. Nor do I want to bring my friends into a dangerous situation but working with them again calls to every basic need. To have them support me as I work through what my heritage means is something I physically long for.

I take a breath.

'In a nutshell, the activities of the Court of Airlie, where this lot live,' I say, nodding my head at the Calahi beside me, 'are under at least partial control of General Siosal – the one who's been leading the abductions, who burned me. The one who ... hurt Will,' I say.

Lochlain's hand moves almost imperceptibly, and the tip of his little finger touches mine. Aeyva looks down, but says nothing. From the other end of the rug, Phoenix glares straight at Lochlain, who stares right back, the current between us prickling.

'The role of General rightfully belongs to Lochlain,' I say, trying to ignore him and Phoenix. 'If he doesn't take it back, he can't formally stop the abductions the Whispers are carrying out while Siosal waits for the ... person who can claim the Throne of the Court of Airlie. To take the role back'—I glance at Lochlain—'he has to challenge General Siosal to a fight to the death. But, to even make the challenge, he needs to have a certain number of people to stand with him.'

Not surprisingly, it's Riley that speaks first.

'Right. Putting aside some of the more confusing, although important I'm sure, terms you used in that little speech – not to mention the totally archaic piece about fighting to the *death* – essentially, you want us to make up the numbers to support ...'

'Lochlain,' I provide.

'Lochlain,' she continues, 'to challenge this asshole in said fight to the death?'

'What makes you think you will win?' asks Phoenix, assessing Lochlain with cold, green eyes.

Lochlain narrows his black and copper ones slightly, quiet tension cracking around me. 'Because I have a very good reason to,' he says, my heart hammering.

'What's the risk, Lish?' It's Will asking this time, his gaze flicking between Phoenix, Lochlain, and me.

'It's a bit of an unknown,' I say. 'There doesn't seem to be a precedent for having so many from outside the Realm. But, according to the rules, all you would have to do is to literally stand with us while Lochlain makes the challenge so the Custodian of the Throne, and General Siosal, can see we have the numbers. If Lochlain's successful, you would also need to be at his swearing in ceremony. In practice, though, I would put nothing past Siosal,' I say. I look at Ciara. 'And humans aren't necessarily respected across all parts of the Realm,' I say remembering those that were sacrificed at the Giving.

'Why?' Phoenix says through gritted teeth and I meet his gaze, conscious of everyone else's on me, too. I relax my barrier a little to get a better read on him and the concern for me is clear. I don't know how to tell him I'm only half-human.

'I've been fine, Phoenix,' I say, gently. 'But I know others haven't been. The girls that aren't killed in the compound are sometimes bought for sacrificing.'

They collectively inhale and Will's hand instinctively moves around Sofia's waist, her gold-brown skin gleaming in the sunshine, as he looks to the four Calahi.

'It's a hard thing for us to explain,' Ciara starts, sorrow clear on her face. 'Our own views are so different to the Calahi that do this. But, essentially, those Calahi who believe it's reasonable, use humans to do what they can't. Or won't.' She looks at the Calahi around her. 'It's a practice we have to stop. To do that, we need Lochlain to be General. In that role, he can put an immediate stop to some of these more horrific practices, most easily the actions of the Whispers. From there, he can also ensure the safety of the rightful Queen of Airlie, who can bring further change.'

Aeyva joins the conversation for the first time when I make no comment on Ciara's reference to the Queen. Even though I know Ciara has told both her and Rory. I struggle to suck air into my lungs around the weight of responsibility being Queen means. 'To be clear, not one of us has, or will, ever condone the behaviour and, if you come to the Realm with us, we will ensure your safety as we do hers.' She jerks her head in my direction.

'It's your people that have been trailing us, isn't it?' Will asks and Lochlain simply nods once.

Blaire looks at me for a moment. 'Why is this important to you, Lish?' she asks.

I don't look at anyone but Blaire and I know she will understand what – who – the flush in my skin is for. But it's more than that. More than him.

'Because ... General Siosal has been involved in more awful things than we can possibly count, including the death of my mother.' Will closes his eyes momentarily as I look at the Calahi around me. 'And these four have become important to me and I will support them if I can. But I do not expect the same of you. Ever,' I say. 'And the Realm ...'—I search for the words—'it means something to me, too, and I don't think its people should be subjected to General Siosal. Plus, the obvious one of Lochlain becoming General means no more women will be taken and ... I will be free of Siosal.' I say.

Lochlain shifts as his emotions become too complex for me to decipher as well as keep track of the conversation.

Hayes's blue eyes miss nothing. 'What aren't you saying?'

I swallow. Lochlain's fingertip presses slightly harder into mine and I draw comfort from his proximity. Rory gives me a reassuring wink when I catch his eye and I look back to my friends.

'I am – I think I am the Queen they've been looking for.'

Silence.

'Well,' I fumble, 'my mum might have been – was, I think – the Queen but she ran and—' I can't finish.

My friends look between me and Calahi, searching for the punchline that won't come. Ciara fills in the blanks.

'Lish's mother was Queen of the Realm when she was betrothed to General Siosal—'

'The asshole?' Riley asks.

'Yes. But she ran, pregnant with someone else's young one – pregnant with Lish. Her death, and no other young, makes Lish the Queen.' She pauses to see if any of them can summon a coherent question. 'Siosal believes he is still owed a bonding – a ... marriage, I think you call it – and Lish is what is left of the appropriate blood line.'

My veins ice over hearing Ciara say it out loud.

'That ... might take us a minute to wrap our minds around,' Blaire says. 'I didn't even think monarchs existed anymore. Although'—her eyes widen—'I guess I didn't know magic worlds existed, either.'

Hayes clears his throat, glancing at Lochlain before the warmth of his attention settles on me. 'And if he dies because of our support?' He nods his head at Lochlain.

I exhale through my nose.

'I'll never forgive myself,' I say quietly, glancing at Aeyva as the thought makes it hard to breathe. Her eyes shift to Lochlain, and I catch the subtle dip of her chin. I don't see what warranted it nor Lochlain's reaction, but a small amount of tension leaves him.

Several moments of silence pass, the processing clear on most of their faces. Hayes looks around the group from the Realm.

'I will stand with you, Lish,' he says in a low, resigned voice.

'As will I,' Riley says. 'The Guard's getting pretty stale, anyway. I need some adventure,' she says. Will and Phoenix look at each other.

'We're both in,' Will says, 'but I will talk to Sofia before—'

'I'm in, Will,' Sofia interrupts, 'I was in before we even arrived,' she says smiling at me.

Lochlain looks stunned. 'I—' he starts.

'The words you're looking for are "thank you",' Phoenix says, and Blaire frowns at him. 'To be clear,' he addresses Lochlain, 'we are doing this for her and only her.'

'That's settled then,' Aeyva stands brushing her legs off. 'I'll brief you on the Realm on the way.'

CHAPTER TWENTY-NINE

Ciara's house is crowded in a way it hasn't been previously as we gather the night before the challenge. We sit around the fire after dinner, all space on the floor and couches taken up as everyone sprawls in front of the heat. I look around at this funny little group, my eyes landing on Nico lying asleep across the laps of both Will and Phoenix. It's hard not to feel like I missed out there. Nico was an addition I wasn't expecting but it makes sense that where Sofia goes, he goes.

The others bubble with quiet disbelief at the few snippets they've seen of Elenlea. Aeyva dispersed their guest status between a number of contacts, primarily from other courts, to avoid too much attention on the Royalists, and they each wear a medallion around their necks. The absence of one on my own tells me more about myself than I have wanted to admit for a long time.

Across from me, Lochlain bounces his knee slightly. I don't miss the quiet glare Riley gives him. I'd told her about Lochlain's bonding to Aeyva because I needed someone to know – really know – what that would mean to me.

I catch Ciara's eye and she starts to usher everyone out, claiming she needs a good night's sleep before tomorrow. Rory readies to see my friends back to the house they are staying in, also organised by Aeyva. Hayes and Will wish Lochlain luck and he thanks them for their support. Hayes takes my face in his warm hands on his way out.

'He'll be fine, Lish,' he whispers. 'I can see what's there and you deserve to have it.' He squeezes my hand. 'It will be okay.' Tears well up at how well he knows me. And the truth he doesn't quite speak. Tomorrow is a huge risk.

'Nothing happened when Phoenix and I ... it still hasn't ... ' I trail off. A dull ache in my chest tightens at what they all must think of me.

'You don't have to remind me, Lish,' he says. He gives me a firm embrace before heading out.

Phoenix has been loitering and the others wait for him by the hall to the back door. I watch as he makes his way to Lochlain, the tension thick around me. Aeyva watches closely, her posture totally casual. He shakes Lochlain's hand.

'I hope you do well tomorrow,' Phoenix says without releasing his grip, 'for her sake. But we know about your wife.'

I immediately regret telling Riley about Aeyva as Lochlain's guilt fills the room and shadows his face.

'If you survive tomorrow,' Phoenix continues, still holding Lochlain's hand firmly, 'and you hurt her again, I will kill you myself and your Court of Airlie can go to hell.'

Lochlain takes a deep breath and clasps Phoenix's shoulder. I take an involuntary step forward.

'I understand,' he says. His eyes flick to the others who are all watching, Riley with her eyes still narrowed at him. 'I would not try to stop any of you,' he says, sincerity in his voice.

Ciara hugs Lochlain on her way to bed with stern instructions that he not stay up too long. She gives Aeyva a long look and disappears up the stairs.

And then it is just the three of us.

'We need to talk,' Aeyva says.

Shit.

'Alone.' She looks at Lochlain. His eyes drag between us before he nods at Aeyva, and follows Ciara's exit up the stairs.

'I'll make us some tea.'

I hope my voice sounds neutral, despite my pounding heart. There is no way out of this, and I owe it to her, really. He's not mine, despite what he's said about how he feels. And she deserves to tell the story I so desperately want to hear, even as my gut twists at what it might be.

With steaming mugs, Aeyva and I head out to the deck and I watch the stars above us. The cool night air kissing any exposed skin.

'Lochlain,' she says, and I force myself to focus on her, palms sweating. Her steel and blue eyes are not as cold as I imagine they can be. Silver hair twists up into a messy bun, showing off her tattoos. She reminds me of Riley in a way, even putting aside that their eyes are similar shades. There is a strength and a frankness in both of them I envy.

'Lochlain,' she says again, watching me, 'is my bonded partner.'

My throat constricts and the vice tightens around my chest. I scramble for something to say but I come up empty handed. In the end, I decide it's better to let her talk. I'm probably lucky she's decided to have this discussion with words and not weapons. There must have been more to them once. And yet ...

'Yes,' I say.

'We were bonded a long, long time ago and vowed to look after each other for as long as time required,' she says. 'We have each taken those particular vows seriously.'

I nod.

'I'd like you to know how we came to be bonded.'

'Okay,' I say, not sure I'm ready to hear this story despite the anticipation pounding behind my ribs.

'When I was young. Really young,' she starts, 'I loved a boy who loved me back, every bit as fiercely. But he was just as young as I was and when we found out I was ... expecting, he didn't take it well.' My cheeks flush as my stomach sinks, this is so much worse than I'd hoped. 'I know now he was also under extreme pressure from his parents but, at the time, all I knew was that I was with child and the boy I loved with all my heart had skipped town without so much as a goodbye.

'Back then, it was a sinful thing to be an unbonded female with young coming and any opportunities for me to find work, or provide for my young one and I, were very slim,' she says. 'With no bonded partner, it was likely I would be begging on the street for food.'

I open my mouth, but she continues.

'I never thought I'd love anyone else as I did that boy. My best friend in the world knew this, and asked me to bond him,' she says. I blink at her slowly, the hope I have been nurturing about Lochlain warming slightly. 'We waited as long as we could for the father, who I still loved, to return but Lochlain didn't want anyone to find out we weren't bonding for the normal reasons.

'So, we were formally bonded – although we obviously couldn't declare ourselves Soul Accords,' she says and suddenly looks out at the sky. 'Not long after, I lost the baby and Lochlain helped me pick up the pieces of my soul. Those that could be retrieved, anyway.'

I can't stop the tears that come to my eyes imaging that pain, but I have no words of comfort that feel adequate and I take her hand instead. She squeezes it once before taking it away again.

'Neither of us expected the other to not see anyone else, obviously – we knew we were just very good friends. But Lochlain promised to never tell anyone of our arrangement, of my loss. That would always be my decision. At the time, I thought I would never feel anything for anyone ever again and so I promised to only release him from the bonding if he found someone worthy of him.'

My heart skips a beat, but I stay silent.

'But making his vow to not expose me, also meant he couldn't be open with anyone else. Most of his dear ones either didn't care he was bonded or didn't stick around long enough to find out,' she says. 'And I certainly haven't been in such ... close proximity to them. But you—'

'I'm not his ... dear one, Aeyva, I assure you nothing has happened,' I say. 'But—'

I don't need to tell her I wanted it to. That I feel an intimacy with him, despite the fact we haven't been physical with each other. How their relationship didn't add up to me. It's all over her face that she already knows.

'You're missing it, Lish, that's the whole point. I wouldn't have cared if it did, but it impressed me that it didn't.'

I sit back. 'You were *testing* me?'

She purses her lips slightly in a non-committal expression. 'Not purposefully,' she says, 'but you and Lochlain ... it's not an easy thing you want to start, Lish.' Unease stirs quietly in my mind. 'But it became clear that you have pretty deep feelings for him and yet you respected him and the thought of his bonding enough to stay away,' she says.

She looks at me then and I brace myself at the look on her face. 'And now, even when you thought you couldn't have him, you're still prepared to stand by him. By us. I should have told you before now. I was stubborn about it and – I'm sorry. I just – I needed to know I could trust you with him before I could share my deepest hurt. To be frank with you, I'm still not sure I *can* trust you with him. But it's also very obvious that his attention is divided, and he cannot walk into tomorrow without having talked openly with you.'

I walk over to the railing at the edge of the deck and lean on my forearms, bent in the middle. 'I ... understand hiding from truths, Aeyva. I wish he hadn't lied but ... I get it.'

She comes to stand next to me.

'He is nothing if not loyal. Even if it hurts him beyond reason. And make no mistake, Lish, it has been hurting him. Mostly because he knows he's been hurting you,' she says. 'Look,' she breathes out her nose, 'I don't really have a right to ask this but, please, don't make him pay for my ... tardiness in telling you. I didn't want either of you to suffer. And, regardless of what future lies ahead for you both, it is imperative he comes out of the challenge alive.'

The weight of her words pulls at my shoulders, and I close my eyes against the lack of faith she has in me. In Lochlain and me.

'Did you ever see him again?' I ask her.

'The father?' she asks.

Rory appears on the deck behind us, having finished his chaperone duties, and she turns to face him. 'Are you checking I'm telling my story, Rory?'

'You know I am, sweetheart. He's waited long enough,' he says. 'It's been painful to watch him try and restrain himself. He deserves this. They will have enough challenges, we don't need to be one of them.'

My face heats.

Without looking at me, she continues. 'I did see the father again, Lish, and he's lucky he survived that first time. But, somehow, we have become best friends,' she says.

'And I will spend every day trying to make it up to her,' Rory says. I look between them as he approaches her and draws her in for a hug. 'You did good, Aeyva. It was past time.'

He shouts up the stairs as we walk through the open deck doors and back into the living area. 'Loch! We're out.'

'We don't do anything that resembles a last goodbye,' Aeyva says quietly to me. 'Night!' she sings out and then I'm on my own.

A stair creaks, and I glance up to find Lochlain slowly making his way down. The room compresses around me, my heart rate rising as I feel him watching me, assessing my reaction to my conversation with Aeyva.

'Shall we sit?' he asks quietly when he reaches me.

We move to what's become our usual couch and I wait him out, my chest just about bursting, but I need him to start.

'So,' he says but doesn't go on.

His face is illuminated by the fire and the lantern that hangs by one of the armchairs. It's dark enough to make his freckles hard to make out, but the copper rings in his eyes are vivid. I haven't worked out all the connections the colour changes mean for his mood. Right now, I have a reasonable idea, but I still refuse to look at his mouth. I need to hear what he has to say first. I keep waiting, not shying away from his gaze.

'You've spoken to Aeyva?' he asks roughly.

'I have.'

'And?'

'I'd like to hear from you first.'

Blood pounds in my ears.

We're facing each other on the couch, me with both legs crossed on the cushion and leaning against the arm and he with one leg on the couch and his arm draped over the back of it, a fist propping up his head. We don't touch but the humming connection between us is impossible to ignore.

'I'm sorry I didn't tell you,' he says. 'Either that I am bonded or the reason for it. I – I wanted to, desperately wanted to, but it wasn't my story to tell, and I had promised her I wouldn't.'

'And?' It's my turn to ask.

'And ...' he says, 'I'm relieved you finally know. But I'm terrified it's too late, anyway.'

I can feel that fluttering against me, my heart flutters for a different reason.

'Too late for what?' I ask.

He blows out a breath. 'For me to know how you feel, how you would have felt if it hadn't been such a mess.'

I frown at him; I'd thought it was pretty obvious how I felt. I'd constantly tried to keep myself suppressed around him, but his emotions leak through to me. I'd assumed mine did the same.

'What do you mean?' I ask.

'Well, there were times, I thought you were ... interested. But—' His embarrassment tinges the space between us, and he runs a hand through his hair.

'Tell me,' I prompt gently.

He takes a deep breath. 'There were times I thought you were interested, okay? In me. But I wasn't sure. We didn't exactly meet under normal circumstances and, then, when you found out about Aeyva I was sure that would be the end of it but then – when I healed you – I hoped, but I couldn't get a proper read on you. And you're the Queen and we—' he stumbles.

'You mean, you can't normally feel me?' I ask.

'Not like I think you can feel me, try as I have to stop that,' he says.

I worry a little bit then. 'What about'—I wave my hands vaguely between us—'the ... crackle here? Is that just me?'

The corners of his mouth go up. 'That is definitely not just you,' he says, 'that's the only thing that's made me think I'm not going totally insane over here on my own.'

'Huh,' I say.

'Huh?' he imitates me. 'I've just laid myself out to you, not very eloquently, I'll grant you that, but 'huh' is your response?' His brows disappear into his curls.

Casting any restraint aside, I take the hand that is holding his head and pull it towards me, placing it over my collar bones, his fingers framing the soft skin of my throat. His eyes hold mine as they darken. He opens his mouth to speak but I briefly press a finger to his lips. Having no idea what I'm doing I give myself over to feeling and I let it wash between us.

Closing my eyes, I let him feel it. The hurt and confusion when Odhran told me about his bonding, the fear I feel when I think of the challenge and the peace I feel in Elenlea, like I don't feel in Rhyton. The way my stomach flips when he walks into a room and my heart has threatened to give me away at every step. How I'd known he was different when we made our way through the wood with Niamh, and the safety I felt when I curled against his chest.

Slowly, I open my eyes to find his again, tears in his lashes. I smile at him as I lean forward to wipe them away.

'Sorry, I should've held back a little.' I realise my own face is wet too. 'I'll get us some tissues,' I say, hopping off the couch.

I grab us water as well, before returning to the lounge and setting the jug and glasses on the small coffee table. Lochlain sits forward with his elbows on his knees, and I stand in front of him, close to his knees.

'You okay?' I ask.

He reaches out and grabs the front of my leggings, tugging me forward so I stand between his legs, and he rests his forehead on the soft part of my stomach. My breath hitches as the warmth from his seeps through the layer of fabric separating us. I lace my fingers in his hair and let it slide between my fingers. His hands run up the back of my knees and thighs until they grip my ass as he presses a little harder into my stomach.

'Thank you, Lish—'he looks up at me like he has the world on his shoulders and runs his hands back down my legs—'for coming back.'

I can't bring myself to let him go. Not tonight. I won't think of it as the last night, our only night, but—

'Are you sure you want to do this?' I ask.

'I have to,' he says. The flames create shadows on his face. 'But I really don't want you to come. He'll notice you and I—' He looks down.

I place two fingers under his chin and lift his face to meet my gaze, his skin soft on the pads of my fingers.

'Lochlain,' I breathe. 'I won't let you face him without my support, too. I'm going, end of story.'

He closes his eyes as I shift my hands to slide around his face and up into the sides of his hair. He presses his own hands against my ass again, a gentle invitation. I let myself drop into him, straddling his lap. The copper rings in his eyes burn bright when he opens them again, scanning my face.

My mouth.

Slowly, I trace the outline of his lips with a finger and they part slightly, his breath hot on my skin. Dropping my hand to his chest, I follow the gentle ridges of his lips with my mouth instead. Pressing soft kisses on his skin until he grips the ends of my hair and I gasp as a shiver runs down my spine. Still holding my hair, Lochlain looks at me again. A moment of stillness passes between us ... and then our mouths find each other.

The softness of his mouth against the desperation of his kiss is only fuel for the heat already pooling in my body.

He slides his hands up the inside of my top, my skin prickling in their wake, and lifts it over my head and down my arms. Tossing it to the floor as he reclaims my mouth. I rock into him, his own desire apparent between my legs, and I smile as a groan escapes his throat. He moves to my neck, running his nose up and towards my ear, and I arch into him. I unlatch my bra and he quickly takes a breast in each hand, his callouses rough on my skin. Lowering his head to my chest he gently takes a nipple in his teeth and bites down. Just hard enough for my own moan to sound.

Carefully slipping myself from him, I shimmy my pants to the floor. His black eyes run the length of my now naked body as I stand before him, and he curses softly. Dropping to my knees between his legs, he watches me as I tug at his pants, lifting his hips to help me take them down.

Straddling him again, I run my tongue along his bottom lip and he nips my own gently in response. I can feel every inch of him against me and my body hums with need.

I still – breathing hard. 'I haven't been taking my birth control since ...' I whisper.

He kisses me again, as if he can't bear our mouths to be parted for more than a moment.

'I take one,' he says, and hot relief pumps through my veins. His tongue is warm where it finds mine. 'For birth control and health,' he whispers between kisses, his hands running up my back and pressing me tightly to his chest.

Pushing his shoulders back into the couch cushions, I raise myself up slightly. Watching his face as I come back down and he slides into me. His eyes roll back slightly and it's an effort to keep mine open at how thoroughly, delightfully, he fills me.

He grips my hips as I move and I lean forward to kiss him, the building in my core drowning everything out but the feel of him. His fingers dig harder into my soft flesh, and I crush my lips to him as I take him further.

Meeting my rhythm, we move as one. Faster. Until Lochlain gives a final, hard slam into me and I cry out. The wave of pleasure emptying my mind. I squeeze around him, and he whispers my name as he comes, pulsing inside me.

Several moments pass, our foreheads resting against each other as we breathe together.

'Will you stay here with me tonight?' he asks softly.

'There is literally nowhere else I'd prefer to be,' I say, my voice husky.

We silently redress ourselves and lie down in front of the fire. I watch the flames behind the glass, every inch of me tingling where his body meets the back of mine as he loops an arm over me. I intertwine my fingers in his and hold his hand at my chest.

'Aeyva told me you're not her Soul Accord,' I say quietly, and he remains still. 'What does that mean?'

He tucks me in tighter to his chest. 'A Soul Accord is ... someone your magic talks to,' his breath tickles my ear as he talks, 'in a way it doesn't with anyone else. It's quite rare, but being Soul Accords doesn't always mean those Calahi will be bonded; and those who bond don't have to be Soul Accords, either – it doesn't mean there's not love in those relationships.'

'It sounds nice,' I whisper, watching the flames. I don't know what else to say, but I tuck the knowledge away into my heart like a secret.

Lochlain's fingers hold mine a little firmer as he presses a kiss into my hair, my skin flushing with warmth all over.

'How come I never see you light this fire?' I ask.

'Just one of the many tricks of the trade.' He laughs softly.

CHAPTER THIRTY

'U gh, you two are so cute it's sickening,' Ciara announces as she starts coffee. The fire is still lit and the morning sun just begins its journey along the edges of the floor. I smile into Lochlain's chest.

'Don't you dare let me find any miscellaneous items of clothing down here, Lochlain.'

She ducks as he throws a cushion over the island bench, laughing quietly. But I don't miss the flicker of deep concern in her expression she tries to cover.

'Good morning,' I mumble, turning back against his chest.

He lifts my chin to look at him and I uncurl my spine. His hair has an effortlessly tousled look, despite sleeping on the floor, his curls mostly intact. His eyes are sleepy and he peers down at me through his dark lashes.

'Good morning to you, too,' he smiles, his perfect mouth pulled wide across his straight, white teeth. Teeth that nipped at my—

'Do you think Ciara would let us stay here all day?' he asks.

'You know full well that's my preference,' she says from the kitchen. 'But we have a Queendom to start taking back today.'

Reality crashes around me.

He places a soft kiss on my nose. 'We'll be okay, Lish.'

The flood of warmth that radiates from my chest in response to his tenderness is completely at odds with the sickness spinning through my centre. I close my eyes.

Please don't die, I beg silently.

I drag myself from the rug. I've spent all night thinking of how to get out of this, but I haven't been able to find a single way around any of the rules of the challenge. I've been over them enough times with Rory to know them by heart. But the only option seems to be finding an opportunity to kill the General before Lochlain has to challenge him. If I can find one, I will take it.

Collecting the others on our way, we walk into town with our hoods thrown back. It's freeing to see the city without it, to show my face. Knowing it is to see Siosal again creates a knot of tension in my stomach. But, around the tightly wound concern, I'm absorbed by the capital of the Court of Airlie, the capital of my Court.

The city gets tighter the closer we move towards the palace where it sits to the north of the city centre.

'How is this real?' Blaire whispers, her eyes sparkling with wonder. 'Those streetlights,' she says, 'aren't even attached to anything.'

I glance at the lanterns that aren't currently emitting any light and smile.

Calahi spill out of cafes and restaurants, sharing meals or drinks on the intricate tables that cover the walkways along the edge of the road we walk on. The deep, green vines that run along the roofline drop down in places as if they reach to caress the Calahi underneath. Large timber and metal signs hover high above the tables, marking the names of the different places. Some of them are words I can make out, others seem to be a collection of symbols or pictures.

To their credit, not one of my friends falters as they get an open view of Elenlea for the first time. My own time here has been unfairly limited, too afraid of Siosal to venture far. Apart from the night I tried to write myself off of course. I wonder what that Calahi will think if he were to find out I am supposed to be their Queen.

Children race down the cobbled stone road beside us, bumping into Lochlain on my left. One of them stops in front of him, halting our progress.

'It's you,' the little girl says. *Young one*, I think as I recall Aeyva's words from last night.

Lochlain glances behind us where I know Rory and Aeyva bring up the rear of our group before he drops to a crouch.

'It's me.' He smiles. 'Who are you?'

She blushes furiously as she gapes at him and an older Calahi approaches, placing a hand on her shoulder. The pale jacket he wears is cut closely to his body, showing the leanness of his form, a large black belt holding up his bright green pants.

'Sorry, sir,' he says.

'No apology necessary,' Lochlain says as he stands. He smiles down at the little girl, who's now twirling her plait in her hand.

The other Calahi gives him a long look before running his gaze across our group. 'Does this mean you are making your challenge?' he asks quietly.

I freeze but Lochlain just nods, the back of his hand brushing mine.

The male grips his shoulder. 'That is the best news I've heard in a long time,' he says quietly. He glances around the street briefly, where I notice a large number of Calahi pausing their meals and conversations to watch us.

'We're all behind you,' he says, pressing the heel of his hand to his chest.

'Oh my god,' Riley breathes behind me and I look back to the Calahi around us.

All of whom stand.

Their hands pressed to their chests in silence as they look at Lochlain.

The large black and gold fences of the palace are open today, as Ciara said they would be, allowing the noble families and other citizens of Airlie access to the Custodian's regular open courts. Some of them participate in the discussions of the day or line up to petition to the Custodian. Many just gather for a day on the palace grounds.

Guards in forest green, the colour of Airlie, are stationed at the entrance, eyes roving the growing numbers of Calahi and their guests. Flicking between faces and weapons, checking for medallions. The wide gravel path ends in a circular shape, studded with a large water fountain. We join the throng of Calahi at the base of sweeping, stone stairs.

I walk with my arm linked in Ciara's, our heads together as if in gossipy conversation. We move forward to keep Lochlain subtly behind us, Aeyva at his side and Rory and the Rhyton team fanning out behind them, watching our flanks. We never heard from Nuala, so my team are his only additional support.

'I used to love coming here,' Ciara says, 'before my father died.'

Killed here, she means. In a challenge just like the one Lochlain is about to make. After everything, him not surviving is not an option I can entertain.

As I take in the elaborate dresses and suits of the Calahi making their way to the entrance of the palace, it's hard to imagine it as a place that holds anything but joy. The palace itself looks to only be three storeys tall, lower than I had expected, but it's long and curves back on itself. From what I understand, there are spectacular gardens on the other side cocooned by the building; but I doubt we'll see those today. Wrapped around the second and third stories are long balconies, divided in sections that don't appear to follow a pattern. A number of Calahi, probably from the more prominent families, watch the rest of the citizens arrive beneath them.

The burning starts as a slight irritation across my chest and the edges of my vision bleed purple as we walk up the steps and into the grand entrance of the palace. My heart hammers in recognition. My body recalling the magic he's used on me before.

Siosal.

'He's here,' I whisper. Ciara's grip on my arm tightens.

I can only hope he is as oblivious of my proximity as Lochlain was to my emotions. But I know and my whole being screams to get away.

A white, marble floor extends throughout the vast entrance and several large, gold doors with intricate engravings punctuate the walls. Two sets of these are open to a cavernous room I can just make out through the crowd. The ceiling above me is painted in a detailed mural I don't have time to take in as we are bustled towards the open doors. More guards in their forest green uniforms monitor this entrance and direct the crowd either to the spectator ring that runs around the outside of the circular room, or the line of petitioners.

I look back to give Lochlain a last encouraging look before he joins the queue, but he's already gone. Ciara and I make our way into the crowd on the right and find a spot we can watch Lochlain and Aeyva. As his formally bonded partner, it is appropriate she be with him in this space. For the first time since I found out about their bonding, I find myself totally at peace with their relationship. Rory finds us and whispers to Ciara who heads in the direction of Hayes.

'What are you doing?' I ask. 'I was supposed to be with Ciara.'

The Calahi around us talk in hushed tones as a sign of respect for the Throne I can't see. Rory stands close enough for me to feel his outline against my side. He leans down slightly.

'I promised Loch I wouldn't leave you alone, so you get me, sweetheart.' He winks.

'What about Aeyva?'

He looks at me.

'Aeyva can handle herself,' he says looking back to the centre of the room.

I nod, not trusting myself to speak as a wave of nausea grips me. My breathing labours and I press slightly into Rory to steady myself. The voice in my head still screaming at me to run as far from here as I can.

'I won't leave you, Lish. You're okay.' He pauses. 'He will be too,' he adds quietly.

'How can you know that?'

He doesn't answer.

I look around but I can't see the rest of our group from here as the crowd packs in tighter. Enormous, beautiful tapestries line the walls and portray a range of different scenes from winged warriors in bloody battles to family portraits. There are a number of crowned people amongst the images and it dawns on me these are stories of each reign. The breath leaves me as I realise my mother's image will be here.

Rory moves us forward a little, Calahi and their guests glaring at us as we push past, but at least now I can make out the raised platform where a handful of decorative chairs sit. The largest of which is obviously the Throne. It's a complicated design of twisted gold and is flanked by smaller, duller looking chairs.

A man strides into the room, stepping up onto the platform in long, black boots. Slim navy pants are covered by a thigh-length black jacket, belted at the waist with a wide, white leather strap. Decorative gold pads cover each shoulder and medals grace his chest, a white gloved hand holds a hat under his arm as he takes a seat on the right, furthest from the Throne. He adjusts the collar of his uniform and a jolt runs through me as I study the chiselled face that's partially hidden by a manicured goatee. He's not Calahi.

I know him.

'Is he always here?' I whisper to Rory.

Before he can respond the shadow of burning in my chest increases so strongly I place a hand on my skin to check it's still healed. And then I see him. The pale man with snow white hair and dark eyebrows. He walks slowly to the platform, savouring the faces that strain to see him. His suit is a pale grey, with purple gems set into the collar of the knee-length jacket. Gradually, he takes a seat in one of the chairs on the throne's left, the closest side to Rory and me.

From here I can see his mauve eyes roaming the room. They move in our direction and I duck my head closer to Rory's chest, my breathing heavy. As well as the pressure of his body against my side, Rory places his hand on my back, as if he knows I need the contact to remain present. I look to Lochlain near the back of the line, Aeyva still with him.

His stature clearly defines him as a soldier, but he is also finely dressed in close fitted black pants and shirt, with a dark blue sash across his left shoulder and pinned at his right hip with a copper pin. His freshly washed hair has now dried and there are more than a few Calahi clearly discussing him.

'The Custodian approaches,' a voice sounds and the Calahi around me bow and curtsy.

I follow their lead and wait to rise until others around me do. Moving my head slightly, I can see the Custodian step up onto the platform. He's an attractive man, older than Siosal, I think, with black, wavy hair brushed back from his face and a long, black cloak. Its gold embroidery catches the light as he moves. He surveys the crowd with a kind smile. Approaching the gold throne, he places a glass box on its seat before he takes the one immediately to the right.

'Begin,' he commands.

Behind the glass is an object, the details of which I can't quite make out. But its shape is that of a crown. I drag my eyes away. Those in the line make their way forward, stopping a polite distance from the platform that is now lined with guards in forest green – a physical barrier between those on the platform and the crowd.

The other chairs remain empty. The petitions from the Calahi of Airlie vary, from transport upgrades to accommodation maintenance issues or they simply bring gifts that are placed on the floor before the Guards. Those with questions or suggestions for city improvements are generally referred to others within the Court. The names of whom I try to hold but start to tangle in my mind.

Time drags and my feet start to ache. The Calahi around us fidget and I hear Lochlain's name whispered more than once. The constant burning in my chest is distracting and several times I have to blink to clear the purple fog in my vision. Rory doesn't seem affected. Lochlain is now third in line. I look back to the platform where General Siosal is waiting. He smiles at me. My throat constricts and I can't look away. I grip Rory instead and he moves subtly into my line of sight.

'That was going to happen sooner or later, stay focused and breathe. Loch's nearly up,' he says.

The reality is suddenly too much. Lochlain is going to die and I can't be part of this. I can't lose him. This Court isn't worth his life, not to me. I twist to Rory, gripping his arm. My vision wavers in purple mist and my gut turns.

'We need to stop this, Rory, Siosal is never going to let him live,' I whisper but the sound is washed away by multiple gasps.

It's Lochlain's turn and the Calahi have realised what he is here to do.

Lochlain and Aeyva step up towards the platform and both bow to the Custodian, who cocks his head.

'To what do I owe this unexpected pleasure, Lochlain?' he asks.

The sound of his name from the Custodian shocks me. But of course he knows him, as the son of the former General. The Calahi who should be in the role now. Lochlain looks only at the Custodian.

'Your Grace,' Lochlain says, his voice completely even. 'I wish to declare a challenge for the role of General. And along with it, the Wolverton Pendant,' he says.

No.

Rory places his fingers over mine where they've stayed clenched on his arm.

A murmur runs through the room and the Custodian holds up his hand for silence. General Siosal watches Lochlain with a small smile.

'And do you have the required numbers of support?' asks the Custodian.

'I do,' replies Lochlain.

'You may present them to me.'

Rory helps me forward as the others make their way through the crowd as well. As we come into view, he removes his hand from my back and I walk alone. General Siosal's eyes follow me to where I stand a step back and to the side of Lochlain. His smile widens as they drop down to my chest and find the medallion we decided I would wear. Not wanting to draw attention to the human – half-human – who can be in the Realm without guest status. Not wishing to declare who I am. Holding his gaze, I lift my chin. Lochlain catches the motion and bristles. But the General knows, there is no longer any point in attempting to hide from him.

Siosal smiles at us like he's greeting old friends. I think the uniformed man narrows his eyes at us slightly, but I don't break my stare with the General to check.

'I see you have some supporters from outside the Realm,' the Custodian says. 'Interesting.'

The uniformed man shifts in his seat.

'I do, Your Grace,' Lochlain replies.

'Well, General Siosal. A challenge has been declared and supported. It is now over to you to defend your title,' the Custodian says without looking at him. Siosal stands slowly and bows to the Custodian.

'So it has, Your Grace, so it has,' he says, still smiling. 'I see, Lochlain,' the name dripping with distaste, 'that you have brought a friend of mine with you.'

I send a wave of stillness to Lochlain but I don't know if it has any impact.

Siosal looks at me. 'I do so look forward to ending this challenge in her presence.'

I watch mutely as Lochlain hands Aeyva his sash and pin. She hands him his sword in return. I hope he's wearing his knives under his shirt as well but I can't be sure, I didn't get a chance to talk to him alone this morning once we left the living room. The things I haven't been able to say or do pressing on my chest.

On the platform, General Siosal makes a show of removing his long jacket and hanging it over the back of the silver chair so the gems are still visible. A sword already hangs at his hip and he gives an almost imperceptible nod to the side of the platform. Rory and I, along with the others, melt away back into the crowd. A ring of red sand is poured in a large circle around Lochlain and Siosal.

The Custodian stands and addresses the masses. 'No one is to enter or leave the ring until the challenge has been completed. Anyone who offers outside assistance faces execution for interfering in Crown matters. Either of you may submit at any time. Weapons and magic are each permitted. Begin,' he says.

Silence is thick in my ears.

Lochlain and General Siosal spend several long moments circling each other. The General talks quietly to Lochlain but I can't hear what he's saying. He's clearly trying to agitate Lochlain and the set of Lochlain's jaw worries me it's working. Eventually, it's Lochlain who moves first, and the two men parry with their swords, the sound of metal clanging around the quiet room. Every now and then someone lets out a gasp but, so far, the challenge is more of an exhibition of swordplay than a fight to the death. I knew Siosal was powerful when I first met him. But to see how he moves in action is something else. He's a good match for Lochlain but neither has yet made a bold move. I realise I don't know Lochlain's strategy. Whether he will tire Siosal and hope he submits, or take him by surprise with the killing blow. The uncertainty pulses in my cheek.

The edge of my vision bleeds purple as Siosal makes an attack on Lochlain, driving him backwards. My heart lurches as he drops Lochlain to one knee and kicks the sword from his hand. Rory grips my arm as I move to go to Lochlain.

My chest kicks in response. This is too fast. Lochlain should never have been brought down so easily.

Lochlain rolls towards his sword and drives it up to block the General's next blow. A blow delivered with such force it could have cleaved him in two. General Siosal pushes his sword with both hands down onto Lochlain's and I understand.

Where the swords meet, the air hisses. The General is shoving his burning magic down his sword and into Lochlain. Who, despite the burning he must feel, refuses to give.

Rory stiffens.

'What is it?' I whisper.

'He's stronger than he should be, his magic ... something's wrong,' he says. The colour drains from his face.

The more magic I can sense from the General, the more my vision wavers until a purple veil covers my eyes. Through the haze I make out dark figures moving amongst the crowd and Rory tenses beside me. Siosal drops his left hand from his sword and holds it out towards Lochlain's throat, the sword held lightly in his other hand. Lochlain inhales sharply, the clatter as his sword drops against the marble is tinny and the only sound in the horrified room. He clutches his throat as he's hoisted into the air like a puppet.

I know then, beyond any doubt.

Siosal will bleed every last drop from Lochlain.

Beside me, Rory is muttering to himself, I think he might be praying. The dark shadows continue to weave through the crowd. Whispers. Around me, the Calahi of Airlie seem to hold their collective breath. A female voice curses. The General's sword joins Lochlain's on the floor as he takes in Lochlain and throws his head back in a laugh. He makes a slicing motion with his right hand and Lochlain's groan reverberates against my skin.

'Oh, Mother,' Rory whispers and, this time, I have to restrain him.

It takes me a moment to see what he sees – the wetness soaking through the front of Lochlain's shirt. The General has attempted to gut him. The world empties around me, only Rory's arms hold me upright as we grip each other. Through the purple veil General Siosal turns to find me.

'For you, Alice,' he laughs, releasing Lochlain to fall heavily to the floor, his blood pooling on the white marble.

I will not panic, I tell myself. Think.

Think.

I can do this. I've healed him before. I took what I knew from that tiny blue bird and channelled it into him. I've made flowers bloom from nothing.

My mother tried to teach me about borrowing power, but I don't know how to do that. Or how it will help me now.

So I focus on what I do know – how I feel. How he feels against my skin. And I imagine I can hold that feeling in my hands and turn into something else. Into healing.

'Rory, brace me,' I say standing in front of him.

He obeys and presses into me from behind, holding my elbows. I close my eyes and plummet deep inside myself searching for my flame. I shape it to the sapphire thread I first found all that time ago with the small bird. The one I found again in the wood when I'd healed Lochlain. It's tiny when I find it and I slowly coax it up, up, up.

Please help me, I beg of it. *Help him.*

In my mind's eye, I see the thread thickening and growing, pulsing with a light fuelled by my fragile gold flame. In the same way I have sent emotions to Phoenix and Nico, I send this light to Lochlain. The dark figures of the Whispers remain in the purple mist. Even though I think I still have my eyes closed, I can feel them weaving through the crowd.

'Rory, they're coming for the others,' I say. Opening my eyes, I focus on Lochlain, collapsed in a heap on the floor.

'I see them,' he says quietly.

He hesitates behind me for a moment, but I can't break my focus on Lochlain, even as my heart threatens to stop beating. I can feel him now and I send the light through and around his body, willing it to heal him. Save him. I'm jostled from behind, someone else taking Rory's place.

'I'm here,' Will whispers and my heart swells in my chest.

The blue threads become a malleable substance I bend to my command, and I send some of it down and around Will and I to ward off any black figures. I will gladly die to save Lochlain but I won't allow any harm to come to Will in the process.

Lochlain doesn't move and I push harder, pressing against Will to hold me upright, not trusting myself to have the strength to stand on my own. I let it flow out of me and into Lochlain. It's a steady stream now and as it gets stronger, my vision darkens. I embrace it. Copper that moves like liquid brushes against my blue stream sending a shiver down my spine. It calls to me and I immediately recognise the feel of it as Lochlain. His magic.

You need to get up Lochlain. Get up, I will him.

The General collects his sword and drags it behind him as he circles Lochlain, the sound of its edge on the marble sending nails down my back. The audience is deathly quiet, waiting for the final blow.

'You didn't really think you would win this challenge, did you?' The General talks loudly enough for all to hear now. 'I defeated your father, remember,' he says. 'The one who was supposed to be the greatest General in our history. And you are no match for him.'

Someone starts to cry quietly behind me. Siosal stalks around Lochlain's blood and nudges him with a boot. Lochlain doesn't move. Pressure builds in my head and I lean harder into Will. The General stops his circling of Lochlain and finds my eyes. He smiles at me as the pressure in my skull threatens to split it in two.

'Hello, Alice,' he says. His mouth doesn't move but his voice is in my ears, in my head. *'I'm sorry it's come to this.'* His eyes find mine. *'He shouldn't have challenged me. I'm stronger than he knows, and I won't give up my position as General. Unless it is to be King.'*

Blue and copper threads dance around me, and I drive them at Lochlain begging him to take them. Use them. I hold the General's gaze.

'Come and meet me, Alice.' His voice is soft. *'Stop hiding behind him. You know you have no choice but to give me what I am due. Your mother shirked her obligations. That is her fault, not mine. And it leaves you to fulfill them.'*

Sweat snakes down my torso.

'Lochlain has been defeated. You know he will die here. But you and I, Alice, we will survive. We are survivors, and I can help you make this Realm all it is supposed to be. You just need to make the right choice,' he says.

Sapphire and copper wavers around me at his transfixing voice in my mind. Will is talking to me from far away but I can't make out what he's saying. Lochlain's face swims before me, his copper and black eyes peeking out from under his dark curls. The chocolate freckles that got me into a little more strife than I'd intended. And the mouth I tried to block from my mind.

'Enter the ring, Alice, come to me.'
Moving, pulled by a force I can't name, I step across the sand.

CHAPTER THIRTY-ONE

Will's hands scrabble to claw me back but I shake him off. As both feet enter the ring, the Calahi behind me exclaim. I look around me once. Their faces frantically search the ring, looking blindly. A clamour of voices rises outside the ring as the onlookers argue if the shield is allowed or not. Whether Siosal has just lost the challenge. Desperately I look for the Custodian, even though I know he can't see me. He waves a hand.

Play on, it seems to say.

'They can't see us, Alice. All that happens here is between you and me, now.' General Siosal's mouth is moving, and it takes me a moment to realise his voice has left my head.

Lochlain groans softly, the sensation of him slowly diminishing on my skin.

I let go then. I let all the sapphire threads I have come together and rush to Lochlain who starts to push himself up, out to the side of me. Relief cools the sweat on my skin but still I push, my breath ragged in my throat. My vision dims to Lochlain and Siosal, the Whispers having disappeared into the darkening purple haze. The General turns, finally releasing my gaze, to find Lochlain now standing on shaky legs.

The General flicks his wrist and purple flame races over Lochlain before he blocks the rest of the blow. He creates a shield in front of himself that spreads the fire wide and around but, through the flames, he is shaking badly. My own hands tremble in response, shaking with Lochlain's tremors.

'You will bond me, Alice. I'm finished waiting.' He looks past Lochlain.

The General lashes out with both hands and Lochlain pushes back with his shield. It's fraying under the General's wall of flames. He's not strong enough to hold it for long. Sapphire and copper bleed together to fill the holes that burn through the shield, and I draw deep within myself to give it all to Lochlain. My muscles ache with the effort. But where there was once a tiny blue thread, I can see no more. I stagger on my feet, almost unable to stand anymore. It's gone, everything is gone.

'It's time, Alice. Give me your word, you will bond with me, and I will leave him unharmed. Give me your word you will not allow him to pursue me, and I let him live.'

I drag my eyes away from General Siosal, where the sweat is just starting to bead along his hairline. Lochlain's panicked gaze finds mine, his desperation sucking me under.

I won't allow him to die here.

Five black figures enter the ring, their eyes flaring as they can finally see what's before them. I blink and realise it's ten figures.

Each of my friends, held by a Whisper. Bile surges, the taste foul in my mouth.

I whirl to Siosal, the words can't leave me fast enough.

'I give you my word.'

A black flare flies between the two of us, piercing my ribs. I gasp, pain searing along my limbs.

Lochlain sinks to his knees, his shield thinning. Large holes appear, the compromised safety of his shield ebbing away with his hope.

General Siosal smiles sadly. 'You took too long, Alice. Unfortunately, you will pay for procrastination.'

Numbness spreads through my veins, my head throbbing.

He nods at the Whispers. Time slows and I wade through it like mud. I try to turn on my heel. Try to move towards them. My family. But I'm too slow.

The sound of a neck snapping echoes in my ears.

NO. Please ...

My gaze flicks between them without seeing, moving too fast to see who. Who did I lose?

And then I find them.

The sparkling blue eyes, eyes the colour of the sky, that know me from the inside. And I watch, powerless, as the light leaves them.

'No!' I scream, the sound ripping my throat.

Not Hayes, not Hayes.

My eyes sting with tears as a hole is ripped through my soul. I sob as I drop to my knees, my chest caving in.

General Siosal lifts his hand to give the next order. He wants me to watch one by one.

Not one of the others moves, rendered motionless by something I can't see. But their faces say it all. I stagger under the weight of their emotions.

No. This can't be it. I won't accept this is it.

I think Lochlain calls to me softly, his light fading but I spin now, looking at the Calahi that line the ring, still wondering what's happening.

Rory and Aeyva smash against the domed shield the General has created, unable to get through.

But, still, Siosal remains watching me, barely showing any exertion at keeping Lochlain down. He rubs at a spot on his neck and smiles sadly. I look back to my family. Back to Hayes. His body crumpled on the floor and something inside me breaks as well.

I scream.

A large, grey wolf prowls through the crowd. Nobody reacts. *Hallucinating*, I think. Shock making itself known. It sits beside me, and my breath becomes harder to draw. But not in fear. I search myself again for something, anything, that I can use. But whatever magic I called has gone.

Perhaps the wolf is to be my guide to wherever comes next. Or Lochlain's, maybe, but I won't let it take anyone else. Nobody else but me.

It nudges its head under my right hand, and I stroke the soft fur there. Siosal doesn't look at it, doesn't notice it, just watches me as his magic pummels towards Lochlain. Sorrow graces his features as the pieces of my heart are ripped away.

'We can be done now,' Siosal says. 'I can see you're hurting as much as I did. Even if you are the reason she ran.' He holds his hand to me. 'Come, we can rule the Realm together. You were meant to be mine.'

Gently, I feel someone take my hand. Resting them both in the wolf's fur. I don't know who it is or what they can do but I know they are standing with me and the wolf. For everything I love. I imagine delving into them with my sapphire stream and drawing out their power as well. Borrowing it.

The person gripping my hand offers a pale gold, the wolf copper, like Lochlain's, and I drive it towards him faster and harder than before. We don't have a lot of time.

I don't have a lot of time.

I can barely see him now, mauve mist thickening around me, black at the edges. But I think he's holding his stomach, where his insides threatened to spill, and driving his failing magic towards the General.

The force between them is incredible and my hair blows back from my face as my chest burns.

Sapphire, copper, and gold explodes around me, surging where I will it – towards the Whispers and I watch them drop to the floor. It's their turn to fall, lifeless, and what remains of my family burst forward in action, released from their binds. I can only point and watch them drag each other out of the ring, obeying my instruction to get out.

Siosal's flames gutter but I can't look at him yet.

I find Lochlain. *Please live.*

The wolf is snarling now, as if warning me of something, but all I can see is the majestic stream and I need to keep it going. *You're not alone, Lochlain.*

Ahead of me, Lochlain stumbles behind his copper magic. The prickle on my skin grows as his strength slowly returns. But I gave my word to Siosal I would not allow Lochlain to harm him. I can physically feel the agreement. There is nothing he can do but protect himself and try and heal. And perhaps watch me die.

I take a deep breath. Time starts to return and Siosal's eyes widen as he takes me in.

Placing a hand on my chest, I grasp the sapphire and copper substance pouring from me and will it to remember. Remember the burning Siosal inflicted on me. The blinding pain. *I remember,* my soul says. *I remember how to burn.*

I do not accept this, I tell myself. *I am the Queen of this Court and I do not accept this.*

I throw the coloured fog I hold in my hand as if I throw my knife, bringing General Siosal to his knees. The wall of flames the General almost had consuming Lochlain disappears in a plume of smoke. I don't dare stop the stream I give Lochlain and I split myself in two, the force trying to push me backwards. Funnelling everything to Lochlain to heal him and to General Siosal to bring him down. The hand squeezes mine and I think someone tells me to stop. My vision now more black than purple.

'No,' I think I say. 'No. I won't leave him.'

The wolf snarls louder and I stroke its fur to calm it.

'It's okay,' I gasp. 'I want to save him. I will save him.'

Lochlain's sword glints where the light catches the blood on the blade. And then I'm next to it, my limbs so heavy I think I might not be able to pick it up. The magic spools away from me, faster and faster and now totally outside my control. My head spins.

I step towards Siosal, my feet heavy, and lift the sword to his throat.

I send every burning I can find down its blade.

'Long live the Queen,' he says, a tear dropping from the corner of his eye.

Then he screams the cry of the burning.

And I am floating. I fumble for the wolf, but I'm made of lead.

I'll just stay here for a while – I – just a while.

The blackness that comes is like a gentle embrace and I welcome it. I'm so tired. The hand I was holding before squeezes mine again and a voice sounds in my head. I think I recognise the murmuring that finds me but it's too far a way to tell.

'Now is not your time, my dear,' the raspy voice says. 'You have a fire in your soul that you need to breathe into. Breathe into your fire and find the Blue Pointed Star. The wolves will guard your path.'

The wolf snarls beside me and its fangs sink into my arm. Warning me. Trying to drag me back.

The blackness tries to take me a second time, but I hold onto the sensation of the teeth in my arm. The white-hot pain that lances through my forearm and up into my shoulder. The sensation of small rivers of blood running over the back of my hand and down my fingers is almost hypnotic, like a caress, but I try not to give in to those and think of the teeth in my flesh.

CHAPTER THIRTY-TWO

'Lish, can you hear me?'

'Lish, it's Blaire. Please come back to us,' her voice breaks. 'Please.'

'Give her time and have faith. Just give her time.'

'You did well my child, you did so well.' An old man talks to me. 'You can wake up now,' he says.

I'm alone. And grateful for it. The room is dark, and it takes me a moment to place it, but it's the room I have been staying in at Ciara's, my robe hanging on the back of the door. I stare at the ceiling for a while as my mind sorts itself. I lift my right arm, the feel of the wolf's fur still between my fingers, where a bright white bandage glows in the dark.

The last memory I have is of holding Lochlain's blade to General Siosal's neck. Bile rises in my throat as I realise I don't know what happened after that.

Tears threaten to come as other images join the fray. The loudest being Hayes's lifeless eyes. I blink them away. I don't know who I want to see first but I don't want them all in here, not in this quiet place. So I get up, slowly, my head spinning, and grab my robe. I don't have the energy to get dressed. In bare feet I quietly make my way to the top of the stairs, their soft voices filtering up to me. I arrive at the bottom of the stairs without them noticing. I guess I haven't stirred in a little while.

'Hi,' I say and several faces whirl to me. Will is out of his seat and embracing me before I can even register who is here.

'Oh god, Lish,' he says against my neck. 'I'm so glad you're awake. You really fucking scared me,' I blink at him as he draws back. 'Are you alright?'

I nod, but it's not the truth, and hug him again. Some of the others come close to embrace me or ask how I am but their features are hard to make out, like I'm watching from somewhere else. Quietly, Lochlain appears at my side and winds his fingers through mine. The sensation grounding me in reality and I stifle a sob, covering my mouth with my free hand.

'I'm so sorry,' I whisper through my fingers. 'I couldn't save him.'

I don't need to tell my team I'm talking about Hayes. They know. The heartbreak is written all over them.

'Let's sit,' Blaire says, and we silently follow her instruction. Moving away from our cluster at the bottom of the stairs. Lochlain never letting go of my hand.

Sitting around the fireplace in Ciara's living room, they all look at me, my Rhyton team and the Calahi, as if I'm about to fall apart. I might be. Distantly, I watch the food appear but I'm not sure who's organised it – or magicked it – but I can't stomach anything anyway. I clear my throat, trying to work out what to ask first.

But I know the most important place to start.

'Siosal?' I ask quietly.

Their gazes shift to Lochlain, waiting.

'He's dead, Lish,' he says, squeezing my hand. He leans into me from where we sit together on one of the couches and tucks a lock of hair behind my ear. 'You did what I couldn't do.'

I look at him for any hint of discomfort that I killed Siosal instead of him, but there's nothing on his face that says that. It's pride I can feel coming off him. Pained pride – he knows what I lost in that room when Hayes died.

'I broke the rules,' I say, looking at them all now, 'when I crossed the sand. When I killed Siosal. What does that mean for the outcome of the challenge?'

I hold my breath against the possibility it's been for nothing, but Rory smiles softly.

'There was quite the outrage after you killed Siosal and the shield finally dropped,' he says. 'Many of the Calahi there were also present at the challenge Siosal made on General Wolverton.' He glances between Lochlain and Ciara. 'They weren't impressed the shield went up at all – started calling foul play pretty early. When word spread that Aeyva and I were trying to break through it, it was clear to them something was wrong.'

'So the shield wasn't allowed?' I ask. 'I thought the Custodian gave the order to continue?'

'It's a grey area,' Aeyva says, her pale eyes full of anger. 'Magic is allowed – the shield was magic. But the challenge is also supposed to play out in view of the Court.'

My pulse starts to climb. I look back at Lochlain.

'So did we win?' I can't help the edge of panic in my voice. 'Are you ... General?' I choke on the title.

'The Custodian wasn't sure how to manage it all after the challenge, when the shield dropped and there were more than the two of us inside the circle,' he says. 'But...'

'But,' Ciara says, tears in her black and gold eyes. 'The Calahi of Airlie stood behind Lochlain and demanded he be appointed.' A tear runs down her face, but she smiles. 'That the role be returned to a Wolverton.'

'So we did it?' I ask, turning back to Lochlain's gaze.

'We did it,' he whispers, leaning in to press a kiss to my forehead. 'But the cost was so high, Lish. I'm sorry.'

I nod because I don't know what to say. Because he's right. The cost was far too high.

'Did you see the Commissioner of the Guard there?' I ask my team.

Blaire looks at me, thinking.

'We did,' she says. 'We've been talking about that a bit, actually.'

'What's the theory?'

'Well, clearly I'm not Hayes,' she smiles sadly. 'But I think it probably explains why the Guard wasn't looking into any of the missing women.'

'Yeah,' I sigh. 'What do you know?' I ask Aeyva.

'We've seen him before,' she says. 'Him being here every now and then was part of an arrangement between the worlds to show a bit of an allegiance, mostly symbolic, really. But he was supposed to keep an eye on any reports of unusual activity in Rhyton that could be magic and make it go away so the Realm would stay secret,' she says.

'No one thinks it's that much of a leap to say he was in bed with the former General,' Riley says. 'The issue will be proving it.'

'Will be?' I ask.

'Of course. None of us can let that go any more than you can.'

'And the Whispers?' I ask. 'How did they ... take you?' I look at my friends, unable to find a better way to ask.

The Calahi look at each other at that, but Riley looks at the ground. 'It was me,' she whispers. 'One of them overpowered me and forced the others to move.'

'It wasn't your fault, Riley,' Ciara's voice is gentle.

I think of how they fell when I killed them. But in the face of Hayes's blue eyes, I can't find any remorse that I did it.

'Will they support you now?' I ask. 'Some of them were clearly supporting Siosal.'

My connection with Lochlain prickles slightly as his face darkens. 'Any who actively supported Siosal with the abductions and at the challenge – when they took your friends – will be weeded out,' he says. 'Thankfully, I think that number will be relatively small. Siosal knew I had supporters in there, but I think he even would have been surprised how many. And, at the end of the day, the Whispers answer to the Throne.'

'Through their new General,' I say, giving him a gentle smile before I sink back into the couch cushions.

We bury Hayes on the hill behind Elenlea. He didn't know anyone here, having only come for me. So the service is just those of us that remain. Will and Riley take turns to talk quietly over his grave, their words striking the rawest part of me. Phoenix coughs and covers his face, taking a step away. Blaire and I hold each other close. Logically, I know we will all process this differently, will have to find different ways to work around the gaping hole. But, for now, we all seem hollowed out. Quiet on the inside and I don't know how to make us whole again. I don't think we ever will be.

We're walking back down the hill when my skin prickles. Pausing to look back into the wood and the darkness that's growing there I wait for a beat.

As the others continue on, not realising I've stopped, amber eyes appear at the edge of the trees. Slowly, I incline my head to the wolf watching my every move.

'Thank you,' I whisper, 'for helping me. For saving him. From the bottom of my heart, I thank you.'

The grey wolf steps forward, slightly further into the light and seems to dip its head at me in return. Its eyes are strangely sorrowful, like it knows what we've just had to do. Like it regrets I couldn't save both of them. I watch its long, furred tail disappear back into the trees before I continue my way back down the hill.

We gather for drinks at Ciara's after the service and share stories of Hayes. The time he pretended to be a jilted lover to rescue Riley from a disastrous date. How he would inhale deeply as he stepped across the threshold to his grandmother's house, knowing he was home. The way his eyes glinted when he solved a problem we couldn't find a way around. Of his hard to provoke but hearty laugh, and his adoration of the woman that raised him. Tears well in my eyes as they land on Blaire's hands. In them she holds the ring of his grandfather's he wore on his little finger, now on a chain to return to his grandmother.

It doesn't take long for the drinks to start flowing and the Calahi to start laughing with us. It feels good to share Hayes with those who didn't really know him, and we laugh as often as we cry. They will remember him for what he gave for their cause but also now a little for the person he was. Lochlain clears his throat and makes a quiet toast to Hayes. My heart breaks all over again and Will and Phoenix nod shallowly in gratitude.

'So,' Riley says, who's sitting next to me. 'You've got magic.'

I turn the glass I hold in my hand. 'Yeah.'

'It was pretty impressive, what you did,' she says.

'It doesn't freak you out?'

She laughs. 'There's a lot of things freaking me out right now,' she says, and I can't help but smile at her. 'That is just one of them. I'm processing.' She takes a sip of her drink.

'Me too,' I say, lifting my brows.

'We'll figure it out,' she says. 'Surely queens are allowed some processing time, too.'

CHAPTER THIRTY-THREE

I'd left it to Ciara to select an outfit for me for Lochlain's swearing in ceremony, having no idea what I should wear to such an occasion. She wanted to help with my hair and make-up as well and I was more than happy to oblige her. In Rhyton, we so rarely got dressed up for formal events, save our graduation from Guard College, and having Ciara dance around me while I sip a glass of wine in my bedroom is quite relaxing.

Her glossy, dark hair is already done up in an intricate braid that starts at the base of her neck and weaves out and around her head like a crown. She's made her eyes up darkly, in colours that bring out the gold, and wears a dressing gown with soft pants underneath. I'd laughed at her when she arrived at my door but she insisted it was better to be comfortable for as long as possible, and I should never wear a shirt that needs to go over my head when having hair and make-up done. So, I have found myself in the same outfit as her. And I have to give it to her, it's very comfortable.

She checks the intricate clock on the wall.

'Right, time to get you into your gown,' she says and disappears down the hall briefly. 'No, you may not come up,' I hear her shout down the stairs. Reappearing in my room with a dress bag in hand. 'So impatient,' she says.

My stomach flutters with nerves. I feel like I'm going on a first date. A really fancy, important first date. She instructs me to strip off and raises her eyebrows slightly at my choice in underwear, the corner of her mouth lifting in a smile, suppressing a laugh.

'I always wear the fancy underwear you bought me, nothing to see here,' I say blushing madly and she laughs out loud then.

'Stand up and close your eyes,' she instructs. 'Hold out your arms.'

The fabric she wriggles up my arms and over my shoulders is cool against my skin. She wraps it around my waist and fastens it behind me before she tells me to open my eyes and make my way to the mirror.

'God, Ciara, you're an artist,' I say, admiring myself. She smiles at me over my shoulder.

'One more thing,' she says as she scoots out the door and returns holding a jewellery box in her hands. 'These belonged to our mother,' she says. 'For saving her son, I think she would've liked you to wear them tonight.'

The earrings are unbelievable. They look like hammered copper, crafted into a long, elegant pattern that would be impossible for human hands to create. At the end of each pendant is an irregular sapphire, about the size of the nail on my little finger. She's pinned my hair back high and loose with slightly curled strands falling around my head. It allows the earrings to be on full display.

Ciara hurries off again to get dressed and I look at myself once more. The dress she's picked out is a cornflower blue that sets off the sapphire earrings I now wear. Long, slightly voluminous sleeves are cuffed at the wrists and the low-cut top hugs my breasts tightly, a ribbon of the same colour looping around my waist and tying at the back. The skirt skims my hips and its yards and yards of fabric swish around my legs. When I bend to put on my copper shoes, I realise there is a thigh high split in the skirt that will take some getting used to. But it's stunning – and it's not lost on me that she's picked accessories that match Lochlain's eyes.

I walk slowly downstairs, so I don't fall down them in these shoes. Lochlain is waiting at the bottom, pacing. He halts mid-pace when he sees me and his mouth opens slightly before he closes it again and holds out his hand to help me down the last step.

'You're—' he says, shaking his head. 'I don't have the words for what you are.'

'Beautiful would be a good start,' I say, raising an eyebrow at him.

'Doesn't do you justice, I'm afraid,' he says, fingering the earrings. 'I see Ciara has helped with this.'

I nod. 'Do you mind?' I ask. 'I'm just borrowing them.'

He draws me close and kisses my forehead, a thrill going through me. 'They're perfect on you,' he says.

I pull away a little and walk around him, letting a hand trail gently behind me across his body. His ceremonial dress is a black suit with long tails on the jacket. The collar stands tall around his neck, where sapphires accentuate the corners. He wears a sash of two strips of colour, sapphire and forest green, that's pinned at his hip by his copper pin. His pants are closely fitted and I wish I could peak under those jacket tails. He has a sword at his side and, as I complete my circle of him, I feel a little out of breath. I place my hand on his chest and step close to him.

'You, Lochlain, are *exquisite*,' I whisper.

He laughs gently and pulls me closer until I'm pressed against the length of him. I trace the contours of his face, around his eye, over his cheek bone and down to his mouth. He bends his head to mine and—

'No time for that,' Ciara says as she makes her way down the stairs. 'We need to get you officially sworn in.'

She wears black velvet like a second skin and it catches the light as she moves. Sapphire-tipped, white feathers fan across her shoulder blades and meet at the base of her neck lightly before the gown disappears in a deep plunge down her back.

'I've decided I don't want the job,' he says, looking at me.

'Of course you have, now move it,' she shoos us through the kitchen and out the front door.

The ceremony itself is short. The Custodian presenting Lochlain to the court as General of Airlie. The Calahi around me clap and cheer, a smile tugging at my mouth. I still can't read other Calahi like I can Lochlain, but I don't need my magic to see how happy they are to have him in this role.

The Custodian asks Lochlain to swear, in the presence of the Throne and citizens of the Court, and the Realm, to protect and serve above all other priorities and motivations.

Lochlain finds me in the crowd, the intensity on his face as he swears fealty sending shivers down my spine. Ciara takes my hand as the Custodian places an amulet of some kind over Lochlain's head and he bows deeply.

Beside me, Ciara tears up as Lochlain tries to make his way to us through the throng of Calahi; but he is frequently stopped and congratulated and asked to share drinks with different groups. Judging he will be a while, we head to the bar.

The throne room looks vastly different from the last time I was here, chandeliers hover high above the crowd and couches and stools set around glass tables punctuate the space. Waiters and waitresses scurry across the marble floor, their trays refilling themselves as they empty. The mood is light and festive and the music from the quartet in the corner is finding its beat in my chest, tempting me with the dance floor.

But nothing can remove the bleeding stain of Hayes's death.

Aeyva's steel-grey gown matches her eyes and she wears her hair down tonight. She seems almost soft without her shaved hair and skull tattoos on display. Almost, that is, until I can see her eyes fierce as ever. Her gaze fixes on Ciara as she walks towards us, nodding in my direction without looking at me. Wordlessly she takes Ciara's hand and waits. Ciara taps her other hand nervously on her knee, not unlike what I have seen Lochlain do, before she gives some unseen message to Aeyva who tugs her gently to dance.

The memory of Lochlain's blood pooling on the floor and the sound of Hayes's neck snapping is a constant reminder of the violence that has taken place here. More mementos of moments I wish I'd never experienced. I regularly find myself seeking Lochlain out in the crowd, to reassure myself he's still standing. Just as my eyes start to flick a little more quickly, unable to find him, a large, tanned hand offers me a pink, sparkly drink.

'Ravishing, does that work?' he whispers, bringing back the goose bumps.

'Congratulations, General.' I smile at him before looking back at Aeyva and Ciara who are holding each other like it's the first and last time. It's hard to tell from this distance but ... I think Ciara's face is damp with tears.

'Did you know about that?' I ask Lochlain. I see him smile from the corner of my eye.

'I had a theory, but Aeyva can be guarded,' he says. 'I would imagine this proves me right. But she's made Ciara wait a long time ... so, we'll see how she responds.'

I sip my drink. 'Judging by the way they're looking at each other, I think she already has.'

'Would you dance with me, Lish?' he asks, serious now.

'Who would I be to refuse the General?'

Lochlain spins me gently around the dance floor, my dress whirling around us. He moves like the magic in his veins and I imagine us as the sapphire and copper threads I wove together the day of the challenge. Each answering the other's move before it's made. The song ends too soon, my chest pounding. Abruptly Lochlain stands a little straighter and inclines his head as he looks over my shoulder. I turn to see who approaches and find myself face to face with the Custodian. I drop into a curtsy, my skirt pooling on the floor not unlike Lochlain's blood. I blink the image away and rise. The fact he should be bowing to me flashes through my mind.

'Your Grace, allow me to introduce Alice Taylor,' Lochlain says, gesturing to me.

'A pleasure to meet you, Mistress Taylor.' His voice is syrupy and the hairs on the back of my neck stand up. 'The first spot on the General's dance card is an enviable one, indeed.' Something about his voice catches my attention but I can't place it. His dark eyes study mine, trying to strip me bare.

A secret knowledge flickers behind his eyes and he smiles. He leaves us, the six guards in forest green uniforms trailing behind him as I watch him walk away.

I jump when Sofia bumps my arm, dragging my attention from the Custodian. 'Dance with us!' she shouts over the music and I grin, happily accepting the hand Nico extends to me, the size of his smile matching the gladness in my heart to see him safe and happy. She and Nico were spared attending the challenge – guarded by Royalists instead – and I'm grateful I haven't added more horror to their lives.

I spend the rest of the night dancing with Riley, Blaire, and Sofia, with the occasional dance with Rory – who is an exceptional, albeit sinful, dancer. It's hard not to notice that he and Riley keep finding each other's gaze, but they say nothing and she is the only one he doesn't dance with. As my feet tire, I make my way to the table where Phoenix and Will are drinking a toast to Hayes, who would have loved an opportunity to dress up and dance.

Phoenix's eyes are sad when they rest on me, and a sinking feeling fills me. Though, when Blaire and Riley come over, ready to call it a night, the sadness from him recedes just a fraction.

I head home with the others, Lochlain promising not to be long, and walk home laughing softly with my friends, shoes in hand.

The streets are quiet, and I notice we are still trailed by Aeyva's guards. The threat of the former General has gone and standing with the new General has all but guaranteed their safety in Airlie. But I guess there might still be others who are loyal to his cause or would like to sacrifice humans at the next Giving.

I walk with my gaze raised, marvelling at the starry night sky, and fall behind a little. The sensation in my chest and the smile on my face as I look up at the sky makes me realise I may, in fact, be home.

Phoenix drops back to walk with me.

'It seems you've found your wolf,' he says.

'What?' I say, looking away from the stars and frowning at him in the low light.

'Your wolf, Lish,' he says. 'I remember that story you told Nico. Of the wolves that will guide you to the blue star.'

My walking slows.

'What do you mean?' I ask, coming to a stop to face him. He looks at me curiously, surprised I haven't put this together already.

'His name is Wolverton, right?'

It's in the stables that Lochlain finds me later. I'd intended to go in and change but I wanted to hold on to the peace I feel with Niamh close by and the gentle caress of night-time in Elenlea.

'How is she?' Lochlain asks as he walks into the stable. It's dark in here but the moon is bright enough that I can make him out in the filtered light.

'Jealous she didn't get to come dancing with the new General but I'm sure she'll forgive you, in time.'

He chuckles in the way that jangles my nerves and stands next to me at Niamh's stall gate. Leaning over slightly, he rubs down her face and she blinks sleepily at him.

'You really do look incredible tonight, Lish, thank you for coming,' he says, turning to face me. I step closer to him and lay my hand on his chest.

'Thank you for having me, I didn't realise being first on your dance card was such an *enviable* position.'

'Really?' he asks. 'I'm surprised you didn't notice all the other bidders.' He laughs. Releasing my hands, he removes the pendant from around his neck.

'Do you remember I told you about the pieces of Roisin's sapphire?' he asks. 'This is the Wolverton piece Benny talked about in his letter. It should have never been in the hands of the previous General and, now that I've got it back, I'd like you to have it.'

'Oh, Lochlain, you can't give that to me.' I hold a hand up at the pendant.

'Then look after it for me,' he says. 'It's not practical for me to wear, anyway.'

He places the copper chain over my head and the pendant falls heavily between my breasts. It's warm from where he's held it in his hand and my heart stutters. Picking up the pendant to examine it, Lochlain briefly creates a small ball of light in the palm of his hand for me to see by.

'Another trick of the trade, I see,' I say, raising an eyebrow at him.

The slightly oblong, irregular piece of sapphire is kept in a cap of copper. An engraving of a wolf winds around it and my chest constricts as Phoenix's words come back to me. Lochlain watches me for a moment, suddenly more serious and runs a finger along my cheek. The strength in his emotions reminds me of my days in the cell when he would sit outside my door. What a long way from that we are.

A thought I've tried to keep buried rises and I force myself to voice it.

'Does this – me as ... and you as General, change'—I wave my hands between us, grappling for the words—'whatever this is.'

I focus on ignoring his feelings, it seems like cheating to try and sort through them, even though I can't help but notice that his breathing changes.

'What do you want it to be?' he whispers.

I look helplessly up at him, at a loss as to how to respond. I want it to be everything. I want him to be – but what am I to a warrior Calahi? Who's kin sacrifice humans at the Giving.

One who believes in the Throne above all else.

But he's also the one I think of to drive away my nightmares, whose face I want to see before all others. The one whose touch simultaneously grounds me and sets me free.

Lochlain's face is inches from mine, close enough for our breath to mingle. I open my mouth, but words fail me. I cup his face in my hand and draw him closer still. The shape of his mouth is visible in the light. The mouth I have tried to avoid before and now don't need to. I trace his soft lips gently with the pad of my ring finger. Over the defined edges and perfect cupid's bow.

He doesn't press me to answer.

'It doesn't change it for me,' he says, and I brace myself for what's coming. Knowing I'm in too deep for any bracing to help. 'But ... others – I'm not deserving of you, Lish,' his voice drops so low I can barely hear him. 'I – you're the Queen.' His eyes widen in disbelief. Not at who I am but at what he feels for me.

Shifting my hand to the back of his head I stand on my toes.

'Let me make something abundantly clear, Lochlain,' I whisper against his mouth, our lips brushing so softly I might have imagined the contact. 'I care if you lie to me again, even by omission. I care how *you* feel about me. I care about the opinions of my closest friends. I do *not* care about some archaic societal constraints a bunch of strangers might like to impose on me.'

He stills for a moment, a wave of something so deep I don't dare to try and name it brushing my senses.

I gently kiss his mouth and he trembles under my touch. He makes a sound in his throat, any semblance of restraint leaving him. His hands are in my hair and roving over my hips and back, pressing me into him as he explores my mouth with his. I take his bottom lip in my teeth and bite, hard enough to draw a sharp inhale from him. His hips drive against mine before he takes a breath, forcing himself to slow and kisses me deeply and slowly. Every inch of my body is aware of where we touch. The rest aches to touch – and be touched. His hand finds the split in my dress and he lifts my knee around his hip, his callused hand like fire on my skin.

I suck the cool air deep into my lungs, tipping my head back as his mouth finds my neck—

'Loch,' Rory calls, his voice cracking across the yard. Lochlain's growl reverberates along my throat.

'Ignore him,' he whispers, kissing me again.

'Loch!' he calls, louder, and it's my turn to groan. We move slightly apart, Lochlain holding me firmly to his side, his thumb rubbing against my hip as Rory enters the stable. He's still wearing his jade suit from the ceremony.

'Ah,' he says, laughing, 'of course.'

'What is it, Rory?' The edge in Lochlain's voice clear.

'Some of the Royalists are insisting on coming by for a night cap to celebrate your appointment—'

'I'm not available, Ror,' Lochlain says pointedly.

Rory just laughs again.

'Listen, I'm sorry, I know how badly you two need some time together, I do.' He smiles and I blush. 'But you know they're going to come anyway. This has been a long-time coming, Loch, and we've all worked hard for it. I thought I should warn you first just in case ...' He gestures at us.

'It's fine,' I say to Lochlain softly. 'Enjoy your night.'

He pins me with an incredulous stare.

'I had every intention of doing just that,' he whispers.

My insides warm at his tone. I turn to him once more and slide my body along his as I stand on my toes.

'I promise I'll let you make it up to me,' I whisper in his ear, gently biting his earlobe to make my point.

His fingers tighten on my lower back.

'I'll see you in there,' Rory says, 'and remember to pace yourself out here.'

He throws his head back and laughs before heading back to the house, still chuckling to himself.

CHAPTER THIRTY-FOUR

'Loch! Lish! Come down here,' Ciara calls from downstairs.

I stretch and groan, arching into Lochlain as he embraces me from behind. Where he has remained since he came to my bed during the night, after his celebratory drinks ended.

'Clearly, you Calahi have no sense of timing,' I grumble, blinking into the morning light. He presses a line of soft kisses against my neck. The memory of last night pressing back in, warming me.

'You don't need to tell me that,' he says. 'But with that tone, she's not—'

Ciara pounds on the door.

'The Custodian is about to make an announcement about your appointment, Loch. You should see this,' she says.

'This might be embarrassing,' Lochlain says. 'But Mother it feels good to have rid Airlie of an insidious traitor to the Crown and,' he looks seriously at me, 'having avenged your mother's lover – your father. She would have been an incredible Queen, Lish.' He hops out of bed and extends a hand to me. 'With Siosal out of the way, Nuala and I will be able to work with the Custodian to correct the Givings. Find out why they're not working as they should.'

He grins.

'Not to mention, start paving the way for you, when you're ready,' he says. 'For the first time in a long time, I am excited for Airlie's future. There's a long road ahead of course, but – we won.'

I take his outstretched hand, self-doubt gnawing at me.

Downstairs, an image of the Custodian, seated next to the throne, fills the living room. I swallow as I am plunged back into the throne room.

Night-coloured, wavy hair is expertly arranged off his face to show his features. His face is slightly lined with age, but it only adds to his attractiveness.

'—every confidence he will fulfill the duties of the role with utmost professionalism and integrity,' he says, obviously talking about Lochlain. The words similar to those he used in his speech last night.

'Father would have been so proud to see this, Loch,' Ciara says quietly, squeezing his arm. He nods slowly.

'As the citizens of the Court and the Realm know, the Court of Airlie has long sought the return of the Queen and her offspring.' His voice is crisp.

My heart beats faster than I thought it could. The memory takes me by surprise. *I'm scared and I don't know why. I need to find –*

'To date,' the Custodian is saying, his hand absently caressing the large staff at side, 'we have not yet found her or any evidence of—'

My head hurts and I can't make it stop. Mummy, how do I make it stop? My ears –

'—increasing our efforts—' his voice is melodic.

Why is it so dark? Mummy, where are you? My head—

'—citizens will be expected to play a role—'

I'm under the table and I can hear them but I can't see. Someone is talking to Mummy but I know not to come out. '—you've been incredibly stupid, of course. But I suppose that can only be expected. You have always shown poor judgement.'

My vision starts to swim and I'm having trouble focusing on what the Custodian is saying.

'—increased the number of Givings to—'

I feel the drop in Lochlain's emotions and Ciara pales.

I can see now and her face is above me, through the crack in the floor. The blood is creeping towards me. A stick stamps on the floor—

'Court of Airlie, I assure you we will find out what happened to the heir and restore our Court to its glory,' he says, stamping his staff for emphasis.

Nausea surges like a volcano and I stumble to the kitchen sink and retch. Lochlain and Ciara take a moment to catch up then they are both at my side – Lochlain rubbing my back. I lean on my elbows at the side of the sink, running the water to wash away the vomit that's still burning in my throat.

'His voice,' I say, talking to the floor. 'I remember his voice.'

Understanding starts to wash through Lochlain.

'It was his staff—' I cover my mouth.

'Lish?' Ciara inquires gently.

I wash my face and stand, my knees still a little wobbly. Ciara steps back to give me space and I look at each of them, their shocked expressions almost matching.

'The Custodian,' I say, tears starting to leak down my cheeks. 'It – it was the Custodian. He used his staff.'

I look up at them through hot tears, overwhelmed with an ache I can't name. The enormity of now knowing the once faceless man – Calahi – who snatched away the life I was supposed to have, splices through every vein in my body. The missing answer I've searched for my whole life. But, instead of taking him to the Commissioner, as I'd always imagined, I *curtsied* to him. The angry bitterness that the Calahi who killed her currently sits in her – *my* – Throne sits in my stomach like acid.

A tornado rips through my mind, lifting the shattered pieces of my reality with another soul-crushing realisation. 'You know this means he's known all along? That he has encouraged the murder of other, completely innocent, women to cover his own depravity?'

The colour hasn't returned to Ciara's face. Black shadows cross Lochlain's. Neither of them answer.

The back door bangs as Aeyva and Rory join us, my Rhyton friends not far behind them.

'Ciara told us,' Rory says, and it takes me a moment to remember that's one of her abilities – communication. 'This puts a bit of a dampener on things,' Rory says.

Aeyva paces slowly, calculating. She pierces me with her steel-grey eyes, pointing a single finger at my chest. 'You need to take your crown. Now. It's the quickest, most straightforward way to remove him. Then we can determine his punishment. The Calahi of Airlie deserve to know the truth.'

It's clear death will be the only option considered. I don't disagree but I blanch.

'I thought you said my heart needed to be in it before I could do that?' The selfishness of the words make me wince as they roll off my tongue.

'Pretty sentiments only apply when there's time,' Aeyva says. 'There is no time, now. 'He killed our Queen. That fundamentally changes how we move forward. He will not give you your crown unless the Calahi of Airlie demand it.' Her eyes narrow. 'Or you kill him. Our Court is dying, *your* Court is dying. And so is the human world. I don't care how we do it, you will take that crown if I have to drag you to it.'

'Aeyv—' Rory says, resigned to her style but gently suggesting she tone it down nonetheless.

I look to him, grateful for the support.

I shake my head.

'She's right,' I say, a fist clenching behind my ribs. 'But I have conditions.'

Rory's face splits into a grin. 'Talking like a queen already.'

'God help us,' Riley says, eyes wide.

Ciara's back steps groan slightly as I make my way out of her house and across the yard. Lochlain's brushing Niamh as I enter the stables. He murmurs to her like he often does, and she almost dozes under his hands.

'Is there somewhere we can go ... before ...' I ask. He slides his eyes to me.

'Before what?' he asks, putting the brush down.

'Before I have to take the Throne and save the world?' I ask flippantly, even as concern starts to gnaw at me. 'I mean, somewhere we can go. Just us,' I say.

He takes Niamh out of her stall and we race out of the city and along the face of the hill it's built into. The warmth of his body behind mine, anchoring me to Niamh as the Realm rushes past, is intoxicating. I lean back into him and we move with Niamh's motion. I'm not ready for the ride to finish when we approach a quaint cottage nestled in a narrow valley.

The white, weatherboard house has a verandah that runs across the front and disappears around each side. Ranch style stables are set back a little way from the house and, like the rest of the hills and meadows that surround Elenlea, everything is so incredibly green.

Dotted along the sea of emerald are tiny yellow flowers and, having dismounted Niamh, I sit near a patch of these and watch the white clouds drift across the blue sky. It's still much cooler here than Rhyton, or anywhere else in Driarn, but the days are warming slightly and the sun on my skin is welcome, instead of something to fear.

Quietly, Lochlain sits beside me in the grass and I distractedly run the stems of the yellow flowers I've picked through my fingers. If I could freeze time, this is a spot I would do it. When the world seems so beautiful and at peace. When the anticipation of what could unfold between Lochlain and me is still exciting and I don't need to experience the hurt that awaits me if I mess it up. Before we head into unknown waters of what lies between us and the tasks I am supposed to complete. Of working out how to get Airlie to support me like they did Lochlain so I can take my Throne. Stop them Giving and find another way to save the Mother. Finding the Star my mother and the librarian spoke of. Working out why that is important.

And how to ensure the Custodian is served justice for his role in my mother's death and Siosal's awful practices.

In truth I've always wanted to make a difference, but I've never known how. Or thought I was brave or smart enough to be one of the few that can change the world. I still don't, but the reality of how few choices there seem to be weighs on me, even as I wonder how much one person can really do.

'It's beautiful here,' I say to distract me from my own thoughts.

'I bought it a long time ago, to have somewhere to escape to,' he says. 'It sounded like what you need now, too.'

He's sitting with his legs outstretched and leans back on his hands. His white shirt stretches across his broad chest; it's easy to make out the impression of the leather straps he wears and the shape of him underneath those. I lie back in the grass, hands beneath my head and look at the sky. Around us, a gentle wood starts and wraps around behind the stable, the cottage sitting just off-centre of this meadow, like it's held in the palm of nature's hand.

'I have a condition,' I say.

'More than no time commitment?'

'Yes. You must promise me it won't change us.' He starts to shake his head and I cut him off. 'I know how you feel about your Realm, Lochlain, and I don't want you to look at me like I'm anything other than me.'

He reaches out and tucks a strand of hair behind my ear before cupping my face.

'Queen or not Lish, you're incredible. And yes, I promise I will always see you that way.'

I smile at him.

'Okay – oh, and'—a thought pops into my head—'I want today.' I lean into his hand and close my eyes. 'Let me have today.' His face splits into a slow grin.

'Oh, yes,' he drawls. 'And what exactly would you like to do with today?'

'I can think of a few things,' I murmur.

Lochlain flips over and prowls towards me on all fours, forcing me to lay down underneath him, which is exactly where I want to be. The flowers around me blow in the breeze and tickle my face. I watch his curls move slightly in the breeze. Behind him the immense stretch of blue is full of endless possibilities.

His chest is warm above me where I place my hand over his heart and I watch it rise and fall, the ridges of his weapon straps moving along with his breath. His eyes are still on my face when I look back up to him.

'What exactly do you want from today, Lish?' he asks again. His voice is a purr and shivers run along my skin in response.

'I want this,' I whisper, pushing slightly on his chest to emphasise my point. 'I want all of this.'

His breath hitches as he places his hand over mine and squeezes gently. 'It might not always be that easy,' he says quietly.

'No doubts. I choose this, Lochlain. I choose you. I made that decision a long time ago.'

He moves to lie on his side and, reaching for my hip, pulls me with him. Tugging me closer until I am lying flush against him. I cup his face in my left hand stroking my thumb over his cheekbone, taking in his chocolate freckles. His black and copper eyes bore into mine, his fingers tense on my hip as the fields that surround us hum against each other.

'And I want this,' I say against his lips before kissing him slowly.

His large, warm hand travels from my hip to the back of my head and he crushes his mouth against mine, his tongue urgent. Pulling back a little, his eyes are dark when they find my own again and he exhales softly. Tilting my head back to reach his face I kiss him deeply again, his lips impossibly soft. I suck his bottom lip gently and he inhales sharply before kissing me harder, his teeth grazing my lips as he bites at them. I trail kisses along his jaw, and, pressing myself closer still, I drag my teeth along the tender part of his neck before placing soft kisses there instead.

'And this,' I murmur where I can feel his pulse racing against my mouth.

The hand that's free roves down my side and grips my ass as he holds me firm to him, warmth seeping through me. I can feel how badly he wants this but I savour the feel of his mouth on mine before I rise to my knees and pull him with me. Knee to knee it's impossible not to notice how much larger than me he is and I run my hands down his torso, his almost wholly black eyes watching me. I lift the bottom of his shirt.

'I want this off,' I say.

He crosses his arms in front of him and grips the hem. His gaze holds mine for a moment before he removes his shirt in a fluid motion.

'Oh—'

The air escapes my lungs and I sit back on my heels.

Painted across his chest is the majestic face of a wolf. One with amber eyes and lustrous black and copper fur dancing in the sunlight. I blink up at him before I rise on my knees again and slowly run my fingers over his tattoo.

'This is – wow,' I say, meeting his eyes. 'What—'

'It's the symbol of my family,' he says roughly, skin prickling under my touch.

I look at him. 'Don't tell me you turn into a wolf on a full moon?'

He smiles wickedly and my insides heat.

'I don't, not anymore. And it didn't require a full moon.'

'You're joking,' I whisper, my fingers continuing their trail, gradually working their way lower and lower down his torso.

'No,' he breathes, the smile gone. 'But, between the decline in nature, the source of our magic, and the Giving, there's just not enough in the bloodline anymore.'

Not knowing what to make of that, either the possibility or the loss he feels, I focus on the feel of him beneath my hands slowly circling between his hips, his shirt now in the grass beside him. His breathing comes harder as I trail his firm chest again and find the buckles to his weapon straps. Letting them fall away, I look at him as I take the waistband of his pants in my hands.

'I want these off too.'

My need for him builds heatedly but I make myself take this slow and feel every sensation. He obliges me with the removal of his pants and kneels before me again. This warrior, in this moment, with his dark hair and eyes, emblazoned with a wolf tattoo and kneeling in a swaying, emerald sea, is simply the most incredible thing I've ever seen.

I take my time to relieve myself of my own clothing as he watches, the intensity in his gaze marking my skin, and kneel before him again wearing only his pendant. The breeze licks at me as I deliberately run my hands along his collarbones and down over his chest. His skin is smooth and soft over his tense muscles.

I kiss my way across his chest and up to the base of his throat. His hands twitch slightly at his sides but he waits for me. Taking his hands, I place them on my waist for him and close my eyes at both the relief and tension they bring. His skin was made to be on mine.

'I want you to touch me,' I whisper.

The connection between us goes taut before each of our edges gives way to the other and we exist in a bubble of time all our own. He runs his hands up my sides, his callouses rough on my skin, and cups my breasts. Trembling with restraint he holds my gaze and gently rolls my nipples in his fingers, the heat in my body flaring to fever in response.

I pull him towards me as I lie back in the grass, his weight finally pressing into me, anchoring me. He runs his nose up my neck and bites my ear, shivers racing down my spine before he lowers himself to my breasts and takes a nipple in his mouth, sucking hard. I arch myself into him.

'I want you, Lochlain.' I slip a hand between us and show him where I want him. 'I want this,' I breathe into his chest and open myself to him. 'I need this. I want you to show me what you want.'

He groans against my neck and takes my mouth as if he can't get enough of it.

'Oh, Lish,' he breathes.

Gently, he pushes against me, giving me a moment to adjust to the feel of him before burying himself where I need him most. A moan escapes my lips at the way he fills me. Slowly, excruciatingly slowly, he begins to move and the tension in my core builds. I push him along with my hips, letting my head fall back in the cool grass.

My breath comes in short gasps. My body takes over and I dig my nails into his back as I start to implode. Breathing shallowly, I grind my hips against him. 'Please,' I moan into his shoulder, 'pl—'.

He moves faster then and I let go of my fear, of my inhibitions, and I free fall over the edge as my body shatters around me. He entwines his hands in my hair, cradling my head and shudders as he finds his own release, murmuring against my neck. Giving himself to me wholly, he lets go of his emotions, dampening my cheeks with their intensity. I wrap my legs around his hips and hold him to me. Never intending to let go.

Gradually, my breathing returns to normal and I release my legs enough for him to lie next to me again in the grass. Laying my head in the soft spot between his shoulder and his chest. My fingers trace over the wolf once more. I'll never get enough of it, of him. I tip my head back to look at him and his eyes find mine. The blackness has given way to the copper again now and the dual rings glint in the gentle sun.

'Does that answer your question?' I ask. He chuckles in the way that makes my insides turn to jelly and I smile into his chest.

'I think it's fair to say we feel the same way,' he says. 'Does that answer your question as well?'

I look up at him again and let his emotions wash over me now he's not holding them so tightly.

'For now,' I say. 'But feel free to tell me all the nice and sexy things in your heart anytime.'

Rolling me back in the grass he leans over and kisses me longingly. 'You are the only nice and sexy thing in my heart, Lish.'

I press my palms against his chest, I like the feel of the movement there. He narrows his eyes at me.

'What?' I ask.

He studies me for a moment and watches the flowers I can feel brushing against my hair as they blow in the breeze.

'Something tells me your heart is going to catch up to being Queen quickly.'

'What makes you say that?'

My face heats at his belief in me. He stands and holds out a hand to help me to my feet. Walking naked through the meadow makes me feel both vulnerable and liberated and goose bumps rise on my skin as he leads me to the cottage. Holding my arms out to the side, I smile at the sky and relish the sun on my skin

Beside me Lochlain laughs freely.

'You are far more Calahi than you realise,' he says, leading me into the cottage and waving his hand at the fire to start as we pass it, something I've never seen him do before. 'Close your eyes,' he instructs gently as we approach a doorway to what seems to be a small bedroom, my body tightening in anticipation.

He pulls me forward through the doorway and turns me around before shuffling us sideways. I feel him stand beside me and his warm arm wraps around my waist holding me to him. He presses his face gently into my hair and I arch into him, my body already starting to respond.

'I think your Calahi heart has already decided where it lies,' he whispers. 'Look,' his breath stirs my hair.

Gasping, I cover my mouth on reflex. My eyes skim over the image in front of me, unsure what to take in first. In the depths of my soul the small gold flame flickers in recognition and my heart thumps under my ribs. Reflected in a dresser mirror before me is a naked woman, her unbound hair falling around her shoulders. Beside her stands Lochlain, his dark eyes meeting the woman's in the reflection.

And the wolf that graces Lochlain's chest.

A wolf whose amber eyes are fixed on the crown of yellow flowers woven in her hair.

Acknowledgements

First and foremost, thank you to you. For reading Amber Wolf and sticking with me until this point. I hope you have enjoyed this story and the characters as much as I have, and I look forward to sharing the rest of their journey with you.

To my husband, who unfailingly supported me through this whole journey and continues to do so. For your endless patience and encouragement and steadfast belief that I should make this happen. For drying my tears when I doubted my ability to bring this book to life and for trying so hard to understand why I love fantasy so much!

To my children, the absolute lights of my life. All of this was inspired by a need to show you that you don't need to be constrained by the societal expectations of you. That you are never too old to break the mould. And that your dreams are important. I hope you follow them relentlessly.

To my Mum and Dad, thank you for the springboard you have given me and the consistent encouragement to push myself out of my comfort zone. None of this would be possible without you. Thank you for your endless reading of my drafts and delving into the abstract with me. And...for not making it weird when you came across all the steamy scenes...

To my 'writing crew'. These are the people without whom my excitement for writing would have fizzled out a long time ago! The people who do everything from fall in love with my characters, lament the ones who are lost and help me work through when it should be 'I' and when its 'me'. For reading, suggesting, workshopping, texting, emailing, video chatting, rereading and everything in between, thank you, thank you, thank you! Some particular call outs I'd like to make here are: Amy Morse (@amymorsebooks) – genuinely one of the kindest, most generous and creative souls on the planet and one I am so grateful to know; and Erin Ogilvie-Fisher (@erinogilviefisher) – a woman whose knowledge of the craft and ability to see the big picture in a story is truly remarkable. AMBER WOLF would not be what it is today without each of you, and the rest of the 'crew', and I am truly thankful for your help in realising this dream.

To my editors, Alexandra Dawning of Dawning Edits (www.dawning edits.com) and Danikka Taylor of Taylor Made Media (www.taylormade media.online). You're both extraordinary people I feel so privileged to have been able to work with and for AMBER WOLF to have had your special love and care to help turn it into a story I still dream about.

To Adrienne Young (www.adrienneyoungbooks.com) who, without even knowing, inspired me to start thinking of myself as a writer; to keep writing; and then write with my soul.

WANT MORE?

AMBER WOLF (DRIARN DUOLOGY, BOOK 1)

FRIEND. GUARD. ORPHAN.
Lish Taylor thinks she knows who she is.
But when her tactical team begins to investigate a series of abductions,
the haunting questions she's carried since her mother's murder come
flooding back. With the case growing increasingly suspicious, Lish leaves
her climate-ravaged city to seek answers, even after she's ordered to stand
down—only to be abducted herself.
Captured by the brutal General Siosal, Lish is determined to free not only
herself, but also the General's other victims. With the enigmatic cell-guard,
Lochlain, as her unexpected ally, Lish's escape catapults her into the hidden
world of the Calahi, where magic pulses through the land. But, even with
its incredible differences, Lish can't ignore that this world is also suffering.
The threads of her investigation soon draw Lish into a war for a dying
kingdom. To survive – and reclaim her future – she must bring those she
loves together and prove that healing a broken world begins with standing
in your truth.

Amber Wolf is an adult, dystopian fantasy with forced proximity, found family, fated mates, climate themes and hidden worlds. If you love family secrets, slow burn open door romance and epic magic, this is for you.

BLUE POINTED STAR (DRIARN DUOLOGY, BOOK 2)

A new queen must save the Realm.

But those who would deny her the crown are strong.

Lish Taylor knows that she is the rightful Queen of Airlie. But, before she can officially claim the throne, she is accused of murdering the previous queen – her mother. Forced to retreat to a neighbouring court, the shadow of regicide at her heels, Lish's only chance to regain her throne, and prevent the collapse of both the Human and Calahi lands, is to reassemble the shattered pieces of the Blue Pointed Star.

Underground assassin, Aeyva Kaylneau, is one step closer to fulfilling her lifelong dream of becoming a Sentinel to the Queen. But Aeyva's past allegiances threaten to jeopardise everything she has worked for, and the secrets she keeps have the potential to not only push away the woman she loves, but bring the entire Court of Airlie to its knees.

As the Human and Calahi realms crumble around them, Lish and Aeyva must unite a network of allies across rival courts and the boundaries of magic, to expose a sinister conspiracy that imperils the very fabric of their worlds. As Queen and her Sentinel, they must show that the future belongs to those who fight for more than power.

Blue Pointed Star is the final book in the Driarn duology (sequel to Amber Wolf). Lovers of fated mates, slow burn open door romance, sapphic romance, found family and becoming who you were always meant to be will adore this thrilling conclusion.

WHEN SECRETS BECKON

Every secret has its price...

Rubilena Lanmiere can barely remember how it felt to live life for herself. Or what it feels like to live a life in the open. Raising her daughter in a world where it's dangerous to be noticed, her days are spent selling forbidden remedies in her grandfather's shop — and paying her brother Theo's debts in an underground fight den.

When their absent mother returns to gift Theo a mysterious medallion, Rubilena and Theo find themselves fleeing their home in Koamah, hunted by the entire Kingdom and its enemies. With the secrets of the medallion painting a deadly target on her brother's back, Rubilena is forced to seek help from a man who once broke her heart, and her trust.

In search of the mystical witches who can free Theo from the medallion's claim, the group find themselves wrapped inextricably in the tendrils of a prophecy. But as the fight for the ultimate knowledge intensifies, the weight of secrets already between them threatens to tear Rubilena and her allies apart.

And they can't be sure if the medallion is seeking to fulfil a deadly prophecy, or save them from the encroaching darkness...

*When Secrets Beckon is a standalone adult, dystopian fantasy with an epic second chance romance, siblings, clashes with royalty, prophecy, witches and a single mum FMC. If you love your fantasy with forced proximity, touch HIM and d*e, and open door romance, this one is for you.*

TRAITORS' CREED (TRAITORS DUOLOGY, BOOK 1)

Truth makes traitors out of even the most dutiful.
Zanteera Island has a secret: it has two prisons. Vana, the one the world knows and fears, and an unnamed compound lined with comforts. Serving her National Duty at Vana's secret counterpart, Luka Brideoake doesn't question the unorthodox disciplinary system, or the VIP status of the criminals. But when the Warden offers her a prestigious new assignment in Parliament, she starts to see the prison and its inmates in an uncomfortable new light.
Then, her childhood best friend and his brother show up sentenced to Vana, and   Luka is forced to go against every rule she's upheld to seek a dangerous new ally. All the while, the Warden's cryptic advice suggests a political web far bigger than Luka could have imagined.
As inmates start to die and the authorities move in, her path intersects with a man as enigmatic as he is powerful. But how much of the life Luka thought she wanted is she prepared to trade...for the truth?

Traitors' Creed is an adult urban fantasy with an epic slow burn romance. If you like your love interests cold to everyone but the FMC, with wings as sharp as blades (literally) and a touch of forced proximity and forbidden romance, this should be your next read. With political intrigue, high stakes and a found family that will sacrifice everything to save each other, you will love Traitors' Creed.

TRAITORS' PROMISE (TRAITORS DUOLOGY, BOOK 2)

Even the greatest escapes don't guarantee freedom.
With the gilded facade of Zanteera Island's prison smouldering in her wake, Luka Brideoake prepares to make her status as a traitor official. But nothing could have readied her for a summons to a second National Duty. This time, in the heart of Nuntainia's poisonous corruption: Parliament House.
Tasked by Quillian with finding the evidence needed to expose the political tyranny, and armed with an invitation printed with government ink, Luka has no option but to report for duty. Alone.
But as the net of her government's lies closes in, Luka risks returning to the island and the prison she didn't burn—Vana. This time, behind bars. With neither time nor magic on her side, Luka will discover just how much she can endure to reveal a truth that will unseat the highest powers.
Traitors' Promise is the final book in the Traitors duology. Full of an epic romance, open door spice, friends to die for, political intrigue, rebellion and high stakes, this is an adult urban fantasy not to miss.

FIND YOUR NEXT READ

All of Lauren's books can be found here, www.laurenparkerrhodes.com/buy, or at all good bookshops and online platforms.

To stay up to date with all new releases (and inside stories...) subscribe here or at www.laurenparkerrhodes.com

Loved this book by Lauren Parker Rhodes?

I'd love you to leave a review wherever you purchased from or on Goodreads! Just a sentence or two, or even just a star rating, will go a long way to supporting this duology and it would mean the world to me.

After all, without readers, stories go unread and unheard.

Escaping to fantasy worlds is a specialty of Lauren's, either creating her own or reading other people's – providing there's a strong romance, Lauren is all in. Living in semi-rural Australia with her husband and two little wildlings, Lauren tries to teach her children of the wonders of nature. About the impact of all our tiny decisions and that, sometimes, it only takes one person to make a difference. When she's not living vicariously through her characters, or kid-wrangling, Lauren can be found at her second home, the coast; feeding her coffee and chocolate addiction; or trying to fit in a yoga class...even though Archie the labrador would much prefer a walk.

Instagram: @laurenparkerrhodes
www.laurenparkerrhodes.com

9 781763 734630